CW01513974

Her Lovely Champion

Sapphic Lady Knights, Volume 2

Mariah Rae Birch

Published by Mariah Rae Birch, 2025.

Table of Contents

To my readers

who asked me to keep writing.

Thank you.

Note

This is an adult story containing subjects that may be triggering, including addiction, child abandonment, panic attacks, subsistence hunting, human and monster violence, grief, discussions surrounding the concept of suicide (no attempts or desire to commit), explicit language, and sexual content. A current and updated list can be found on the author's website: mariahraebirch.com

Please take care of yourself.

CHAPTER 1
Goodbye, Friend

After spending the past twenty years in nearly exclusively her own company, Crown Princess Eliza of Alludan had come to the uncomfortable yet reasonable conclusion that she was not entirely sane.

The dark wood writing desk set with pearl inlay was alternately littered with forgotten scraps of food and parchment, or shining with polish from when she scrubbed it until her fingers bled. Today, it was clean. She selected a quill, opened her ink, and boldly wrote in the perfect penmanship drilled into her skull and hands:

> *If insanity is the absence of normality, which necessitates others to be normal, can one be insane while alone?*

With a sigh, Eliza crossed out the pointless words before crumpling the piece of thin parchment and lobbing it over the grate into the hearth. It landed off-center. Eliza frowned, retrieved it, and threw it again. This time it landed satisfyingly at the heart of the orderly stack of wood she'd arranged earlier. There. Eliza's aim had much improved over the years.

She wandered back to the window and stared out at the desolately pretty outerlands of eastern Alludan. One advantage of being trapped in her tower was that it had an excellent view.

Mountains loomed up like teeth above the gummy forest, the hill lolling like a grassy, green tongue.

Eliza watched the clouds shift across the sky for a while, until all the interesting ones were gone, and she was left with an expanse of blue and a muddle of wispy tangles on the horizon. And it was only noon.

Boredom wasn't something she felt anymore. It was simply something she lived.

She would go see Harriet.

The door to Eliza's room was not locked. After all, locks had no purpose when she couldn't cross the threshold to the outside world. But the tower, at least, was hers.

She descended the eighty-two steps, around and around. One long winter a decade ago, she had named them all. As she stepped on Lady Lena and Lord Lennox, she wondered what the namesakes would think if they knew she was treading on their faces. Eliza chuckled, the sound echoing back to her in a comforting way. Even if it was her own voice, at least it wasn't the blank, empty silence far more terrifying than Harriet was to any of the hopeful knights who had all failed to rescue Eliza.

As Eliza approached Sir William, the sixty-eighth step, Harriet's rumbling snore grew audible. By the time Eliza bounced into the great chamber at the base of the tower,

HER LOVELY CHAMPION

Harriet was awake, slimy drool stringing between the cold stone floor and two of her three deadly jowls.

"Oh dear," Eliza said, extracting her handkerchief. "You have something on your face."

As Eliza approached, all of Harriet's eyes narrowed and she hastily retreated, her deep purple scales screeching as they scraped along the stone.

"I'll leave this here for you," Eliza coaxed, laying the handkerchief on the floor and backing up a few paces.

Head One and Head Two recoiled, but Head Three tilted. Head Three had always been Eliza's favorite—not that she could ever admit that to the others. But then Head Three jerked back as well.

Harriet growled, low and menacing in a chorus of three throats, the sound like boulders churning against a riverbed. It didn't frighten Eliza, simply made her shoulders sag in defeat. No matter what she tried, Harriet hated her. And Eliza had tried endlessly. Eliza couldn't even blame her for it, since Eliza was the great hydra's reason for being trapped here, with nothing more than a small moat to lounge in.

Harriet was only one of the many wild beasts that lived in these outerlands. Eliza liked to think Harriet had ruled her river quite well before the witch had lured and trapped her, casting the shield magic to keep them inside this tower. Eliza wore a second invisible shield, and the same magic that bound them both to this place prevented Harriet from touching Eliza. Or Eliza from touching Harriet. Or anyone.

"Not a good day, then?" Eliza asked, fighting off the clawing wave of despair and hopelessness she couldn't let herself fall into. Again.

Harriet glared at her.

"Maybe tomorrow," Eliza mumbled, shoving her handkerchief back into her sleeve.

She was about to head upstairs when she noticed the armor.

"Is that one new?" She eyed the punctured, stomach-corroded metal slumped against the wall, adding to the gruesome decor. "When did that happen? I didn't know we had another one. You must have enjoyed it."

And Eliza had missed it. It had been nearly two years since she managed to catch a rescue attempt.

In the early days, a veritable army had stormed her tower. But perhaps people were finally starting to forget about her, because they had become more of a rare appearance in recent years.

Eliza steered away from the dark thoughts. Her father loved her. He would never forget about her. She was certain.

She knew the king still lived, though he must have been getting quite old. Eliza was getting rather old herself. She hadn't expected to still be waiting here, past thirty, with several alarming strands of silver in her brown hair. As her age grew, so did the possibility that if—no, *when*—she was eventually rescued, she would greet her hero with a bad back and wrinkled eyes, more likely to call him son than lover. Not that Eliza wanted to call any man lover. But it was the principle of the thing.

That was the second uncomfortable yet reasonable conclusion of the day. Perhaps Eliza would write it down.

Harriet's renewed growl made Eliza halt her climb yet again, and she turned excitedly toward the door.

HER LOVELY CHAMPION

The witch checked on them every month or so. Unlike Harriet, Eliza treasured these days. She should probably have resented or hated the witch, but the witch was the only person Eliza got to interact with, so Eliza could not hate her. It was a relief to have someone who talked back to her when she spoke, no matter what the reply was.

Contrary to the stories Eliza grew up on, the witch did not have a hunch, or any warts, or even dress in all black. Today she wore a deep red gown with a pink floral pattern on it. Looking at her, she didn't seem evil. And speaking to her, she didn't seem particularly evil either. She swished through one of the creaking double oak doors, letting it close with a loud, resounding thud.

Harriet roared, lunging at the petite, middle-aged woman who didn't so much as flinch. The hydra rebounded, her scales scraping again as her own efforts sent her flying back, splashing into her moat. Eliza cringed, wanting to go to her but knowing she couldn't.

The witch glanced almost apologetically at Harriet as she approached Eliza.

"What are you doing down here?" the witch asked.

"Visiting. What's that?" Eliza's excitement spiked when she saw the package the woman was carrying.

"I brought you something."

"What is it?"

"I'll show you upstairs."

Eliza hiked up her skirts to her knees and took the steps two at a time. The palace would have been scandalized, but this was Eliza's tower, and she rather liked to dash.

The witch, however, climbed them at a painfully slow pace, so Eliza still had to wait.

Late-afternoon light poured through one of the three large windows in Eliza's room, catching on the witch's features as she entered. Eliza frowned. The witch's skin was usually pale, but even in the warm light, she appeared slightly green.

"Are you well?" Eliza asked.

"Fine." The witch glanced at her quickly, clearing her throat and holding out the package.

Eliza's flighty mind had already forgotten about it. It rested heavily in her hands as she sank onto her wide, soft bed and unwrapped the velvet cloth.

Midnight blue leather bound the book's creamy pages, clasped closed with three bands of winding iron and silver. The stamped title read: *A History of Glea*. Their neighboring kingdom.

"What do you think?" the witch asked.

"I love it!" Eliza hugged the book.

The witch's mouth twitched. "Only you would. But since you liked the ones of Alludan and Uvaria so much, I thought it would go with your collection."

They both looked at the bookshelves lining the southern wall of Eliza's room, which were nearly living things as they moved so much from Eliza's constant reorganization. They were currently coordinated vertically by color, and horizontally by size. But Eliza would read through this treasure several times first before it found its place with the others.

Happiness bloomed as she ran her hands over the textured leather. Something new. She brought it to her nose and inhaled, the scent of the ink on musky parchment mixing with the tang of metal.

Then she forced herself to put it down. This would be here later, but the witch would not.

"Is that a new gown? I like it very much," Eliza said, simply to say something.

"I agree. I plan to commission several similar." The witch swept through the room, scanning it quickly.

"Who made it?"

"No one you would have known of."

"Oh." Some of Eliza's happiness dimmed at the reminder. She had no idea who the fine dressmakers of this or any kingdom were. "Well, it is pretty."

The witch stumbled, catching herself on the window ledge. Eliza had never seen her falter, and jumped up to help, but the witch threw out a staying hand. "Don't," the witch snapped, and Eliza stilled.

The witch was the only one who could touch Eliza through her shield, but she never did. And she never let Eliza come near her either.

"You aren't well," Eliza said, swallowing her hurt. "Have you seen a physician?"

The witch let out a humorless bark of laughter. "No physician can treat this."

"Is it...the sickness?"

Human magic, which infected witches to give them power, festered over time and ate the mortal within. Known as the green sickness, it was the reason witches were outlawed. Because of what they became once the person inside was gone. Eliza would know. Her mother had been killed by one.

"I will be fine," the witch said, straightening her shoulders. "I just need to purge." She shuddered again and walked briskly to the door.

"Thank you for the book," Eliza called, following the witch's now hastened steps down the spiraling stairs. "Perhaps next time you come, I can tell you about what I've read?" She sounded pathetic to her own ears, desperate for scraps of time in an endless sea of it.

"Perhaps."

Eliza was practically running to keep up with her as they spilled out into the hall below, where Harriet waited, growling malevolently.

Eliza followed the witch right up to the tall doors, where the magical shield pressed Eliza back. It wasn't uncomfortable, unless she tested it, which she had long since given up on. Touching it was like when she would hold her nose and sink beneath the water in her deep bath back at the palace—an enveloping pressure, but with an edge.

"Farewell, Your Highness," the witch said, as she always did. It was a sickeningly familiar phrase.

Eliza watched her until the closing door blocked her from sight. And Eliza was left alone again.

SIR KAYLEN HAD STARED down her own death more than once, and death always blinked first. And after finding clarity in the bottom of too many wine bottles, she wasn't entirely certain that was a good thing.

Which brought her here, staring at the underside of a rotting thatched ceiling, three days—or however long it took her legs to arrive—before death was guaranteed. And Kay found herself rather indifferent. A strange peace came alongside the knowledge that one was going to die.

It had not been a difficult decision to accept the king of Alludan's mission. It had been even easier to accept the promise of payment. The reward for attempting the quest remained constant over the years, even as the supply of willing knights dwindled. But it exceeded over five years of what she earned in wages serving in the queen of Glea's ranks. And over twenty of what the farm made at its prime.

The money she sent home that spring had run out already. Kay didn't have any left to send.

The hardest part was not being able to say goodbye. But they would understand. One day, they would both understand.

"I wish you'd rethink this," Sir Hugo said, his northern Glea accent as thick as the air as he leaned in the doorway to the attic of the inn, the angle of the early sun highlighting the gaps in the walls. This attic was the type of space that managed to be drafty in winter, suffocating in summer, and never anywhere near comfortable. But it had been cheap, and only one of the other six narrow beds had been claimed.

"And I wish you'd realize I'm not going to," Kay replied calmly, pushing herself up.

She'd slept fully clothed, including her chainmail and sword. As noted, this place was cheap. But she had at least forgone the shoulder pauldrons, bracers, and breastplate overnight. She quickly pulled them on, the leather straps and buckles supple and worn, her body having molded them into shape with wear. Kay would have left them behind to be sold along with the rest of her full set, but Sir Hugo had sworn he would fight her if she tried to embark completely armorless, and Kay hadn't been in the mood.

Kay stood from the last bed she would ever lie in. She would sleep on the forest floor for the next few nights, and then it wouldn't matter anymore. At least, not to Kay.

Sir Hugo's dark hair flopped rakishly in his face, making him look younger than his thirty-odd years. The dimples and sparkling eyes got him out of as many situations as they got him into. Her best friend since her first day as a wet-eared knight, he'd pulled her out of her own misery more than she cared to admit.

Sir Hugo wrinkled his nose. "What is that smell?" he asked, looking around.

"What smell?"

"The one that's making my eyes water."

Kay inhaled wet straw and rot, mice and stale food, and the scent that lingered from too many people in one space. She shrugged.

Sir Hugo gestured questioningly at the sleeping form in the other bed.

"He's alive," Kay assured him. "I checked."

"You should have accepted the actual room I offered. Or bunked with me. You know I wouldn't have minded."

"You're already doing enough." Kay slung her lightweight bag over her shoulder. "Let's get out of here."

"With the greatest pleasure."

He didn't wait for her, and Kay cracked a small smile, following him down the ramshackle steps that solidified into polished ones on the lower levels.

"At least let me buy you breakfast," he said when they got to the main room of the inn that was also the village tavern. "Please, Kay." He looked pained, and Kay relented.

"Fine. If I can take it with me."

Sir Hugo approached the bar as Kay waited near the door. Only a few people sat taking a meal in this sleepy yet hardened town, which was the last stop of civilization before the mountains. The stone wall surrounding the settlement was lined with a shallow moat to keep out unwanted beasts. And beyond that, in an unseen valley of those mountains, stood the witch's tower.

The few patrons eyed both Sir Hugo and Kay curiously. This town had seen plenty of knights, but presumably most wearing Alludan armor, not Glea. The two kingdoms shared a long border, though only two routes—south by the sea and north above the mountain range—were reliably safe to pass through, skirting the outerlands. Alludan and Glea had been close allies for many generations. And Kay was no longer certain which she belonged to more.

A noticeboard hung nearby. Between an illustration of a suspected witch who could alter memories, and a warning of bandits on the roads north, a stack of superseded announcements was stuck haphazardly with more and more pins, the oldest ones browned and curling. Each one bore a name, title, and date. Knights who had perished in the quest to rescue the princess. In one month's time, when Kay did not return, a new sheet would be pinned up bearing her name. That was somehow comforting.

"Here," Sir Hugo said gruffly, shoving a large cloth-wrapped package at Kay.

Kay frowned. "This is food for several days."

"Yes, exactly. Because I know you didn't pack any. Am I wrong?"

"I didn't see the point of eating."

Sir Hugo sighed. "Maybe because you are about to fight for your life and need fuel for that? If you even make it to the tower without becoming something's breakfast."

Kay shrugged, but she did tuck the food in the leather bag slung over her shoulder. The sun was growing brighter, and Kay was eager to get going.

They walked out and around to the stables off the end of the inn. Kay ran her hand along the neck of her dependable steed. They'd been through a lot together.

"I hope you're happy in your new home, buddy," Kay told him as he nuzzled at her chest until the sensation sank inside, twisting. Before Kay could feel it too deeply, she stepped back, turning to Sir Hugo, who was watching her with a bleak expression.

"You are truly doing it," he stated as if he hadn't been riding with her for the past week for this express purpose. As if he was only now realizing that fact.

Kay handed him three things. One was a pathetically light pouch of coins, the second a small grass-woven doll, and the last a folded piece of parchment. "Please bring these to them. Ma can't read, so you'll have to do it for her."

Sir Hugo pulled her into a bone-crushing hug that only her armor saved her from. Kay held him back just as tight.

"I'm gonna miss you, you heather-headed hag," he whispered into her hair, and Kay smiled, feeling his fondness through the sadness.

"Back at you, you dreadfully dull dog."

"You blue bilious beast."

"You numb-nut nance."

"Hey now." Sir Hugo released her. "There is nothing numb about my nuts. That was low."

Kay managed a huff of laughter, and then she sobered. "Thank you. For everything."

"Take care, you fine friend."

Kay nodded, hoisted her bag higher on her shoulder, and walked toward the rising sun.

CHAPTER 2

The Witch's Confession

Harriet's furious roar woke Eliza from her rather pleasant daydream.

Eliza was sprawled on her back beneath her bed, and not entirely sure why. Then she remembered.

The spider she'd been trying to befriend was hiding from her under here somewhere. A feather from her down-filled mattress poked out, which reminded Eliza of the last winter ball before her capture. A beautiful stuffed swan had commanded the center of the table. Eliza asked her father if she could have a swan as a pet. He'd smiled indulgently, patted her cheek, and promised her. But if her swan had ever arrived, it had been too late.

If Eliza could grow wings, would the magic that contained her here apply to the window? Did the shield extend that far up? Could she fly away? But then she would have to deal with the wings themselves, which would need to be rather massive to carry her weight. She might not even fit out the window. So perhaps that was not a good plan after all.

Harriet roared again and Eliza shimmied out from beneath the bed. Harriet's fury could only mean one thing: the witch was here.

Had it been a month already? Eliza frequently lost track of time, but she could have sworn it had only been a few days since the witch had brought her the book. Eliza thumbed through the pages of her newest and favorite treasure. Yes. She had only read it once. Surely it hadn't been a month.

As the witch appeared at the top of her stairs, Eliza was simply happy to see her as always.

"Why do you look like that?" the witch asked.

"Like what?" Eliza glanced at herself in the mirror on the opposite wall. "Oh." Eliza rubbed at the dust and cobwebs sticking frustratingly to her hair and the lace trimming her gown. "How are you? Were you able to commission some more gowns? I was wondering if—"

The witch seized Eliza's wrist, cutting off her rambling questions and frantic brushing. The witch never touched her.

"Listen to me," the witch said, face and tone intense.

Eliza swallowed. She listened, and she also looked closer. A sickly pallor tinted the woman's skin, and the bones in her hands and cheeks stood out too sharply. "I don't have long."

"Are you all right?"

"No, I'm not. The sickness is taking me. Do you understand?"

Eliza nodded, her heart accelerating.

"I will die soon," the witch announced, and Eliza blanched.

"Can't we do anything?"

A baffled smile tugged at the witch's pallid lips. "You are such an odd child. No, there is nothing to be done. I tried to purge but I...couldn't do it. It's too strong now, and I can't resist much longer." Sweat broke out on her forehead, tinged green. Green like magic. "I must tell you why you are here."

"You stole me. I already know this," Eliza said gently, covering the witch's trembling hand, distracted by how cold and clammy it was. Was that normal? Eliza hadn't touched someone in a long time.

The witch released her and shook her head sharply. "I took you, not stole. And it wasn't for some petty reason your father proclaimed. He hired me."

"What?"

"You heard me."

Eliza would not believe it. The witch was confused by her sickness. "Whyever would he do that? My father loves me." He had always doted on Eliza, and his fond smiles remained Eliza's strongest memories of her time before. The memories Eliza clung to when the loneliness threatened to overwhelm her.

"Perhaps. But he also loved your mother."

"What about my mother?"

"He didn't love her at the end."

"Of course he did. But she was killed by a malignant." Killed by the very thing the woman in front of Eliza would soon become. Eliza involuntarily stepped back.

"In a manner of speaking, she was."

None of the witch's words made sense. "What are you trying to tell me?"

"I'm warning you that you don't know the whole story. Be careful whom you trust."

Eliza stared at the witch, who was her captor and also the closest thing she had to a friend. A friend who was growing greener with each moment.

"Perhaps you should sit down," Eliza said.

Something flickered across the witch's features and her hand rushed at Eliza's throat. Eliza jerked out of her grasp, the witch's fingernails scraping against Eliza's skin.

"Sorry," the witch breathed, blinking rapidly. "It's already happening. The magic is claiming me." Her words picked up speed and urgency. "The magic that shields you from the outside world will end with me. You will be free, but you will also be unprotected. I have paid for the next several weeks of food but will not be able to ensure it is delivered. Be prepared that it will stop coming. Don't attempt to stay here through the winter."

The witch's features flickered again and she lurched, leaning toward Eliza as her feet carried her farther away, some battle happening within her. "I'll run as far as I can. But if you see my face again, know it won't be me. Do whatever you must do to get away."

Eliza rubbed at her throat, where the witch's hand had tried to squeeze. "You aren't actually evil, you know." Eliza had never truly believed she was.

"That doesn't matter. To everyone else I am, and always will be. And I'm more dangerous now than I ever was. Goodbye, Your Highness."

"Wait!" Eliza called. "Will you tell me your name?" It was something the witch had never given her.

HER LOVELY CHAMPION

The witch's knuckles whitened as they gripped the doorframe, the decorated wood that lined it splintering with her unnaturally imbued strength. "Layla."

Eliza repeated the name as Layla's somewhat labored footsteps echoed. Eliza didn't follow this time.

She moved to the window that faced the front of the tower and watched Layla break into a stumbling sprint across the meadow, her new gown billowing behind her. Clouds threatened, casting the world in dark, stormy gloom as the witch vanished into the trees.

Eliza's head spun from what she had learned, uncertain if she should believe it. She sat heavily on her bed, the rain thrumming on the slate roof above her.

This had by far been the worst visit by the witch in eighteen years.

Eliza didn't know how long she sat there, listening to the rain. She was never good at telling things like time.

Downstairs, Harriet roared again, but it wasn't like any roar Eliza had heard before. It wasn't fury or rage or sorrow. It was relief. It was joy.

The front doors banged open, sending a tremor through the whole structure.

Eliza returned to the window to witness a sight she never thought she would.

Harriet lumbered over the grass, her form slithering and powerful amongst the rain-dappled field. The shield magic that held her here was gone. Head Three glanced back and up, right at Eliza, before Harriet plunged into the river running through the valley basin, and she was gone. Finally free.

Eliza cried for her, tears staining her cheeks and she didn't bother to wipe them away. She was glad, and terribly sad, that Harriet and the witch were both gone.

Eliza would never see either again. It was a ridiculous notion to wish she could.

She should have been happy. Instead, she simply felt lonelier than she had when she woke that morning.

It was true, and yet it made no sense. Was that it? If Harriet was free, that meant Eliza was too.

After all this time, it was over so calmly. So quietly.

Eliza had never been rescued, after all.

On shaking legs, Eliza descended her stairs, moving like in a dream all the way down to the empty hall. It had never been empty before.

Thunder rumbled, rolling in and booming around the space.

The double front doors stood twice Eliza's height, built of thick wood enforced by iron braces and scarred by Harriet's furious attempts to break them, though they were not the cause of her imprisonment. Now those scars caught and channeled the falling water, grooves in nothing more than wood and metal.

Eliza stopped short at the threshold to the world. The view looked different from down here. When she waved her hand in front of her, nothing pressed back, only air. She crept her toes forward to where the stone turned to grass. Chest pounding, she stepped. Rain hit her face for the first time in so many years.

She was free. How utterly overwhelming.

Eliza turned and fled back upstairs.

HER LOVELY CHAMPION

THE MOUNTAINS OF EASTERN Alludan were beautiful in late summer. Kay's boots crushed the cheery wildflowers littering the slopes, petals of blues, whites, and pinks sticking to her damp boots with morning dew. They were the same varieties she used to run through briefly in her youth, before the weight of the world crushed her too.

Her mind started to wander toward home, but Kay firmly redirected it.

> *Sing, my darling,*
> *my heart, my starling...*

The old lullaby rang in her head.

As she crested the saddle between two hills, she saw it.

The tower rose from a valley dotted with patches of trees and brush. Dark smooth stone made up its walls, devoid of any ornament or charming vine. It stood dispassionately as a beacon of death.

Kay focused on her feet. One in front of the other as she descended toward her tomb. The sky, which had been clear when she woke, had darkened with afternoon storms, clouds materializing overhead. A river rushed loudly, covering the sound of her footfalls and the increasingly loud thump of her heart.

> *When I say goodnight, it won't be the last time.*
> *When the sun returns, so will I...*

Only when she reached the windswept field and stared up at the tower looming above her did she allow herself to think about what she was doing. But thinking about it didn't alter her steps, just made her palms clammy.

Goodbye, my starling, goodbye.

Two great doors at the base of the tower stood open, welcoming her in. Kay drew her sword. It wouldn't be much of a fight, but it felt wrong not to defend herself at all.

Kay had been a knight for five years, and a soldier for nearly five before. She understood the value of her sword, and of what she was. But she'd never liked it. That mantle she carried would finally be put down. That fate she had accepted but never wanted would end. With this one act, she could do more for her family than ever before.

As she reached the doors, a sudden jumble of memories of home spattered through her mind. Pa in the fields, grinning as he took off his sweaty hat. Luka helping him, whole and tall, freckles stretching around a matching smile. Finley laughing, catching at Kay's hand as Ma called, waving for them to come inside. Stella toddling, arms outstretched.

This was for them. The ones who were left.

Kay adjusted her grip on the hilt of her sword, straightened her shoulders, and stepped through the doors.

CHAPTER 3
An Unusual Battle

Kay braced to be assaulted at once, but the vast room was eerily quiet. Absolutely still.

She took another step, spine tingling with anticipation.

A moat ran a ring around the side of the chamber, and not a ripple disturbed the surface. The rusted remains of armor and weapons shadowed the walls, a few corroded piles of crushed helmets and shields shoved into the corners.

The space was empty. Vacant. And that was so much worse than facing the raging beast.

Kay's shoulders knotted as she moved forward, her footsteps reverberating back at her.

Where was the beast? She was prepared to meet it. She'd already decided and settled her mind on it.

"Show yourself," Kay called, and that, too, came back at her, mocking. Kay turned in a circle.

Silence spiraled, until a faint clattering rang from somewhere high above. Kay snapped her head upward, scanning the rafters. She had expected the hydra to be enormous and impossible to hide, but Kay could adapt. After all, no one who had faced it could give an accurate description, could they? Small things could be just as deadly as large ones.

Kay softened her knees and circled to the side, eyes straining through the darkness as she looked for her fate.

ELIZA CURLED ON HER side on the bed. She hadn't moved much since both of the beings she knew had abandoned her, though the sun had set and risen again at least once. She should probably get up and eat.

How long would the food continue to come? What would she do when it didn't?

When Eliza was younger and the darkness closed around her, she had thought about trying to kill the witch to end her entrapment. But those had been passing fanciful ideas and she never planned to actually do it or, if she did, for it to work.

Eliza was not a stranger to death. She had seen plenty of knights perish to Harriet, and the remnants afterward. But those people were unknown to her. Even when Eliza's mother had died, they had never been close. While the king had doted on Eliza, the queen had been distant at best. Not much changed for Eliza when she died only a month before Eliza's capture. Or so Eliza had thought.

Her pulse sped up. What had the witch meant? She'd said her father had not loved her mother at the end, but that couldn't be right. Eliza had seen his grief. He had retreated, barely speaking to Eliza at all.

Had Eliza been in danger too? If true, was that why her father had orchestrated her capture? To keep her safe? But from whom? From what?

All she had were questions, and no one to answer.

Eliza was now free and yet had never been more trapped. Every time she thought about getting up and walking out of the tower, she panicked. What was she supposed to do out there? Which way would she walk? What would she do when night fell?

All manner of dangerous beasts lived in the woods. These were the outerlands, where the creatures that fed and ate nightmares roamed. She had seen and heard a few from her window and knew stories of the rest from when she was young.

A faint sound echoed up from the main chamber. The only reason Eliza heard it at all was because she had been motionless for so long.

She sat up. Was her mind playing tricks on her? Had someone truly come?

Or had one of those deadly creatures wandered into her tower? Too late, she realized she hadn't shut the front door. She'd never needed to before.

Eliza glanced around, fear quickening her movements as she searched for a weapon to defend herself. Something heavy.

Her gaze landed on her new history. Perhaps not the best choice, but it was something.

Gripping the large tome, she tiptoed down the steps. Eliza would throw the book to distract the beast, close the door at the base of the stairs, and run back up to her room.

Then...what?

Eliza would figure that out later.

Light filled the lowest part of the stairwell, pouring through from the open doors across the chamber. Eliza paused, adjusted her grip on the book, and flung herself down the last few steps.

A person stood facing away from her, sword in hand, like a drawing from one of her storybooks. Like what she'd always dreamed of, and been waiting nearly twenty years for.

The knight whirled, sword raised and fabric swishing as the book that had already left Eliza's hands slammed into their face.

"Oh! I'm sorry!" Eliza rushed forward as the knight reeled backward, stumbling away from her. Eliza pursued, arms outstretched. "Here, take this."

Eliza offered her handkerchief, as she had to Harriet. Only it wasn't a hydra staring back, with blood slowly trickling from her nose.

Curly red hair draped in a frizzy, flyaway braid over the knight's shoulder. Beneath a simple wool cloak, she wore a partial set of silver armor etched with scrolling patterns Eliza quickly recognized as that of Glea. Eliza had become somewhat of an expert in armor since it gave Harriet indigestion, so she usually spat it back up. But Eliza had never encountered it on a woman, except in illustrations of the lady knights of Glea. Like inside the book she'd just thrown.

Was this even real? Or had Eliza's mind finally betrayed her and created a champion?

"I didn't mean to hit you," Eliza promised. "I thought you were a beast."

The lady knight's eyes widened and she lowered her sword, taking another step back.

"Your Highness." The knight dropped to a knee and bowed her head. Then she straightened and turned toward the door again, throwing a protective arm out between Eliza and the empty room. "Get back."

"Why?"

"The hydra."

"Harriet is gone." The words were harder to say than Eliza had expected.

"Gone?"

"I mean, she's taller than a house. Where do you think she's hiding in here?" Eliza managed a small laugh at the thought, and the knight's fair, freckled cheeks pinkened.

Eliza curled her hand around the knight's arm to reassure herself this wasn't a hallucination, slightly shocked when her fingers connected with cool, textured metal.

Eliza was about the same height as the other woman, though not as sturdily built. "I am so glad you're here. You have no idea. Though I wasn't expecting...you."

"No?" The knight tensed at Eliza's touch. "Did someone already slay the hydra?"

"Oh no. Harriet is fine, thank goodness."

"Might she be coming back?" The knight sounded strangely hopeful, turning to gaze at the open doors.

"She's long gone." Eliza tugged at the arm she held. "What's your name?"

The knight cleared her throat and sheathed her sword. "Sir Kaylen, Your Highness. At your service." She bowed again.

Sir Kaylen. What a wonderful name. The woman's accent was a strange mix of rough and lilting, and the most beautiful sound Eliza had heard in years. Eliza vibrated with excitement.

"I am Princess Eliza, but you already know that. Please, take this."

Eliza shoved her handkerchief in Sir Kaylen's face, who hesitantly accepted, pressing it to her nose with a wince. "Thanks."

Eliza was delighted. "Come upstairs. I have so many questions for you!"

CHAPTER 4
An Unwise Venture

Princess Eliza turned and ran up the stairs curving out of sight. Kay swallowed, her body waiting for another attack.

But nothing attacked her. Except for that book which, judging by the pain, might have cracked her nose. She clutched the darkening handkerchief to her face.

Kay had not been prepared to meet the princess. She'd never imagined getting so far, let alone finding the princess unguarded.

Kay stooped to retrieve the enormous book that had collided nicely with her face. Glancing around, uncertain about what else to do, she started up the steps.

They went on forever, finally ending in a single, high-ceilinged room. The princess waited just inside the door and Kay nearly walked into her. Kay hastily bowed and stepped sideways.

The princess smiled brightly. She was much older than Kay had imagined her, but of course, it made sense she would be. Princess Eliza had been captured when she was fifteen years old, and that was nearly twenty years ago.

The pink silk gown complimented her smooth, warm-toned skin. However, said gown was creased and rumpled, and exhaustion ringed beneath heavily fringed eyes. Her dark chestnut hair fell loose and mussed, one pin barely clinging to a strand, reaching toward where a discarded tiara rested on the unmade bed.

Kay's sinking instincts from earlier returned. Something was terribly wrong.

"What has happened?" Kay asked.

"Oh, um." Princess Eliza bit her lip, hands fluttering around each other. "There's been a change of circumstances."

"What sort of change?"

"The witch. She's dead." Princess Eliza shook herself and hurried to a large desk.

The witch was dead. The hydra was gone. Kay was still bewilderingly alive. And the princess was... "When?"

"Yesterday. I think. Or the day before?" The princess bent, diving elbow-deep in a drawer. "Where is it?" she asked absently. "I know I had it last year."

Kay had a headache. This was not how today was supposed to go.

"I found it!" The princess straightened triumphantly, holding up a carefully bound stack of parchment nearly the size of the book Kay gripped. Kay reactively stepped back as the princess looked down at the top page. "I already asked your name...Where are you from, Sir Kaylen?"

"I was born not far from here, in the borderlands of eastern Alludan, Your Highness."

The princess frowned. "But your armor is from Glea."

"It is. I am a knight of Glea."

The princess sighed, looking down at her page again. "I'm already getting distracted. That wasn't one of my questions. Sorry."

She looked oddly distressed, and Kay slowly approached. "Perhaps we can go through your list later, Your Highness. I need to understand what has happened. If the witch is dead, and the hydra is gone, does that mean you are able to leave freely?"

The princess hugged her bound list to her chest. "It seems so."

If the princess was free, that meant she didn't need rescue. Would the king honor the payment? If only Kay had arrived a few days earlier.

Why Kay still expected things to work as she'd planned, she didn't know.

Her nose and cheekbone throbbed, but the bleeding had stopped. The fine handkerchief was thoroughly ruined, and Kay hastily wrapped it in her own rough one and shoved it in her pocket.

The princess didn't notice her move. She was staring at the window, her face turned away, but her eyes glued to the spot.

Kay waited, but the princess remained frozen, simply staring at the window as the time crawled by.

"Your Highness?"

The princess startled. "What?"

Despite herself, Kay felt bad for her. She was clearly shaken by something. "Would you like to tell me about what happened?" Kay offered.

The princess looked at her with large brown eyes. "She's gone."

Kay nodded. "I imagine that's a relief. She was your captor."

"Yes, but..." The princess trailed off as she reached out to pick a moss remnant from Kay's messy braid. Elegant fingers lingered, brushing lightly down the strands that fell over Kay's breastplate. Kay's heart accelerated unnecessarily. When she cleared her throat, the princess snatched her hand back.

"But now you are here. And you can take me home," the princess added, smiling cautiously. She had a narrow gap in her front teeth, which Kay found unreasonably charming.

Kay swallowed. "I don't believe that is wise, Your Highness."

"Why not?"

"I'm not prepared," Kay admitted, that fact cringing through her. "You should wait here, and I'll return to the nearest town and arrange—"

"No." The princess shook her head vigorously, her hand clamping around Kay's arm again. "I won't stay here alone. Not another day. I'm coming with you."

Kay was not equipped to go anywhere, and certainly not with a princess. She had no food left, no supplies, no transportation, and no money. She also had no choice.

"Do you have any boots, or a simpler gown?" Kay asked, assessing the princess's silk skirts and delicate slippers as she tried to figure out what she was going to do with her.

"They are all like these."

"What about a cloak?"

"I've never needed one."

"Right. May I examine your room for supplies?"

The princess nodded easily and finally released her grip on Kay's arm, but she followed Kay's steps only one behind, watching her intently. Unnerved, Kay kept her focus on the room.

A small food box contained a hard loaf of bread, some strong cheese, and several fresh apples. She slipped those into her own pouch and took a finespun wool blanket from the bed, rolling it up and slinging it over her shoulder.

Then she asked the question that should have stayed in her mouth, but she couldn't afford to keep there.

"Is there anything of value here you wouldn't mind parting with? Perhaps a necklace or something?"

"Would you like one?" The princess put a hand to her head. "Of course, I should give you something for rescuing me." She hurried to the wide dressing table and pulled out a jewelry box. "I'm making quite a mess of this being rescued thing, aren't I?"

"No, Your Highness." Kay was the one who had glanced at *mess* and hurtled right past on to *unsalvageable disaster*.

The princess considered her jewelry box, and then presented Kay with a silver chain cascading with ruby pendants. "Please accept this as a token of my gratitude," she said with all seriousness.

Kay stared at the beautiful, rare piece. She was about to explain, but simply nodded and accepted it. It would be easy to break apart, at least. "Thank you."

ELIZA STOOD AT THE threshold of her tower for the second time in as many days.

She looked at the expanse in front of her, and then back at the stairs on the other side of the cavernous hall. Eliza had repeated each name as she stepped on them for the last time, saying goodbye to her old, inanimate friends. They said nothing back, of course. Because they were made of stone—not friends at all, but worn slabs of rock a silly, desperate girl had ascribed personality to.

Harriet's hall gaped silent and dark, like the past years. The familiar misery of these walls offered a bleak safety in their own way. Eliza didn't *have* to leave, right? A tiny, deceitful, cowardly part of her wanted to stay.

Eliza shook herself and turned back to the outside. There was just so much of it.

"Princess?"

Sir Kaylen watched her, and Eliza realized she was still being silly. She wasn't a child, and she wasn't alone. With a deep breath, Eliza stepped off stone and onto earth.

The weight of Sir Kaylen's cloak hung around Eliza's shoulders, unfamiliar and comforting, like a sort of hug. It smelled of damp wool, moss, and something Eliza could not name. She inhaled and took another step. Being free was incredible, and frightening, but Sir Kaylen stood sturdily beside her.

The sun broke through the temperamental clouds and highlighted the woman's fiery hair, catching the frizz and turning into a glowing aura. Eliza had to force herself to look away, or she might have stood there and stared for the rest of the afternoon.

"Where is your horse?" Eliza asked.

"I don't have one."

"What do you mean you don't have one?" In all of Eliza's imagined rescues, her champion always had a horse.

"Well, I did. But I sent him to be sold several days back."

"Why?"

"I didn't expect I would be needing him again."

Eliza stared at her.

"Your Highness, I must be entirely honest with you," Sir Kaylen said, her cheeks turning that fascinating pink once more. "I was not prepared to live past this morning, let alone take you to safety. I truly think it would be best if—"

"Don't," Eliza said. "Don't tell me to stay here." Now that she had left, she couldn't stand the thought of returning.

Eliza was torn between the desire to retreat and the need to reach for the human in front of her. Her body compromised by freezing in place, only a handful of paces from her former prison.

Sir Kaylen bent, and at first Eliza thought she was bowing, but instead the knight held out Eliza's list. Eliza didn't recall carrying it down with her or dropping it. She had completely forgotten, and hadn't even asked the first three questions.

She was a mess, and her mind was more of one. What must Sir Kaylen think of her? After all this time, Eliza was ruining her own rescue. She blew out a frustrated breath.

"Forgive me," Sir Kaylen said, clearly misinterpreting the cause of Eliza's annoyance.

"It doesn't matter. If you don't have a horse, we will venture on foot. Lead the way." Eliza tried to sound confident and gallant, and likely failed.

Eliza struggled to keep up with Sir Kaylen's long, purposeful strides up the gentle slope of the valley. Eliza was used to climbing her stairs and crossing her room endlessly but could not recall a time when she'd walked so far in a straight line. It was disorienting and she kept getting distracted by how the tall grass caught at her skirts.

When they neared the river, the rush grew deafening. Eliza looked in vain for a sign of Harriet. She wondered if she would always look for her in every river she saw.

They entered the forest where the trees grew thick and grasping, and much bigger from on the ground than from above. Birds and insects and squirrels screamed from all angles. The scents of the forest clogged Eliza's nose, full of decay and new life, and she struggled to get the air into her lungs. Everything was too loud and too close.

Sir Kaylen appeared right in front of Eliza's blurring vision. Eliza reached for her, not sure where to grab, and settled for shoulders covered in sloped metal.

"Breathe with me," Sir Kaylen said, her voice strong but not harsh.

Eliza breathed—in and out—following the exaggerated rise and fall of Sir Kaylen's shoulders.

Hands framed Eliza's waist. Touch was not something Eliza was used to anymore, and her skin seemed to catch fire through the layers of fabric between them.

Sir Kaylen's eyes were the most beautiful green, like the grass in autumn when it started to yellow and brown.

The world steadied around them, but Eliza didn't look away.

Sir Kaylen dropped her head, hiding her lovely gaze as she released Eliza like the fire there burned her. "Please forgive my familiarity, Your Highness."

"Not at all. Thank you." The heat moved up to Eliza's cheeks.

Sir Kaylen retrieved the blanket and bag she'd dropped on the ground. "Do you want to rest?" Sir Kaylen watched the forest floor rather than Eliza. Eliza wanted the woman to look at her again.

They hadn't made it far into the trees, the light of the field clearly visible.

"How far do we have to go?" Eliza asked.

"It will take us several days to reach the nearest village. The palace is much, much farther."

Eliza's mind caught on the way Sir Kaylen pronounced *farther*. It curled off her tongue charmingly, though not all of Sir Kaylen's speech was like that, as if her accent couldn't decide if it should be Alludan or Glea. Eliza liked it. It made the knight more real, and too unique for Eliza's brain to conjure up.

Eliza rolled the word around in her head, her mouth mimicking the shape of it.

"Princess?"

Eliza blinked, taking a moment to remember what Sir Kaylen had said, rather than simply the way she had said it.

"We'd best keep going," Eliza announced.

"I would suggest you return to the safety of the tower, but I don't fancy having any other parts of my face broken today." Sir Kaylen glanced at Eliza's bound list as she turned and started walking again.

"Are you teasing me?" Eliza asked, delighted by the notion.

"I would not dream of it."

"I am sorry about your nose. I honestly didn't mean to do that."

"My nose would testify to the contrary."

"Does it still hurt?"

"Like someone stuffed a hive of bees up there."

Eliza snorted at the analogy. "I broke my nose several years ago. I tripped on the stairs, and it bled for days."

"Days?" Sir Kaylen paused and frowned at her. "Didn't you have any help? Servants? Physicians?"

Eliza shook her head. "The witch would visit every month. And someone would deliver food to the base each week. The witch was the only one who could get close to me. The shield magic stopped everyone else. I saw the knights from a distance, sometimes. But none of them made it far."

"That must have been lonely."

Eliza huffed. "That's an understatement. So if I say anything odd, ignore me. I'm not used to anyone listening."

A somewhat awkward silence fell as they resumed walking.

When the world grew too loud again and Eliza's chest constricted, Sir Kaylen slowed. "Perhaps you would like to ask me some of your questions?"

Eliza brightened at the thought, but then she frowned. "I don't think I can read and walk at the same time."

"There must be hundreds of questions in there. I'm certain you can remember at least a few."

"But if I go out of order, I might miss some."

Eliza ran her thumb along the careful, expanded binding on the list of questions she had started writing when she was fifteen years old, waiting for this very day when she could ask them of her rescuer. It had been a comfort, especially during those first years. Something to look forward to. Something she could control.

Now her rescuer stood in front of her. The circumstances were different than she had expected, but she would make the most of them anyway. She'd waited too long not to.

"Hold my hand," Eliza said, reaching for Sir Kaylen's and thrilling at the warm skin that touched her own before it disappeared, and Sir Kaylen retreated.

"Your Highness?" Sir Kaylen looked at her in a way that made Eliza's cheeks heat again. She was being odd, wasn't she?

"So I can read and not trip."

Sir Kaylen cleared her throat and hoisted the blanket higher on her other shoulder. "Loop your arm through mine. So you can have both hands to hold the pages."

CHAPTER 5
Into the Woods

Kay waited with trepidation as the princess linked their arms together. The princess was clearly overwhelmed, and no wonder, if she had been as isolated as she had said. Kay knew the princess had been locked away, but she hadn't expected her to be completely alone. She was a princess, after all. To finally be free after so many years would be a shock to the senses.

Kay had immediately recognized the panic setting into her earlier, and could see it threatening again now.

The daylight wouldn't last forever, and Kay needed to distract her. "I believe we were on question number four, Your Highness."

Princess Eliza nodded and pressed herself closer as she gripped the pages with both hands. The curve of softness beneath blush silk grazed Kay's arm.

She was briefly taken aback by the flicker of desire it coaxed in her.

Sir Hugo had thrown all manner of pretty women at Kay on their whole journey here, claiming a quick lay would do her good, what with going off to die and everything. It had been the farthest thing from what Kay had wanted. And she still didn't. The princess simply looked quite fetching in her fine gown beneath Kay's old, humble cloak.

Fetching, traumatized, and very royal. And entirely forbidden to someone like Kay.

"How old are you?" Princess Eliza asked.

"I am twenty-nine years old."

"Really? You look older."

Ouch. Kay's face must have betrayed her because the princess slowed and her grip on Kay tightened.

"Oh, that was rude. I'm sorry. I didn't mean to insult you."

"It's fine. I'm certain it's true."

"Well, I am thirty-three."

"You look much younger."

The princess laughed, and the sound tickled something pleasurable in Kay. "Are you teasing me again?"

"Not at all." Perhaps Kay was, just a little. It was brazen of her, but it had worked last time, as it did now, their steps returning to normal strides. In truth, the princess looked exactly her age. And it looked good.

"Who is your family?"

Kay's insides clenched. "Next question."

"What?"

"It's not something I wish to talk about."

"Why not?"

"Next question."

"Are you truly refusing to answer?"

"Are you ordering me to, Your Highness?"

"No, I just…" The princess bit her lip and looked down. "We'll come back to that one. Um, when did you become a knight?"

"Five years ago."

"And what heroic deed earned you the title?"

"I managed not to die."

The princess watched her expectantly. "And? There must be more to the story."

"Not really. I was in a brutal battle, and fortunate when most were not. I helped pull out one of the queen's favorite knights. The kingdom needed more after that, and I was convenient."

A frown appeared on the princess's face. "You saved someone? That sounds like you were worthy, not convenient."

What a disarmingly kind thing to say.

Kay hadn't felt heroic or worthy as she had fled with Sir Brigal through the night from their fallen regiment, covered in their own and others' blood and all manner of filth. But dying there would not have served any purpose. So she ran.

She didn't regret it, but wasn't exactly proud either. But it had pleased Queen Viola of Glea.

Kay stepped over a fallen tree first and helped the princess clamber over it, freeing her silk hem as it caught on a branch.

"What's your favorite food?"

That being the follow-up question on the princess's list amused Kay. "All food is my favorite."

The princess didn't like that answer, frowning as she hooked her arm back through Kay's. "You aren't very good at answering my questions."

Kay almost chuckled. "Sorry. Why don't you tell me your favorite instead."

The princess's frown deepened as she stared ahead of them. "I would say anything hot. I haven't had much hot food since I was captured. You are right. Maybe that isn't so easy to answer."

Yet her answer tugged at something in Kay. "When you get back to the palace, you will have all the hot food you like. I am certain."

A new shadow crossed the princess's expression. "I hope so. Did you, um, see my father before you set out to rescue me?"

"I saw one of his stewards. I'm sure the king is too busy to meet with mere knights."

The princess nodded and fell silent. She clutched Kay's arm and her list, but paused her questions, a faraway look on her face.

Kay led her onward, weaving between the trees and sparse undergrowth and along the undulating hills, staying quiet to not disrupt whatever was going on behind those startlingly pretty eyes.

PERHAPS ELIZA HAD TRULY lost the ability to interact with time correctly, because one moment she was walking up the hill, thinking of her father and what the witch had told her, and the next the world was growing dark around her.

She stood in a clearing beside a rushing stream, her arm tingling from where it cinched around Sir Kaylen's, and her legs aching.

"How long have we been walking?"

"All afternoon."

"Oh." Eliza tried to drop her arm, but it didn't cooperate until Sir Kaylen extracted her own. Sir Kaylen also carried Eliza's list. "Sorry, I get distracted easily."

"It's all right."

Sir Kaylen shrugged off her satchel and approached the swift current, kneeling to fill a flask. Eliza gratefully gulped down the icy liquid that chilled her parched throat. Still disoriented from the long time in her own mind, she stepped toward a stump, but her exhausted, stiff legs had a mind of their own. She was tipping toward the damp earth when sturdy arms caught her.

Eliza was an utter disaster.

Sir Kaylen deposited her on a nearby log and then turned to gather large stones from the riverbed into a ring. Eliza drank in each movement as she had done her water. What other interesting sights had Eliza missed while retreated into her head?

The fire crackled cheerily, stoked to life by Sir Kaylen's skilled hands. Starting a fire was not something Eliza had had the faintest idea how to do before she was forced to learn fast that first winter in the tower. She had never done it in the woods before, though. It seemed terribly unsafe with no hearth, but she would trust that the knight knew what she was doing. The sun had set, and the sky beyond the treetops was a warm pink that wouldn't be warm long.

Several nearby tree trunks bore dark burn scars. Eliza pointed them out. "What are those?" she asked, hoping the answer wasn't what she thought.

"Flamewalkers."

Fear pricked Eliza's insides as she pictured the hulking, flaming beasts she had seen lighting up the nights from her window. "Should we move our camp?"

"You'll find the same in any other part of the forest. This sign looks old. Believe me, we are safest near the water with them. Though the water has its own dangers."

Eliza didn't have much choice but to believe her. Sir Kaylen stated these things as if they were nothing to worry about.

Eliza shivered.

Sir Kaylen stood and offered her hand. "Come sit by the fire."

Eliza accepted, startled anew by the warmth and texture of Sir Kaylen's skin.

Eliza was not used to her comfort being cared about by anyone but herself. Though perhaps that wasn't entirely fair. Layla had cared, in her way. Eliza had been alone, but she had never worried about her safety. The witch gave her new gowns when she outgrew her last. She brought her books like her histories, and parchment and ink.

The more she thought about it, Eliza realized Layla had cared for her in ways Eliza had taken for granted. And Eliza could never thank her.

Eliza sank cross-legged on the blanket Sir Kaylen had brought from her tower. Their food for the night consisted of stale bread and cheese—a meal Eliza had eaten endlessly. Sir Kaylen ripped the small loaf unevenly in two, keeping the much smaller one for herself and passing Eliza the larger.

"Give me your knife," Eliza said.

Sir Kaylen froze, the bread partway to her mouth. She raised an eyebrow. "Is that another order?" But she reached for the knife at her belt beside the hilt of her sword.

"Sorry. May I please borrow your knife?" Had Eliza always been so rude? Perhaps she had.

She used the knife to slice the bread longways and then shaved the sharp cheese onto the stale interior, skewering one half on the blade and holding it over the flames. In the tower, she had bent the top part of the hearth grate for this purpose, but she didn't have that here, obviously.

"It either dries or burns before it gets melty, usually, but it's warm at least," Eliza explained. "And it makes the crust easier to get through after a week."

Sir Kaylen watched her for a few more moments, and then she tore her own bread and broke some cheese onto it, resting it on one of the stones around the flames. She had to use her hands, but didn't comment.

"That's a much better idea!" Eliza pulled back her mildly warmed bread and placed it on the rock beside Sir Kaylen's, passing the knife back. "Thank you."

Sir Kaylen quirked a small smile at her. And they sat in companionable silence, staring at their mismatched, simple dinner starting to bubble, the cheese slumping and releasing delicious oils into the structure of the bread.

A soft hum filled Eliza's ears. At first, she thought she was imagining it. But no, it was coming from Sir Kaylen.

"What's that?" Eliza asked.

The sound stopped and Sir Kaylen glanced at her. "What?"

"Were you humming?"

"No."

"Oh. Sorry." All the new sounds that day must have frazzled Eliza's senses.

She reached for her bread, and had to wait for it to cool before she bit into it. It tasted better than it ever had. Perhaps the rock added something.

She glanced over at Sir Kaylen to find her hands empty. She had eaten her whole chunk already and was collecting the crumb fragments from the hot rock and the blanket before tipping them into her mouth.

Eliza remembered the winter she was twenty-one, when the food had not arrived for two whole weeks, and she hunted for crumbs like that too. Every scrap had been precious. Sir Kaylen was a woman who knew what it was to be without food.

The fire smoldered lower, but Sir Kaylen made no move to add more wood. "We shouldn't burn it at night," Sir Kaylen stated ominously.

Eliza shivered in anticipation of the chill, but knew the fire might attract flamewalkers—or something else—so she didn't protest when Sir Kaylen stood and approached the small river while undoing the three buckles at either side of her breastplate. The front and back halves opened and came away like the shell of a clam. She pulled it over her head, dipping the curved plates into the running water to capture the current.

The doused fire sizzled and steamed, blurring the darkness with a billow of hot, humid gray between them. As it disappeared, cold crept over Eliza's cheek and down her neck.

It was going to be a long night.

CHAPTER 6

A Swampy Encounter

What had Kay gotten herself into?

She lay on her side on the bare earth, near the bundle of blanket that was Crown Princess Eliza.

Kay didn't expect she would find sleep at all tonight. Her mind spun in too many directions and her ears listened too hard for signs of threats in these woods.

She'd put her breastplate back on, just in case. It wasn't comfortable, but that wasn't the point.

Kay hadn't worried last night, or any of the ones since she left Sir Hugo and her horse. It had not mattered if danger found her. But Kay was not alone anymore. Whether Kay liked it or not, she was now responsible for the safety of the royal heir of her homeland. It was theoretically what she had signed up for, but no one—least of all Kay—expected it to happen. Life had apparently decided it wasn't finished making a fool of Kay. And all she could do was keep going.

The small sound should not have stood out over the others of the forest, but was distinct for its deliberate quietness.

Ever so slowly, Kay tilted her head back.

Through the trees, a shadow loomed darker than the rest.

Kay stopped breathing and it appeared larger. They were being stalked. Was it a dreamhound, lured by Princess Eliza's slumber?

Kay only had a moment to decide. Should she fight, or should they run? A second shape formed to flank the first.

She could have stood at least a chance against one. But likely not two.

If she survived, Kay might lose her head for what she was about to do.

Kay launched herself toward the river, scooping a sleeping, blanketed princess over her shoulder as she plunged them into the icy water.

The princess shrieked and bucked, and Kay lost her footing in the swift current churning past her thighs. Stumbling forward, she landed hard on the opposite bank.

"Run," she huffed as she shoved the princess ahead, away from herself and the water.

To Kay's great relief, the princess listened, disentangling from the blanket and Kay and sprinting into the dense trees.

Kay didn't look back, but she didn't need to. She could hear the beasts' pursuit—howls, splashing, and heavy paws beating the ground.

They crested a small rise and hurtled down the opposite slope, the princess just ahead of Kay and the hounds too close behind. The princess slipped, and Kay reached for her as her own feet hit slick, damp earth, moving at a different rate than the rest of her. They both lost their footing but didn't stop moving as the slope steepened and trees thinned, sliding past in a blur.

The ground disappeared altogether as Kay wrapped herself around the woman she clutched, twisting during a gut-lurching moment of freefall, and braced to catch whatever landing they hurtled toward.

Stagnant water swallowed them briefly before the silty bottom rejected them back into the unwelcoming night air.

A swamp.

Howls repeated above them, from somewhere out of sight beyond the short cliff they had tumbled over.

Kay grabbed the princess's arm, who was trying to get her feet under her.

"Hold your breath," Kay ordered.

The princess stilled. Wide, dark eyes caught the waxing moonlight, and she nodded. Kay inhaled. And then she dropped once more, dragging the princess down with her.

THE TERRIFYING WORLD vanished as pungent water enveloped Eliza again. Her lungs immediately cried out, and she instinctively struggled, but strong arms tightened around her waist, the weight of a metal-clad body at her back keeping her submerged.

Sir Kaylen's touch was the only thing holding Eliza to reality. Panic filled Eliza at the thought of her letting go, and of the darkness all around, both horrifyingly familiar and strange. She struggled again, but Sir Kaylen held firm.

An eternity passed. Eliza's chest burned. The thick, brackish water was everywhere, seeping into her nose and ears, until she imagined it filling her brain.

She couldn't stand it any longer. If she didn't breathe, it wouldn't matter if whatever was chasing them found them.

Eliza thrashed out of Sir Kaylen's grasp, gasping in a fresh lungful of air and quite a bit of swamp. A dripping Sir Kaylen emerged beside her, scrambling onto her knees and looking around.

Eliza couldn't see much through the veil of slime or hear anything over the thundering of her own body. She wiped at her face with equally filthy hands. She'd never been more disgusting.

Eliza needed a moment to compose herself and recover, but Sir Kaylen wasn't giving it to her, hauling her up.

"Wait," Eliza panted.

"We must keep moving. I don't know where they went. And I don't want to overstay our welcome in this swamp."

That got Eliza's legs to move. The water dragged at the sodden cloak and her skirts, the fabric slick and heavy as she tried to gather it in her numb, frigid hands. Sir Kaylen bent, reaching around her and bunching the hem up to Eliza's waist.

"Forgive me, Your Highness," Sir Kaylen whispered as she propelled Eliza and her skirts onward.

Eliza huffed out a slightly hysterical laugh. "I think we're past formalities."

They waded through changing water and muck. Sparse trees jutted from the hills rising on all sides, leaving them far too exposed. A large nocturne bird swooped and landed on a dead branch protruding from the water, which creaked and bobbed as they passed. The scavenger's piercing, chilling call echoed around them. Every shadow leered. Every croak made Eliza's heart race as they crossed the swamp and stepped onto solid ground on the other side of the low basin.

Sir Kaylen kept a secure arm around her the whole way. Eliza had no idea what she would have done if she attempted this journey on her own, and was now realizing why Sir Kaylen had protested attempting it on foot. But it was too late for regret now.

They crested over another ridge and into a new valley, finding a rushing, thankfully clear stream. Only then did Sir Kaylen stop. Eliza shuddered violently, as Sir Kaylen did the same.

"It'll be dawn soon," Sir Kaylen said, her voice following her shiver, looking up at the sky turning from deep midnight to pale purple. "A fire's a risk, but I don't fancy our chances if we don't get warm."

Eliza nodded, her teeth chattering, and helped find wood.

The flame that flared bright and young was welcome, but not strong enough. Eliza leaned as close as she dared. Beside her, Sir Kaylen struggled out of her armor, yanking off the pieces and dragging the shirt of chainmail over her head.

Eliza fumbled for the lacing on her own gown. Like all the others she owned, it was designed to be done in the front to make it easy to dress and undress herself. But her hands shook frighteningly. Frustrated, she yanked at the end of the cord with her teeth, the bitterness of the swamp souring her mouth.

Wordlessly, Sir Kaylen moved to help, her fingers also unsteady but more effective. Eliza stilled as the backs of the knight's knuckles grazed the skin of her neckline and then dipped a trail down beneath the lacing, efficiently loosening the gown to Eliza's navel.

Eliza's belly swooped. She wished her skin weren't so numb so she could feel the sensation better.

"Thanks," Eliza whispered breathlessly and shimmied out of the ruined garment, leaving her in a thin silk shift. She considered removing that too, but felt far too exposed with nothing on. At least it would dry faster than the several layers.

Sir Kaylen added more wood to the fire, and slowly, Eliza felt it.

Sir Kaylen huddled beside her, watchful eyes scanning the forest. The only thing covering her torso was a worn undershirt. Eliza had not noticed Sir Kaylen's figure much beneath all the metal, but it was obvious now even in the flickering light of the fire.

It was rude to stare. But Eliza would much rather die staring at Sir Kaylen than awaiting death, or giving in to the dark hopelessness that lured her.

The woman's arms were sculpted like a statue, the muscles curving beneath the thin, wet fabric clinging to them.

Eliza wanted those arms to surround her again and hide her away from this dangerous world she was no longer certain she wished to be free in.

CHAPTER 7

Up the Mountain

They heated water inside Kay's breastplate over the flames and washed away as much of the swamp and scent of stagnant decay as they could.

Kay attempted to focus on herself and not watch the princess cup the water in her hands, letting it track down the stretches of exposed skin on her neck and forearms.

Dawn brightened with the first rays of morning, shining deceptively prettily through the crisping trees. Kay wasn't entirely sure where they were anymore. They had lost the blanket, the small amount of food, and all of Kay's supplies from her bag. Now all Kay had was her flint on a simple chain around her neck, a small hip flask, a knife, and a sword.

With a sinking feeling, she reached for the pocket she wore tied at her waist. It was open, the necklace from the princess gone, probably lost somewhere in the swamp. Even if they reached civilization, they would have next to nothing to offer for help.

They were fucked.

Trust the land 'neath your feet for it grew you up strong.
You may wander far but it's here you belong...

"You *are* humming!"

Kay cut off the melody that she hadn't realized was coming out of her, cursing the habit that clung to her despite her efforts. "Sorry."

"Why did you stop?"

Kay cleared her throat. "It's annoying."

"It's nice." The princess smiled sweetly. "Do you also sing?"

"No," Kay lied, returning her attention to the forest around them.

The princess stood and wrung out her ruined silk gown that had gone from blush to brown in one swamp crossing.

"I'm sorry we lost your list," Kay said quietly, distracted again by the way the drying fabric of a fine silk shift fluttered and clung at the same time.

The princess shrugged, glancing back through the trees the way they had run from. "The ordering of the questions feels much less important now."

"Thank you for listening last night. And for trusting me."

"Is there a reason I should not trust you?"

"No. But I'm very glad you did, Your Highness."

"And I thought I told you we are past that. Call me Eliza."

Kay was not certain she would be able to, but it was a nice gesture.

"That's what friends do, right?" Princess Eliza asked, sounding slightly unsure.

"Are we friends?" Kay couldn't decide if she should be alarmed or flattered.

"Currently you are the only person I know. So I would like to be."

Kay nodded. "All right."

The princess beamed. Even wearing traces of swamp, she really was beautiful.

Kay looked quickly away.

ELIZA'S LEGS BURNED as the tree line fell behind, replaced by brush and rock and the mountain peak looming above them. The sun chased away the chill of the night and sweat collected uncomfortably in the crevices of her skin.

They were climbing high to look for the closest settlement, to know which direction to go in. At least, Sir Kaylen would know.

Sir Kaylen led the way with sure strides, and Eliza did her best to keep up. Through her delicate, shredded slippers, the soles of her feet were growing painfully tender.

"I need a break," Eliza managed, sinking onto a slanted rock. She winced as she pulled up her stained hem and inspected her feet.

"You should have said something earlier." Sir Kaylen knelt in front of her. "May I?" Sir Kaylen's hand hovered over Eliza's stockinged ankle.

Eliza nodded and Sir Kaylen cradled Eliza's heel, slipping off the dainty shoe whose thin wooden sole had split.

"They are still damp, and so it won't be pleasant, but they will protect your feet better," Sir Kaylen explained as she sat back and tugged off one of her tall leather boots.

"But what about you?" Eliza asked.

"We'll trade."

"You don't want these."

"It's not about want, Your Highness."

"Eliza," Eliza corrected.

Sir Kaylen met her gaze. "Eliza."

Her name on Sir Kaylen's lips, in her liltingly unusual accent, made Eliza's belly flip.

Eliza was so captivated by the sudden force of those green eyes, she didn't realize Kaylen had slipped off her other shoe until the echo of the touch bled through the thin material over her battered skin.

Eliza reminded herself to move and speak.

"We will each take one boot," Eliza declared, reaching for the left one.

It was as Sir Kaylen had warned: damp. Also warmed from the heat of Sir Kaylen's leg. Eliza's own foot was apparently smaller than Sir Kaylen's, leaving the footbed loose, but the sole was sturdy and would protect her, as Sir Kaylen had also said. As Sir Kaylen had also done both last night and this morning.

Eliza stood, slipping back on her other ruined slipper. It was an uneven, uncomfortable pairing, but better than before.

"Let me know if you change your mind and want both," Sir Kaylen said. "And we can switch later."

HER LOVELY CHAMPION

On Sir Kaylen's left foot, she wore only a thick woolen sock, which instantly picked up everything on the ground. The top of her big toe peeped through a hole that had obviously been repaired before.

They both would have looked comical, but Eliza had no desire to laugh. A bruise bloomed across the bridge of Sir Kaylen's nose and cheekbone where Eliza had hit her with the book. Scorch marks from their fire darkened her silver breastplate, and her hair was a wild thing escaping her head. Sir Kaylen was nothing like the composed, regal knights and nobles Eliza had been told to dream of.

Eliza reached for her, simply needing to touch her. To make sure she was real, and Eliza was here, and this wasn't some cruel, wonderful delusion. "May I take your arm again? Or your hand?"

Sir Kaylen held out her elbow, and Eliza curled her fingers around the solidity that wasn't only from metal. Yes, Sir Kaylen was entirely real, and Eliza's heart drummed faster than usual.

After a while, Sir Kaylen started to hum. Eliza didn't recognize the tune, but she listened raptly, enjoying the sound. Sir Kaylen's eyes roamed their surroundings as they climbed, the hum looping, ebbing, and flowing, and she seemed unaware she was doing it.

Above them, the clear sky cracked. Eliza smiled as a thunderwing bird swooped, chased by its mate. Energy crackled off their wings, which stretched as long as Eliza's arms.

One cold winter, a pair had roosted on the roof of Eliza's tower, in the crook above her chimney. She loved listening to the shuffle of their talons on the slate and the rumble of their ruffling wings. She'd burned through all her wood trying to keep them warm up there, and then shivered in her blankets for two days waiting for her next delivery. By the time it arrived, the pair had moved on.

Eliza wondered now if these might be the same ones as they twirled and dove out of sight around the curve of the slope up ahead.

Eliza wished she still had her list. It was a frivolous thing to be upset about, given the circumstances, but Eliza hated the idea of it languishing on the bank of that stream, to be found by anyone, before it rotted away.

"What's wrong?" Sir Kaylen had stopped humming and watched Eliza closely.

Eliza would never know the exact ordering of her questions anymore, so she would do her best. "Do you like your name, or would you change it if you could?"

Sir Kaylen blinked at her. "I've never minded my name. But in a way, I did change it, when I earned my title. If that counts."

"And what were you before that?" Eliza was curious about where Sir Kaylen came from, but Sir Kaylen wasn't about to tell her.

"Not a 'sir.' What about you? Do you like yours?"

"I was named after my grandmother, so I've always thought it sounded old and stuffy."

"I think it's pretty."

The soft declaration as Sir Kaylen's gaze danced over Eliza's face made it feel like the knight was talking about more than the name. Eliza's insides fluttered again. Did Sir Kaylen like women too?

"What would you change it to?" Sir Kaylen asked, and Eliza forced herself to concentrate.

"I know it's rather common, but I've always loved the name Stella."

Sir Kaylen stopped abruptly, and Eliza jerked to a halt, locked with her arm. Sir Kaylen stared intensely at the trees below them.

Eliza pressed closer, looking too for signs of danger. But she saw nothing. "What is it?"

Sir Kaylen cleared her throat. "Nothing. That's a pretty name too." Her words were quick and clipped. "This is high enough. Let's look for a place to camp."

CHAPTER 8
A Dreadful Hope

Kay stared out at the rolling hills and valleys, waiting for dusk to gather. They were wasting daylight, but knowing a direction was better than aimlessly wandering with a hope and a wish.

Princess Eliza was curled behind Kay in the shallow cave at the base of a rocky cliff, fast asleep on a prickly bed of evergreen branches. Kay was glad she could rest.

Hunger rumbled through Kay's stomach around the handful of underripe berries from earlier. It was a sensation she was unpleasantly acquainted with.

Tall mountain grasses rustled in the breeze near her singular boot. Kay pulled out her knife and cut several handfuls before she could think much about it, sitting back on a jutting rock.

Kay had thought the doll she sent with Sir Hugo would be the last, but everything had changed now.

Kay had never expected to be alive to see the king's reward. If they somehow managed to return to the palace, and the king still honored it, everything could change again.

Something tentative and fragile took root in her breast as she twisted the grass, adding and layering more to extend the length of her working piece. Perhaps Kay could stay home longer. And when she inevitably had to leave, perhaps she could bring them to Glea for a while, to be closer to her.

Kay squeezed her eyes shut as an emotion too big to contain filled her chest. It wasn't pain, for once. It was dreadful, terrifying hope. A soul-killing desire for something that had hurt her too many times to trust. Hope she might live free of fear of waking to a letter saying another person she loved had died, and she hadn't been there.

When I say goodnight, it won't be the last time.
When the sun returns, so will I.
So fly, my starling, goodbye...

Kay noticed her own hum this time. She breathed deeply, subduing and smoothing her mind, until those fanciful thoughts were safely secured in their corner, behind the stone walls where they belonged. She couldn't indulge in them. They would only break her heart more when they weren't possible. So instead, she braided and twisted the grass into a figure of a girl.

"What are you doing?"

Kay dropped the half-finished doll, and it unraveled. The princess crouched right beside her, watching. Discomfort washed through Kay as she glanced around.

She should not have been startled. The princess should not have been able to sneak up on her.

"It's nothing," Kay said hurriedly, gathering up the now tangle of grass and tucking it out of sight.

"It doesn't look like nothing."

Shame at the flippant response loosened Kay's tongue. "You're right. It isn't."

"You're making something?"

"I was. But I'll need to start over now."

"Was that my fault?"

"It was all mine. Did you sleep?"

Princess Eliza scooted closer, tucking her dirty stockinged feet on the edge of Kay's rock and hugging her knees. "Show me. Please."

A please was so much worse than a demand.

Kay reached for the grass, untangling and re-sectioning it. She started again with a hank of about ten strands. "This is when the grass is best. See how it's yellow on the outside but has a faint green core? It's dry enough that it shouldn't rot, but fresh enough that it bends without becoming brittle."

Eliza watched in apparent fascination as the figure took shape again. "Where did you learn to do this?"

"From a boy I knew long ago."

"What was his name?"

"Finley."

Kay hadn't spoken his name in a long time. It felt odd, and both acidic and sweet in her mouth. The emotions and memories clamored, but Kay's weary walls held strong.

"Who was Finley?"

What a complicated question. "My best friend, I suppose. Briefly, my husband." Old pain and resentment burned, licking at the gaps in the stone of her emotional walls.

Eliza's eyes widened. "Why brief?"

"He died."

"Oh. I'm so sorry." Eliza touched Kay's arm, and Kay stilled.

"That was many years ago." Kay forced herself to smile because the princess looked sad and unsure. "We should never have married to start with. Anyway, he was the one who taught me to make these dolls."

"Are you making this one for someone particular?" Eliza asked, and Kay nodded. "Someone back home?"

Kay nodded again. "I send them, when I can."

"To...?"

"Someone." Kay shot the princess a sideways look, silently asking her not to press the matter, and she listened, returning her attention from Kay's face to her hands.

"Well, they are very lucky, whoever they are. To have your care."

It was the second distressingly kind thing the princess had said to her. Kay flooded with the sudden desire to cup her soft cheek and kiss her.

Kay throttled that disastrous thought and shoved it roughly behind her walls too.

SLEEPING IN THE LOW cave was like lying beneath her bed, and Eliza did not mind it at all. It was, however, extremely dark once the sun set.

Sir Kaylen had pointed out several clusters of lights dimly visible. Eliza had been thoroughly distracted by the much closer flicker. A flamewalker illuminated the night, steadily moving through the landscape, its flames burning but not spreading, following its form. Eliza huddled closer to Sir Kaylen.

Once morning came, Eliza would be hopeless to know where they were, but Sir Kaylen said they could reach the nearest town in only a day or two. Eliza would believe her and follow wherever she led.

Perhaps Eliza should have been warier of putting her trust in the hands of a woman she had met only the day before. But Eliza had always been in others' hands, and Sir Kaylen's were proving very capable.

When Eliza was a child, all aspects of her life had been dictated and ordered, not that she'd always adhered. When she was in the tower, she experienced a certain new freedom within the walls, despite being trapped. And there she depended on the witch and the people who brought the wood to keep her warm and the food to fill her belly.

At least with Sir Kaylen, Eliza had made the choice to trust her. Nothing was stopping Eliza from standing up and walking away. Eliza could leave.

She didn't want to.

Sir Kaylen rested on her side in the shallow cave entrance, behind a partial wall of stacked stones. The knight slept curling inward and shielding Eliza from the faint breeze that brought an extra chill. Eliza muffled the chuckle that bubbled in her throat. Her new shield was much more corporeal and attractive than her previous one.

Eliza gathered Sir Kaylen's cloak tighter around herself, inhaling the scent of it and the tangy pine beneath her, and shifted just a little closer, several needles jabbing.

The sound of another person's breathing was a comfort Eliza had not realized she had missed. She adored it.

It was too dark to see Sir Kaylen's face.

"Are you awake?" Eliza whispered.

"I am now."

"Sorry."

Sir Kaylen let out a puff that might have been a laugh. "I was already awake. What is it?"

"What are your thoughts on magic?"

"My thoughts? That's a pretty broad question."

"Do you believe witches are evil?"

"I believe malignants are, and we should do what we can to prevent them. I've seen what their strength and mindlessness can do."

Eliza recalled how the witch had so easily splintered her doorframe with a single hand. "But what about before? When they are still witches?"

"People can be evil too. Witches are born of infected blood, not made by choice, so I imagine some may be good and others not. But they are all dangerous, simply for what they become."

"Have you ever met a witch?"

"Several."

"What were they like?"

"Mostly quiet. Though I wasn't trying to have lengthy conversations with them."

"What were their powers?"

"I didn't ask."

Eliza swallowed. "Did you kill them?"

"No."

"Would you?"

"If I had to. Magic is outlawed in Glea as well." Sir Kaylen shifted. "Why are you asking me this?"

"Because I want to know."

"Magic may not be a choice, but actions are. I believe the witch who captured you must have been evil."

Eliza swallowed again.

"Don't you?" Sir Kaylen added when Eliza didn't reply right away.

"I don't, actually. I sort of miss her." The words hung in the dim silence between them. "I know that sounds ridiculous, but she was the only person I knew. She was never cruel to me. She took care of me. And she revealed something that may change my perspective on things. It seems it wasn't as simple as her capturing me because she wanted to."

"Then why did she do it?" Sir Kaylen's voice was careful.

"I probably shouldn't tell you that."

"Do you forgive her?"

Eliza hadn't expected that question. The witch had still imprisoned Eliza and Harriet, regardless of the circumstances. "If I had learned when she had captured me, I don't think I could. But now...I don't know."

"Forgiving the dead is hard. They cannot give us any closure or assurances. We must simply make do with what they gave in life."

Sir Kaylen's words drooped with an old weight. Eliza reached out in the dark, searching for the woman's hand. Sir Kaylen twitched when Eliza found her, but didn't pull away as Eliza curled their fingers together.

It was more intimate than Eliza had planned. Her belly fluttered and she wondered if she should not have. Sir Kaylen had spoken earlier of her dead husband. So perhaps it was only intimate for Eliza.

Sir Kaylen's callused fingers tightened around Eliza's briefly. The pulse of comfort settled her.

Eliza feared she might like her new friend a bit too much.

CHAPTER 9
Brushes with Death

Kay slowly shifted her weight to get a better angle on the partridge hiding ineffectively in the brush. The stone in her palm warmed and she readjusted her grip. She didn't have a bow, but had learned long ago she didn't need one. The stone wouldn't kill the bird, but would stun it for long enough. The thrum of the nearby river masked the sound of Kay's heartbeat and steady breath.

The partridge never saw it coming. Kay pounced, ending it with a single stroke of her knife. A few frantic flaps of wings beat at Kay's hand before the already dead bird stilled. Blood dripped onto the forest floor and rushed through Kay's veins as her body reacted to the quick brutality of the hunt. They needed this food. It wasn't enough, but it was something.

Princess Eliza hovered on the edge of Kay's sight between the sunset-crested trees.

"Shall I start a fire?" Eliza asked, surprising Kay.

Kay sat back on her heels and reached for her flint, pulling it over her head and handing it to Eliza with stained fingers.

Kay prepared the carcass, her hands thankfully knowing what to do as the rest of her distractedly watched the princess struggle with the flint for a while, but she figured it out. Feathers clung to Kay's skin and tumbled over the ground as the breeze caught and carried them away.

Eliza's fire was crackling heartily on the riverbank when Kay finished and joined her. "Thank you," Kay said.

Eliza picked a bit of down from Kay's hair, which resembled a nest more with each day. "I'd rather make the fire than hunt. I don't think I could kill it."

"You could."

Eliza eyed the limp bird in Kay's hand. "Well, I'd much rather not."

Kay envied the princess for being able to say that, and the luxury to choose. "Then you don't have to."

Using her knife again, Kay stripped several young sapling branches to create a makeshift roasting spit, the green boughs resistant to the flames licking near them. Her stomach rumbled with anticipation as the meat warmed and sizzled, and she approached the small river.

She washed her hands in the chilling water, burying her fingers into the mix of silt and gravel to scrub away the evidence. The forest rustled around her, quiet and deceptively peaceful.

A few mottled feathers stuck to Kay's boot. Kay collected and rinsed them clean, rubbing them down and back into shape. Then she pulled out the doll she'd made the night before, tucking the ends between the strands to make a little skirt. Kay allowed herself to imagine delivering this one in person.

One day. When this was over. After she brought the princess safely back to the palace.

Kay blinked rapidly and slipped the doll back in her pocket before rejoining Eliza at the fire.

"How does it look?" Kay asked.

Eliza bit her lip. "I don't know. I've never cooked raw meat before."

With her snarled hair, crunchy gown, and dirty fingernails, it was easy for Kay to forget exactly who Princess Eliza was.

"I'll show you. If you'd like."

Eliza smiled, the charming gap in her teeth flashing. "I would like that."

Kay sliced into the largest part of the breast. "It needs more time," Kay explained as she showed her, failing not to let the touch of Eliza's shoulder against her own affect her as the princess leaned in to look. "The thickest parts will take the longest. But see here, this part is done."

"Can we eat that now, then?" Eliza asked earnestly, and Kay's stomach rumbled in agreement.

"Ideally I'd leave it whole." But Kay didn't want to wait either, not caring if it was drier than it needed to be today. She carved off the legs and wings, the meat burning at her fingertips.

Kay watched with pleasure and amusement as the princess enthusiastically devoured her portion of the unseasoned gamey meat. The sight should not have warmed Kay's insides. Kay pretended to rotate the spit, resettling to put more physical distance between them.

They threw the bones into the fire. Eliza smiled at her again, and Kay's still-hungry stomach jittered. *Stop it.*

The princess's smile froze. Kay's muscles tensed, her hair raising as she turned to follow her gaze.

A woman stood between the trees, her floral gown torn and ragged.

Not a woman—what used to be one.

The malignant watched them with sunken, unseeing eyes, a green glow ringing the sockets and resonating from within. It must have been young, because it was still very human-like in appearance.

Kay stood, drawing her sword. She wouldn't be able to kill it, but she could slow it down.

Malignants hated two things: fire and metal. Kay had both.

"Layla?" Eliza whispered.

Kay glanced at her and understood. This was her witch. *Fuck.*

"That's not her," Kay told her quietly as she carefully unfastened her right bracer, and the malignant took a step closer, sightless gaze fixed on them. Kay pressed the bracer into Eliza's hands. "Don't let it get close."

Kay reached down to the fire, grabbed the end of a thin log being eaten away by flame, and chucked it. The log broke as it rolled toward the malignant. And in its wake, smoke caught. Kay took another, ignoring the heat licking her hand, and tossed it on their other side. Using her elbows, somewhat protected temporarily by her chainmail shirt, she shoved and scattered the rest of their fire in a crescent around them, keeping the water to their back. The flames flicked and caught on the drying leaves, guttering against the damp ones and creating a weak barrier.

The malignant circled them as the fire burned brighter. Kay looped her arm around a motionless Eliza's waist and pulled her back toward the water. "That's not her," Kay repeated intently into Eliza's ear.

Eliza inhaled and nodded, readjusting her grip on Kay's bracer. "I know."

A new light caught the corner of Kay's eye, and a fresh chill of fear ran down her neck.

A flamewalker, perhaps the same one they had seen the night before, lumbered toward them. Twice as tall as Kay, its coal-black body was composed of too many legs, like thick charred roots extending from a tangle of white and blue flame. It didn't have a face in the traditional sense, but Kay sensed it watching them. It must have been lured by the crackling fire spreading around them in the dusk.

Kay had attracted a new monster by trying to evade the first.

The malignant retreated a few trees, shifting its focus onto the walking mass of heat.

The flamewalker reached their burning shield and paused, extending one long, twisting limb.

And it consumed the fire. Like a dry rag dipped in water, the flames traveled up its leg, abandoning the forest floor and leaving behind a blackened, charred ring. Fresh flame twined with the others flickering on the creature's body. The flamewalker burned brighter. Grew larger.

Would it be satisfied with that? Kay kept her arm around Eliza, backing slowly down the riverbank. Flamewalkers fed off heat. And Kay and Eliza were unfortunately warm-blooded.

For a moment, Kay thought it might let them leave. But its form swung back toward them and stepped, too large to skitter, its many legs weaving. Pursuing.

"Get in the water," Kay told Eliza.

Kay altered her backward path, trying to draw it away. The flamewalker slowed, shifting its mass that might have been a head between them. But it continued toward Eliza, who retreated, splashing ankle-deep into the swift current.

With a muttered curse, Kay attacked. She carved into one of its surprisingly dense legs, the intense heat of its body already singeing her hair and skin. The sword in her hand burned briefly before going cold as ice, and Kay nearly dropped it.

The flamewalker hissed, fire licking higher into the darkening sky, as it turned its full attention on Kay.

SIR KAYLEN SCRAMBLED back over the uneven ground as the flamewalker descended on her. Eliza had to do something. Her eyes flicked back to the witch.

No. Not the witch—the malignant. Eliza's heart pounded faster. It looked like Layla, but she had told Eliza herself. It wasn't her.

Eliza's unbooted, numbing foot nudged a loose river rock and she plunged her hand through the icy water for it. She hit the flamewalker squarely in the main flare of its body. She was grateful for the many years of throwing practice.

She hurled another rock at one of its legs, which jerked, sizzling where the water made contact.

The flamewalker swayed toward Eliza, and Sir Kaylen sliced again, this time completing the cut she had started before. One of its limbs crumbled away, disintegrating into charred ash.

"Look out!" Eliza shrieked as the malignant darted forward.

Sir Kaylen twisted just as the malignant reached for her. She blocked the crushing grasp that was meant for her throat with her sword, forced back by the blow. The top of the blade crumpled.

The malignant screamed and recoiled, three fingers nearly severed, gashes dripping a ghastly green liquid and not nearly enough blood.

Eliza dropped the newest rock she'd gathered and hurled the metal bracer instead. It was an odd shape, but Eliza hit. The malignant let out another unearthly shriek, its horrifying eyes snapping onto Eliza. They held no recognition.

Sir Kaylen swung with the base of her damaged sword, and Eliza's stomach dropped along with Layla's head.

Again, there should have been more blood. But as the green glow spilled from the neck stump instead, the stumbling body righted itself, and then turned and bent, reaching for its severed part. Sir Kaylen kicked ruthlessly, rolling the head between the maze of burning flamewalker legs. The malignant couldn't scream anymore, but Eliza still felt its fury as the fair hair that had once been Layla's began to smoke. Already re-attached fingers stretched desperately, but the malignant was reluctant to get too close to the flames.

The flamewalker finally noticed its competition. Sir Kaylen ducked around them both, splashing into the water and seizing Eliza's arm. And they ran.

They followed the river, plunging deeper into the valley as the night closed around them, leaving Eliza's former captor and friend behind.

Eliza shook herself. It wasn't her. Layla had already died. That thing was simply her shell.

Eliza's legs and lungs burned with effort as she cursed her skirts and hiked them higher. And it was a good thing, because it kept her mind and body focused on the present and the fear rushing through her instead of processing what she'd seen and done.

They didn't stop until Eliza's exhausted body forced her to. She would have fallen on her face if Sir Kaylen hadn't caught her, both staggering to a halt. Listening.

All was quiet, except for the rush of the river and their heaving breaths.

Eliza sagged into Sir Kaylen's hold.

"Let's sit," Sir Kaylen said, guiding Eliza down to the rocky bank of the river and collapsing onto her back beside her. "Just for a moment."

"I think we'll need more than one."

Sir Kaylen chuckled breathlessly. "Fine. Several moments." Then she stiffened as Eliza curled into her side.

"Shall I move?" Eliza asked, hoping Sir Kaylen would say no.

"No."

They recovered somewhat, feet soaked and sweat chilling. And Eliza's mind had time to think, which wasn't a good thing.

"You did well," Sir Kaylen said, as if Eliza had spoken aloud. Had she spoken?

"I hit her."

"Yes, you have very good aim with cumbersome objects."

Eliza's fingertips traced the bruise on Sir Kaylen's cheek, barely visible in the gray light. "I've said I'm sorry. I really am, you know."

Even Sir Kaylen's breathing seemed to freeze, and Eliza reluctantly let her hand fall. "I'm not complaining. It's why we escaped."

Eliza wasn't so certain. She just remembered the shrieks. Eliza had hurt the witch. And then Sir Kaylen had... "Do you think she's truly gone now?" Eliza whispered, thinking of the bright flames.

"A flamewalker is one of the few things hot enough to actually kill a malignant. Let's hope so."

But Eliza couldn't quite manage to hope for that. Part of her mind understood while rejecting the notion at the same time.

"That wasn't the person you knew," Sir Kaylen said again.

"I know that. But it looked like her." She kept seeing Layla's head tumbling, over and over.

"I understand." Eliza barely heard the quiet whisper, but something made Eliza believe Sir Kaylen did.

She was tucked into Sir Kaylen's side. Almost in a hug. Eliza reached for the comforting warmth of her hand to block out the dark thoughts in her own head, but Sir Kaylen hissed and twisted away.

"Are you hurt?" Eliza asked, grabbing her arm and leaning closer.

A trail of small white blisters crossed the back of Sir Kaylen's hand and down her palm, following the line of her sword guard and hilt.

"I'm fine," Sir Kaylen said, pulling away and standing. "We should keep going."

"We should treat it."

"It'll wait for tomorrow."

"No, it won't." Eliza was not willing to let it go. "I've read that sap from a weeping tree can heal wounds. Is that true?"

"It can protect, at least."

Eliza looked around at all the forest that loomed the same. "Right. Um, do you happen to know what a weeping tree looks like?"

Sir Kaylen led them a short distance to a hunched tree trailing branches nearly to the ground. Pushing past the curtain of leaves, she carved a line through the trunk with a flash of her knife.

"Let me do it," Eliza said, capturing Sir Kaylen's wrist again. "Please," she added, and Sir Kaylen let her.

The sap was thick and sticky on Eliza's fingers. As carefully as she could, she drew the substance over the raised welts. Sir Kaylen hummed a few breathy notes into the quiet darkness, tickling Eliza's forehead. Eliza hadn't realized how close she'd stepped.

"Did I do it right?" Eliza asked, brushing her thumb over Sir Kaylen's chapped knuckles instead of letting go. Eliza wanted to study and catalogue each nick and scar on the woman's skin. Every freckle dotting her complexion, erased by the moonlight and its shadows.

"Good. Thanks." Sir Kaylen cleared her throat and withdrew her hand. "Let's get as far as we can tonight."

CHAPTER 10
New Old Friends

As they crested the last hill in late afternoon, Kay had never been more relieved to see smoke and evidence of other people. It had taken two days and one more perilous night since leaving the shelter of the mountainside cave to reach the village.

Shallow moats of stagnant water surrounded the ripening fields that edged town, as was common with these settlements that bordered the outerlands. Narrow walkways resting barely submerged acted as bridges, enough to dampen Kay's sock, but also to deter a flamewalker. Kay was thoroughly thankful to be standing on the inner ring of it.

"While we are here, I'm Kay, and you are Ellie. Follow my lead. And don't tell anyone who you are," Kay instructed as she handed Eliza across.

Princess Eliza frowned at her. "But if we tell them who I am, won't they be more likely to help us?"

"No one has seen you in nearly twenty years. They would have no reason to believe us, and if they did, it would put you at risk."

Eliza scowled deeper. "Risk?"

"Not everyone would be incentivized to help you." It was a rather callous thing to point out, but Eliza deserved to understand.

Eliza huffed. "Fine."

When they neared the entrance to the walled town, Eliza paused and tugged off the boot she was wearing today and passed it over. "Take this back. We'll look silly."

Kay opened her mouth to point out they already looked ridiculous. Instead, she accepted, and then hooked one elbow behind Eliza's knees and the other her low back, scooping Eliza up into her arms as she straightened. Eliza let out a surprised little gasp, followed by a delighted laugh as she grabbed at Kay's neck.

"What are you doing?" Eliza asked.

"I would think that was obvious."

"You can't carry me everywhere."

"True, but I can carry you twenty paces to that town."

Kay didn't set Eliza down until they reached the latticed iron gate, rusted ajar only barely the width of shoulders, a few weeds tangling around the base. Kay poked her head through.

"I suppose they don't get many visitors," Eliza said as Kay helped her squeeze past.

"At least not from this direction."

The town was sparse, the size of the outer wall more ambitious than the prosperity of its inhabitants.

A young woman straightened from an overrun garden and watched them approach.

"Good afternoon," Kay greeted. "My name is Sir Kay, and this is my wife, Lady Ellie. We ran into a spot of trouble on our travels. Is there an inn or place for us to rest in this charming town?"

The words felt disingenuous as they left Kay's lips. The woman's eyes remained narrowed, but she nodded up the dirt path that nearly passed as a road. "Center of town. Called the Prancing Frog."

Kay inclined her head politely with thanks.

"Wife?" Eliza hissed as Kay carried her onward.

"It's more believable than my sister." Kay looked pointedly at the princess's warm, smooth skin compared to her speckled, fair complexion. "We certainly could be siblings by marriage or adoption, but that requires more explaining. When it comes to lies, the simpler the better."

"And why are you so good at lying?"

"Believe me, I'm not."

Eliza laughed again. "Believe you?"

The sensation of laughter against Kay's chest helped her arms stay strong as Eliza grew progressively heavier. Kay was fatigued, sleep-deprived, and ravenous, but she would not allow the princess to walk in shredded stockings that might as well not have been there at all.

The village reminded Kay of the weeds growing around its rusted gate—a bit run-down, yet sturdy and stringy, and determined to survive where others might not. A few children careened around the side of a building but stopped short to stare. A man passed them, looking more confused than anything. Another woman hurried by without sparing them a single glance.

At the heart of the town lay a small square, and the swinging sign for the Prancing Frog Tavern and Inn. Kay nudged the door open with her foot, surprised to find it somewhat busy.

The man behind the bar eyed them as Eliza slid down Kay's front to stand on the floor, clinging close. Kay should not have enjoyed it. Her arms were glad for the break, but the rest of her traitorous body was not.

"Good afternoon," Kay said again, and she repeated her brief story, trying not to let it carry to the eavesdroppers. "Do you have a room?"

"Do you have coin?"

Kay hesitated. "I have my armor. And I can work."

The man turned his back, placing a tankard on a tall shelf. "I don't need armor or help. The taxman only takes gold ludans."

"But you must help us!" Eliza blurted, her hands tightening on Kay, and her own tightened back in warning.

The man raised an eyebrow. "Must I, my *lady*? I'm full up tonight."

He clearly did not believe their story, and given their state, Kay couldn't blame him. They probably looked like thieves, or worse.

"It's all right, my darling," Kay said to Eliza, the endearment tripping too naturally off her tongue. "We will figure something out."

When Kay reached for the door, the inn owner surprised Kay by speaking again. "You might try the blacksmith, just down the lane. She sometimes takes people in, and may have more use for that armor than me."

"Thank you," Kay said, meaning it.

"He was so rude," Eliza huffed as they followed the lane along the side of the inn as instructed.

"He was actually quite kind."

The forge and humble stone house beside it backed against the crumbling town wall, overrun by a dense tangle of tree limbs as the forest on the other side reclaimed it. Smoke belched up and mingled with the darkening sky.

One wall of the forge was open for ventilation. A blacksmith worked on the far side, the glow of an intense fire outlining broad shoulders.

It wasn't the blacksmith who noticed them first, however. A strikingly beautiful woman emerged from the doorway of the adjoining house. She wore a low-cut gown made of simple cloth, which still looked entirely out of place in this border village.

As she approached, her steps slowed, eyes traveling over Kay's armor. "Leon," she called loudly. "We have guests."

The blacksmith turned. Her fair hair was pulled high on her head, soot darkening one cheek and a deep scar decorating the other. She looked vaguely familiar, though Kay could not place her.

As she too swept Kay's armor, her face hardened. Almost casually, she curled her hand around a glowing iron from the fire. Kay tucked Eliza behind her as her injured hand reached for the damaged sword on her belt.

"What do you want?" the blacksmith, Leon, asked.

"Shelter. And no trouble." Kay squinted, unable to recall where she had seen the distinctive woman.

"Try the inn."

"We did. He sent us here. I'm afraid we don't have any money, but I know how to work hard, and you may have anything on my person other than my sword."

"You would sell your armor, sir?"

Kay held her gaze. "I would do much more than that for some food and shelter for my wife."

Leon glanced at Eliza. "I have no use for Glea armor."

"Then turn it into something else. You are a blacksmith, are you not?" Kay challenged, not certain if it would earn her a fight or respect, but taking the chance. It earned her only a stony stare.

"Please," Eliza said, stepping out from behind Kay and looking between the strangers. "For one night? My name is Ellie." Eliza stuttered over the lie, and Kay cringed internally. "And this is Sir Kay. We have been in the woods, attacked by a flamewalker, a malignant, and, and—what were they?" She looked at Kay with wide eyes.

"Dreamhounds chased us off camp several days ago. We are just trying to get home."

Two sets of eyes studied them intently, taking in everything from Eliza's stockinged, scratched feet to their tangled hair. Leon and the woman shared a look that spoke words Kay couldn't understand. With a nod, Leon replaced the iron in the fire.

"I'm Della," the beautiful woman said. "Follow me."

THE INSIDE OF THE STONE house was warm, cozy, and chaotically colorful. Swatches and bolts of rich and simple fabric alike scattered the main room, a partially draped dress former standing in the corner. Della moved a shimmering armful of expensive silk off the kitchen table and gestured for them to sit. Eliza sank gratefully onto the bench, every bit of her aching with exhaustion.

"How about some food?" Della asked, and Eliza almost cried as she nodded vigorously. She didn't mind that it was yet again bread and cheese, along with some fresh carrots and pickled beets.

A wet nose nudged Eliza's wrist, and she yelped, looking down to see a gray-faced dog staring hopefully at her.

"That's Ham," Della said. "Ignore him. He's not hungry. He just acts like it."

"Hello," Eliza greeted the dog, tentatively stroking the wiry hair on Ham's head as he stared balefully at her. He pressed into her leg, resting his chin on her knee. Eliza appreciated the contact, and her skirts were already ruined.

"Is that Uvarian silk?" Della asked, eyeing Eliza's gown as Eliza dove into the food in front of her.

"It is. And it used to be pink, but then a swamp happened. It's destroyed, I'm afraid."

"Perhaps not."

As Della studied Eliza's form, Eliza studied Della's face. The angles should have been too sharp to complement each other, but they fit together pleasingly.

The large, handsome blacksmith also entered and sat down directly opposite them. Leon folded her burly arms and observed them as they ate rather indelicately. Eliza was too hungry to care if it was impolite. The scar on Leon's face gave her a menacing appearance, though her expression was not as harsh as it had been in the forge.

The elderly dog abandoned Eliza and wagged his way around to Leon, the happy motion of his tail making his already unsteady legs wobble more.

Leon's smile transformed her features. Della rolled her eyes to the ceiling as Leon not-so-sneakily snuck a piece of cheese beneath the table.

"Sir Kay, was it?" Leon asked, and Sir Kaylen nodded around a mouthful of bread. "What's a knight of Glea doing wandering in the borderlands of Alludan?"

It took Sir Kaylen a moment to swallow down her overambitious bite. Eliza passed her the cup of water Della had served and earned a tiny, appreciative smile.

"I'm originally from the town of Embers Hollow, close to Griffin's Gap. Do you know it?"

Eliza wondered if that was the truth, or part of the lie.

"North of Rosewood?"

"Exactly. We recently married in Glea, and I'm bringing Ellie home to meet my family."

Leon raised an eyebrow. "Through the center of the outerlands?"

"No, from the south and making our way up. But we ran into trouble and got lost."

"Quite a lot of trouble."

Sir Kaylen's cheeks darkened.

"We didn't go looking for trouble," Eliza interjected, needing to defend Sir Kaylen. "We were...distracted at the time."

Beside her, Della snorted, her eyes amused as she roamed Eliza's figure once more, but not for studying her gown. "I bet you were."

Eliza realized what she had implied. She wasn't sure if she should be offended or flattered by Della's reaction, but a flush spread from her cheeks down her chest. The prospect of distracting Sir Kaylen was entirely appealing.

"How long have you been a knight?" Leon asked Sir Kaylen.

"Five years."

Leon and Della shared another look, and they both visibly relaxed, Leon's demeanor becoming more open and friendly. She fed Ham another piece of cheese when Della wasn't looking.

Sir Kaylen offered to help in the forge, and Leon agreed after another searching look. Panic flared in Eliza's chest when Sir Kaylen stood.

"I'll be right outside, darling," Sir Kaylen assured her as she captured Eliza's hand, pressing her lips to the back in an intimate way that had heat returning to Eliza's skin.

And then Sir Kaylen disappeared out the door, leaving Eliza alone with a stranger.

Eliza focused on not staring at Della, even though she wanted to. Eliza had so many questions, but she was afraid to ask the wrong ones and give away their lies. Before she could sort through what was safe, Della took pity on her.

"I'll start some water for a bath."

CHAPTER 11
No Small Feat

Kay unclasped her armor as she followed Leon back to the forge. Kay was mostly certain she was there to do work and not get murdered by the hard-eyed woman.

"Thank you," Kay said, just in case. "I know what it is you are sharing with us, and I appreciate it. More than you know."

"Oh, I know. Della and I have also been forced to find our feet with nothing. More than once. We help when we can. And why James at the inn sent you here."

"Where would you like these?"

Leon eyed the armor with something like distaste and jerked her head at a scorched wooden table. Kay lay the pieces down. They were her signifier of who and what she was, and all she had done. Of all she had sacrificed. But that was how life was. It gave a little and took far more, no matter what she did. Kay had not lied when she said she would let the armor go if it meant securing the help of these people.

Leon nodded at the stack of wood lining the far wall. "Grab some more fuel."

Kay watched Leon move through the space and followed her directions. "Were you a soldier?"

"Why do you ask that?"

"You have the bearing of one. I was as well. Enlisted for several years before my knighthood."

Leon took a moment before answering. "Yes, I was. A long time ago."

Leon was nearly a decade older than Kay, she guessed. But something about her reminded Kay of when she was a new recruit, a vague memory she could not grasp. And her words held the hint of a lilt. "In Glea?"

"No." Leon's response made it clear that line of conversation was over.

Leon lay a sheet of freshly formed gold on the anvil, grabbed a chisel, and hammered off two strips. Kay fetched more wood as the strips became rings, and Leon set each with a single dark gem, cursing quietly at the fiddly task.

"I don't normally do jewelry, but these are a favor," Leon explained. "Grab those pliers."

Kay handed them over.

"Do you and your wife not wear bands?" Leon asked.

Kay ran her thumb over the inside of her finger that had never worn one. Her mind caught on the memory of empty promises. "Well, um. It was a rather hasty ceremony. And with traveling, I haven't gotten around to it," Kay finished lamely, hoping the heat of the forge would disguise the discomfort rising in her cheeks.

Leon saw through Kay's babble and somehow found the closest thing to the truth. She surprised Kay by resting a hand on her shoulder. "There is no shame in not having funds for a ring. Della and I have never worn them, and she is no less my wife. When these damned things are done, let me see what I can do about that sword of yours."

They worked mostly in silence until the remains of the day faded and they headed back inside the house.

Eliza's stained gown was draped over a chair and had been replaced on Eliza's person with a simple one made of earthy berry-colored linen. She sat near the hearth, struggling to run a comb through her long, wet hair while chuckling at something Della had said.

The sight both warmed Kay's insides and made them clench as the familiar scent of humble, hearty food filled her nose.

Eliza turned her smile on Kay. "Look!" Eliza hitched up her skirt and Kay stared at shapely calves before realizing what Eliza was showing her. "Shoes!" Eliza wiggled her ankle, and a half boot of worn leather.

"Perfect. And much needed." Kay glanced at Della. "Thank you."

"They were a trade. I'm going to have fun picking apart that gown. The silk alone is worth far more."

Eliza bounced over to Kay on her newly clad toes. "I missed you," she said sweetly, rubbing her thumb over a spot on Kay's cheek. "You're turning all manner of new colors, darling."

They were acting. Eliza was pretending. But for a moment, it didn't feel like a lie. Like a fool, Kay briefly leaned into the tender touch.

"The water should still be somewhat warm, if you want to clean up. Go on back," Della told Kay, breaking the spell.

Eliza grabbed Kay's elbow, leading her into a compact room that held a bed, trunk, and small metal basin with several hands of water in it near a second crackling hearth.

"How are things going?" Kay whispered as the door closed.

"Della is so interesting! Very kind, and also a bit wicked. Remind me to tell you later what she called Prince Valin of Glea!"

"Perhaps you shouldn't tell me," Kay muttered, toeing off her worn boots and unbuckling her belt. Though Kay had little opinion on the prince, he was still the son of her queen.

She paused when she reached the laces of her kirtle. Eliza watched her intently.

"Do you mind?"

"Oh. Yes." Eliza perched on the edge of the bed, turning her head away.

Kay sighed in relief as she slipped off the last bits of clothing she had worn for too long. She dunked her whole head first, fingers catching in the snarls of her hair as she crouched in the shallow basin, letting the tepid water run down her skin. Using a rag and crescent of soap, she scrubbed off the last old bits of swamp, fresh sweat, and soot. Her hand stung as the water washed away the sap from the tender blisters. She'd need to bandage it properly, and soon.

"How did things go out in the forge?" Eliza asked the wall, working at her hair with the comb.

"I get the sense our hosts do not care much for knights. Or Glea."

"Why would that be? Alludan and Glea have always been allies. We still are, right?" Eliza stilled.

"We are," Kay hurried to assure her.

"But they are helping us."

"Yes, and I'm glad. It also makes me uneasy."

Eliza glanced at her. "Why?"

"I don't like owing people who dislike me. And there's something about Leon, like I've seen her before, but I don't remember. It's bothering me."

"Well, if you are from the area, maybe you ran into her when you were younger?"

Kay made a noncommittal noise.

"What will we do now?" Eliza asked.

"I'll ask about finding someone heading on the road toward the capital. But even if we must walk, the forests are safer in the direction we're going. We'll be heading away from the outerlands, not through them."

"Did you really grow up in Embers Hollow?"

Kay had hoped the princess had not caught that. "Yes."

"I have never been there. I've never even heard of it. What's it like?"

"A place you should be glad you never have. Will you pass me that towel?"

Eliza collected the damp towel she had used earlier from a hook on the wall. Kay angled sideways and covered herself as much as she could with her arms where she crouched, her skin prickling as Eliza's eyes roamed the marks on her hip. Kay braced herself for questions, but Eliza simply held out the towel, her gaze skittering over the rest of Kay's skin. Too exposed and seen, Kay used the towel as a shield as she stepped out of the tub.

"Are you finished with the comb?" Kay asked, grasping for something to say.

"Almost. You can have it."

"I may need my sword, but I'll try the comb first."

Eliza's eyes widened. "Don't cut off your hair! It's so pretty and wild."

"I may not have much choice."

Eliza ran her fingers over the wet mess that snarled easily on a calm day with good care. "We'll get it combed," she promised.

And Kay almost believed her.

FOR THE FIRST TIME in days, Eliza felt like the princess she was. Della, Leon, and the old dog had gone to bed in their room, leaving Eliza and Sir Kaylen with several blankets and pillows in front of the main hearth.

Eliza curled in them snugly, warm and full, watching Kaylen struggle with her hair in the firelight. It truly had matted terribly.

"Let me try," Eliza hissed, pushing up and grabbing for the comb.

Sir Kaylen jerked her hand back. "I've got it."

"Please?"

Kaylen reluctantly handed her the comb. "It's no use. I'll cut it tomorrow."

"Don't you dare."

"Or what? It's my hair."

It was, and none of Eliza's business. But the striking red curls had been one of the first things she noticed about Sir

Kaylen, and Eliza hated the idea of them being cut when Eliza was determined to save them.

"Turn around," Eliza demanded.

Kaylen huffed, but she complied. "Your princess is showing."

That made Eliza pause. "I'm sorry. I don't mean to be so rude and bossy."

"Again, I wasn't complaining. Just be mindful of it around others, or you'll give us away."

"So you think people would believe who I am if I started ordering them about and making decrees?"

Kaylen chuckled softly. "It would be a dangerous plan either way."

"But I would have you at my side to defend me." Eliza stared intently at Sir Kaylen's profile.

"You would."

Eliza's belly fluttered. She gathered the hanks of hair and lay them carefully down Kaylen's back. They fell past her natural waist and Eliza's eyes drifted to the gentle flare of hips. Eliza remembered what she had looked like earlier. All that skin on display.

The quiet murmuring of her name brought Eliza back to herself.

Eliza focused on the hair, starting at the ends. As Kaylen's mane dried, it frizzed and tangled even more, but Eliza was determined. Soon, soothing, absent humming wrapped around them. Eliza tried to stifle her yawn.

Kaylen turned and caught Eliza's wrist with her freshly bandaged hand. "Let's sleep."

"No." Eliza snatched her wrist away as Kaylen leaned forward, reaching for the comb again. Eliza lost her balance and toppled back, Kaylen falling on top of her.

Eliza forgot about the comb as the weight of Kaylen in just a loose tunic pressed her into the blanket beneath them.

Their noses nearly brushed as Kaylen stared down at her, fields of grass glistening with morning dew. As those eyes raked across Eliza's face, they lingered on her lips.

Did Kaylen want to kiss her too?

Eliza was about to press their mouths together and find out, when Kaylen abruptly pushed off her, returning to face the flickering hearth.

Eliza sat up, the comb still clutched victoriously in her hand. "Please let me try. Let me do this for you."

Kaylen didn't look at her, but she nodded, and Eliza set to work.

She tried to be gentle, but several of the mats required a lot of strain. Kaylen didn't complain, just handed over her knife. "Use it as you need."

After a while, Eliza admitted she would need to do something.

As strategically and carefully as she could, she sliced through and away a few sections beyond hope, until she could at last run a stroke through the heap of separated curls without catching.

"There," Eliza announced, entirely too proud of her meager accomplishment.

Kaylen tentatively ran her hand over her head. The hairstyle was somewhat shaggy and asymmetrically thinned, but once it was braided, no one would notice much.

"Thanks," Kaylen murmured, giving her a soft look that melted Eliza's insides. Eliza's lips tingled to feel Kaylen's. "Now, please, let's sleep."

They settled down on their backs, side by side. Eliza's eyes grew heavy, her hand reaching for Kaylen's uninjured one as she had done for the past several nights, and she fell asleep smiling.

CHAPTER 12

A Good Day for a Wedding

Leon took Kay into the heart of the village in the morning. The cool wariness of the day before was nowhere to be found as everyone greeted Leon cheerfully, some warmth even rubbing off on Kay by association.

"The butcher and tanner are getting married tonight," Leon explained, gesturing at the commotion in the center square. "It will be quite the party, knowing them."

A large, beefy man jogged across to them, several beads of sweat clinging to his brow.

"I have them right here, Bram," Leon assured him, handing over a small leather pouch.

Bram tipped out the pair of wedding bands into his palm. He stared for a moment, his eyes glistening. "They're perfect."

Leon placed a calming hand on Bram's shoulder. "You will do fine."

Bram's gaze shifted over to Kay, and he inclined in a bow. "You must be the knight who arrived yesterday."

Kay was unsurprised he already knew. Small towns worked like that. "This is Sir Kay," Leon introduced. "And this is Bram the Butcher, one of the lucky grooms."

Bram shook Kay's bandaged hand with a firm grip, and Kay gritted her teeth to suppress her wince. "It would be an honor if you and your lady would attend tonight, sir."

Kay forced a smile. "We would be delighted."

Bram lumbered off, looking panicked again.

After asking around, they eventually found a merchant with a wagon willing to take Kay and Eliza northwest as far as Rosewood the following day. It wasn't exactly the direction Kay was hoping for, but it was progress, if indirect. Rosewood was a larger town than this one, so their chances of finding something else there would be better. Especially after being able to sleep through the night and no longer looking like they had crawled through a swamp.

Kay had been hesitant to leave Eliza that morning, but Eliza had promised to stay in the house or with Della. Kay didn't know these people, and while they had been kind, that did not eliminate the chance they had forces stronger than good intentions behind them. But Eliza was clearly fatigued from the days of travel, and Kay wanted her to rest while she could. It was a risk, but one Kay needed to take. She was used to leaving behind the people she cared for.

Not that she cared for Eliza like that. She was simply responsible for her.

Since they would be relying on Leon and Della's hospitality for another night, Kay was determined to be useful. She helped Leon and several others assemble a wooden platform in the square and then climbed up onto a roof to hang strings of drying flowers from the eaves.

A loud throat clearing made Kay pause in her task of tying a frustratingly short end, and she peered over the edge of the roof.

Eliza and Della stood on the stoop below them. Kay raised a quick eyebrow at Eliza, silently asking if everything was all right, and Eliza beamed in reply. Della, however, glared at Leon with sharp exasperation.

"Oh. Fuck," Leon muttered from beside Kay, glancing up at the sky. She swung off the roof, dropping beside her wife. "Sorry, love."

"How many times..." Della hissed. "I told you to be home by noon."

Leon kissed her, open-mouthed and in front of everyone. Kay couldn't help but stare as passion visibly sparked between them. Leon whispered something that sounded like, "I'll make it up to you."

"You'd better." But Della's glare had softened into a smirk.

Kay finished tying off the strand she held and followed Leon down to the ground. Eliza continued to smile, and Kay sensed eyes on them. She needed to do something to greet her "wife," so she captured Eliza's hand, pressing her lips to Eliza's fingers before flipping them and kissing her palm. It was meant to be sufficiently intimate, and instead felt too real, as it had last night.

The princess caught her breath and looked at Kay with convincing desire in her eyes. And Kay reminded herself repeatedly this was Princess Eliza. It was a game. Eliza was not hers to kiss.

"Love is in the air." Someone chuckled as they walked past. "A good day for a wedding."

ELIZA HAD ATTENDED several weddings when she was a girl, but none had been like this. Those had been formal affairs, and she'd been sent away before anything interesting could happen.

This was loud, joyful, and a bit rowdy. In the wake of the ceremony, food was being laid on mismatched tables as music filled the air above a deafening swell of voices and laughter. Eliza drank it in. Faced with so many people, she hardly knew where to look.

Well, that wasn't entirely true, because her focus kept returning to the woman who was still the most fascinating creature among them.

Kaylen wore a borrowed green tunic, which brought out the color of her eyes in the fading sunset. She brushed Eliza's damp cheek. "Are you better now?"

Eliza sniffed. When everyone else started crying during the ceremony, Eliza's own tears had joined in for no reason. "I'm not sad," Eliza protested.

"I know." Kaylen smiled gently, sitting beside her on the bench near the edge of the festive central square.

Someone started a new song, a chorus of varied voices ringing through the crowd. Kaylen's lips moved along, but Eliza couldn't hear her over the others. When she leaned closer, Kaylen stopped.

Kaylen's leg started to jitter.

"Was your wedding like this?" Eliza asked.

Kaylen stilled. "No. *Our* wedding was much quieter."

Oh. Right. "It was a small affair," Eliza asked as a statement.

Kaylen nodded.

"But we had family with us."

Kaylen shook her head, and Eliza's chest squeezed. "They were all back home," Kaylen murmured. "We got married quickly in a soldiers' camp."

"Do you wish we could have had something different? Grander?" Eliza watched Kaylen closely.

"I don't know."

Eliza rolled her eyes. "You really need to work on answering questions better."

"Sorry, darling."

Eliza enjoyed the endearment far too much. "Have you ever thought of marrying again?"

"No."

"Why not? You're still young."

Kaylen's smile turned lightly mocking. "But I look much older."

"I didn't mean that!"

The warm sound of Kaylen's laugh was mostly swallowed by the crowd. "It's not that." The amusement faded and Kaylen looked down. "It didn't go well last time."

Before Eliza could ask what she meant, they were interrupted.

"Now this will put hair on your chest, my lady," Della said, materializing in front of them and holding out two tankards. "I highly recommend it."

Eliza took her tankard curiously. She swallowed a large gulp, and her eyes watered from the intense, bitter ale.

Della suddenly seized a woman, pulling her into a tight hug. "Netty. I didn't think you'd make it back in time. How was the trip?"

"Good, as always." The new stranger studied Eliza and Kaylen closely. "And you have guests. From Glea, I hear."

Della introduced her sister to them. Eliza was certain she would forget all the names learned today, wishing desperately she could write them down. But when she'd asked earlier, Della had told her they didn't keep any parchment or ink. It was an expensive luxury Eliza had taken for granted, along with everything else she'd had as a child and later in her tower.

She drank the strong ale. It grew less bitter the more she consumed, and the world took on an enjoyable buzzing. But Kaylen was not drinking hers. The tankard rested full on the bench between them, and Kaylen's leg started bouncing again.

"You don't like it?" Eliza asked, gesturing to the undrunk drink as their hosts wandered off, leaving Kaylen and Eliza relatively alone.

"It's better I don't." Kaylen gave her a sideways look, her gaze flicking toward the gathering of people dancing nearby.

Eliza scooted closer. "What do you mean?"

Kaylen licked her lips. "I don't drink."

Eliza gazed into her own mostly empty tankard. "Are you philosophically opposed? Should I not either?"

Kaylen crooked that soft smile at Eliza again, sending Eliza's unsteady belly sloshing. "No, you go ahead. I just..." She looked down at the tankard for a moment. "It's too easy for me to get lost inside it." Kaylen's skin was warm and newly familiar. Kaylen spoke to their twined hands, running her thumb over Eliza's knuckle. "There are things I like too much to forget."

Eliza ached to know what those things were.

Kaylen cleared her throat and pasted on a strained smile, pulling Eliza to her feet. "Will my new wife honor me with a dance?"

Eliza veered forward and Kaylen steadied her. "If you promise you know how to lead well. I hated when my partners stepped on my toes."

"I can assure you I am terrible."

Eliza laughed as Kaylen led her to the edge of the dancing.

Della and Leon swayed together nearby, eyes only for each other and not at all in line with the upbeat music. When Leon pressed her mouth to Della's ear, Della grinned, and then stooped and swept the strapping woman off her feet with shocking ease.

The look Leon gave her wife as Della carried her behind the nearest building made Eliza's face heat again. It was smoldering and adoring, and held a thousand promises.

What would it be like to have someone look at her like that?

Kaylen pulled Eliza closer. Her emerald eyes glittered in the firelight, and for a moment, Eliza saw what she wanted. Then Eliza blinked and it was gone. She was only fooling herself.

The current dance was a formation, like what Eliza had learned at her father's court. "Aren't we supposed to change partners?" Eliza asked when the row shifted.

Kaylen pressed her hand into Eliza's back and stepped them away. "We are newlyweds. I'm feeling possessive."

Eliza raised her eyebrows, surprised by the thrill those words sent through her. The thought of this woman desiring to possess her was more intoxicating than the ale. Eliza looped her arms around Kaylen's neck and leaned scandalously close. "Is that so?"

No, of course it wasn't so. But Eliza pretended.

Kaylen's hand skimmed down to Eliza's hip, leaving a trail of fire. The music faded and Eliza's heartbeat replaced the rhythm. Eliza forgot to move her feet and they stumbled as Kaylen stepped into her.

"Sorry," they both muttered together.

Eliza laughed again, suddenly nervous, her body extremely aware of Kaylen's as their chests brushed.

A slower ballad began. Kaylen's strong neck and shoulders were solid beneath Eliza's forearms.

"I like this place," Eliza said. "I'm no longer convinced we should leave tomorrow."

Kaylen stiffened. "Are you saying you don't want to return to the palace?"

Eliza sighed. She did want to return. The palace was her home. But she rather liked the fantasy of staying here with these new, kind, interesting people. Where she wasn't Princess Eliza, but Lady Ellie. "I think you should call me El from now on."

"That's not your name," Kaylen said harshly, and Eliza flinched. "And you cannot stay here."

"Why not?" Eliza challenged, stung by Kaylen's change in demeanor.

"What would you do? How would you live?"

"I don't know." Eliza hadn't thought about it, because it hadn't been a genuine plan, but now she wanted to dig her heels in.

"You will be expected at the palace."

"Actually, I won't. No one knows I'm free except for us. Because you told me to keep my mouth shut."

"I didn't—" Kaylen clenched her jaw. "I'm taking you to your father."

"What if I won't go? Will you throw me over your shoulder?" The thought was not entirely unpleasant.

Kaylen's face remained impassive. It had been a joke, but now Eliza wasn't so sure Kaylen wouldn't.

"Why do you care so much?" Eliza asked. "What's in it for you? Glory?"

"Not glory, no."

"What, then? A few gold ludans?" Eliza threw it out there to provoke her, but when Kaylen did not deny it, Eliza's gut tightened. She pulled free of Kaylen's arms. "How much is the reward, anyway?"

"Six hundred ludans to attempt," Kaylen answered easily, and the number sank through Eliza. Was that all she was worth to her father? To her kingdom? To Kaylen?

Eliza had assumed the knights who tried to rescue her were doing so to earnestly free her. She had naively not expected anyone who succeeded to have done it for the money. Especially not Kaylen. But Eliza had only known her for a short time. Eliza's skin itched at knowing the monetary price assigned to her freedom, and it didn't even feel like very much, compared to the years of her life she'd been deprived of.

She shouldn't have asked.

She shouldn't have drunk that entire tankard of ale either. It soured in her stomach and fuzzied the world.

The only direction she had was away. In the alley darkened more by the dusk, she tripped, but a hand steadied her elbow. She whirled around to find Kaylen supporting her.

"Get away from me," Eliza bit out, pulling free.

"No."

"Oh, that's right. You wouldn't want your bag of gold to spill, and that's all I am to you."

Kaylen sighed, and it irritated Eliza. "Sit down. Let's talk."

Eliza ran instead, but not very well. Kaylen followed. Eliza made it around the back of a barn, where she stumbled again on apparently nothing, and Kaylen steadied her.

"Fine," Eliza snapped, and reluctantly let Kaylen steer her onto an upended barrel. Kaylen perched on the one beside her, and Eliza folded her arms. "You really had me fooled. I thought you were kind, but you're greedy and selfish. Stop sighing at me!"

"Are you done?"

"Done with you! I've changed my mind. I'll find someone else to take me home to the palace."

Silence stretched as Eliza stewed, not certain if she meant the words or not. Kaylen's breathing sharpened, following the faint cadence of her calming hum. Eliza scowled harder, annoyed that she still liked it.

"I know you're upset," Kaylen said finally.

"Well spotted."

"But that reward is not the value of your life." Kaylen's words were rough with something Eliza should have listened to. "It's mine."

"What?"

"I won't lie and say I accepted this quest for any other reason than that I'm utterly broke. I had nothing when we met, because I have nothing."

Eliza blinked through the darkness. "But you are a knight."

"I am. A destitute one. And people I love are relying on that reward. I was prepared to die for it. I *planned* to die for it. So don't treat it like some inconsequential thing. Your Highness."

Eliza flinched at the hard edge to Kaylen's voice. Anger morphed into shame, prickling Eliza's scalp. "I didn't mean...I don't know what I meant. You're right. My princess is showing, and it seems she's horrid tonight."

"No, she's just hurt. And a little drunk."

"Sorry." Eliza wished she could fold herself into the barrel beneath her and disappear at Kaylen's understanding.

"It's fine."

"I didn't think before I spoke. I told you I'm bad at...being listened to. Ignore me."

"I don't think that's possible."

Eliza wanted to hug Kaylen. So she did. It was an awkward angle, until Kaylen stood so she could wrap both arms around Eliza. They fit together, and Eliza naturally parted her knees so Kaylen could stand between them.

"You're worth far more than any amount of gold," Kaylen whispered into the side of Eliza's head. "I just also need the gold very badly."

Kaylen's words warmed Eliza. "You're worth more too, you know."

"I'm actually not."

"But you are."

One of Kaylen's hands found Eliza's lower back. A delighted thrill replaced Eliza's earlier confusion. Her inner thighs brushed Kaylen's hips, and Eliza wanted more. She wanted Kaylen's hands to reach lower. To reach everywhere.

"Kay?" Eliza breathed, and Kaylen froze. "Can I call you Kay? Even when we're not pretending?"

"Sure." But her hands fell away, and Kaylen stepped back. "Let's get some rest while we can."

CHAPTER 13
A Bit Late

The cart rumbled and jostled them about as they bumped along the dirt road toward Rosewood. The merchant, a cheerful man named Dillon, drove as his young son dozed on the other side of the cart.

Kay was unusually optimistic about the day. For the first time since she said goodbye to Sir Hugo and her horse, she was rested, fed, and wearing washed clothes. Leon had even hammered out Kay's damaged sword. It wasn't a perfect fix, but the blade was functional again. The only thing presently weighing heavy on Kay was the desire to look sideways at where Eliza sat, the movement of the cart doing incredible things to the neckline of her new gown.

"I liked them," Eliza said, gazing back at the walls of the village disappearing behind them.

"They were very generous," Kay agreed, glancing at the rattling sack by her feet. Leon had handed it to her as she climbed into the cart.

"I have thought about it, and I don't want Glea armor after all," Leon had said with a crooked smile.

It had not been a small gesture, and Kay couldn't quite get over it. But perhaps the not-so-muffled sounds from the bedroom last night had something to do with the woman's generosity that morning.

"When we get to the palace, I'll make sure to have something sent to them as a thank you." Eliza looked at Kay. "That would be good, right?"

Kay assured her it would.

The road took them up the valley and over a ridge with views toward the hills and flats of central Alludan. They did not turn that direction, however, continuing north and through the foothills. The dense forest encroached upon the road on one side, then the other, then both, narrowing down to barely a lane before opening again.

Kay shifted on the bale of hay, which provided some cushion from the ruts of the road. As the two mules navigated the turns, Eliza slid and pressed against Kay's side, and Kay eventually wrapped an arm around her to keep her steady.

The child woke and laughed as he tumbled back and forth, much to the exasperation of his parent.

"You'll hurt yourself! Hold on," Dillon reprimanded.

Kay tensed to reach out and snag the young boy close too.

Thankfully, he listened. And his attention, no longer occupied by the reckless game he had been playing, shifted squarely onto Kay.

"Are you a real knight?" he asked, his face speckled with even more freckles than Kay's and capped with a head of messy hair.

"I am."

"Then why don't you have a horse?"

Kay's mouth twitched and she glanced at Eliza. "I keep having to explain that a horse is not actually a requirement to be a knight. We parted ways last week."

"You talk funny."

"Ralphie!" Dillon scolded and looked apologetically at Kay.

"It's all right," Kay said.

"Have you fought in battles?" the boy asked.

Kay nodded.

"Awesome!"

Kay smiled sadly back. That would not have been a word she associated with it. But he was young. Kay would not be the one to disillusion him. Life had a way of doing that already.

Beside Kay, Eliza traveled with her eyes alternately wide open, staring around them at everything, to throwing her head back when they reached the patches of sun. She was beautiful both ways. Kay marveled at how bright and resilient Eliza remained through everything.

Kay's hand splayed over Eliza's side, keeping her close. For a brief, careless moment, Kay imagined what it would be like to call Eliza hers.

The sun passed behind a cloud as the cart dipped. Eliza blinked open her eyes, swaying into Kay as Kay shifted to brace them. Kay's nose bumped Eliza's cheek, sun-warmed and smooth. Kay's head tilted, her body responding. Eliza curled one hand around Kay's arm, the other gripping her upper thigh.

The cart lurched to a stop. Entirely distracted, Kay tumbled with Eliza into the straw-strewn bottom. It knocked the sense back into Kay, saving her from the disastrous temptation to taste Eliza's lips.

"What's happening?" asked the young boy loudly as he clambered up onto the bench with his father.

Kay was about to ask that same question, when a new, unfamiliar voice spoke. "Good morning."

Kay tightened her hold on Eliza, pressing her down onto the floor of the cart.

"Nice day, ain't it?" the new voice said, false friendliness ringing through each word.

Kay had grown up near these woods. She knew what they had driven into, and it wouldn't end well for someone. They had traded magical monsters for human ones.

Kay made eye contact with Eliza and mouthed, "Stay down."

Eliza nodded.

Kay stood slowly, making deliberate noise so she wouldn't startle an arrow loose.

Three figures blocked the road at the bottom of the dip. Trees lined the roadsides, and Kay assumed more bandits lurked beyond her sight. The man in front was dressed simply but clean, while the two behind him looked little better than Kay and Eliza had when they'd left the forest two days ago.

Kay wished she wore her armor, but at least she had her chainmail shirt on.

"Is there a problem?" Kay asked. She let the simple hills accent she'd tried to shake for the past eight years now lace her own voice, as she rested her hand casually on her sword hilt.

The two henchmen blanched, both stepping back and glancing at each other. The leader, however, did not.

"No problem that cannot be fixed with a quick change of hands."

Kay was glad to see Dillon was holding both his son and a long dagger. He was a local as well, and no fool.

"Well, I'll have a problem if you don't step aside," Kay said.

She could see his mind working, calculating her, the child, the weapons, and how much trouble this was worth. "You think you're a knight or somethin'?"

Kay smiled. "Somethin'."

"She is a knight!" the boy piped up boldly, and his father shushed him. "She has armor and everything!"

The man smiled back coldly. "Is that so?"

ELIZA WAS DETERMINED to be quiet, not even breathing. But the hay itched her skin, and one piece tickled her nose. As she twitched away from it, her lungs took a needed inhale.

Kaylen shifted her foot, and Eliza knew she had heard.

A hand seized Eliza's ankle. With a shriek, Eliza grabbed for Kaylen's boots, but only brushed the worn leather before she was yanked back and tipped out of the bed of the cart, like one of the sacks lining the sides.

The grip circling Eliza's wrist tightened. Like bindings from a lifetime ago, in an endless darkness. The darkness appeared now, blocking out the bright sunny day.

Eliza struggled, fighting to stay in the present, twisting to see her captor. She caught sight of a ruddy, red-haired woman, just as a reshaped, sharpened sword blade pressed into that throat.

"Hands off, or I'll take them off after your head," Kaylen snarled, her voice helping to burn back some of the encroaching, clawing panic closing Eliza's lungs.

Eliza's captor's hard countenance melted into one of surprise. "Kaylen?"

They knew each other? Kaylen's deadly expression didn't change, and neither did the pressure of her steady weapon.

A new man appeared over Kaylen's shoulder. Eliza made an incoherent sound of alarm as the woman holding her hissed, "Don't!" but it was too late. He lunged.

Without removing her sword, Kaylen shifted, rolling beneath the strike. His blade slithered against chainmail and sheared off an additional lock of Kaylen's newly shaggy hair.

The fluttering, falling curl shuddered down Eliza's spine.

Kaylen's left hand flashed with her knife as she stabbed back, and the man crumpled with a cry, the hilt protruding from his leg.

"Hands fucking off," Kaylen gritted out.

The stranger released Eliza. Kaylen wrapped her free arm protectively around Eliza's waist, backing them into the side of the cart. Only then did Kaylen let the attacker's hasty retreat succeed.

"It's me—Maggie," the stranger said.

"I know."

"I haven't seen you in years," Maggie said, hand coming up to cover the shallow cut Kaylen's sword had left on her skin.

"Uh-huh." Kaylen was done being polite, her face fierce and hold almost painful as she clutched Eliza close. Eliza clung right back, no desire to be anywhere else. Her heart hammered through her chest, but the threatening panic eased. Kaylen had her.

Maggie must have realized Kaylen was done as well, because she retreated another pace. "Let's go, boys," she called to the other three, who were circling around the front of the cart. The man Kaylen had stabbed lay whimpering on the ground. "Misunderstanding."

"There's only a few of them," the clean man said, his gaze intent.

"I said *let's go*." Maggie smiled nervously at Kaylen. "Didn't realize you were back. Give my best to Aunt Ruth, yeah?"

Kaylen just stared her down as Maggie roughly grabbed the clean man and they dragged their bleeding companion away, disappearing into the trees, where the others already fled.

"You hurt?" Kaylen murmured, her grip gentling.

Eliza shook her head.

"Are you and your son all right?" Kaylen asked the driver as two more matching sets of wide eyes stared at Kaylen with something a bit like awe.

"Yes. Thank you, sir," Dillon said.

"That was awesome," the boy whispered earnestly, and Eliza managed a shaky laugh.

"I shall drive, or ride up there with you," Kaylen stated, authority and confidence radiating off her, the lilt of her modulated accent returning to its delightful mix. She reached for the sack that contained her armor, buckling on her one remaining bracer, and Eliza was finally forced to relinquish her hold on Kaylen's hand. Eliza wanted to stay pressed against Kaylen for the rest of the day.

Perhaps longer.

IT WAS GROWING DARK when they rolled into Rosewood. As the largest town in this low-populated section of the borderlands, Kay had visited a few times, but she didn't know it well. Dillon offered for Kay and Eliza to stay with him, apparently grateful for Kay's presence on the road that day. And Kay had no better option than to accept.

They pulled up in front of his home, a narrow two-story structure near the edge of town and crammed between a shared barn on one side and another house on the other.

"There's an excellent tavern at the end of the lane. Let me buy you a drink and a meal," Dillon said hopefully as Kay handed Eliza down from the cart.

Kay's stomach rumbled. "A meal would be wonderful."

She regretted agreeing as soon as they stepped into the small, busy tavern. The violence of earlier lingered in her body, keeping her on edge, and the familiar atmosphere wasn't helping. She kept a hand on Eliza's waist, unwilling to let her out of reach here.

As they squeezed around a table in the corner, Kay hastily assessed the other patrons. Most greeted Dillon with a nod, and they all eyed Kay and her armor with curiosity.

Dillon pushed a tankard of ale toward Kay, and she forced a smile. "Thanks."

Ale wasn't as difficult as wine. She'd never liked it as much, though it had worked fine when no wine could be found. Or when the wine ran out. The scent both turned her stomach and tempted her. Swallowing hard, Kay angled her head away. The wood table was smooth and hard beneath her drumming fingers.

*When the fields are sown
with seeds of our own,
we'll never be parted, my darling...*

Eliza's light touch stilled Kay's jittering knee. Kay cleared her throat, hoping no one else had noticed her humming.

Eliza sipped from her own water and placed it in front of Kay, casually taking the tankard of ale for herself and moving it farther away. Dark, gritty shame licked Kay's insides.

Kay was fine. She didn't need Eliza's help. Kay could handle herself. She hadn't touched a drop in two years, and had more than enough opportunity.

She should never have told Eliza about her problem.

And yet the scent of it called to her anyway.

"So, you knew who those ruffians were?" Dillon asked, eyeing her curiously.

"Only the one. And I don't know her, but we have an unfortunate connection by blood. The bad side of the family, you could say."

"I would say! A bandit related to a knight! Regardless, I can't express how grateful I am you were with us today. Things seem to have gotten worse recently. More news of thieves and brigands on the roads."

"Yes, well, with the drought this spring and Uvaria choking our markets since that new trade deal, I imagine things are difficult for many around here."

Everyone stared at Kay, so she reached for the tankard in front of her, relieved and disappointed it was only water.

"Right. Of course, you would have your pulse on the economy of the area. Do you own a large estate, sir?"

"Quite small, actually," Kay hedged. It wasn't entirely a lie, though not truthful anymore. "What is it you trade in again? Tell me more about that."

Kay pretended to listen as their food arrived and she finished every scrap, barely stopping herself from licking the bowl. Dillon liked to talk, and Kay was glad of it.

Eliza listened with apparent interest to what he told them about the trade of source resin from the mountains to a distiller in the flatlands for processing.

Around them, the crowd gradually changed over from others looking for a meal to those looking for a drink or some entertainment. A musician strummed and sang over the drone of chatter.

Dillon asked to stay and share another drink, but Kay quickly declined. "My lady and I are quite tired from the day."

"Of course," Dillon agreed, clearly disappointed. Kay regretted leading him on to believe she was a worthwhile person to invest time into ingratiating. But regret was not stronger than the security of a roof and warm hospitality.

Dillon offered them his own room, but Kay firmly refused. So they found themselves in a small one on the second floor. A narrow bed sat beneath the window. It was perfect.

As soon as the door closed, Kay leaned against it and her shoulders relaxed. She closed her eyes too, but sensed Eliza watching her.

Eliza was right in front of her. Kay heard her feet on the floor and almost felt her heat. Still, Kay kept her eyes shut.

"Are you avoiding me?" Eliza whispered.

"Yes."

"Oh."

Kay sighed and finally looked at her. "Sorry. It's just been a long day."

"I know. I was there."

Eliza was right. The candle Eliza held was the only light in the room, and it cast warm shadows over her face.

"How are you?" Kay asked. She should have asked already.

"I'm alive, and we have a bed. That's nice." Eliza smiled, but something was off.

Kay reached out before she could think better of it, tucking a strand of hair behind Eliza's ear. She waited.

"What you said earlier," Eliza continued. "About it being a hard time for people. Is that true?"

"Things have always been hard, but the last few years they've been getting worse."

Eliza nodded slowly. "I feel so out of touch. These are my people, and I had no idea they were here, let alone their troubles. And I have no idea what I might do about it."

"Well, you have been in a tower for eighteen years. It's a very reasonable excuse."

"I'm not looking for an excuse. I'm going to be queen one day. I've been alive for so long with nothing to show for it. And I'm afraid I'll always be behind."

"It's a bit late in the day for this sort of conversation, isn't it?"

Eliza laughed. "Isn't it the perfect time? Deep philosophical questions are best answered at night, I've heard."

Kay's fingers caught at Eliza's sleeve as she stood too close. "I'm far from a philosopher, but I have a feeling you'll do just fine. You have a good heart. That's a lot better than a bad one with experience."

Eliza's eyes glistened as she smiled. "I like your heart too."

Eliza placed her hand in the center of Kay's chest, and the heart she spoke of stopped beating. Then thundered. Her mind knew she couldn't feel Eliza's touch through her breastplate, but her skin swore she could.

"I've missed so many experiences," Eliza murmured. "So many things I want to learn. And re-learn."

Kay's body was very awake. She tensed, resisting closing the alarmingly minimal distance between them. To kiss Eliza's kind lips and offer herself up for Eliza's education. But Kay couldn't afford to.

Eliza's eyes fell to Kay's mouth. Kay froze, waiting, but Eliza simply continued to stare, the light of the candle washing over her features. Kay barely breathed as the wax softened and dripped down the stubby taper.

Kay's damaged hand contemplated the curve of Eliza's waist.

Then Kay gently nudged her away, slipping past into the relative safety of the room beyond.

Eliza was worse than wine, and Kay couldn't fall into her.

Kay shed her armor and reached inside her mind for the soothing song she carried with her.

It was a chilly night, and no hearth graced the room, just a stack of slowly warming stones that continued the chimney from the room below and radiated warmth. But the woolen blankets were thick.

Eliza shivered, shifting closer in their narrow bed. After another shiver, Kay wrapped an arm around her.

For warmth.

CHAPTER 14
Wander Far

Eliza clung to Kaylen as they moved through the clamoring streets. People called, carts splashed mud, and shutters banged above. Children laughed and shrieked over honking animals.

In life before the tower, Rosewood would have seemed quite quaint, but now it bustled like a metropolis. So many faces and sounds and scents.

"Sorry," the man Kaylen was speaking to said with a regretful shake of his head. "Not leaving that way for another week."

Kaylen thanked him and moved on through the main town square. He was the fifth person they had asked.

Kaylen glanced up at the sky, already shining with midmorning. "Let's start walking and hope someone will pick us up along the road."

An elderly woman intercepted Eliza, a smile cracking through her face cheerfully as she held out a bouquet of vibrant blue blooms. "Pretty flowers for a pretty lady?"

"Oh, thank you!" Eliza accepted them with an answering smile, inhaling their faint scent.

"Just half a ludan for a whole bushel. You won't find finer this side of the capital."

Eliza's smile faded, now seeing the stand of colorful flowers behind the woman. Of course she was trying to sell them. Eliza quickly handed the bouquet back. "They are lovely. But not today."

"You sure?" The old woman turned her attention to Kaylen. "Your lady seems to like them. Wouldn't want to disappoint her, would you, sir?"

Kaylen glanced sideways at Eliza, her posture tense. "Perhaps another time," she murmured and tugged Eliza onward.

They followed the main road out of town, which took them past the outer wall and into rolling hills of fields and patches of trees, as the mountains of the outerlands loomed behind and above it all.

As they walked the deserted road, Eliza still held Kaylen's hand, having no desire to let go. Eliza was growing decadently used to her presence. Awaking that morning with Kaylen's steady exhales tickling the back of her neck, Kaylen's knee slotted with Eliza's and arm heavy at her waist, Eliza had been frighteningly content.

They paused by a bridge over a shallow stream, and Kaylen finally pulled free.

"I'll be right back," Kaylen muttered before hurrying a short way up the bank.

Eliza's disappointment vanished when she realized what Kaylen was doing.

Kaylen returned with a small bunch of spindly blue flowers. "They aren't the same, but..." Kaylen held them out, watching her questioningly.

The pale petals fluttered in the faint breeze, far more beautiful than the ones from the square. Because they were from Kaylen. Eliza closed her fingers around the stems, brushing over Kaylen's scarred knuckles. Heart expanding into her throat, Eliza leaned forward and pressed a quick kiss to Kaylen's freckled cheek. "Thank you."

Kaylen cleared her throat, not quite meeting Eliza's gaze. "You seemed to like the others, so."

Kaylen abruptly turned and started walking again. Eliza grinned, inhaling the strong, wild scent of her new favorite flowers. Giddy with happiness at the thoughtful gesture, Eliza looped her arm through Kaylen's and tried not to skip up the road.

Not long after, they heard the cart behind them.

"Good day," Kaylen called as she waved the driver down. "Where are you headed? Might you have room for two more?"

The driver slowed, squinting at them, his gaze as wiry and sharp as his frame. "Where are you wantin' to go?"

"Toward the capital."

The driver rubbed his mouth, studying Kaylen's armor. His eyes shifted and lingered over Eliza, and she found herself pressed closer to Kaylen.

"Just so happens, we're headed that way. Hop in." He jerked his head at the back of the cart, smaller and rougher than Dillon's and draped in stained cloth, and where two other men already rode. "But don't touch anything."

"How far are you going?" Kaylen asked, not moving.

"Graymill."

Eliza recognized the name and looked excitedly at Kaylen. "That's close to the palace," Eliza whispered.

"Sure is," the man said, grinning toothily at her. "Your carriage awaits, my lady."

Kaylen hesitated, her jaw tensing, and she kept an arm wrapped tightly around Eliza even after they were settled on a hard cloth-covered barrel. A strong, acrid scent filled Eliza's nose.

The driver whistled as the cart lurched into motion. The pressure of Kaylen's grip increased as the new strangers eyed them.

"Don't leave my side, no matter what anyone says," Kaylen whispered into Eliza's ear.

Eliza wasn't about to. She clutched her drooping bouquet and leaned into Kaylen's hold as the cart turned at a fork.

Eliza had never ridden in an open cart before yesterday. She found the comfort lacking but the views and fresh air superior to the stuffy carriages of her youth.

"Why are we going north?" Kaylen called after a while. "Last time I checked, Graymill was west."

"The road directly west is rutted. This way is better."

Kaylen shook her head almost imperceptibly at Eliza, her eyes returning to the back of the man's balding head and flicking between the other strangers. Eliza twisted around, but Rosewood was already far out of sight. As the cart jolted up from a dip, one of the cloths slipped. A shimmer of pearlescent hide caught the sun, gleaming.

Kaylen suddenly grabbed Eliza's free hand, bringing it up to her face as she leaned forward. "We'll have to lanolin your hands, darling. They are getting dry in this weather." Eliza opened her mouth but Kaylen shook her head minutely again, her eyes warning, and Eliza fell silent as one of the other men furtively adjusted the cloth back.

"Where'd you get that armor?" the same stranger finally asked Kaylen.

"A smith."

"Looks genuine."

"It is."

The men glanced at each other, something in their expressions setting Eliza's hair on end, but they didn't speak again.

Uneasiness filled her, though she wasn't truly afraid. Kaylen would protect her if these men meant them any harm. Like Kaylen had protected Eliza every day before now.

They rumbled onward. The road forked again, the larger path to the west wide and well-traveled.

They continued driving north.

As the cart picked up speed trundling down toward a valley, Kaylen leaned in, nuzzling Eliza's cheek. Eliza immediately responded to the intimate touch, her heart accelerating and forgetting about anything besides the faint brush of Kaylen's lips as Kaylen pressed them to Eliza's ear.

"After the bridge, when I say go, you jump. Out the back. Aim for the grass on the side."

Disoriented and feeling foolish, Eliza stared from Kaylen to the swiftly moving ground disappearing behind them. But she remembered what she had just told herself. Kaylen would protect her. She nodded.

They reached the bottom of the hill, the wheels rattling over the stone bridge and slogging as they hit the steep slope rising on the other side.

Kaylen shifted her grip on Eliza's waist. "Go."

Eliza hesitated, and belatedly jumped. She almost made it to the grass.

Dirt and rocks scraped as she landed, tumbling to a stop just shy of the swift river. Eliza struggled to her feet, something rushing in her blood to get up, suppressing any pain.

And then Kaylen was there with her, taking her hand.

They ran into the trees and down the slope of the valley that turned to a ravine, shunted by the river. Voices cursed after them and Eliza pushed her feet faster, until the babble of the forest was the only sound.

Eliza stumbled, the rush fading as her body grew louder. Pain throbbed up her arm and shoulder, and Kaylen caught her as she grew unsteady.

Laying Eliza gently down on the bank of the river, Kaylen's touch skimmed over her, and Eliza reveled in it, until Kaylen got to her sleeve.

"I'm sorry," Kaylen said, pushing up the fabric to reveal a nasty scrape.

"For what?"

"For getting in that cart, and getting you hurt."

"I was the one who hesitated."

Kaylen's entire focus fixed on the stinging injury as she carefully and tenderly washed it. Eliza could have done it herself, but she liked that Kaylen was doing it. Taking care of her.

"What was under that cloth?" Eliza finally asked, not certain she wanted to know.

"Based on the smell, something dead a while."

"They were hunters?"

"I doubt they were the ones who killed it. Hide like that is worth a lot. Are you hurt anywhere else?"

Eliza did a quick mental sweep of her own body. She reached for her skirt, finding another tender scrape on her knee, but the skin had not broken.

Kaylen's gaze riveted on Eliza's exposed legs.

"I'll be fine," Eliza promised.

Kaylen nodded quickly and looked away. "Good."

Eliza's insides fluttered.

They stood, yet again alone and lost in the woods.

A patch of pale blue caught Eliza's attention. She'd lost her bouquet, but more of the flowers grew in the shade along the bank. She plucked one.

"For you this time," Eliza said, tucking it behind Kaylen's ear and lingering, one curl wrapping around Eliza's finger as if it wanted her to stay as well.

Kaylen stilled, her intense green eyes capturing Eliza's.

The river shattered, a massive coil of scales bursting through the surface. Water soaked Eliza's gown and dripped onto her face as she stared up at the head looming above.

"No!" Eliza grabbed Kaylen's arm, staying her sword, as the head was joined by two identical ones. "It's Harriet."

Six familiar eyes bore down on them. Harriet sparkled, her once muted purple and ash coloring turned violet and silver by the sun.

"You're so pretty in the light," Eliza whispered, happiness flooding her. "Is this your new river now?"

Eliza wasn't certain Harriet understood her words, but that had never stopped Eliza from speaking to her.

Cautiously, Eliza reached up.

Head Three glared at her for several heartbeats before slowly lowering. When Harriet nudged Eliza's palm with her great snout, Eliza choked on something between a sob and a gasp. She'd never been able to touch Harriet before.

Eliza ran her second hand over the slope of Harriet's nose, her arm not even as long as Harriet's jaw. Her scales were smooth, cold, and almost soft. Tears burned Eliza's eyes.

Then she heard the growling beside them.

Kaylen hauled Eliza farther back onto the bank, breaking Eliza's fleeting contact with the hydra.

Heads One and Two continued to growl, slitted eyes fixed on Kaylen's armor and drawn sword.

"No," Eliza repeated firmly, stepping in front of Kaylen as Kaylen tried to step in front of Eliza. They collided rather painfully. "No, Harriet. Not this one. This one is mine."

Head One lunged toward them, but Head Three slammed into One's jaw, diverting its strike.

"Get back!" Kaylen spun Eliza away from the water, placing herself between Eliza and Harriet as the hydra swung around toward them.

"Don't hurt her!" Eliza cried, not certain whom she was talking to. Panic clogged her throat as Kaylen reeled backward, sword gleaming, and Head One and Head Two lunged again with fangs bared.

Head Three hooked under the other necks, wrestling them sideways as jaws snapped at the air above Kaylen's head. Harriet tumbled, fighting with herself as she disappeared into the current again.

Eliza didn't have time to whisper her goodbye as Kaylen looped her arm around Eliza's middle and hauled her bodily away from the water.

"Run." Kaylen's order brooked no argument, and Eliza listened. They ran again, not along the river but directly away from it, up the slope of the valley.

"Where are we going?" Eliza panted.

"Away."

"How far away?"

Kaylen finally slowed. "I don't know." Her shoulders sagged briefly. "I've never run from a hydra who answers to Harriet."

Eliza couldn't tell if Kaylen was angry with her. "We don't have to run from her."

"The growling and lunging were pretty compelling."

"Head One is just like that."

Kaylen looked at her, and Eliza wanted to flinch away from the intensity of it, and also to step closer.

Eliza had never feared Harriet. But nothing was stopping her from harming Eliza anymore. Or Kaylen.

"Sorry," Eliza mumbled, repeating that scene in her mind and realizing how reckless she had just been. "If we see her again, I won't try to pet her."

Kaylen huffed, her expression cracking into bewilderment. "Good."

They walked on, falling into another shallow valley and then climbing back up. Kaylen remained quiet, and Eliza fretted that Kaylen really was upset with her, and probably for good reason.

The trees thinned as they reached a grassy, windy ridge.

The new valley looked the same as the last to Eliza. "Where to now?"

Kaylen didn't answer immediately, her gaze on the hill across from them. "That way," she eventually said, gesturing to the side, but her attention hadn't strayed.

Gathering her courage, Eliza reached out for Kaylen's hand, relieved when Kaylen didn't pull away. Eliza stroked her thumb over the back of Kaylen's. "What is it?"

When Kaylen answered, her voice was so quiet Eliza almost didn't hear. "My home is on the other side of that hill."

Eliza's heart leapt with excitement. "Really? Let's go there."

"No." Kaylen shook her head jerkily.

"Don't you want to?"

"It's out of our way."

"Not much."

"It'll take even longer to get back to the palace."

"So? You told me you had people you love there. Was that true?"

Kaylen flinched, which confused Eliza more. "Yes."

"Then why not go there?"

Kaylen remained quiet.

"How long has it been since you were home?" Eliza asked.

"Almost two years," Kaylen whispered.

"Why would you stay away so long?"

Anger flashed across Kaylen's face and she yanked her hand away. "You have no idea what you're talking about."

Eliza swallowed, the words stinging. "I know I don't. That's why I'm asking."

Kaylen ran a hand over her eyes, shoulders set with tension.

"Will you tell me so I understand?"

Kaylen stared at the hill for several more heartbeats. "It's complicated."

"Why?"

Kaylen did not answer that either.

"You want to go back, don't you?" Eliza confirmed, knowing she did.

Kaylen looked longingly at the hill.

"Do I need to order you to take me to your home?" Eliza prompted.

Kaylen didn't smile. Instead, she closed her eyes. "Maybe," she breathed.

"Very well. Take me home, Sir Kaylen."

KAY'S PALM GREW CLAMMY in Eliza's as they crested the final ridge. Embers Hollow sat sadly below them, sickeningly familiar. It wasn't a town so much as a few buildings scattered through the valley, with the manor looming on the hill.

Kay hadn't been prepared to come home. She wasn't ready. And yet here she was. Her walls trembled as the emotions she tried to control sieged her. Her feet carried her down the slope, a painful eagerness filling her chest.

Kay didn't want Eliza to see this place, or to add Eliza's presence to the memories here. It already held enough. But Ma and Stella were somewhere out of sight. Kaylen hadn't thought she would ever see them again.

She struggled not to run.

She passed the field where Finley had kissed her for the first time, and climbed over the fence Pa had helped repair when Luka accidentally drove a cart too close to it. The wood used to be bright and mismatched, but it had faded and weathered to blend with the rest now, the only evidence in the minds of those who remembered.

The crooked house sat welcoming and terribly sad. Kay couldn't breathe and her feet quickened. The wooden door was worn, Kay's hands finding the groove in the handle like it was yesterday.

"Ma?"

Kay hadn't expected so much gray. She should have, as it had been there when she left last time, but now only a trace of Ma's original red was visible on her light head. More evidence of how much time had passed. Of how much Kay had missed.

Ma stared at her. "Kaylen."

And suddenly Kay was in her mother's tight embrace, the scent of her washing over her. It was the hardest and best thing in the world to be home. For a moment, Kay was ten years younger, and then twenty, being hugged by her mother.

But Kay wasn't younger, and nothing was as it had been.

Tears burned but she blinked them away as she frantically swept the darkened space.

"Where is she?" Kay whispered.

"The brook."

Kay immediately opened her mouth to protest it wasn't safe. To demand if Stella knew not to wade into the water. But she bit her tongue. Kay had no right to question Ma. Not after everything. If Kay had been here more than a handful of times in eight long years, she would have known the answer.

Ma pulled back and cupped Kay's cheeks, a delighted smile cracking her face. "You are truly here! Oh, my dear. The strangest thing is, I had the most terrible dream just last week that you were never coming home. But it's only my worry. Look at you."

Kay's already troubled stomach clenched. She almost hadn't come back.

"How are you?" Kay asked, drinking in Ma's face, which had aged more than her years called for.

"Managing. As always."

Eliza stood near the door, watching them with wide eyes. Shame and defiance both reared their ugly heads. What must Eliza think of Kay's home?

"Ma, this is..." Kay stumbled over how to introduce her. She should have made a plan, but her mind had gone blank of anything when it knew she was coming home.

"El," Eliza stated firmly and bobbed a small curtsy. "Nice to meet you."

"Oh!" Ma turned her full attention to Eliza and the shine of happiness in her eyes made Kay instantly regret bringing her. "I'm Ruth." She pulled a startled Eliza into a hug. Eliza accepted quickly, hugging her back.

"You've found someone?" Ma asked Kay, so hopeful, clutching Eliza's hands. Kay wasn't sure how to answer—hating to lie, and not able to tell the truth. Eliza smiled at her and Kay blurted out the easiest thing.

"Yes."

CHAPTER 15
A Mother's Love

Y*es.* Eliza should not have loved that single word. Kaylen looked a bit ill as she said it, but Eliza warmed all over at Kaylen's claiming of her.

Ruth beamed and pulled Eliza into another hug. Eliza eagerly accepted the physical affection so freely given. It made sense that Kaylen's mother would also be kind, like her daughter.

Eliza could not deny the state of the small cottage surprised her. When they had entered the valley, she expected Kaylen to lead her to the large manor house on the hill, not to this leaning timber home on a mostly barren patch of land.

"Ma?"

A young girl whirled into the doorway. Eliza wasn't good at determining children's ages, but she guessed she was less than ten. A riot of red hair frizzed away from her small head, like Kaylen's, and the lighter version on Ruth. But she wasn't looking at Ruth.

Kaylen dropped to her knees as the girl threw herself at her. Kaylen's face disappeared in the tangle of hair, some immense weight falling from her shoulders that Eliza had not seen until it was gone. As she hugged...her daughter?

Kaylen cupped the girl's cheeks like her own mother had, her eyes full of wonder. "Hi, my little starling." Tears spilled unhindered down Kaylen's face and Eliza's own welled at the sight.

"You're here! When did you come?" The girl beamed. "Will you stay home now?"

Kaylen flinched. "Not quite yet. But I wanted to come by and see you. You're so tall."

The girl's smile vanished, like a flame snuffed. She nodded seriously.

Kaylen swallowed with apparent difficulty. "I brought you something." She fumbled in her pocket and pulled out the woven grass doll.

The little girl looked at the offering for a long moment. "Thanks. But I'm getting a bit old to play dolls."

"Of course you are," Kaylen whispered, trying for a smile, which just highlighted the shattered expression in her eyes. "Silly me."

"That's all right. I don't mind," the girl said magnanimously, taking the doll. "I'll put it with the others."

She climbed onto a bench to reach a long shelf, placing the gift beside a row of dozens just like it, but all unique in their own ways. A few had faded scraps of ribbon or colored feathers adorning them. One wore an oversized seashell necklace. The oldest ones on the far end were battered and dirty from use, and starting to crumble. Eliza knew Kaylen must have made each one. They were evidence of her love, even if Kaylen had not told Eliza about the child. Why hadn't Kaylen told her?

Kaylen remained kneeling, the weight so briefly absent now resettled on her. Ruth touched Kaylen's heavy shoulder.

"She always tells everyone when one arrives. They mean a lot," Ruth said gently.

Kaylen leaned her head into her mother's side before she shoved to her feet, brushing aggressively at her salty face.

Eliza reached for Kaylen's hand. She wasn't certain if Kaylen would accept, but Eliza needed to offer her some support. Kaylen gripped her so tight Eliza thought her fingers might break.

Kaylen glanced at Eliza, clearing her throat. "There is someone you should meet. Stella, this is El. El, this is my daughter, Stella."

Stella—the name that Eliza had flippantly, unknowingly told Kaylen was common.

Eliza smiled at the little girl. "How do you do."

Stella gazed at their clasped hands and up at Eliza with large eyes too old for her face. "Are you the reason my ma has been gone?"

"She's not the reason," Kaylen said hurriedly. "But it won't be as long this time. What if...what if I were home again by midwinter? Then we could celebrate. Together."

"That would be wonderful!" Ruth said. "Wouldn't it, Stella?"

Stella looked between them slowly, wariness on her young face. "I'm going back to the brook," she announced as she ran out the door again.

Kaylen stepped forward, tension bunching her whole body as Stella disappeared, but Ruth stopped her with another hand on her shoulder. "Give her a moment. It's a shock for her."

"I shouldn't have come," Kaylen muttered.

"Nonsense, of course you should. This is your home. And we both miss you so much. Do you mean it about midwinter?"

"I hope so." Kaylen glanced toward Eliza. "And I'll be sending a lot more back soon. I don't have it yet, but I will. I promise."

Kaylen had told Eliza people relied on the reward. Eliza hadn't truly understood, but she thought she did now.

Ruth sighed, her smiling face pinching. "How long will you stay?"

"For tonight at least." Kaylen's gaze snagged on a bucket in the corner, and she frowned up at the darkened, rotting patch of the ceiling. "When did that start?"

"This spring."

"I'll fix it."

"Leave it. It'll be dusk soon."

"I'll fix it."

"Can I help?" Eliza asked as Kaylen pulled her hand free.

"No, I'll do it." Kaylen finally looked at Eliza, eyes brewing with a desperate storm. "I need to fix it."

Eliza nodded, letting her slip outside.

Ruth touched Eliza's shoulder, smiling sadly. "Sit down, dear. Let me look at your arm."

Eliza had forgotten about the minor injury, though when mentioned, the sensation came rushing back. She sat at the large, worn table covered in scratches and stains. Two long benches rested beneath, designed to hold many more people than the two who occupied the space now.

"Tell me about yourself, my lady."

Eliza opened her mouth, but snapped it shut. "Why did you call me that?"

Ruth smiled indulgently as she re-cleaned Eliza's scrape with a warm cloth. "Your clothes are common, but your posture and bearing are not. And I rather fancy my Kaylen falling for a beautiful noble lady." Ruth's expression grew sad again. "She's been through so much. As I am sure you know. She needs more happiness in her life. And so, if you can do that for her, you have my blessing wholeheartedly."

Eliza stammered, overwhelmed yet again by the love of a mother. Kaylen had been so secretive about her family, and Eliza wondered why. They seemed wonderful.

"Are you the reason she will be able to return soon?"

It was the opposite of the question Stella asked. And Eliza thought she was, though not in the way Ruth likely meant. At least, the reward for her rescue was. "I hope so."

"Then you have my blessing ten times over." Ruth's eyes shone, and Eliza's own grew wet again as a ladder thudded against the outside wall.

ELIZA STARTLED AS STELLA burst back through the door, holding a bloody fish aloft in triumph. The sunset highlighted the hole in the roof Kaylen was making before re-thatching.

"Look what I caught, Gram!"

"Very nice," Ruth praised. "Shall we add it to our soup?"

Kaylen appeared in the doorway, wiping her hands on her kirtle, the roof forgotten and eyes on Stella.

"Look!" Stella swung the fish around to show Kaylen, narrowly missing Eliza's face.

"Where did you catch it?" Kaylen asked, her expression soft.

"The hole by the old oak."

"That's a good spot. Your father caught a pike as tall as you are there once."

"Ted says my father was a no-good wastrel bastard."

"Stella!" Ruth scolded and Eliza's mouth slackened. "You shouldn't listen to or repeat such things."

Kaylen looked stricken, but recovered herself quickly. "Ted never did like your father much." She cleared her throat. "That fish looks like it needs cleaning. Shall I help you with that?"

"No, I've got it." Stella dropped the fish on the table, which wriggled as if still alive as Stella drew a curved knife from a block.

"You sure do," Kaylen breathed as she watched.

Eliza stood hastily, going to Kaylen, mostly to be with her, and a tiny bit so Eliza didn't get fish remnants on her skirt.

"Do you want to sit?" Eliza asked, not sure how to help.

Kaylen shook her head. "I should finish the roof."

As Kaylen slipped back out the door, Ruth sighed and gently reprimanded Stella. "You shouldn't speak like that in front of your mother."

"But he's the reason—"

"Hush."

Intensely curious, Eliza held her tongue with difficulty and did what she could to help with the soup, which was nothing, because it was already done. She was as useless as she was out of place here. An intense mixture of dark longing and fluttery hope filled her, somehow missing something she hadn't realized she'd never had—a family.

No, that wasn't right. Eliza had her father. He always loved her. At least, she'd thought he had. He had, hadn't he?

"Where're you from?" Stella asked Eliza, swinging her legs as she sat across from her.

"I've spent most of my life quite secluded. In the mountains."

"You're really pretty."

"Thank you." Eliza was inexplicably pleased by the compliment until Stella finished her thought.

"Do you think if I were pretty, Ma would take me with her too?"

Something thudded outside. Eliza hoped that was a coincidence and Kaylen hadn't heard that.

"We've talked about this, Stella," Ruth said firmly. "Your mother is a knight. She cannot take you with her."

Stella sighed loudly and looked down, and then violently decapitated her fish.

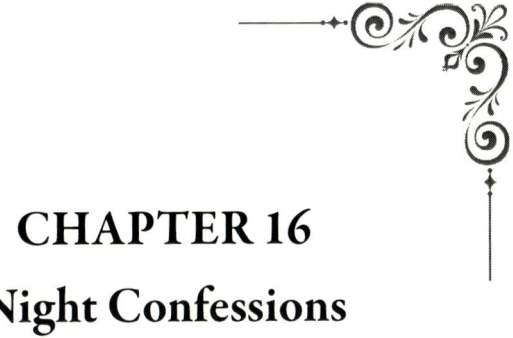

CHAPTER 16
Night Confessions

The smooth clay warmed in Kay's palm, its dark contents swirling.

Ted always kept a stash hidden in the back of his woodshed. It had been easy to slip over there and find it after everyone had gone to sleep, Ma and Stella in the bed, and Eliza curled on as many blankets as Kay could find.

Tomorrow Kay would get up, keep going, and pretend everything was fine. But tonight, a storm raged in her chest, churning like the swill in her hand. She wasn't certain the storm would stay contained, and didn't want to be around anyone if it didn't.

The jug's cork had come out easily, lost somewhere in the scrubby grass.

Kay stared out at the land that was now nothing more than a glorified garden, with Ma's aching hands gnarled and no one around to help. The land that used to be Kay's.

The lullaby from earlier filled Kay's throat and she let it out, singing to the dying field. It would always be the sound of this place.

The sound of home.

Sing, my darling,
my heart, my starling.
When I say goodnight, it won't be the last time.
When the sun returns, so will I.
So fly, my starling, goodbye.

Trust the land 'neath your feet for it grew you up
strong.
You may wander far but it's here you belong.
You may reach for the stars, but the stars always fall
back to the land that grew you up tall.

Sing, my darling,
my heart, my starling.
Goodbye, goodbye, goodbye...

"I knew you'd sing beautifully."

Kay let the song fade.

She briefly considered trying to hide. Trying to run. But Kay was so tired.

Footsteps approached, followed by the quiet rustle of skirts as Eliza climbed over the creaking fence and sank down beside Kay, leaning her back against the uneven slats.

"What are you doing out here?" Eliza whispered.

"Sitting."

"Are you drinking that?"

"No."

"Why do you have it, then?"

Kay wasn't sure how to explain. "Because we used to always raid Ted's stash."

It was reckless to play with her control, but perhaps the storm wanted to taunt her. Eliza's eyes bored holes into the side of Kay's head, and then she reached out and took the jug.

Eliza choked and spat out the small taste. "That's terrible!"

"It really is."

"Why didn't you warn me?"

Kay shrugged.

The glug of the jug emptying filled the night as the cheap spirits soaked into the unfertile earth. Poisoning it more.

"That was a waste," Kay said flatly.

It was better there.

They sat in silence for a while, listening to the night.

"Why didn't you tell me about her?" Eliza finally asked.

Kay closed her eyes. "Because I don't tell people."

"Why not?"

"People ask questions. It's hard enough without having to talk about it."

It was easier to pretend Kay didn't have a home. She was ashamed of that, but she'd learned to compartmentalize her life away so that it wouldn't consume her. When Kay was at home or thinking of home, she could regulate it. Control it. Protect it. The rest of the time, she was simply Sir Kaylen.

"Will you talk about it with me now?"

Kay didn't want to talk. But her battered walls were off duty tonight, leaving her wallowing chin-deep already. "What do you want to know?"

"I take it her father was Finley?"

Kay nodded. "Finley and I were always close. When his mother died, he lived with us. We did everything together. Went to Glea and enlisted together when the farm started to fail. And we...found comfort in each other. When I realized I was carrying her, he convinced me I should come home for the birth. That he'd follow. That he'd take care of us." Kay's mouth twisted bitterly. "I was so young and stupid back then."

"I'm sure you weren't stupid."

"Yes, I was. He had a betting problem. Cards, dice, tournaments—anything someone would take odds on. I knew, and I married him anyway. Stupidly."

"Why?" Eliza whispered.

"Because he asked. And because I loved him, though not in the way he loved me. Or, the way he claimed. He was very persuasive when he wanted to be." His charming, infectious grin flashed in Kay's mind. Even as the memories of him faded, that smile lingered. "So I married him. And then I left him alone." The regret and anger burned away the brief fondness, as it always did. "He finally showed up with debt collectors chasing him. He stayed long enough to hold Stella once. Promised he'd win everything back for us." Kay huffed in resentful amusement. "I never saw him again. Got himself killed in the next skirmish, they told me. Sometimes I...sometimes I wonder if he even tried to live."

Kay hadn't been there to see it happen. Or to stop it. She had been at home, burdening her already overburdened family, not knowing how to soothe the screaming infant who had Finley's eyes.

HER LOVELY CHAMPION

Eliza was holding one of Kay's hands in both of hers, rubbing a comforting pattern on her battered knuckles. "But you went back to Glea?" Eliza prompted gently.

"We still needed money. It was the whole reason we went in the first place, because an extra set of hands here wasn't worth nearly as much, and neither of us had the stomach for crime. I didn't have the stomach of a soldier either, but this life made my body strong, and they offered to pay for that. And Finley's debts didn't die with him. Because he'd led them straight here. To me. So yes, I left." Kay closed her eyes again, tears spilling as she allowed herself to remember. "I told myself it would be temporary. A year or two. Stella was so young, she wouldn't remember. Wouldn't know I was gone. I tried to come back every few months, at first. But it's a long journey, wasting time and money. I couldn't always get leave to come and could never stay long. She deserves so much more than a day or two. I don't try to stay away. But maybe part of me does. When I'm here, I know I'll just have to leave again. I never wanted to leave." Kay looked at Eliza, needing her to understand what Kay couldn't explain. Needing Eliza to not judge her as others had done. As she did herself.

"I know you love her," Eliza said. "I may be silly and sheltered, but even I can tell. I knew you loved her before I knew she existed. When you made that doll."

The doll. Fresh tears spilled from Kay's tightly shut eyes again, her throat raw. "I don't know my daughter."

"You haven't had time to."

"Time I'll never get back." Kay knew she should stop talking, but the words spilled. Now that they had started, she couldn't stop these horrifying words that swirled in the hollow pit inside her. "I don't know how to be a mother. Or if I should even try. Or if that's even what I am. She calls me Ma but I don't deserve that name. I haven't been here to earn it."

"I don't think it's something you earn," Eliza said kindly, wrapping her arm around Kay's shoulders.

Kay rested her face into the comforting crook of Eliza's neck. "Sometimes when I look at her, I see Finley. And it's fucking hard, because I still miss him and wish I could kill him myself. But I also see my father. And my brother."

"Where are they?"

"Dead. And I wasn't here for that either."

Eliza shifted so she could hold Kay with both arms. "Do you regret deciding to leave?"

"No. And every single day." Kay's head knew she couldn't stay. She knew she couldn't support Ma and Stella from here. But her heart didn't feel like it on nights like this.

"My mother was around my whole life, until she died just before my capture," Eliza said, running her fingers lightly over Kay's hair. "But she was a stranger to me. I would rather have known I was loved, I think."

Kay tightened her hold on Eliza, inhaling the scent of her skin. "You deserve to be loved."

"So do you."

Kay heard the words, but she wasn't ready to listen to them. She hurt too much.

"Come back inside. Let's sleep," Eliza said, but Kay didn't move. Eliza held her like she cared. Like Kay mattered. "If you don't get up, I might have to carry you," Eliza warned.

"I'd like to see you try."

Eliza grabbed the backs of Kay's knees and lifted. She got Kay an arm's length off the ground but was way overbalanced, and Kay caught them before they slammed into the fence.

It startled a laugh from Kay, and that felt strange. But good.

"That would have worked if you weren't so heavy," Eliza protested as they both stood.

"Maybe I'll let you try tomorrow."

Then Eliza surprised her yet again by leaning in and pressing a kiss to Kay's tear-stained cheek. Kay caught her breath, desire flaring and not caring about things like titles and reasons, searching for Eliza's eyes and lips in the moonlit night. But Eliza had already pulled away, taking Kay's hand and leading her back toward the house.

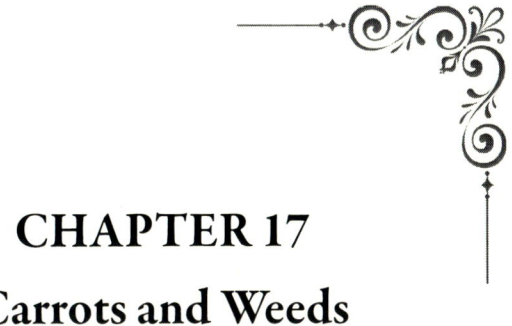

CHAPTER 17
Carrots and Weeds

"Are you going to marry my ma?"

Eliza dropped the carrot she was scrubbing, having to fumble for it in the basin. Stella watched her with that same quiet seriousness she had shown yesterday, which didn't belong on her young face.

Eliza glanced around the empty house, hoping Kaylen or Ruth would appear and rescue her from having to answer. But they were outside in the small field. Eliza was out of her depth with people in general after her long isolation, and Stella, who was so important to Kaylen, was ten times as intimidating. Eliza didn't want to say the wrong thing.

"We have not decided that we will," Eliza settled on. "But if we did, what would you think about that?"

Stella picked up another carrot and considered her answer. "Gram says you're a lady. Does that mean you have a big house somewhere?"

"I do have a very big house." If the palace could be considered a house. It couldn't, in any fairness, but for their purposes, Eliza would count it.

"And would I get to come live there?"

Eliza's heart started beating even faster. "Would you like to?" When Stella nodded, her expression earnest, Eliza's chest ached. "Your ma would like that too."

Stella grabbed a large kitchen knife and chopped through the root with small hands. "One day, I'm gonna be a knight."

"Is that so?"

"Then I can go with her. And she won't leave me. And we'll both take care of Gram." Stella paused her vegetable butchering and looked up. "Can Gram come live with us in your big fancy house too?"

Eliza swallowed hard and nodded back. What else could she do?

Eliza stared down at her hands and promised herself she would make sure Kaylen never had to worry about sending money home to her family. Eliza was useless in many ways. But she *was* the crown princess, and that would count for something again when she claimed that title.

"Do you need help cutting that? I can show you, if you want," Stella offered, pointing at the carrot Eliza was holding limply.

"Oh. Um, yes please. I would like that."

Stella got a second, duller knife and handed it to Eliza. "You just..." Stella frowned at her own carrot. "Do what I do."

Eliza bit her lips to keep from laughing, doing her best to replicate the lopsided cuts Stella was making.

"I thought you might be like Lady Velma, but you aren't," Stella continued, picking out another orange victim. "You're much nicer."

"That's good. Who's Lady Velma?"

"The lady who lives on the hill. She owns the farm now, because of my father."

"Your father?" Eliza tried to follow Stella's explanation and haphazard chopping.

"Gram and Ma used to own it, but they sold it to her to pay the bad men coming after the no-good wastrel bastard. But now we have to pay her too. I like her gowns, but she isn't very nice when she comes by."

"I see." Eliza's insides twisted. She saw enough.

"Why don't you wear nice gowns if you're a lady?"

"I usually do, but I got this one recently from a friend. I rather like it. What do you think?"

Stella scrunched her lips to the side. "I'd like silk better."

Eliza smiled. "I think you'd like my friend too."

"Have you ever been to the royal palace?"

"I have."

"Really?" Stella stared at her with excited eyes. "What's it like?"

Eliza started to explain but had a better idea. "How about I show you?"

KAY KNELT IN THE DIRT, pulling away the stringy, stubborn weeds. Her hands already ached from fighting the roots, skin stinging from the small cuts they left.

"Go inside, Ma. I'll get this."

Ma sat back on her heels and gave Kay a hard look. "You go inside and see your daughter and beautiful bride."

"She's not my bride," Kay mumbled.

163

"But she will be."

Kay shook her head, grabbing at another tough stem. "We've not made those promises."

"You can't lie to me, Kay," Ma said, with a knowing smile. "You brought her here, which means you love her."

Kay choked on nothing. "I didn't—I don't—" She breathed deeply. "I won't let anything distract me from what I need to do. What I owe you."

"Owe us," Ma echoed, shaking her head with a bone-deep sadness on her face. Kay recognized it because it was how Kay felt. "You already do too much."

Kay ripped the weed too hard, and it tore at the junction of the earth, leaving the roots embedded. "I don't do nearly enough. You are here raising her and keeping this field going all on your own."

"And I wouldn't have it any other way, other than to see my daughter more. Another set of hands here would have been helpful too, though."

"Not much," Kay said firmly, reluctant to dredge up the old argument.

"Why not stay for a season and see? We'll make do."

"With what?" Kay bit back the snarl that burned her throat as another weed ripped. "I'm trying."

Ma's rough, gnarled hands covered Kay's. "And I am grateful for you every single day, my sweet Kay. Don't ever think we don't know what you do for us."

"I heard her," Kay rasped, blinking through the sudden haze in her eyes. "She thinks I leave her because I want to."

"No, she doesn't. She's just eight and misses you. It's been two years." The gentle reproach in Ma's tone punched Kay down further. "That's a long time for someone her age."

It was a long time for Kay too. "Things will be different soon."

"You said that two years ago."

"But I mean it this time. I'm working on something, and I'll have more than I ever have. What if I could bring you both with me next year? To Glea?"

Ma turned her gaze out over the struggling field. "But this is our home. We've always been here."

And Kay had always known Ma wouldn't go. It might break her heart to leave the land she was born on, and then raised and lost a family on. Kay wouldn't do that to her. So Kay would need to figure out a way to be home more. With the reward, she could, for a while.

"Come on," Ma said, standing and brushing the dirt from her knees. "These weeds will wait for tomorrow. Let's go inside and see what our girls have made for us."

Kay couldn't love the sound of that. Eliza wasn't hers. And Stella wasn't truly hers either.

Kay almost told Ma who Eliza was. But then Kay would have to admit what she had done, and she wasn't ready for Ma's tears again.

She followed Ma along the side of the field, only to find two figures crouching on the ground together. Eliza held a stick in her elegant hand as she carved into the dirt. When they got closer, Kay saw Eliza had created a sprawling drawing of the Alludan palace, along with the courtyard and gardens. The surface and materials were crude, but her forms were confident. Kay couldn't help but stare at them as Stella did, in awe.

"Oh, sorry," Eliza said, her hand faltering as she looked up at them. "There's no parchment, and I wanted to show Stella what the palace looks like."

"It's beautiful," Kay said, and Eliza smiled almost shyly.

"I enjoy drawing. And I've had a lot of time to practice."

Stella stood and grabbed at Kay's hand. Kay's heart swelled, until Stella seemed to second-guess it. Kay squeezed tight, hoping Stella would never let go.

"When I live with you in your big fancy house, can we go see the palace?" Stella asked.

"Big fancy house?"

"Lady El's. When you get married and we can live with you."

Kay snapped her gaze to Eliza's, who looked back wide-eyed. She silently shook her head with a shrug. A fresh flash of anger gutted Kay for a moment. Eliza had no right to tell Stella things like that. But then Kay looked down at Stella, who smiled hopefully back up. Kay's mind traced the face that was all new and so familiar. "Yes."

Kay shouldn't promise, but she'd find a way to keep some part of it. One day, she would take Stella to see the palace.

"I'm afraid we got rather distracted from cooking," Eliza said, wringing her hands nervously. "I'll get right back to it."

"It's all right, dear," Ma told her, taking her arm and leading her inside.

As Kay sat at the table with her family, something frighteningly like joy filled her. It terrified Kay, because she couldn't trust it. It would only hurt more when she lost it. When she left again.

And soon Kay would lose Eliza too. Kay had only known her a short time. They were never supposed to have met. It shouldn't have hollowed Kay's torso at the thought of parting from her.

Kay didn't see a princess anymore when she looked at Eliza in her family's home, chopping carrots. And that was a problem.

The sooner they arrived in the capital, the better. Kay could collect her reward and come home again. For longer.

They needed a horse. Only one person around here would have one to spare. Kay hated to go to her for anything, but she would. As with so many things in her life, she didn't truly have a choice.

"We'll leave in the morning," Kay announced.

Three sets of eyes looked at her with disappointment, like Kay was the vilest of villains. And perhaps she was.

"No!" Stella shoved to her feet, her eyes brimming, and slashing Kay to pieces.

"Stella," Ma said gently, but Stella shook her off and scrambled away.

"No!" she shrieked loud enough to shatter glass and dashed out the door.

Kay stood to go after her.

"Wait, Kay. Give her time."

"I don't have time," Kay snapped, and instantly regretted it. She leaned down to press a quick kiss to her mother's cheek. "Where's she going?"

"The brook." Ma's expression was so full of sadness and understanding, Kay couldn't stand it. She turned away and went after her daughter.

Red hair flashed through the trees in the falling dusk, and Kay followed it, right to where Ma had said.

Stella huddled on the bank, between the smooth, knotted roots of the old tree. Kay carefully approached and sat nearby.

"I hate you!" Stella seethed.

Kay shuddered, the words branding across her skin forever. She shut her eyes and clutched at the walls in her mind. Kay had hurled those same words at her own mother when she was young and angry. She hadn't meant them back then. Perhaps Stella didn't truly mean them now either. Though Kay couldn't blame her if she did. *She's just eight and misses you.*

Stella sobbed, great ugly things that jerked her small shoulders. Kay's own twitched to hold her, but she didn't know if Stella wanted to be held by Kay. So Kay sat, simply being there, not knowing how to explain, or to apologize, or to be what Stella needed her to be.

The lullaby looped from her throat, and Kay didn't try to stop it tonight.

Slowly, they both calmed in the quiet, only broken by the babble of water and Kay's hum.

"I don't want to leave," Kay eventually said. "I've never wanted to leave you."

Stella peeked over her arms, which were folded protectively over her knees, her eyes as puffy and red as her hair. "But you do leave."

"I do," Kay agreed, because it was the awful truth.

"Then why?"

"Because I cannot stay. Not yet. But that has never been your fault." Kay shifted closer, and Stella didn't move away.

Feeling like she was carving open her chest, Kay reached out her scarred hand that had done things she hoped Stella never had to understand. Stella glanced at it before she launched herself forward, throwing her arms around Kay's neck.

Kay caught her, sagging in relief and turning her gaze up at the pinpricks of light in the darkening night. "I would rip the stars from the sky for you, my starling. I'm just...working on making my ladder."

"I don't want stars. I want you."

"I know." Kay struggled to get the words past her thick throat. She ran her unworthy palm over Stella's ever-tangled hair. "But in the meantime, be thinking about which ones you might like, all right? Then when I come back next time, you can show me. And we'll work on it."

CHAPTER 18
A Lavender Lie

K ay pulled on her chainmail and reached for her remaining armor. Her breastplate was still blackened from their fire, but she was preparing for battle and refused to look as desperate as she was.

"Where are you going?" Eliza asked as Ma and Stella prepared for bed.

"To run an errand."

"Right now? Should I come with you?"

"Stay. Get some rest. I won't be long." At least, Kay hoped she wouldn't.

The night was clear and chilly, and Kay didn't bother with a torch as she walked along the overgrown dirt lane, the moon as her guide.

The manor stood grand and imposing against the hill, decadent light pouring from the windows. Her fist landed heavy as she knocked on the door, which was answered by a tall, thin man.

"Sir Kaylen, to see Lady Velma," Kay said, focusing on her diction.

The man arched an eyebrow. "Oh, I know who you are. Come in. Sir." The last word was tacked on as a begrudging afterthought. "I shall ask if the lady will see you."

Kay waited in the entry, the dark wood paneling on the walls absorbing the light. Kay had only been inside a few times, but tonight, the shadows flickered darker.

After an unnecessarily long time, Lady Velma appeared at the top of the stairs. She descended unhurriedly and Kay was forced to look up at her.

Not much older than Kay, Lady Velma would have been pretty, if she had been anyone else. If she didn't own Kay's home and everything in it. And if she had ever been something near kind.

"Kaylen. What an unexpected surprise," Lady Velma said, a smile curving her red lips.

Kay bowed. "My lady."

"It's been a while. Come, join me in the sitting room." Kay followed her into a similarly dark room. Lady Velma moved to a cabinet. "What would you like to drink?"

"Nothing, thank you."

Lady Velma ignored that, pouring a rich wine into two goblets and handing one to Kay. The aroma of it wound around Kay's control and tickled the back of her throat. She cleared it and set the goblet aside as Lady Velma sank elegantly into a soft sofa and Kay perched rigidly on the opposite one.

"I heard you were back," Lady Velma said, sipping slowly. "And with a woman. Who is she?"

"No one," Kay lied, and hating the words, but needing to shield Eliza from Lady Velma's curiosity. "A distant relative I'm escorting."

"You sound more like a foreigner each time we meet, but you don't have to pretend with me. We both know exactly where you come from, Kaylen."

Kay gritted her teeth. "I would like to borrow a horse," Kay said. No point to drag this out.

"Borrow?" Lady Velma's eyes sharpened.

"Fine. I would like to hire a horse."

"Do you have funds to hire one? Last I checked, you were rather short on those."

Kay swallowed. "I don't have the funds on me. But I will. I can have the animal returned to you by the end of the month, along with payment."

Lady Velma languidly sipped more wine, watching Kay closely. "But a month is so far away. What will you give me now?"

"What do you want?"

Lady Velma's eyes tracked Kay's body. "What you have always refused me."

Kay fought the bile rising. "I am not for sale."

"Pity."

Lady Velma drank more of her wine. She had Kay cornered and knew it.

Kay's heart thundered. Could she do it? She'd done worse things.

"I would settle for a kiss," Lady Velma said, smiling coyly. "Just one kiss for a horse?"

Just one kiss. So little for so much. Kay glanced longingly at the goblet beside her. She wished she could drain it and get lost in the dark earthiness of it, so she wouldn't hear her own words as she spoke them. "Very well."

Lady Velma's smile made Kay's stomach roll as she stood, turning away from the wine that her hand twitched to reach for. The overpowering scent of bottled lavender filled Kay's nose instead as Lady Velma stepped close. Kay took a deep breath, forcing her mind to go blank as she leaned in and pressed a quick, closed-mouth kiss to painted lips.

When Kay pulled back, a long-nailed hand gripped her nape.

"Are you trying to cheat me?" Lady Velma asked, tone dangerous. "I would not recommend that. I am not satisfied with your payment. Kiss me like you mean it, Sir Kaylen."

Kay could never mean it with Lady Velma. She yearned to kiss only one mouth in this world, and it was in her home right now. Waiting for her. Depending on her. Kay looked at false lips and imagined they were Eliza's. The angle was wrong. Kay should have had to tip her own head back ever so slightly and bring Eliza's mouth down. Perhaps Kay was standing on a slope.

Kay couldn't have the real Eliza. So she closed her eyes and kissed a pretend one.

The wine Kay had avoided so well earlier touched her tongue, igniting the need to have more of it. Eliza's face felt wrong beneath Kay's hands, threatening to shatter her fantasy, but Kay clung desperately to it. They were standing in a field of blooming lavender and Eliza had just told Kay something disarmingly kind, as she was wont to do.

Eliza made a mewling sound, but it wasn't right. Hands slid over Kay's hips, but it wasn't Eliza's touch.

The illusion shattered and Kay wrenched away. Shame filled her mouth, dirty and used, knowing she had used Eliza too in the worst sort of way.

"I'll collect the horse in the morning," Kay said.

Breathing hard, she showed herself out.

KAYLEN HAD NOT COME back.

The peaceful sounds of Stella and Ruth sleeping in the bed jarred against Eliza's worry, which started spiraling out of control as the night deepened. She was about to throw off the blankets and do something incredibly foolish like go looking for her when the door opened, and Kaylen slipped inside. She took her time removing her armor, placing it quietly in the corner.

"Where in the world have you been?" Eliza hissed as Kaylen joined her, and Eliza caught the scent of lavender. "Why do you smell like that?"

"I don't."

"Yes, you do. You smell like perfume." Kaylen didn't answer, and something dark and unsettled filled Eliza's stomach. "What sort of *errand* did you run?"

"Go to sleep, Eliza."

Kaylen rolled so her back was to Eliza and the glow of the fire. Eliza's mind reeled. Kaylen had visited someone. A woman? Someone from her past? Why hadn't she told Eliza about it? When Eliza touched Kaylen's shoulder, it shuddered.

"Are you all right?" Eliza asked, the worry returning.

"No."

Eliza tucked herself into Kaylen's back and wrapped her arm around her waist. Kaylen covered Eliza's hand and threaded their fingers.

Eliza wasn't sure how to process what she felt for Kaylen. It was growing rapidly, wild at times, and it had changed here. Eliza had known Kaylen had a big heart before, but now she saw the evidence all around. Eliza would happily hold Kaylen forever. And the thought of Kaylen holding someone else...

"I'm sorry," Kaylen whispered, and Eliza's stomach lurched.

"What for?"

Kaylen shook her head, which moved against Eliza's cheek as she rested them together. Kaylen's natural scent was stronger now than the strange perfume.

So what if Kaylen had been with a woman tonight? Hot, angry fire burned through Eliza, despite her attempt to smother it. Kaylen didn't owe Eliza an explanation of where she had been. But Eliza wanted one.

"Where were you?" Eliza tried once more.

Kaylen shifted their clasped hands higher, so Eliza's palm rested over Kaylen's big heart. Eliza's own sped up.

Since Kaylen wasn't pulling away, Eliza simply enjoyed holding her while she could.

CHAPTER 19
Undeserved

Kaylen slipped away again in the early morning. Eliza stirred to rise with her, but Kaylen pressed her back down with a gentle hand on her shoulder. "Sleep."

Eliza rested her head and the next thing she knew, the sounds of something dropping, followed by Stella giggling and Ruth shushing, woke her.

When Kaylen returned, the giggling ceased.

The mood remained strained and sober as they ate a quick porridge. Eliza's heart hung heavy as she watched Stella lean toward Kaylen's side where she sat beside her on the bench, and Kaylen's slanted posture right back, both desperate for a last little bit of contact.

"I'll be back soon," Kaylen whispered into the top of Stella's hair when it was time for a goodbye no one was ready for. "Remember what we talked about? Go outside at night and look. I'll look too."

Stella was silent, and that was worse than sobbing and screaming.

When they reached the doorway, Kaylen got stuck in it as she looked back at her mother and her daughter.

Eliza took Kaylen's hand. "Soon," she repeated the promise.

Eliza nudged Kaylen past the threshold and then shut the door so Kaylen wouldn't have to.

Kaylen's strides lengthened until she was practically running. They hurried to the end of the lane, where it split and went up the hill to the manor house. A docile brown horse stood saddled and bridled, and tied to the fence. Kaylen dropped Eliza's hand to unhitch it.

"What are you doing?" Eliza asked.

"This is Pepper. Our horse."

"We don't have a horse."

"We do now."

The unsettled sensation from last night returned, smoldering through Eliza. "Is this the errand you ran?"

Kaylen nodded jerkily. She wasn't looking at Eliza.

"Where did you get her?" Eliza pressed.

Kaylen's gaze flicked to the manor.

"Lady Velma?"

Kaylen's head snapped toward her. "How do you know her name?"

"Stella."

Kaylen sighed. "Let's go. We're wasting light."

Eliza stepped closer. "Are you—"

"No, I'm not all right. Now let's go."

"How did you pay for this horse?"

"It doesn't matter."

The strong scent of lavender perfume returned to Eliza's nose. "Did you—you didn't..." Eliza's question died beneath Kaylen's searing gaze.

"What?" Kaylen asked, sharp challenge in her tone.

Eliza forced the words out. "You lay with her."

Kaylen's face twitched. "So what if I did?"

The burn turned painful in a flash, the admission slapping Eliza across the face. "How could you?"

"How?"

Eliza physically retreated from the fury in the single word.

"How dare you ask me that," Kaylen spat, her speech curling back to a rough Alludan accent.

Eliza backed up until she hit the fence, and Kaylen stalked her.

"I've done far worse than fuck someone for a horse, and I will again. Because unlike you, I was born in that." Kaylen flung her arm toward the dying farm. "So don't you dare judge me for doing what I must to protect the ones I love."

Eliza's tears ran hot on her cheeks. A confusing mix of shame and anger bubbled in her as Kaylen's hands landed on the fence on either side of Eliza, pinning her in place. Eliza wanted to both escape and reach for the furious woman in front of her. "I'm not judging you. I think I'm jealous."

Kaylen's eyes widened briefly. Then she squeezed them shut. "Don't say that."

"Why not? It's the truth."

Kaylen abruptly pushed off the fence, turning away. "Get on the horse, Your Highness."

The use of her title in Kaylen's quiet voice hurt far worse than any of the words spat in anger.

Eliza's head spun and her body screamed with need. She bizarrely wanted Kaylen to turn back and press her against the fence again. Instead, Kaylen stood facing away, her shoulders set with tension.

Eliza's trembling legs carried her to the horse, and she mounted, her body remembering the motion despite the years. Kaylen swung up behind her, and the contact down Eliza's back was comforting and also made her confusion worse.

Instead of guiding the horse forward, Kaylen reached around Eliza to wipe gently at the tears. "I shouldn't have raised my voice at you. Please forgive me."

Eliza's heart thudded twice. "I think I deserved that."

"You never deserve to be yelled at." Kaylen's cheeks were flushed, gaze cast down. "I'm not used to being with anyone when I leave. I wish I could say I'm not always like this, but...You shouldn't have to deal with me. I'm sorry."

"There's nothing to deal with. I'm just a silly princess, remember? This is one of those times when you should ignore me."

"I could never ignore you."

Eliza's stomach flipped, and she did what she had been dreaming of for days.

Eliza kissed her.

It was an awkward position, with Eliza twisting back and Kaylen leaning around. It was also terrible timing, with Eliza's face still wet and Kaylen's heart grieving. But there was nothing awkward or terrible about the sharp gasp from Kaylen's parting lips, or the fierceness of Kaylen's tongue.

Eliza's senses couldn't decide what to focus on—teeth grazing her lower lip, or the hand circling possessively around her rib cage, or the one trailing fire from her burning cheek down her neck.

Kaylen pulled away. Eliza swayed, following her retreating lips, but was forced to grab the saddle as Kaylen nudged the horse to start moving.

Eliza panted. "Should I not have done that?" she asked, staring unseeing at the road ahead of them.

"Probably not."

Eliza shut her eyes, the guilt returning until Kaylen brought her mouth to Eliza's ear and breathed the sultry, roughened words against her skin.

"Because I wanna do it again."

Fresh desire rushed through Eliza. They were completely flush. Eliza wished the breastplate weren't in the way of feeling Kaylen's chest against her back, but she could feel the rest of her. Kaylen's thighs pressed into Eliza's.

Had Kaylen's thighs pressed against Lady Velma's last night?

Eliza's whole body tensed.

"El?"

The name both helped and didn't. "I'm fine." Eliza made her eyes focus on the world around them as they rode along the valley.

The hooves crunched in the tense silence.

"How long is the journey now?" Eliza asked to break it.

"We could make it to the palace in four hard days of riding, but with both of us on one horse, a bit longer."

Eliza's heart sped up at the thought of arriving at the palace. Of seeing her father and learning if what the witch told her was true. And of Kaylen leaving her.

"We'll get there as soon as we can," Kaylen said to reassure Eliza but doing the opposite.

Eliza nodded and tried not to dread reaching where she had longed to be for the last eighteen years.

IT HAD BEEN A SWEET sort of torture to be pressed against Eliza in the saddle all day. But it had distracted Kay's mind as home fell farther and farther behind her. Kay was always alone when she left. But she wasn't alone today.

A dilapidated barn slumped on the edge of an overgrown field, threatened by the tangled forest beyond. It looked uninviting as Kay steered their horse off the road and toward it, but a damaged roof was better than none. The sun already drooped below the cloud-studded horizon.

Kay helped Eliza dismount, steadying her.

"I haven't been saddle sore in a long time," Eliza said, smiling.

Kay's lips remembered the taste of that smile. She shouldn't remember. Kay tried to scrub it from her mind and banish it to the hollow part of herself behind her walls, which were shaky today in the wake of everything.

Kay grabbed the blanket and bundle of food they had brought from home, seeing Ma's worn hands wrapping it that morning. Kay squeezed her eyes shut, reaching for her walls again. It was food and warmth. Not much, but it was what they needed.

The barn doors stood askew, one rusted stiff and the other sunk into the earth, leaving enough room to pass through into the darkened, mostly empty space, only old hay and animal musk lingering. Eliza slipped a hand around Kay's elbow, staying close.

An apology rose to Kay's lips. She couldn't do any better. So she would make it as comfortable as possible.

Leaving Eliza inside with their supplies, Kay hurried into the trees, taking a moment to simply feel the weight of her sword in her hand and the movement of her arms as she hacked down some boughs to cushion and insulate the ground, yet again without a bed to offer. She led their horse through the narrow barn doors and hitched her inside, and then spread the blanket and unwrapped the food. Bread and cheese, and not even a fire to warm it.

Eliza huffed. "Well?"

Kay looked up at her. "What?"

"Are you going to do it again or not?"

CHAPTER 20
The Barn

Eliza had waited all day for Kaylen to kiss her again. She had wanted her to when they stopped at midday. She had hoped she would a mile back when they watered the horse in the soft sunset light. But Kaylen had not. And now Eliza watched her doing everything she could to make Eliza comfortable, and Eliza was ready to scream at her to stop. She burned to feel Kaylen's passionate lips on her again.

Kaylen sat beside her, a piece of bread frozen halfway to her mouth. "We should eat."

Eliza pushed up onto her knees and braced her hands on either side of Kaylen's hips, leaning forward as Kaylen leaned frustratingly back. "I'm not hungry for food."

"Fuck." Kaylen dropped the bread, seized Eliza's face, and claimed her mouth.

They both overbalanced. Eliza's heart tumbled after them as she climbed on top of Kaylen, straddling her lap. Ravenous for every piece of her, Eliza scrambled for the buckles at Kaylen's sides.

Kaylen was so sweet. But she was also tangy, and salty, and bitter sometimes. It was a heady combination, and Eliza was determined to consume all of her.

Kaylen's hands covered Eliza's, tangling their fingers as she pulled them away from the frustrating fastenings of the breastplate. As Kaylen tilted her head back, Eliza took the opportunity to press her mouth to Kaylen's throat. A rapid pulse drummed against her lips, but Kaylen still gripped Eliza's hands, not letting her back to the task of freeing Kaylen from her aggravating armor.

"We shouldn't do this," Kaylen whispered, her eyes closed.

Eliza stilled. "Oh." The chill of rejection swept through her. She sat up and scooted back as Kaylen did too. "I'm sorry."

"Don't be."

"Was it something I did?"

"No."

Throat thick, Eliza reached for the bread, not having an appetite but knowing she should eat. Tension hung around them in thick silence.

"Is it because of last night?" Eliza asked, not able to keep the question in her mouth, and regretting asking as soon as it left.

"I didn't lie with her."

"You didn't?" Relief flooded Eliza's limbs.

"No. But I did kiss her."

The relief evaporated. The image of Kaylen kissing a shadowy, beautiful woman appeared in her mind. "Did you want to?" Kaylen's face hardened and Eliza winced. "Sorry. I shouldn't have asked that."

"When I did, you should know. I'm sorry. But I thought of you."

The heat returned. Eliza barely resisted throwing herself at Kaylen again. "Why would you be sorry for that?"

"I have no right to ask this, and you don't need to answer, but have you—that is, that wasn't your first kiss, right?"

Charmed by the uncharacteristically tongue-tied Kaylen, Eliza scooted closer. "I was fifteen when I was captured. Were you unkissed when you were fifteen?"

"Hardly. But we've had very different lives."

"We have. But no, you are not my first kiss. That summer before the witch came for me, I spent much of it out in the gardens, getting my gown muddy with the second-born princess of Uvaria. What?" Eliza laughed at Kaylen's expression. "Have I shocked you?"

Kaylen's small smile eased the remaining tension in Eliza's breast. "Maybe a little."

Eliza reached for Kaylen, needing to touch her again. She traced over the smattering of charming freckles on Kaylen's nose and cheek, some nearly invisible and others dark and drawing Eliza's eyes and fingers. Eliza grew lost in them.

She blinked, her eyes dry and straining to see in the fading light. How long had she been staring?

Eliza dropped her hand. "Was that all you were worried about?"

Or was Kaylen rightfully reluctant because Eliza was the sort of person who interrupted important conversations to stare at freckles?

"This complicates things," Kaylen said.

"We're already complicated, aren't we?"

Like a moth drawn to fire, Eliza leaned in. Kaylen released a strangled sound as Eliza brushed their lips together. Eliza could feel the passion behind Kaylen's hesitant response.

"We've already kissed. So a few more cannot make anything worse, right?" Eliza pushed.

"I'm no philosopher, as I've already told you. But that sounds reasonable."

Kaylen captured Eliza's chin, tipping Eliza's face so she could kiss her better. Deeper. Nudging Eliza's jaw open. And Eliza loved it.

Eliza had wondered sometimes, in the dark loneliness of her tower, if she had died and simply never noticed. But she knew now she was entirely, gloriously alive.

She delighted in learning Kaylen's mouth with her own, then with her thumb, tracing the line of Kaylen's lip. The lower one was fuller than the upper. Kaylen's quickening breath against Eliza's fingertips sent spirals of pleasure through her. She reached her other hand into Kaylen's hair, hooking her fingers through the untamed mass of curls she adored so much. Kaylen hummed, not her lullaby, but a single needy note, and Eliza tightened her grip.

The name tumbled helplessly from Eliza's lips. "Kay."

HER LOVELY CHAMPION

THE SLIGHT TUG ON KAY'S scalp shocked desire all the way to her toes.

This was all they were doing. Kay could put a box around it and keep it secure, tucked behind her walls. It didn't have to spill out, and she could revisit it when she needed to. In quiet, lonely moments.

Kay knew it was a terrible idea even as she convinced herself.

Kay's hand found its way around the back of Eliza's neck. Eliza made another diabolically wonderful sound of pleasure and Kay pulled her down to the blanket again, lavishing her jaw and throat.

The light salt of her skin, and the faint scent of horse and fresh-cut pine, mixed with Eliza's own scent.

They should stop.

Eliza uttered Kay's name again. It was an invocation, a promise, and a question, all wrapped up in one.

Kay thrummed and clenched to answer. But she reined in her escalating desire. Gentled her grasping touch. Calmed her rushing pulse.

She drew back so she could search for Eliza's dark eyes in the darkening night and got distracted by slightly swollen lips.

They rested on their sides, Eliza's head pillowed poorly by Kay's metal-clad arm. Kay should remove her armor, which was digging into her ribs and shoulder in this position. They should sleep. But Kay didn't move, clinging to the moment and this woman who was so dangerous to Kay. This woman who was a crown princess lying on branches and rotting straw.

"I wish I could do better," Kay whispered. "You should have a hot meal and bed, in a room at an inn."

Eliza shifted closer. "But we are here, and you are with me. So I'm happy with our barn."

Kay's breath left in a rush. Why did Eliza have to say things like that? It wasn't fair. It would have been so much easier if Eliza were unlikable.

It would have been even easier to nudge the hip she brushed, spread Eliza out like their picnic, and devour her until neither of them could take any more.

Kay wouldn't do that in this crumbling barn, and she wouldn't do it anywhere else either. She reluctantly pulled away and shed her armor. When she returned to Eliza, wrapping them up in the blanket, Eliza sighed contentedly and wound herself around Kay.

For warmth. Like before. It was only practical.

When Kay was certain Eliza had fallen asleep, she allowed herself to press a kiss to the top of Eliza's head. "Good night, El."

CHAPTER 21
A Fine Friend

The foothills of eastern Alludan gentled as they traveled west on rough and dusty roads Eliza had never been on before. Kaylen steered them into the woods to avoid the few other carts or riders when they spotted them in time. When they didn't, Kaylen told Eliza to keep her head down and not make eye contact.

"You said yourself that no one will recognize me," Eliza protested. She still resented the idea that she might be in danger in her own kingdom after thinking for so long that everyone missed her. Everyone had, in fact, seemed to get on fine without her.

"I'm just as concerned that they will not," Kaylen said.

Kaylen tilted Eliza's face away as they rode into the ditch to evade a cart bouncing in the opposite direction. Eliza instinctively leaned into the touch, forgetting she was supposed to be hiding, as she fixated on where Kaylen brushed her skin.

Eliza shook off the sensation. She knew she was unusually surly this morning, and begrudgingly admitted it was because Kaylen had refused to do more than kiss her last night. Physical intimacy would complicate things, as Kaylen said, and undoubtedly make things harder when they had to say goodbye. But it would already be hard.

Eliza's existence had been so small and dull for so long. Now that she was free, she longed to experience everything. She would have to work on a compelling argument to persuade Kaylen to her way of thinking. They only had a few days left together before things would change again, and Eliza planned to make the most of them.

The road bent sharply around a rocky outcropping, so they didn't see the rider until he was right in front of them. Kaylen directed their horse aside, but Eliza was too startled to turn away soon enough and looked straight at the man.

Dark hair flopped rakishly over his brow. But he didn't even glance at Eliza.

He stopped so fast his horse nearly bucked. "Kay?"

Kaylen slipped the reins into Eliza's hands and was already on the ground as the stranger leapt down. Eliza had a moment of alarm as the large man grabbed Kaylen, but only to crush her into a strangling hug, which she returned.

"What in the eight kingdoms, Kay?" he asked, a thick northern Glea accent curling his words as he planted a wet kiss on her forehead. "You're supposed to be dead."

Eliza bristled. She didn't know who this man was, aside from apparently a knight of Glea, but she wouldn't stand for him calling Kaylen *Kay* and kissing her. She swung her legs over and slid from the saddle.

Kaylen grinned at him. "Can't get rid of me after all."

"But how?" His eyes shifted to Eliza, flicked to Kaylen, and back. "Um, pardon the ridiculous question, but should I be kneeling right now?"

"You should, but not here." Kaylen looked furtively around and ushered Eliza and their horse to the side of the empty road, dipping into the trees.

The man gaped at Kaylen and glanced nervously at Eliza as he followed.

"Hugo, this is Her Royal Highness Princess Eliza. Eliza, this is my friend, Sir Hugo of the Honorable House of Haymore." Kaylen gestured between them.

The knight stared, slack-jawed, for another moment before he dropped to his knee as promised and bowed his head. "Your Highness."

It was what Eliza should have expected but felt strange after so long. "Thank you. Please stand, Sir Hugo."

Sir Hugo returned his stare to Kaylen. "You truly did it. I cannot believe you did it."

"Not exactly." Kaylen shifted uncomfortably.

"Are you seriously going to deny it? Because the evidence is standing right in front of us." He bowed again, his attention distracted between Eliza and Kaylen. "Your Highness."

"It's a long story." Kaylen frowned. "What are you doing here?"

"I was on my way to your family, actually." Sir Hugo rubbed the back of his neck sheepishly. "I was planning to deliver the news first, along with what you sent, and maybe a bit more. To make sure I reached them before word from elsewhere."

Kaylen was the one to hug him this time, the clank of armor loud as she squeezed him tight. "You generous, goutish goat."

Sir Hugo blinked rapidly. "It was the least I could do. You lucky, living liverwad."

Eliza wasn't sure if she should be jealous or scandalized. Their words were insulting, but spoken with fondness. Whoever Sir Hugo was to Kaylen, they were clearly close. And perhaps Eliza was horrible for disliking that.

"Why are you all the way over here? Why didn't you return the way you came?" Sir Hugo asked.

"We ran into a spot of trouble. Several spots."

Sir Hugo nodded. "There's an inn a few miles back. I'm taking you there." He jabbed a finger into the center of Kaylen's chest. "No arguing."

"For once, I will not."

Sir Hugo flashed a grin. "Are you certain you're not someone impersonating Sir Kaylen?"

Kaylen turned to Eliza, starting to reach for her before hesitating. So Eliza did the reaching, taking Kaylen's hand. They didn't speak until they were riding again, falling in behind Sir Hugo.

"Why did you tell him?" Eliza whispered. "I thought no one was supposed to know who I am." Eliza couldn't help the resentfulness in her mouth.

"He was the last person to see me before you. He already knew. Don't worry. I trust him with my life."

HER LOVELY CHAMPION

IN THE QUIET YARD OF the inn, Sir Hugo deposited a familiar coin pouch into Kay's hand. It was, however, unfamiliarly heavy. "Go settle in. I'll deal with the horses. Then I expect that long story."

Kay only accepted because of Eliza.

The innkeeper was all graciousness when Kay asked for her nicest room and paid upfront. The stooped, sharp-eyed woman led them up to a suite which consumed most of the second floor, with a private dining area and separated bedchamber.

"Will you need a hand with your luggage?" the innkeeper asked.

"No, thank you. I'll get it later," Kay lied. "But if there is anything hot in the kitchen to be brought up, we'll take that. And I have a friend who will be joining us."

"Of course, sir." The innkeeper eyed Kay curiously. "We don't see many like you around here."

Kay wasn't certain if she was speaking of the Glea armor, or the woman beneath it. "We're just passing through."

When the door finally shut, Kay focused on Eliza, who had been unusually quiet on the ride.

"Who is Sir Hugo to you?" Eliza asked, her eyes searching.

"My closest friend."

"How close?"

Kay thought she understood what Eliza was asking. "My love for him has nothing to do with attraction."

"Good."

Eliza grabbed Kay's collar and kissed her.

Kay had told herself she wouldn't. The dark delight of the barn last night had been a dream best left there. But the relief of being in a warm, dry, safe place with the promise of food and a bed addled Kay's mind.

Eliza's lips turned fierce. Possessive. And Kay was lost.

Kay spun them, pressing Eliza's back against the closed door. Eliza grinned, hitching her leg over Kay's hip and shimmying herself higher. Climbing Kay. And Kay helped her.

"Yes," Eliza breathed, gripping Kay's neck and looking down at her with eyes that held things Kay both longed and feared to see.

Kay tried to pull back. "We shouldn't—"

"I don't want restraint and reasons. I want more."

Kay tried to hold her in place, but Eliza would not be still, squirming and tempting Kay's wonderfully full hands to knead and slip where she shouldn't, and then tumble them into the large bed in the adjoining room.

A knock near Eliza's head saved Kay from that truly terrible impulse. Setting Eliza back on her feet, Kay wrenched away, gathering her breath and sense as she opened the door.

Hugo stood outside, along with two servers with steaming trays. Kay gestured them in, trying to act like she hadn't been kissing the crown princess of their kingdom, who was looking delightfully flustered.

Kay didn't miss the bottle of wine one young man carried in, or how Hugo pushed it back into his hands with a shake of his head. Kay was both grateful and irritated as she followed him to the table.

Hugo waited until the servers had left before bowing deeply to Eliza. "Your Highness."

"Call me El. Or Lady Ellie, if you must."

Hugo glanced uncertainly at Kay.

"Lady Ellie will do," Kay said. "And I'll tell you what's happened, but first, let's eat."

They all sat at the table and dug into the richly buttered vegetables and gamey, well-seasoned partridge. Kay had never tasted anything better.

Hugo watched them with bemusement and then a touch of alarm as Eliza and Kay both inhaled their servings. Kay wordlessly refilled Eliza's plate when it was nearly clean, along with her own. She ate until she knew she should stop, and then ate a bit more.

She forced her hands to her sides to prevent herself from continuing.

Eliza sagged, slumping in a very unprincessly way as she smiled contentedly, stifling a yawn.

"Go on and rest," Kay said gently, nodding at the door behind them that led to the small bedchamber of the suite. "We're not going anywhere today."

Eliza blinked sleepily. "You won't go anywhere either, right?"

"I'll be right here."

Hugo stood as Eliza did, and Kay realized she should as well. She was so used to Eliza. Too comfortable with her. She grabbed the arms of her chair to rise, but Eliza placed a firm hand on her shoulder. "You should rest too."

"I will. I'll come check on you soon."

Eliza disappeared into the adjoining room, shutting the door quietly. Would she climb into the bed clothed, or would she undress? Was she pulling at the laces down her back right now? Should Kay go help her?

"You're killing me, Kay," Hugo said, his eyes brimming with curiosity.

Kay slammed the door on her thoughts, which had started wandering down a delightful path toward a sun-drenched Eliza sprawled in the bed. "Sorry."

"How have you managed to get here with nothing?"

Kay gave him a brief summary of their path and how they had reached it.

"Whose horse is it? A fine creature."

"Lady Velma's."

Hugo narrowed his eyes. "That snake. Tell me you stole it from her. Would serve her right after she swindled you out of your land."

Kay huffed around a smile. "I did not steal it."

Hugo looked at the closed door to the bedchamber, and back at Kay with raised eyebrows. Kay took a long drink of water. He studied her while she avoided his eye. "Kay..."

"What?"

"You and the princess seem fond of each other."

"We've been through a lot in a short time. Nearly dying together creates a bond. As you know."

Hugo nodded slowly, watching her closely. "But does it make your eyes burn with desire?"

Kay glared at him. "My eyes do nothing of the sort."

"Well, hers do. Don't tell me you don't know it."

Kay didn't have a good reply for that.

"I know you," Hugo said, reaching across the table to grip Kay's forearm. "You love so much and so easily. It's your greatest flaw and my favorite thing about you. And it can make you a blithering fool sometimes."

"Thanks," Kay snapped.

"What I'm saying is, she is the crown princess, and that comes with a kingdom's worth of expectations that will be stronger than yours."

"I know that. I have no expectations, because we aren't anything. I'm simply returning her to the palace as planned."

"I don't want you to get hurt."

"I'm used to it."

Kay regretted the bitter quip as soon as it left her mouth. Hugo hauled her to her feet so he could crush her in one of his wonderful hugs.

"Get some sleep," Hugo said gruffly. "Can I get you a second room for yourself?"

Kay shook her head. "I'll be fine."

"Are you saying that because you don't want to pay for it, or because you don't want it?"

"I don't want to leave her." The words fell from her mouth and hit her chest. Kay had meant she didn't want Eliza to feel unsafe, or to leave her unguarded, but Hugo's eyes told her he knew it was more than that.

"Rest. I won't bother you, but come find me if you need. Otherwise, I'll see you in the morning."

When Hugo closed the main door, Kay approached the other.

Eliza was fully dressed, curled in the center of the bed in a puddle of sun. It was better than Kay had imagined, the light and shadows of the tree branches outside shifting across and bronzing her skin.

Quietly stripping off her armor, Kay moved to the chair by the window.

"What are you doing?" Eliza mumbled, fluttering her long eyelashes at Kay and extending her hand. "Come here."

"I didn't mean to disturb you."

"Come here."

Kay complied, sinking onto the decadently soft bed. Eliza wrapped around her, snuggling her face into Kay's neck.

It was plenty warm, leaving no practical need to cuddle.

Kay ignored that inconvenient thought, for now, and closed her eyes.

CHAPTER 22
Bathtime

The last rays of sun were disappearing beyond the window when Eliza surfaced from her deep, dreamless nap, still wrapped in Kaylen's arms. Eliza wouldn't have ever moved, but she had to pee.

She managed to slip away without waking Kaylen. It took her a moment to find the chamber pot hiding behind a decorative screen.

A sound from the next room caught her attention. She peered through the gap to see the remnants of their meal from earlier being cleared away.

"Excuse me." Eliza intercepted the young woman. "Would it be possible to have a bath prepared?"

The woman nodded and bobbed. "Of course, my lady. We'll start the water and be up right away."

Eliza waited impatiently. How strange it was to have others to do things for her again. In her tower, she would haul only as much water as she strictly needed up from the well in the corner of Harriet's hall, but the prospect of a true bath was irresistible.

A line of people entered, carrying staggeringly heavy, steaming buckets, enough to fill the deep brass tub below the window. So much effort for something so luxurious. One bucket would have done, but Eliza was simply too excited to slip beneath the water's surface.

She peeled off her gown and shift, and stepped into the tub with a sigh.

For a moment, she was fifteen again—silly and pampered and blissfully unaware of it. Eliza cringed at her younger self. She hadn't known better, and hadn't had anyone to show her.

Then the witch had taken her, and she learned what it meant to take care of herself more, at the cost of missing out on everything else, like human connection. Eliza was still silly, but more aware of it.

And now she had Kaylen. Eliza smiled as the door to the bedchamber opened and a sleep-creased Kaylen emerged.

"When did all this happen?" Kaylen asked, her eyes widening as she took in the table and steaming bath. "I can't believe I slept through it. I'm sorry."

"Don't be sorry."

"I'm not very good protection if I sleep through an attack."

"Kind people making me a bath is hardly an attack."

"But what if they were not kind?"

"Then I would have screamed. You don't have to be perfect all the time. You can need to sleep, like normal humans do."

Kaylen looked away. "I'm far from perfect, anytime."

Eliza narrowed her eyes, wanting to get up and shake Kaylen, but too warm and cozy in the water. And she grew warmer as Kaylen's eyes returned to her, lingering. Eliza was mostly hidden by the rim of the tub, and the dim lighting of the hearth and a few candles.

"Join me," Eliza said. She had seen Kaylen briefly and inadequately a few times, and Eliza was eager to see her again.

Kaylen's gaze flickered. "I don't want to crowd you. I'll wait for you to finish."

"Kaylen."

"What?"

"Do you want to take a bath? Yes or no?"

"Yes."

"Then take the bath. Don't wait until it's cold. Do something for yourself."

Kaylen hesitated before she took a small step into the room. "Just a bath?" The question was so quiet. Almost vulnerable.

Eliza had planned for it to be a bath, followed by a continuation of what they had started against the door earlier, but the wary look on Kaylen's face made Eliza nod. "Just a bath," she promised.

Kaylen's hands went to the laces on her kirtle. Eliza clung raptly to the edge of the tub, drinking in each motion as Kaylen slowly revealed herself. Her skin was pale and scattered with more of the freckles that marked her face, her figure sculpted with muscle that came from a lifetime of hard work.

She wore scars too. Some inflicted, like a jagged line near her collarbone and white slashes on her forearms. And some old and natural ones on her abdomen and hips. Eliza longed to trace each one.

Kaylen hastily stepped into the tub, and Eliza drew her knees up to give her room.

It was a tight fit, the water nearly spilling over as Kaylen huddled on the other end. Their legs brushed and Kaylen jerked.

Eliza smiled, extending one foot. Exploring. Kaylen jerked again, sloshing the water.

"I would not have offered if I didn't want to share," Eliza told her, reaching for the cloth. "Now turn around so I can wash your back."

"I can do it."

"But I want to do it. Let me, please."

Kaylen swallowed. "All right."

A surge of triumph and pleasure at Kaylen's surrender flooded Eliza and she sternly reminded herself this was only a bath. But it wasn't only a bath. Kaylen was allowing Eliza to take care of her, the way Kaylen took care of Eliza and everyone else. And Eliza didn't think Kaylen allowed many people that.

Kaylen's back and shoulders tensed, pebbling as Eliza ran the cloth and her trailing fingers over them. Her skin was textured beneath the smattering of fascinating dots. Eliza started to count.

"El?"

Eliza blinked, losing track after fifty-eight. Kaylen was looking at her over her shoulder as the cloth languished uselessly in the depths of the tub.

"Sorry." Eliza retrieved it. "I got lost in my head there."

Eliza cringed yet again, but this time at her current self. She sometimes still forgot that she didn't have endless time, though she thought she was doing better at not wandering into her own reality.

Eliza smoothed the cloth over Kaylen's shoulders and down her arms. Scooting her legs on either side of Kaylen, she leaned forward so she could reach around to Kaylen's scarred collarbone.

"What happened here?" Eliza asked, following it with her fingers and struggling not to get distracted again by the new texture and warm, slick skin.

"A war pike made it beneath my breastplate. The angle was only glancing, not piercing."

Eliza shuddered. "You were lucky."

"I was. There have been many times I should have died, by all accounts."

"Like to Harriet?"

Kaylen huffed, the motion and sound pleasing Eliza. "Did you give the hydra that name?"

"I asked the witch what her name was, but she said she didn't have one. I tried out a few, and Harriet stuck. Head Three always looked at me when I said it."

Eliza dragged the cloth a bit lower, over the swelling tops of Kaylen's breasts. Kaylen cleared her throat and grabbed Eliza's wrist, stealing the cloth from her grip.

"Thanks. I've got the rest."

Kaylen shifted forward, away from her. It stung, but Eliza had promised it was only a bath.

She didn't know why Kaylen was so reluctant for more. When Kaylen did kiss her, the intensity of her desire was unmistakable. Eliza didn't believe Kaylen was that good of a liar.

Kaylen rubbed herself down quickly and efficiently, facing away from Eliza, and Eliza tried not to be disappointed by that as well. The water was growing tepid, and she shivered, turning her gaze to the window. The moon stared back, large and nearly full. How many times had Eliza stared at that moon and wondered who else was doing so at the same time? It had felt like a connection, though it had been a foolish notion. One of many she'd clung to.

When she turned back to Kaylen, she found her sitting sideways, eyes on Eliza. The heat of earlier returned, despite the water.

ELIZA WAS BREATHTAKING. The surface of the water trapped the dim light, but it was clear enough. She sprawled, her arms draped along the rim of the tub, knees bent. Kay told herself to look away.

When Eliza had pressed into her back earlier, Kay had needed to ball her fists to keep from reaching for her. Kay gripped the tub now for the same reason.

One of Eliza's feet crept along the bottom of the tub until it covered Kay's. A small touch. A simple one. And one that made Kay's heart race.

Kay scooped up the foot, resting it on the top of her thigh. Eliza's eyes widened as Kay ran her knuckle down the inside of Eliza's arch. When Eliza sighed, dropping her head back, Kay did it again.

This was all right. The box around their kisses was growing larger, but this could fit there. It was only a foot rub, just like this was only a bath. It didn't mean anything.

Kay told herself that, but it didn't feel like nothing to her wrinkling fingers as the water moved with them over Eliza's toes. Eliza twitched, her little gasp melting into a giggle.

Eliza was ticklish. Kay wished she didn't know that.

She ran her fingers beneath Eliza's toes again, and was rewarded with a reactive kick as Eliza twitched away, water sloshing as she pushed up.

"Stop it!" Eliza laughed.

Kay's smirk faded as Eliza stood, Kay's full attention riveting on the glistening water tracking down so much flawless skin. Eliza stepped out of the tub and reached for a towel draped over the arm of the chair, her long limbs elegant, and the curve and indent of her spine making Kay swallow hard.

Kay shook herself and dripped out after Eliza, grabbing the second towel. She wrapped it around her torso as if it could somehow protect her. Eliza slipped into her shift, plucked an apple from the platter on the table, and breezed gracefully into the bedroom. Taking a moment to wrestle her desire into submission, Kay pulled on her undershirt, snuffed the candles, and followed.

Eliza sat propped up against the headboard, her loose hair tumbling over her shoulder, the dark locks stark against her pale shift in the night. She patted the spot beside her as the apple crunched beneath her teeth. That had no right to be so arousing.

The sheets slid smooth and cool against Kay's damp legs. Eliza brushed a clinging curl of hair off Kay's neck, where the steam of the bath had frizzed and stuck it. Then Eliza held the fruit up to Kay's lips.

As the tartness flooded Kay's tongue, Eliza shifted closer.

"Are you trying to seduce me?" Kay rasped.

"If you have to ask, I must not be doing a very good job."

"You're doing fine."

The heat of the bath condensed and pooled between Kay's legs as Eliza's lips traced Kay's cheek to the curve of her ear. "Would anything work better? What do you like? Because I wanna try everything you do."

Kay bit back a groan, crushing the fine blanket in her fists.

Eliza stilled. "Do you want me to stop?"

Kay knew very well what the correct response was, but didn't give it.

Eliza pulled back, studying her in the darkness. "I'll stop."

Crunch.

"I thought you were going to stop," Kay grated.

"I'm not doing anything."

Kay sighed. "You don't have to try to seduce me. That's the problem."

"Sorry."

Eliza rolled away. Then the slow, careful sound of a crunchy apple being eaten quietly filled the darkness. For some reason, it made Kay's heart clench and her lips smile. And it worked more surely than any planned seduction, as Kay forgot why she shouldn't kiss the enchanting woman beside her until they were both breathless.

Kay found Eliza's waist, plucked the apple from her hand, and kissed her.

Eliza gasped and welcomed her, fisting Kay's hair and the front of her shirt as Kay's tongue invaded past the sweetness clinging to Eliza's lips.

They fit together. Nothing more than a layer of loose linen and silk separated them as Kay's thigh pressed between Eliza's eager ones.

Kay savored the sensation for a moment. It was so tempting to see and feel this woman as only El, the woman Kay was a fool for. But she was also Princess Eliza. Things weren't that simple.

Kay had left enough people she loved behind in her lifetime. She couldn't let Eliza be another one. And since leaving her was inevitable, Kay couldn't let herself love.

Perhaps if they hadn't known each other, or if she were someone else, Kay could have indulged in the pleasure of Eliza's body and had it mean nothing. But they did know each other.

Kay pressed their foreheads together as she eased away. Eliza resisted, clinging to the fabric of Kay's shirt. Kay placed the apple back in Eliza's grasping palm, though it wasn't apple Eliza was looking for.

"Is that all?" Eliza asked as she rolled to her side, chasing Kay.

"Forgive me. I shouldn't have done that."

"You shouldn't have stopped."
"It won't happen again."
"But I want it to."

CHAPTER 23
The Happy News

Eliza stared at the outline of Kaylen beside her. Her body still wore the press of Kaylen's, and craved it again. But Kaylen was retreating, and Eliza didn't know how to hold on to her.

Eliza knew she shouldn't fix her heart on this lovely, reluctant knight. But her heart had a mind of its own. And it needed Kaylen to want her back.

Eliza sat up, pushing off the blanket and finding the cool floor with her feet.

"Where are you going?" Kaylen asked.

Eliza wasn't certain, but refused to lie sadly in the dark and feel sorry for herself. She'd done enough of that in her life.

Restless, she returned to the main room, taking another bite of her apple before remembering that Kaylen's teeth and mouth had touched this fruit too.

Eliza set the apple on the table and reached blindly for something else. Whatever she was about to find was intercepted by Kaylen's hand.

"I've upset you," Kaylen said.

Eliza pulled free and immediately longed to be captured again. The thought made her shiver. But when Kaylen held her, Eliza didn't feel alone.

"Maybe I'm hungry again."

"Are you?"

"No."

She relaxed as Kaylen's arms circled her waist. Eliza loved how much of Kaylen she could feel. The undershirt Kaylen wore fell to her upper thighs, and their bare feet brushed, and then their knees as Eliza stepped closer.

"It's not because I'm not tempted," Kaylen murmured. "Come back to bed. We should sleep."

"Will you at least hold me tonight?" Eliza was afraid to be cold and alone again.

Kaylen led her back to the bed, one hand remaining on her hip. Eliza liked it. She liked it more when Kaylen followed her right in under the blanket, wrapping securely around her back.

It was enough for now.

SIR HUGO PULLED KAY into a tight hug as they stood at the mouth of the stables in the early morning.

"You have no idea how glad I am to be able to do this again," he said, squeezing tighter before releasing her. He ruffled the top of her hair and grinned. "You smelly, salty simp."

"Thank you," Kay said, too grateful to formulate a better response.

"I'll stop in on your family on my way back to Glea. I can't spend all my time chasing after you in a foreign kingdom, you know. Don't look like that. I was joking."

"I'll pay you back for everything when I can."

Hugo shook his head, like he didn't know what he would do with her, before he turned his attention to Eliza, bowing a bit too deeply for discretion. "You are in the best hands with Sir Kaylen, Your Highness," he whispered.

"I agree." Eliza smiled, and Kay's insides twisted.

"Take care, Kay."

Then Hugo mounted his horse and rode away.

Every muscle in Kay's body tensed, gripped with the terrible sensation she would never see him again.

"You're all right," Eliza said, running her fingers soothingly over Kay's neck.

Kay nodded jerkily. She helped Eliza mount their own horse and swung up behind, perhaps holding the reins too tightly and crowding Eliza too much as they turned in the opposite direction.

"Have you been on this road before?" Eliza asked.

"Um, I have. A few times."

"I wonder how many people have traveled it. What do you think?"

Kay thought Eliza was trying to distract her. She pressed a quick kiss to Eliza's cheek. "You're the philosopher. You tell me."

Eliza did, and it worked. Kay managed a smile as Eliza talked of everything and nothing, and Kay simply enjoyed listening to her.

It was only midafternoon again when the road took them past a charming village on a rushing river.

"Let's stop here for today," Eliza said.

"We can make it a few more villages before sundown."

"But I want to stop here."

"Why?"

"Because."

"That's not a reason."

"Yes, it is. Please?"

Kay sighed. She turned down the lane that ran along the waterfront and main street dotted with large shade trees. A hanging sign welcomed them to the truly uninspired River Inn. But it did have an inviting appeal. Kay led their horse to the stable and tipped the too-skinny groom too much.

Kay tugged Eliza closer as they entered the busy tavern room.

"Long live the king! Long live the princess!" shouted someone, and everyone echoed it.

Eliza and Kay shared a look before Kay managed to catch the bartender's attention. He welcomed them with a wide grin and curious glance over Kay.

"Travelers! Do you need drink, sir? Food? A room? Or good cheer?"

"A room at least," Kay said. "Though the cheer seems high indeed."

"Have you not heard?"

"Heard what?"

"Princess Annabelle was born yesterday. At long last, the kingdom has an heir again."

"What of Princess Eliza?" Eliza asked, her eyes wide.

"What? The one in the tower?" The barkeeper shrugged carelessly. "What good does she do any of us?"

"One private room," Kay said quickly, tightening her hold on Eliza's waist. "My wife and I have come a long distance and are tired."

"Of course."

They followed him up the stairs to a room that faced the river, smaller than the one last night but far more than Kay would ever dream to splurge on for herself. But it wasn't for her.

Kay steered Eliza to the bed. "Are you well?"

Eliza licked her lips as Kay sat beside her. "I guess all these years I've expected that people missed me."

"Don't listen to him."

"No, I think he was right. What good have I done, locked away for so long?" Eliza looked down and chewed on her lip. "Did you know about the new princess?"

"I had heard the queen was with child."

"Why didn't you tell me?"

Guilt itched at Kay. "I haven't thought of it much. But I should have told you." The child was Eliza's sister, after all. Kay suddenly wondered if the king would be so eager for his first daughter back with his new one born. Kay chastised herself as she pushed the awful thought away.

"It's just another reminder of how long it's been," Eliza whispered. "The closer we get to the palace, the more I'm realizing what I'm heading toward. A father I don't know anymore and a whole family I've never met."

"Your father has spent many fortunes and sent as many people to die to free you. Don't think you haven't been missed."

Eliza didn't answer.

Kay swallowed, her hand moving to her side. "I have something for you."

Eliza lifted her head. "Oh?"

"Don't get your hopes up." Kay pulled out a doll she had woven in the barn two nights ago, in the early dawn as sleep had eluded her. It wasn't a good one, since all she'd had to work with was old hay remnants and darkness. But she'd thought it might make Eliza smile.

Eliza didn't smile. She stared at the asymmetrical doll on Kay's palm and Kay knew she'd made a mistake. "Never mind. It's stupid. I didn't mean—"

Eliza snatched it as Kay tried to hide it again. "I love it."

"I can make you a better one."

"I don't need a better one. Thank you." Eliza leaned forward and Kay angled at the last moment, catching the kiss on her cheek instead of her mouth.

"Anytime."

"Do you think this inn might have parchment and ink?"

"Do you have more lists to write?" Kay asked to lighten the mood, glad of the abrupt subject change.

"Something like that."

"We can ask."

Kay stood and Eliza took her arm as they made their way downstairs into the busy, cheerful tavern once more. Snatches of conversation drifted past their ears.

"...About time we had some good news."

"I didn't think the old king had it in him. Wonder if he did. Guess we'll see when the babe is presented." That treasonous statement was met with a shushing sound.

Anger flared in Kay and she hurried Eliza away. It didn't take long to retrieve the excessively expensive parchment and ink, but Kay wasn't certain it was worth it based on Eliza's drawn expression as they disappeared back up the steps.

CHAPTER 24
Trapped

E liza woke back in her tower.

Her room appeared untouched, the new history of Glea resting on her desk. Her bookshelves were still ordered by color. Her washbasin was full. Beyond the window, the sky was the same gloomy overcast, broken by flares of sunlight, as it had been when she'd left.

Eliza frowned, disoriented, her hope sinking through the floor.

No. It couldn't be true. Where was Kaylen?

Eliza ran to the stairs, her feet echoing as she threw herself down them. They narrowed. The stone closed around her. She lost track of the names of whom she was stepping on, and kept going. Surely she should have reached the bottom by now.

With each step, the walls of the stairwell grew closer. She turned to go back up, but all she saw was curling blackness, which lunged at her. Chasing her.

A panicked sob escaped her throat and she ran onward, down, down. But she wasn't fast enough.

Tendrils of darkness wrapped around Eliza's wrists and snaked over her eyes, forcing open her mouth...

Eliza woke in the River Inn.

She flailed up from the center of the bed, trying to escape. It was a dream. Only a dream. Her skin itched where the darkness had touched her.

Eliza searched for Kaylen in the empty room, and her absence smothered Eliza like a blanket of ice. Eliza had not been alone since Kaylen had found her. Kaylen had left her briefly a few times, but never truly alone.

On shaking legs, Eliza climbed down from the bed and tugged the handle of the door. It didn't budge.

The fist around her lungs tightened. Familiar darkness curled behind her, following her from the dream, smoke licking the edges of her mind.

She was trapped. Again.

Eliza had to get out of here.

They were only one short story up. The ground was right there. She could reach it.

Eliza swung her legs out of the window, her bare toes searching desperately for purchase on the frustratingly smooth exterior wall, extending down until she reached a tiny lip of the window below. Her palms were clammy and slippery as she gripped the sill.

Across the room, the lock scraped.

A figure swung open the door, backlit by a flaring bracket in the hall, juggling a basket and two steaming bowls. The bread tumbled as the figure unceremoniously dropped the items and lunged toward Eliza, the darkness flanking.

Eliza let go.

A flower bed cushioned her fall. She rolled and scrambled onto her hands and knees, trying to get away. Someone cursed loudly and then landed next to her, red curls vibrant in the light spilling from the tavern right behind them.

"Eliza, wait."

Eliza froze, panting. The darkness started slinking away, retreating as the reality of Kaylen reached for her.

When Kaylen's hand cupped her cheek, Eliza breathed easier. Then Kaylen hauled Eliza into the safety of her strong arms.

"You're all right," Kaylen murmured, holding her close.

Kaylen's scent filled Eliza's nose as she buried it in Kaylen's neck. Eliza wouldn't have thought she'd love the combination of sweat, hay, and wool.

Her legs started to tingle where they were bunched beneath her, and Eliza absently wondered how long she'd been out here.

"May I take you back inside?" Kaylen asked.

Eliza nodded, still clinging to Kaylen's neck as Kaylen gathered her up. She vaguely noticed the murmurs as they passed through the busy tavern. Kaylen ignored them and carried Eliza up the steps.

"What happened?" Kaylen asked, resting Eliza on the bed in their benign room once more that held no darkness, just regular shadows and a fire and a few candles.

"I had a dream," Eliza managed. "And then the door. It wouldn't open."

"I'm so sorry. I thought you'd be hungry. It wasn't to keep you inside. Did the lock jam?"

"What?"

"The lock. You can flip it open from this side."

Eliza tried to follow Kaylen's words. She looked at the door again. She hadn't noticed that.

The fading panic morphed into embarrassment, and she covered her face with her hands. "No, I'm just useless."

"Don't say that." Kaylen retrieved the bread from the floorboards and rested it beside the partially spilled soup on the small table. "It's not fancy, but it was the hot option. Though I don't think it is anymore," Kaylen explained, sounding absurdly apologetic.

Kaylen had remembered. Eliza's heart stuttered at the small act that wasn't small at all. Like the charmingly imperfect doll in Eliza's pocket. Eliza pulled it out to make sure she hadn't damaged it in her ill-advised escape attempt.

Eliza caught Kaylen's hand as she moved past, holding on until her pulse returned to a more normal rhythm.

The soup was still somewhat warm. Suddenly ravenous, Eliza inhaled it gratefully, brushing off Kaylen's offer to go back and get them non-floor bread. Eliza didn't care. And she wasn't ready for Kaylen to leave her again. But eventually, Kaylen would leave her for good.

The soup sloshed dangerously in Eliza's stomach.

"I'm going to take these back downstairs," Kaylen said, collecting the empty bowls, her eyes searching. "Will you be all right here?"

Eliza almost insisted on going with her. But Eliza didn't want Kaylen to have to ask that question. It was ridiculous. "I'll be fine," Eliza promised. She would need to learn to be alone again. And she hated that.

She also hated every single moment, every heartbeat, as she waited for Kaylen to return. The sounds from the tavern below drifted up to her, and it did help a little to know other people were so near, though she was glad she could not hear their exact words.

Eliza wasn't trapped. She wasn't truly alone.

She glanced at the upside-down sheet of parchment on her side of the bed which she had started sketching on earlier. Annoyed at herself, and to keep away from the jittery, treacherous thoughts in her head, she retrieved the parchment and ink, sitting back at the small table.

After far too long, Kaylen closed the door again, on the correct side once more. Eliza relaxed. She stood, hiding the parchment behind her back.

"Are you ready for your gift?" Eliza asked.

Kaylen's answering smile faltered, replaced by a bewildered expression. "My what?"

"Come here."

Kaylen approached warily, like she thought Eliza was holding a knife. Eliza had tried to think of a clever way to present it, but was too eager and simply ended up thrusting it into Kaylen's face.

Kaylen took the drawing.

When Kaylen didn't say anything, Eliza hurried to explain. "It's your home. I don't know how to make dolls, but I can draw. You should have someone to give you things too."

The sheet of cheap parchment trembled in Kaylen's hand. "El."

One syllable held so much.

When Kaylen finally looked at Eliza, her eyes glittered with unshed emotion. "What do I do with it? How do I keep it safe?"

She looked adorably lost, so Eliza rolled it into a scroll for her before Kaylen carefully slid it into her coin pouch and set it gently on the table, as if it were made of glass. It was a quick sketch, but Kaylen looked at it like it was a masterpiece. And Eliza thought she might have fallen a little bit more in love with the woman. It was a disastrous notion, but no less true for it.

"Thank you," Kaylen said roughly.

Eliza couldn't help herself. She framed Kaylen's face and kissed her.

Kaylen's passion ignited to meet Eliza's, and it thrilled Eliza to know Kaylen still desired her too, even if she was stubborn and refused to take her. Eliza would have to convince her.

Eliza walked backward, drawing Kaylen forward, until they reached the side of the bed. Kaylen had removed her armor earlier and still wore too many layers. Eliza hungrily followed the lines of her hips up to the undersides of her breasts, but only got a tantalizing brush before Kaylen stepped away, a sharp gasp on her lips.

They stared at each other, Kaylen's cheeks delightfully flushed already. But Eliza knew it was another no.

"Why not?" Eliza demanded, a prickly mix of hurt and guilt in her belly, which Kaylen had filled with warm soup because she had listened to Eliza the very first day they met.

"You're still upset."

"Don't make this about that. Please," Eliza said, mortified by her earlier meltdown. "Unless it really is about that." Perhaps Kaylen didn't truly want her anymore.

"It isn't." Kaylen closed her beautiful eyes. "You are the crown princess."

"And you are the knight who rescued me. Isn't that how the stories go? The knight gets the princess?"

"I didn't rescue you. I just showed up at the wrong time."

"The *right* time. I would never have survived on my own." Eliza bunched her hands in her skirt instead of throwing herself at this frustrating woman like she wanted to. "You are my champion. I want to be your prize."

Kaylen watched her with an intensity that made Eliza's already quickened pulse race. Some internal battle raged on in the fields of Kaylen's eyes.

Eliza cheated. "Please."

Kaylen's face twitched into focused hunger. Eliza vibrated as Kaylen took a step closer. Then another.

Kaylen stopped right in front of her. She hovered her mouth over Eliza's lips, but didn't kiss her. After a tantalizingly long hesitation, Kaylen slowly traced along Eliza's jaw and down her neck, her breath creating the only connection. Not touching but burning a path against Eliza anyway, one wisp of hair tickling her throat.

"Kay..."

"Sit."

The command weakened Eliza's limbs, and she dropped onto the edge of the bed. Eliza looked up at Kaylen, thrumming with excitement for whatever Kaylen would give her.

"Just this," Kaylen whispered, almost to herself, as she knelt. "Just once."

Eliza nodded, uncaring what she was agreeing with, entirely entranced as Kaylen's gaze pinned her, and her hand grasped her hem.

Fabric and cool air dragged sensually up Eliza's shins. Knees. Thighs. Eliza's heart thrashed wildly as Kaylen nudged her legs apart with barely a touch.

Kaylen finally dropped her eyes from Eliza's, and time stopped as Kaylen simply looked at her. Eliza wasn't shy, but she had a moment of uncertainty. Until the brush of Kaylen's frizzy hair, stroke of exploring fingers, and the heat of her mouth chased away all thought in Eliza's head.

Eliza toppled backward. Her hands fisted the blanket beneath her, toes clenching in the fabric over Kaylen's muscled shoulders as she scrabbled for something to keep her rooted to the earth. Kaylen made a pleased hum.

Eliza glanced down. The sight of her skirts rucked around her waist and Kaylen's head between her bent, bare knees was exquisite. Eliza needed to draw it and capture the memory, because the sensations would leave her too soon.

Kaylen seemed unhurried, yet Eliza couldn't wait any longer. She was tired of waiting. She sank her hands into Kaylen's hair to keep her where she wanted. Kaylen hummed again, the sound rumbling through Eliza. And Eliza let herself go—tumbling, falling. Kaylen would catch her.

The wooden ceiling came into focus as Eliza melted into the bed beneath her, Kaylen's strong hand curling around and gripping her thigh, keeping her safe. Anchoring her so she wouldn't float away.

Eliza laughed breathlessly.

KAY RAN HER NOSE ALONG Eliza's skin, inhaling her. Tasting her and craving more. Wanting her again and afraid she would always want her.

This had been a gloriously terrible mistake.

Eliza's fingers burrowed deeper into Kay's hair, tugging. It jolted through Kay's whole body. Eliza guided her higher, so Kay reluctantly left the protective cradle of Eliza's legs and faced her. Eliza grinned, flushed and beautiful, and Kay's chest squeezed.

When Eliza tried to draw her down for a kiss, Kay stiffened her arms, avoiding her eyes. When Eliza's hands started to wander past her shoulders, Kay rolled off and stared at the ceiling.

Eliza's face appeared above her. "What's wrong?"

"Nothing."

Eliza scowled. "You're pulling away again."

The box full of lines Kay should not have crossed with Eliza was growing heavy. This had been about Eliza's pleasure. It wasn't about Kay, and so she told herself it could fit inside, beside dimly lit baths and searing, apple-sweetened kisses. Kay's walls alone couldn't hold Eliza back. And Kay knew if she let Eliza touch her, the box would splinter, and everything would spill out. She would be utterly lost.

Kay kept her eyes on the ceiling as the bed eased and Eliza stood. Fabric rustled. Kay chanced a glance to see Eliza slipping out of her gown, down to her shift. She returned to the other side of the bed and climbed under the blanket, where Kay rested the wrong way, taking up far too much space. Kay started to sit up but Eliza stopped her, adjusting so Eliza's stomach pillowed Kay's head.

"May I touch you like this?" Eliza whispered, her fingers threading carefully through Kay's hair.

Kay swallowed and nodded, the light scrape and drag of Eliza's fingernails on her scalp sending fresh tingles through her.

It was just a head rub. And it was arousing and relaxing at the same time. Kay lay still, enjoying it and knowing she shouldn't.

"I'm sorry if I pushed you into doing something you didn't want," Eliza said, her voice quiet and sad.

"Oh, I want," Kay assured her, turning her head so she could look up at Eliza. "That's the problem."

"Are you being selfless again? Trying to protect me or something?"

"I'm protecting myself."

"You think I'll hurt you? I won't."

"You won't have to."

Eliza's breath caught. "Will you kiss me again?"

Kay rolled onto her forearm. It would add to the many others. What was one more? Or ten?

Eliza sighed against her mouth so prettily. Arched into her so eagerly. Clung to her so desperately. Who was Kay to not give her everything?

If not for the blanket pinned between and separating them, Kay might have slipped her hands down and made Eliza shudder for her again. She wanted to—oh, how she wanted—but it wouldn't solve anything. It couldn't fix the truth. It would only break Kay more in the end. So she rested on her arms above Eliza and plundered her mouth, searching for the answer to how to let her go, and finding only more reasons not to.

CHAPTER 25
Like That

The rest of their journey back to the palace slipped by too quickly, the days both glorious and the worst in Eliza's recent memory.

Eliza's body was a constant riot of confusion, relishing each touch Kaylen granted her, and missing the ones she did not. True to her promise, it really had been "just once." Kaylen's kisses were brief, and she pulled away when Eliza pushed for more. She held herself back with an infuriating control, which Eliza couldn't seem to tempt away.

Eliza would have felt rejected, except then Kaylen would wrap around her as they slept, keeping the nightmares of darkness at bay, and banishing them with soft words and candles if they slipped through.

Since it was all Kaylen would give her, Eliza greedily took it.

Eliza found herself asking to stop earlier each day. The first two afternoons, Kaylen tried to argue, but Eliza put her foot down and let her princess out. So they had stopped.

Eliza knew she was only delaying the inevitable, but she wasn't ready for their time together to end.

As the roads grew wider and busier, Eliza realized with a shock she recognized a town. She had passed through it when she was a girl, recalling the town square but not the reason they had been there.

"It's still morning. We cannot stop here for the night," Kaylen said, misinterpreting Eliza's interest.

"I wasn't going to suggest we do." Eliza was affronted and irrationally annoyed by Kaylen's assumption, though she worried it was far too reasonable. She rather liked the idea, now that Kaylen had taken away the option.

Kaylen made a small disbelieving sound, and it poked at Eliza's irritation.

"I wasn't!"

"All right."

They made it past the village, the road narrowing and broadening as the river and silty bluff allowed. As it climbed to get away from the water, Eliza caught her first sight of the palace since she had left.

Built centuries ago to be as intimidating as it was impenetrable, the dark basalt towers and connecting buttresses were unmistakable, rising like a rib cage from hips of a smoky city and skirts of gently rolling fields.

"Welcome home," Kaylen murmured.

ELIZA WAS QUIET, AND Kay didn't like it.

"What are you most looking forward to?" Kay asked as the road fell back down and the palace dropped out of sight.

"I should say my father."

"But what would you rather say?"

Eliza glanced over her shoulder, a small, fond smile touching her lips. "Still my father. But also the unlimited hot baths and silk sheets. And as much paper and ink as I want." Eliza reclined against Kay's front more, and Kay's blood rushed at the innocent contact. "Oh, and new books."

"On philosophy?" Kay teased and Eliza elbowed her gently.

"Yes, actually."

"You should write one."

Eliza scoffed. "Who would read that?"

"Many people. Or you could just write it for yourself. What would you put in your book?"

Kay listened, enjoying the sound of Eliza's voice and the rumble of it against her torso. She briefly and recklessly closed her eyes, soaking it up, taking it into herself to hold on to.

Kay had noticed Eliza slowing them down, and Kay felt their time evaporating as well. Her arms reflexively closed tighter.

She couldn't allow her heart to sway her. They needed to return to the palace. Eliza belonged there. And Kay most definitely did not.

They crested another gentle hill and the palace reappeared, a little larger.

Eliza fell silent again.

"Do you truly not want to return?" Kay asked, not certain what she would do if Eliza said no.

"I do. Of course, I do. But..." Eliza chewed on her lip. "Do you remember when I told you there was more to the story of my capture?"

"Yes."

"I still shouldn't tell you."

Kay waited, and it didn't take long.

"All right, if I tell you, do you swear you will never, ever repeat it?"

"I swear it."

Eliza looked around the deserted road. "The witch said she was paid to capture me."

Kay's grip on Eliza intensified. "Who paid her?"

Rage caught in Kay's chest at whoever it was. She had assumed the witch was to blame. Everyone said so. It had been revenge on the king for...something. Kay hadn't paid attention to the details. But if someone else wished Eliza ill, Kay would deal with them.

"My father."

Kay stopped the horse. She stared at Eliza's profile. "That cannot be true."

"That's what I thought at first."

Kay's heart started beating wildly. "The witch must have lied. Or been mistaken who it was."

"She implied it had to do with my mother's death."

"Wasn't your mother killed by a malignant?"

Eliza winced and Kay regretted her direct question.

"She was. Maybe he thought I was also in danger, and hired the witch to take me away. To keep me safe."

"From the malignant who was already dead?"

"I...don't know."

Kay's head spun, her gut sinking beneath the hooves carrying them. It couldn't be true.

But what if it was?

Eliza took the reins from Kay's limp hand. "Come on. Let's stop for a while."

Eliza led the horse off the road and Kay slid down, sitting hard on the earth where she landed.

"But if your father arranged for you to be captured in the first place, why would he send so many knights to get you back? Why would he send me?"

Was it all a lie? Was Kay bringing back the daughter the king didn't want to see free? Would he honor the payment after all? Had Kay's promise to Stella to see her soon been a lie too?

And another sickening thought occurred to her. "Will it be safe for you at the palace?" Would the king send Eliza back for whatever reason he'd sent her in the first place?

Eliza bit her lip. "I've asked the same question. But I believe so. I have to go back. You've said it all along."

This changed nothing about the practicalities of their situation. They had no other destination or information.

"You said there's more to the story," Kay said, clutching at the threads of hope that this wasn't a fatally flawed venture.

Eliza nodded hurriedly. "I don't know all the pieces. The witch was rather vague on the details. Maybe it was supposed to be temporary, but something went wrong."

Kay had a hard time believing that, but it sounded nice.

"Will you stay with me when I meet him again?" Eliza asked hesitantly.

Kay took Eliza's hand and rubbed her thumbs over the backs of Eliza's knuckles. "I promise."

Eliza smiled, undeserved relief in her eyes.

When Eliza asked to stop early again, Kay did not protest. She yearned for more time, but time was something she never had enough of. She would take the gift of one more afternoon.

THE SPRAWLING TOWN was only a half day's ride from the palace. Streets turned from dirt to cobble and back, narrowing between drooping, smoke-stained buildings as Kaylen led Eliza and their horse on foot.

A group of five children suddenly appeared and rushed past, snatching at Eliza's waist and wrist as Kaylen spun her out of the way. Eliza gasped, stumbling into Kaylen's hold, the echoes of small fingers stinging.

"What was that?" Eliza whispered, staring at the backs of the racing children disappearing down an alley.

"Looking for jewelry. Let's find a better part of town."

Eliza's numb feet followed Kaylen's lead. She was shaken by the sudden contact, even if it hadn't hurt. And by the thought of why those children might need to snatch jewelry.

As they approached a noticeboard, Eliza slowed to stare at the rustling pages tacked there. The ornate decree of Princess Annabelle's birth was plastered in the center, over the crumpled edges of wanted posters. A depiction and warning of a witch who could create visions caught Eliza's eye. Beside that was an old, stained flyer for...her. A reward for rescuing Princess Eliza. Payment for an attempt, to be awarded to the surviving family. Six hundred gold ludans, exactly as Kaylen had said.

Even in the advertisement, her rescue was written off as pointless, the knight already assumed dead. Eliza couldn't stand the idea of Kaylen being another one. Heat pricked at Eliza's skin and eyes.

Kaylen wrapped her arm around Eliza and turned her away.

They passed several peddlers of various items on the streets. Eliza hesitated, trying to listen and see what they had, but Kaylen ushered her onward. As they rounded a corner, a man's voice rang out over the others. This time, Eliza got a good look.

A cage woven of thick, knotted branches, not much larger than Eliza's head, closed around desperate, constricted wings.

"Fancy a thunderwing, my lady?" the man holding it called to Eliza, shaking it. Inside, light cracked and flashed. "Caught in the outerlands last week it was. Intelligent birds, they make excellent pets and companions!"

Through the weave, a small, beady eye met Eliza's.

Eliza's throat closed. "Let it out."

"Best not to do that until you get home, or it'll fly off," the man said, his smile oily.

The pressure of Kaylen's hand on Eliza's waist increased, but Eliza dug in her heels, the thrum of the wings echoing through her, growing louder with each beat. "I said let it out."

"Are you interested in buying it or not?" the man asked, his eyes narrowing and glancing at Kaylen.

"No," Kaylen stated firmly. She tugged on Eliza, but Eliza slipped from her grasp.

Eliza reached for the cage, already feeling the spidering wicker pressing painfully into her own flesh.

The cage bounced away as the man retreated, holding it aloft. "Watch it, or I'll call the guards on you!"

Eliza didn't listen. The bird flashed with light again as Kaylen's arms closed around her, but not for comfort. "We can't afford it. Let's go," Kaylen murmured in her ear, trying to haul her away.

Eliza fought, shoving at Kaylen's shoulders. "No!" The bird was trapped, its scream shattering Eliza's ears. Eliza was trapped.

"El, look at me." Kaylen's green eyes overtook Eliza's vision. "Breathe."

Eliza sucked in thick air. "Please," she managed.

Kaylen's beautiful eyes disappeared as she mumbled a curse. "How much?" Kaylen asked the man harshly, still holding Eliza.

"Twenty ludans."

"I don't have twenty. Ten."

The man scoffed, his face hard as he clutched the shaking cage to his horrid chest. "I won't take any less than fifteen, after that stunt. I won't be swayed by tears, and haven't decided not to call the guards. I bet they'd be interested in learning where you got that armor, *sir*."

Eliza's frantic mind only partially comprehended the words.

"Eleven and three pence. It's all I have," Kaylen gritted out through her teeth.

The man huffed. "Fine."

Kaylen finally released Eliza and reached beneath her breastplate for her coin pouch, where she'd tucked it earlier for safety. Eliza trembled, gaze on the bird as the man counted the ludans out twice, before he thrust the cage at Kaylen. When Eliza reached for it again, Kaylen gave it over.

But Eliza's shaking fingers couldn't work the door. The feathers sparked with light and faint heat against her skin as she sank to the dirty cobbles, failing to free the bird. "It's all right," she whispered to herself as much as to the creature. "You'll be out soon."

Her vision blurred with hot tears.

Kaylen crouched in front of her and opened the door.

The bird floundered out, its wings slicing at Eliza's face as it flapped upward and away, disappearing over the nearby roof.

Eliza panted, staring after it, her insides aching.

She clutched the empty cage, a few feathers stuck between the joints where they'd been ripped out in the thunderwing's struggles.

Eliza doubled over and threw up.

ELIZA WAS SITTING ON something hard in a narrow alley. She blinked dazedly, not remembering how she got there.

Their horse stood patiently beside her, and Kaylen paced the three steps between the dirty walls painted with the sunset. She was muttering. Humming. A breathy, familiar tune.

Eliza swallowed around her fuzzy mouth, heart beating too fast. As the recollection crept over her of what had just happened—what Eliza had done and what Kaylen had done for her—it quickened more.

"Kay?"

Kaylen halted her agitated pattern. "Are you feeling better?"

The question felt careful, and Eliza hated it. "Yes." She stood, and her foot knocked into the cage, sending it clattering over the cobbles and jittering up Eliza's spine. "Thank you."

Kaylen didn't tell her it was all right. She didn't say anything at all as she handed Eliza the small flask of water, which helped to wash out the sharp taste in Eliza's mouth.

Eliza glanced at the sky again. It would be night soon. "Was that truly all of our money?" Eliza asked, her empty stomach protesting as the water sank toward it.

"All of *my* money, Eliza." Kaylen finally looked at her. "Or rather, Hugo's. Which I'll have to repay." She turned away and started pacing again. "That was meant for hot food and a bed tonight. And for part of this horse, and for getting home. But now it's flying somewhere in the clouds."

Eliza's stomach cramped harder. "I'll make it right. I'll pay you back." Eliza reached for Kaylen, catching her arm to stop her movements. "I'm sorry." Fresh tears stung Eliza's eyes. "It was in that cage, and—"

"I know." Kaylen covered Eliza's hand with her own. "I understand why. I'm not angry with you."

"You seem angry."

"I'm angry at the fucking world. That you were trapped for so long. That I'm so broke. That tomorrow—"

"What?" Eliza's heart climbed up her throat.

Kaylen shook her head. "Come on. I have a shaved half ludan in my boot. Let's see if someone will take that in the seedy part of this town."

THE INN'S NARROW STAIRS moaned as they climbed them. But at least the illegal coin Kay discovered in her change the day before had managed to get them a basic meal and a private room, which both turned out to be small and damp. Kay didn't mind for herself. But she minded for Eliza.

Kay watched Eliza closely, worried about her after that afternoon. Perhaps Kay should have been angrier, but how could she be? Some terrors lived on in the body long after the danger was gone. Remembering the look on Eliza's face as she'd made herself physically ill over the bird, Kay kept her hand at Eliza's waist until the door was safely closed.

Kay had just finished pulling off her armor, resting it in the corner of the cramped space, when Eliza crowded her. Eliza braced her hands against the wood on either side of Kay's head.

"What—"

Eliza stopped the question with her mouth, the kiss both demanding and questioning.

She pulled back, eyes glittering with a desperate mix of longing and panic, and Kay feared her own were mirrors. They shouldn't muddy the already filthy waters between them with anything more. If Kay were better, perhaps she would have listened to her own logic.

Kay gripped Eliza's waist and hauled her closer. Kay burned to feel Eliza shake beneath her touch once more. This would be their last night. Her last chance.

Eliza breathed Kay's name, weaving her fingers into Kay's hair. What might have been an innocent touch in another lifetime now made Kay wild.

She eased Eliza away and Eliza sighed, until Kay bent into Eliza's hip, tossing her over her shoulder and carrying her the two steps to the narrow bed. Eliza laughed, as Kay had hoped. As Kay tipped her down gently, the ropes beneath straw and wool creaked.

Kay was on the edge of losing control, sliding her own body along Eliza's. She needed to see Eliza again. Her hands dipped beneath Eliza's back, fumbling for her laces and more skin. When Eliza realized what Kay wanted, she enthusiastically helped, frantically throwing off the layers that covered her tempting figure, until she was beautifully bare in the evening light.

Kay memorized every swell of skin she could reach with her lips, watching it pebble in the wake of her touch. Eliza arched beneath her, daring fingers raking across Kay's shoulders. One foot snaked around to Kay's calf, sliding up to the back of her thigh, as a hand slipped along Kay's hip.

It felt too good.

Kay lifted off Eliza's hungry, welcoming body.

Eliza released another frustrated huff. She glared up at Kay, reaching for her again, but Kay caught her wrist and pushed it down, pinning her.

They locked eyes, and Eliza's flickered as her frustration flared into desire.

"Do you like that?" Kay asked.

Eliza nodded.

Kay ran her free hand along Eliza's side, over one of her breasts. Eliza's moan burned through Kay's blood. "Do I need to hold you down so you don't touch?"

Kay had meant it teasingly, but Eliza gasped and squirmed, nodding again.

Kay carefully positioned the wrist she held above Eliza's head and captured her other. Eliza resisted, trying to grope at Kay as she passed within reach, but Kay easily overpowered her.

"This is a game," Kay said, making sure Eliza met her eyes and understood. "Just say so and I'll let you go."

"I know you will."

Kay crossed Eliza's hands so she could hold them both with one of her own, leaving a free one to roam over Eliza's heated skin.

Eliza tested Kay's grip, arching into her light, skimming touch. Her feet started to wander again, so Kay trapped them with her shins. Kay shuddered at the sight of Eliza beneath her.

Eliza panted. "Touch me."

Kay ran her nose along Eliza's jaw. "Is that an order, Your Highness?"

"Yes," Eliza sighed, and it sounded more like a plea.

Kay grazed her teeth along the shell of Eliza's ear as she slipped her free hand between Eliza's legs.

Eliza's keen burrowed into her. Kay wasn't sure where her box was anymore. All she knew was she needed Eliza to make that sound again.

ELIZA WAS READY TO burst out of her body and crawl into Kaylen's. She was splayed open and completely vulnerable, and had never been safer. Kaylen had her. Held her. And Eliza didn't want to be anywhere else.

Kaylen's clothes dragged against Eliza's oversensitive skin. Her brimming pleasure started to spill over, but Eliza wasn't ready for it to end yet. She'd been too hasty before and wanted it to last. She couldn't face Kaylen's retreat and distance after, like last time. Eliza screwed her eyes shut and tried to draw back, but Kaylen was everywhere, and it was no use.

She rode the waves of her bittersweet pleasure, clinging to them as they slipped through her fingers. She couldn't even do this right.

The tears leaked from beneath her closed eyelids.

"El?"

Eliza's wrists were free, and she hated that. Kaylen moved off her. Away. As Eliza had known she would.

"Did I hurt you? Eliza, look at me." Panic tinged Kaylen's voice as she cupped Eliza's damp cheeks. Eliza forced her eyes open, though she wasn't ready to look at Kaylen yet.

"Was that too much? I didn't—I thought—" Then Kaylen's hands were gone entirely as she stumbled away from her. "Fuck. I'm sorry."

Why was Kaylen sorry? Eliza finally looked at her, to see her back hitting the wall, face stricken.

Still fully clothed, Kaylen hadn't even removed her boots.

Eliza was suddenly far too exposed. What had thrilled her moments before now made her need to hide. She reached blindly for her discarded shift, clutching it pointlessly to herself as she rolled away, the blanket coarse and itchy beneath her. She searched for a scrap of comfort in Kaylen's cold absence.

"What can I do? Do you want me to leave?" Kaylen whispered. "Or do you want me to hold you?"

"That's a stupid question," Eliza mumbled, the tears choking her. "You should always hold me."

The bed dipped and Kaylen was there. Eliza turned into her, latching on.

Kaylen ran her hand over Eliza's hair. "Did you not like that?"

"I liked it."

"Then why are you crying?"

"Because—" Eliza stopped the careless words before they could leave her mouth.

Because she didn't want Kaylen to leave her. Not tomorrow. Not ever. But Eliza couldn't say that. It would be entirely unfair, if honest. It would only add to the unearned guilt Kaylen carried with her, the invisible weight that Eliza now saw. Eliza was already selfish enough.

Kaylen's heart was far too big for her. Even now, Kaylen saw Eliza's tears and decided they were her responsibility to fix.

"Because I'm hungry," Eliza lied.

"I'll get us some more food. Somehow."

"Not yet."

Eliza did not let go for the rest of the night.

CHAPTER 26

An Unexpected Oath

As they rode up the grand central road toward the outer wall of the Alludan palace, a wave of memories hit Eliza. Dizzy and sick at the same time, she gripped Kaylen's arm cradling her.

Banners of red and gold fluttered from nearly every tower. The tall gates stood open, but guards blocked the path, with more on the smooth dark walls on either side. Kaylen gave her name to the two who greeted them.

"And what business do you have, Sir Kaylen?"

"I am the business," Eliza said, raising her chin.

The guards stared blankly at her.

"I have an appointment with His Majesty's steward, Maxwell," Kaylen said, tightening her hold on Eliza.

Surely now was the time to declare her identity. Eliza was about to demand they let them in. But the guards looked at her without recognition. They didn't know who she was. And part of Eliza wondered what it would be like to keep it that way. She could turn around and leave, and no one would know.

But that wouldn't serve anyone. Kaylen needed her reward, and Eliza needed answers. And a bath.

The guards glanced between Kaylen and Eliza.

"If you fetch him, he will recognize me," Kaylen stated confidently.

The guard studied her for another moment and then waved them past, looking bored.

Kaylen maneuvered their horse into the courtyard, riding over to the stables echoing with snorts and some laughter where several grooms were running about. Eliza barely noticed, her eyes traveling over the palace.

The central keep was surrounded by additional towers, connected by suspended halls bridging the various wings. Like a spider's web. Would Eliza grow trapped inside this one now too?

The gentle circles Kaylen rubbed on Eliza's arm helped her breathe. Eliza sought out the windows she used to look out of. She recalled running along those halls so long ago. It was exactly as she remembered.

Eliza couldn't find the words to express how grateful she was that Kaylen was with her as they approached the front entrance steps. But it was blocked by more guards, who eyed them stonily. Eliza had a better idea.

She dragged Kaylen back toward the stable block, skirting around it instead of through.

"What are you doing?" Kaylen asked.

"There's an easier way in."

Ducking through the rows of hanging linens and steaming vats of scented soap and starch in the rear courtyard, they entered the kitchens. Chefs and cooks barked at one another as metal clinked and wood thunked. The carcass of something large was being butchered near the door, a cleaver adding to the rhythm of the heart of the palace. The scents of herbs, fresh bread, and sizzling lard chased them through the busy series of connected rooms. They didn't exactly blend in, but the people back here were too busy to be bothered by them much. Eliza walked with purpose, like she knew where she was going. Because she did.

Her feet remembered the way. She stopped a maid in a staircase as they climbed higher. "Do you know if the king is in his study?"

The maid looked confused, glancing between her and Kaylen. "In the meeting hall, my lady? With his council. They recently went in."

Eliza thanked her and hurried on, up into the central entrance chamber of the main keep, Kaylen's hand clutched firmly in her own.

"Perhaps we should request an audience the proper way," Kaylen hissed.

"That'll take forever. I'm afraid you're right, and no one will believe me if I just say who I am."

Again, the main doors would be guarded and she didn't feel like convincing anyone. So she didn't aim for the wide steps that led to the front doors of the king's meeting chamber. She opened the nondescript one on the side and climbed the short staircase that led to another low archway and the servants' access.

She paused and listened, her heart rising. Voices drifted to her from the room that lay beyond. Eliza had hidden here when she was younger, listening and not understanding what was happening.

Her father's voice was as distinct now as it had been then. Eliza closed her eyes, a mixture of excitement, longing, and resentment slamming into her. She had missed him and his voice so much over the years. Was she going to let her doubts and a few words alter the memories of her own father?

Kaylen squeezed her hand in support, and then released her. Eliza took a steadying breath, straightened her spine, and finished the last few steps into the king's hall.

KAY WAS GOING TO DIE for Eliza after all, just not the way she had planned. She couldn't quite believe she was barging into the king's private meeting unannounced. Eliza would likely get away with it unscathed, but Kay wasn't certain a lowly knight would. But Eliza had asked Kay to stay with her, and Kay had promised. Hugo had been right. Kay was an utter fool.

Afternoon light poured through tall, colored windows onto five figures gathered around a table.

No one noticed them at first. Then a guard on the opposite side of the room started forward, and the movement made the king turn.

"Father?" Eliza's voice held on a quaver.

The king simply stared, the lines around his mouth and eyes etching deeper. His white hair fell from beneath his crown to just past his stooped shoulders.

The guard's feet faltered, his gaze flicking over Eliza. He shifted his focus to Kay, and she saw confusion, but also determination to do something. He seized Kay's arm, and a second guard grabbed her other. Kay deserved to be restrained for having the audacity to enter as she had.

Eliza, however, disagreed.

"Unhand her!" she demanded, the full force of her princess shining through. "She is with me."

The guards looked at each other, and to their king.

The elderly monarch spared a glance over Kay, and he nodded. Kay was released and immediately forgotten as everyone refocused on Eliza.

"How?" the king asked, his deep voice sounding as shocked as he looked.

"Sir Kaylen rescued me," Eliza replied, the only one still paying attention to Kay, reaching for her. "The knight whom you sent for me."

Kay awkwardly leaned so Eliza's hand slipped into her arm instead of her palm, so they wouldn't scandalize their audience. She hated the flash of hurt on Eliza's face.

The *princess's* face.

Kay had to start thinking of her properly.

The king frowned at Kay again, and turned to the same steward, Maxwell, whom Kay had met with briefly when she accepted the mission. Kay hoped her bravado at the gates had been true and he would recognize her. Luckily, she was quite distinctive.

"This is Sir Kaylen, Your Majesty," the man said. "The most recent knight to accept the quest."

"I see."

"Aren't you happy to see me?" Eliza asked as she watched the king.

The king cleared his throat and recovered himself. He straightened and suddenly looked ten years younger. "Of course. Come here, my child."

He opened his arms and Eliza hesitantly approached. They embraced briefly. It looked stiff and formal, and nothing like the great bear hugs Kay's father used to give.

When the king smiled, it was brittle. "You have returned. After so long. What a joyous thing to be blessed with two daughters again."

Eliza's smile was also strained. "Yes, I hear I have a sister."

"Indeed." The king looked fully at Kay for the first time, and she dropped to a knee and bowed her head. "Sir Kayden?"

"Kaylen, Your Majesty," the steward, Maxwell, whispered hastily. "Of Glea."

The king's eyes and mouth sharpened. "We can't have that." The king nodded at one of the knights who had grabbed Kay earlier. "Sir Grimhook, take Sir Kaylen's current armor to the smith and have a full set of Alludan steel made right away. Top priority."

The knight hauled Kay upright and brusquely unfastened her remaining bracer as the king reached for the ornamental sword at his belt. Kay had a moment of fear that he would cut her down, until his words registered.

"It is not customary for our kingdom to bestow knighthood on a lady, but under the circumstances...Take a knee, Kaylen."

Kay found herself on her knee again, her armor gone, looking up at the king of her homeland.

"Do you, Lady Kaylen of...?"

"Embers Hollow, Your Majesty. But I am not—"

"Of Embers Hollow, do you swear fealty to the kingdom of Alludan, to myself, and to my heirs, promising your steadfast loyalty and devotion, to defend us against all that desire to harm us, and forsaking all previous such vows?"

Kay hesitated, wholly unprepared. She had sworn fealty to Queen Viola of Glea, and had never expected to do so again. Eliza looked back at her with wide eyes.

"I swear, Your Majesty," Kay promised, understanding it was not truly a question. But the vow was real, and as it passed her lips, Kay wasn't certain how she felt about that.

"Then for your heroic deeds for our kingdom, I declare you Sir Kaylen, Honorable Knight of Alludan. Rise, Sir Kaylen."

Kay stood numbly.

"There." The king re-sheathed the sword. "Now, at least, you have the correct title. Or Queen Viola would never let me live it down." He turned back to Maxwell. "Go and spread the word, and draw up a new announcement to be distributed across the kingdom. Princess Eliza is home."

CHAPTER 27
Stuffed

An unfamiliar reflection stared back at Eliza. Apparently, her old room had been repurposed a decade ago. Now she stood in a rich guest room in another wing as strangers touched her. Brushed her hair. Painted her lips. Tugged the laces of the velvet gown being fitted and altered for her on the spot.

And Kaylen was gone. She'd been whisked away in the opposite direction, looking more dazed than Eliza was. Eliza wanted to demand she stay with her, but forced her mouth shut and complied with her father's direction.

Kaylen wouldn't leave without saying goodbye first. Eliza clung to that knowledge, needing to believe it, because the rest of her memories she'd long held as truth seemed to be disintegrating.

"Your Highness, the king is ready for you to join them," a young maid named Amber said.

Eliza wasn't ready. But she was hungry for the food she knew would be served. Eliza followed Amber along the hallway bridging back to the main keep.

She needed to speak with her father. She also dreaded the prospect. He had said words to indicate he was glad she was home, but it was not the welcome she had imagined since she was fifteen. She had an awful sinking feeling the witch had been telling the truth.

Unlike the massive banquet hall, this second dining chamber held a table to fit around twenty people, though only two others were in attendance tonight.

The king was there, looking every bit eighteen years older than Eliza remembered. His frailness frightened her slightly. Rising alongside him was a woman around Eliza's own age, a glittering crown set in her fair hair. Eliza should not have been surprised. A younger wife made sense if the purpose was to create another heir. But Eliza had a hard time accepting that this woman was technically her mother. At least the queen didn't seem *younger* than Eliza.

Eliza curtsied and the queen mirrored her, but her mouth was thin and her expression wary. They were strangers.

The king was a stranger too. And Eliza didn't feel as she had expected seeing him again. She felt oddly hollow around a faint queasiness.

She took her seat and waited impatiently for the servers to come.

"Congratulations," Eliza said when no one else spoke, looking across at the queen. "On your daughter. Annabelle, right?"

The queen smiled tightly. "Yes."

"Will I get to meet her soon?"

The king and queen shared a look.

"She is young," the king said. "Not ready for visitors yet."

Eliza swallowed the hurt. "Of course. Well, it's a very pretty name," Eliza managed. "Father, when I was named, did you choose or did my mother?"

The king froze, and Eliza watched his reaction closely. He reached for his wine. "You were named for my own mother," the king finally stated.

It wasn't an answer, but it gave Eliza a fragment of information she had been looking for. He wasn't keen to talk about his previous wife.

She glanced around in the silence. "Are they going to bring the food soon?"

"We are waiting for one guest to join us."

As the words were spoken, the doors to the room opened.

Eliza barely recognized Kaylen. Her red hair was constrained in a nearly elegant pile on her head, and she wore a deep emerald gown that looked lovely with her coloring, and yet all wrong on her as she stepped forward. She was stunning, but clearly uncomfortable, like she had been stuffed into an actor's costume meant for someone else.

As Kaylen bowed deeply, Eliza appreciated the delightful view the neckline of that gown offered. But then Kaylen frowned and curtsied awkwardly as well. She was adorable. Eliza's ribs squeezed her expanding heart.

KAY WAS HAVING THE strangest day. She had woken with Eliza in her arms at a rundown inn, prepared to say goodbye to her. Now she was being seated beside her at the king of Alludan's table, no longer a knight of Glea, and just as poor as she had been.

That last part wasn't strange.

Eliza smiled at her with warmth and relief, and Kay couldn't help but smile back. Then she quickly dropped her eyes and head.

When the king raised a hand, food appeared immediately. Along with wine. Kay's mouth watered for it.

"Take that away, for both of us," Eliza told the server, turning to the king's raised eyebrow. "I am unaccustomed to drinking after my time in the tower and have resolved not to partake. And Sir Kaylen is persuaded to my thinking as well."

Discomfort twisted in Kay's gut. Eliza shouldn't have to lie for her. But after the day she had had, Kay would be grateful.

Eliza dug into her soup course with enthusiasm, and Kay had to restrain herself from doing the same. The fabric of her sleeve tightened around her bicep as she bent her elbow.

From across the table, the queen was eyeing Kay closely, lingering on the long scar marring Kay's upper chest, which the gown's wide, low neckline exposed. Kay was bursting out of the thing, but in all the wrong ways.

"Sir Kaylen," the king started, and Kay quickly set down her unused spoon again, stomach rumbling. "You said earlier you were from Embers Hollow?"

"Yes, Your Majesty."

"So you are from Alludan, then. Why did you go to Glea?"

"I went as part of Alludan's shared regiment when Glea needed soldiers many years ago."

"You were enlisted? What rank?"

"Foot soldier, Your Majesty."

"I see." A tiny frown creased the king's brow and he shared a glance with his wife.

Kay shifted uncomfortably, knowing she didn't belong. The king had assumed she was of noble blood, and Kay tried to explain earlier, but it had all happened so fast.

"Sir Kaylen is the most selfless person I have ever known," Eliza stated confidently into the renewed awkward silence. "She gave me the boots off her own feet when my slippers wore through."

A flush crept up Kay's neck, which was far too much on display with her hair pulled tightly back. The slippers had only worn through because Kay had made the princess walk her way out.

Kay waited for the king to ask about the rescue. To ask for the story of their journey and expose Kay's inadequacy more, but he avoided it instead.

"Now that you have returned, we must celebrate," the king said, choosing to ignore her words completely. "We have a ball planned in twelve days' time to honor Annabelle's birth. But it seems it shall be a celebration of two daughters." He looked at his wife. "Won't that be nice, my dear?"

The queen glared sharply at her husband, who smiled blandly back, his eyes troubled. "Yes, of course."

The pair had not expected Eliza to return, and their words did not mask the truth. Neither were happy she had.

Kay fought the urge to both sink into the ground, and also to stand up and yell that they were the lucky ones to have Eliza back.

Kay wasn't quite reckless enough to take Eliza's hand, so she shifted her leg sideways beneath the table. When Kay's foot covered Eliza's, Eliza smiled. And for a moment, everything was all right.

"You shall, of course, attend the ball as well, Sir Kaylen, and be honored publicly with your title," the king continued.

Kay's stomach dropped. She would need to remain in the capital for another twelve days?

She got to remain in the capital for another twelve days. Where Eliza was. And Kay would see her at least once more, at the ball.

Kay could find a cheap place to stay for that long. If she could get the reward. The steward, Maxwell, had evaporated that afternoon when Kay had asked after him.

"It will be my honor, Your Majesty," Kay said because she couldn't think of anything else to say.

"And she will stay here in the palace until then," Eliza stated, looking at her father.

"Yes, that's fine," he agreed, waving his hand as if it made no difference.

Kay was overwhelmed again by it all. Another twelve days in the palace sounded dreadful. But she would be near Eliza.

The second course was served before Kay had the chance to touch her soup.

CHAPTER 28
An Uncertain Path

Eliza rolled over for the hundredth time in luxurious silk sheets, entirely too alone. The waning moon shone into her room, but it didn't hold the comfort it used to. She missed Kaylen's presence beside her.

After spending over half her life alone, it had only taken a few short weeks to grow dependent on Kaylen. Eliza would need to get used to being without her. Even if Eliza could figure out a way to keep her, they couldn't spend every moment together. But they still had moments left.

Eliza tossed back the covers. Somewhere in this palace, Kaylen was lying in another bed.

Eliza shoved her feet into a pair of silk slippers and shrugged on a robe.

When she reached for the door handle, it was locked.

She forced herself to breathe through the moment of panic. One of the many things Kaylen had done in each room they stayed in was to show Eliza how the locks worked, so she always knew how to get out. But this lock was different. She couldn't find an inside way to open it.

Anger flared alongside the renewed panic—very real this time.

"Let me out!" Eliza cried, knowing someone was outside. Her own voice sounded thin as dark smoke laced the corners of her vision.

She pounded on the heavy wood, her throat closing, until the lock clicked and released. Eliza twisted the handle and threw the door open, met with the shocked face of Sir Grimhook, the knight who had grabbed Kaylen earlier.

"Your Highness—"

"Don't you dare lock my door ever again." Eliza pushed into the hall, trying to get away from the darkness.

"Your Highness, it was for your own safety."

"Which room is Sir Kaylen in?"

"Sir Kaylen?"

"I know you know. Which room?"

"The scarlet room, in the north tower."

Eliza hurried toward the stairs that would take her to the connecting bridge there.

"Your Highness, it is late," the knight protested.

"Yes, I am aware of that. I'm not quite that silly."

Eliza did not slow, and he rattled loudly after her.

Eliza shook with agitation as she moved through the quiet halls and into the north tower. It wasn't used as frequently, a chill hanging in the air and seeping through the soles of her slippers. Why had Kaylen been put here and not in Eliza's wing? She would make sure to correct it tomorrow.

HER LOVELY CHAMPION

THE LIGHTS OF ALLUDAN'S capital city, which shared its name, flickered below Kay's window and illuminated the sky, making it difficult to see the stars.

Had Stella listened to her? Was Stella looking up too?

Kay hoped she was sleeping peacefully.

Kay's life had changed irrevocably today. Her rank and position as a knight of Glea had been stripped from her, and she hadn't had a chance to protest. While it had been replaced by another, Kay didn't yet know what that meant.

What did the king expect of her? Would she be a true knight here? She'd never thought it possible to be a knight of Alludan. The lady knights of Glea were generally looked at with bemusement by the other kingdoms. Until they faced them in combat, when the only thing that mattered was either winning, or staying alive.

Would Kay be able to compete in tournaments? After forsaking her previous vows to Glea, Kay would be far from welcome back there. The kingdoms of Alludan and Glea were longstanding allies and generally friendly, but not *that* forgiving. Kay didn't enjoy tournaments, but they paid when she did well enough.

With the reward she was due from the crown, they could be comfortable for a while. But Kay knew it wouldn't last forever. They could hire help for the farm, but it was barely profitable in good years, no matter what Ma wanted to believe. Kay would take the time she had, but eventually she would need to leave again.

She would figure it out when the time came. She always had.

Someone knocked on her door. Kay frowned, crossing the expansive room to find Eliza at the threshold with a panting knight on her heels.

"Your Highness," Kay said, starting to bow, but Eliza stopped her with a hand on her chin.

"Don't." The wild flicker on Eliza's face was visible now she was so close.

"What happened?" Kay folded Eliza into her arms, not caring that the knight was watching. If Eliza was upset, Kay would fix it. "Tell me."

"Can I sleep with you?" Eliza asked, and Kay's blood rushed quicker.

"Um..."

Eliza pulled away only enough to push Kay backward into the room and shut the door behind them. "Please? My bed is so big and empty and I can't relax."

"Will your father have me beheaded for sleeping with his daughter?"

"Don't even joke about that, Kay." Eliza's voice was strained and thin.

"It wasn't a joke."

"It'll be fine. All I'm asking is to sleep."

Kay shouldn't agree. "Of course."

Eliza visibly calmed and rewarded Kay with a smile, her mouth curving through the darkness. Then she turned and climbed into Kay's untouched bed.

"I didn't wake you," Eliza whispered as Kay slipped in beside her. It wasn't a question. Eliza's hands slid around Kay's neck, into her hair as Eliza snuggled closer. "I missed you today."

Kay had missed Eliza too. "It was strange being apart."

"I didn't like it at all."

Kay squeezed her eyes shut. She really wished Eliza wouldn't say things like that. "Are you happy to be home?"

"This place doesn't feel like home anymore."

"It will. Once you get used to it again." Kay ran a soothing hand over Eliza's back as Eliza yawned into the pillow. "Do you feel safe here?" Kay asked, not sure it was quite the right question.

"I think so. I didn't have a chance to talk to my father, but he isn't happy to see me. I just don't know why."

"Then he's a fool."

Eliza sucked in a gasp, and released it on a pleased puff, eliminating the space between their bodies. "That's a rather treasonous thing to say, Sir Kaylen, Honorable Knight of Alludan."

"I was focusing on the 'heirs' part of that vow earlier."

"Thank you. For everything."

"You don't have to thank me."

"Well, I just did anyway."

Kay smiled as Eliza tucked her face into the crook of Kay's shoulder and sighed contentedly. Kay relaxed, at peace for tonight.

Kay would start behaving properly tomorrow.

She pressed her lips to the top of her princess's head. "Night, El."

CHAPTER 29

Around in Circles

When Eliza tried to catch her father during his breakfast, she was informed he had already eaten. So, following the vague and unhelpful description that he was walking "in the garden," she headed out in the hopes of finding him.

Sir Grimhook trailed behind her. He had been standing unhappily outside Kaylen's door when Eliza had slipped out before dawn. Now they wandered down graveled paths and between trees and well-groomed hedges.

Eliza's parents used to sit by a small pond on the far side of the gardens to get away from the prying eyes. Naturally Eliza had followed them there as often as she could.

She hadn't been wanted then either, but she had been more innocently oblivious.

Eliza headed there now, with no real expectation it would work, but needing to choose a direction.

To her surprise, when she reached the pond, the king sat on the stone bench on the same side he always had. Eliza wondered if it was a common habit of his, or if Eliza's return had stirred up old memories. His head was lowered, but he looked up when they approached, Sir Grimhook's clanking impossible to ignore.

For a moment he stared at Eliza as he had the day before, flickering with something like horror. Not the softly fond expression he used to give her. It made Eliza want to curl up into a ball and hide.

"You look so much like her," he said, eventually.

"You never used to say that. Have I really changed that much?"

His eyes remained haunted. "Yes."

"I actually wanted to speak to you about her."

The king's expression changed, closing and withdrawing as he stood. "I have a busy schedule."

"I've been back for less than a day. Can you take just a moment to have a conversation with me?" Eliza's throat ached with confusion.

"The schedule was set before we knew you would be here. I was not expecting you to arrive."

"Perhaps you should have been. Since you sent a knight to rescue me."

"I have sent dozens of knights, my dear."

The endearment stung, mocking her because it was obvious now that it wasn't true. "Why did you even bother?"

"Enjoy the gardens, Eliza."

His cold dismissal hurt, and Eliza couldn't quite convince herself it didn't as he walked away without another word to her.

Eliza kicked angrily at a young tree, and instantly regretted it as her toe flared with pain and the innocent sapling shook. It was childish, because Eliza felt like a child.

Time had apparently halted when she'd been placed in that tower, and she was still fifteen and silly.

Instead, she was thirty-three and silly.

She trudged back to the palace, missing Kaylen already, though she had only been gone from her arms a short time. How was Eliza going to cope when Kaylen finally left her?

To distract herself from that distressing prospect, Eliza wandered her former home, trying to reconnect to it. To feel it. The dark walls ate up much of the natural light, despite the generous windows. She climbed to the next floor and crossed to the west tower, roaming along the galleries she hadn't paid much attention to as a child. She passed the mounted foot of a dragon with claws curling as long as Eliza's arm. Her feet quickened past a bust of a hydra. This one was painted darker than Harriet had been, but still too much like her.

As Eliza approached a giant plinth covered in ashes, she frowned and inspected the plaque. It described a flamewalker's body, preserved by magic for twenty years until the magic had died with the witch who froze it. Eliza's stomach soured. The kingdom condemned magic yet had used a witch's abilities for its purposes here. What else would it use it for?

Elaborate tapestries lined the walls in the adjoining hall, illuminated by tall windows. Eliza vaguely remembered them. All but one.

She stopped in front of the largest near the far end, the exposure to the sun starting to fade the colorful threads already, though it couldn't have been more than eighteen years old.

Script woven into the top of the piece read: *The Lost Princess*.

The scene was about Eliza. And it was all wrong.

A hydra lunged from the base of the tower, not contained at all, with at least five distinct heads. The bodies of dismembered knights scattered the ground around her. An old, hunched woman looked on, smiling. Was that supposed to be Layla?

But Eliza's attention was drawn to the girl leaning from the upper window. Eliza remembered that blue gown. It had been the one she'd worn when she was captured. Eliza had tried to wear her favorite pink gown that morning, but her maid discovered a tear near the hem, and so Eliza had donned the blue instead.

At some point over the years, Eliza's mind closed to the memory of that day, and she rarely thought of the details anymore. Like how she'd grown unusually sleepy that fateful afternoon. She'd fallen into her bed for a nap, woken only when hands had seized her. Eliza rubbed at her wrists now, feeling where they'd been bound, blinking rapidly against the ghost of the cool silk blindfold. She'd been forced to swallow something several times. She recalled the sensation of riding in a carriage. And when she had been untied and freed from the enveloping darkness, she was in the tower.

Could Layla have organized and executed all that by herself?

The girl in the tapestry looked down on the carnage and her situation serenely. Pretty. Young. Hopeful.

Hot anger seared Eliza's throat. A reckless need to do *something* seized her.

HER LOVELY CHAMPION

The priceless blue vase from the pedestal beside her shattered satisfyingly as it hit the floor. Eliza grabbed the largest shard and slashed it across the scene in front of her, slicing through the lying threads. She hacked at it until the image of herself was unrecognizable, and then she removed two of Harriet's extraneous heads for good measure.

"Your Highness, you are bleeding!"

Eliza blinked, finally hearing Sir Grimhook. Her palm bled from where she gripped the sharp shard. The bloody piece fell to her feet like the rest. Like the bodies of the knights in the tapestry in front of her.

She accepted Sir Grimhook's handkerchief, pressing it to the shallow cut.

"Please, Your Highness. The resident physician should see you," Sir Grimhook said, as though Eliza had been stabbed through the chest.

Eliza puffed out a humorless laugh. She hadn't had help from a physician in years. Her hand barely stung. "It's a shallow cut."

Sir Grimhook tried to usher her back down the hall without touching her, wafting his hands near her arm. It reminded Eliza of when she'd had the shield on her. She brushed against his prostrating arm as she relented and started walking.

Just to assure herself she could.

KAY FINISHED FASTENING her new gauntlet, completing the full set. Her former Glea armor was nowhere to be found. The Alludan armor was heavier, but moved well as she tested it, swinging her arms and bending.

The smith had done a decent job of recreating the fit of her old breastplate, though she could see where they had altered an existing piece. Alludan smiths were unaccustomed to armoring a woman's figure. The other pieces would need to be fitted a bit better as well, but they worked for now.

Kay tried to like it as she studied herself in the tall mirror propped in the corner of her room. When that didn't work, she at least tried to observe it objectively. It was sleeker. Newer. And without the ornamentation and etching of her former set. But she missed her old pieces. They had seen her through a lot.

They were the price the king demanded, and so Kay would pay.

She turned and abruptly left her room.

Wandering her way through the halls and stairs, Kay tried to figure out where she was. She spotted a maid standing near a corner, staring at her.

"I'm looking for the king's steward, Maxwell. Can you point me in the direction of his office?"

The maid blushed. "Yes, sir. Shall I take you there?"

"No need, I'm sure you are busy. Just tell me, thanks."

The young woman pointed Kay down the hall and to a staircase that would lead to the central keep of the palace. "You must be very brave, to have rescued the princess," she added before Kay could leave.

"The princess is the brave one," Kay corrected as she fled. "I got lucky."

From the main entrance hall, Kay muddled her way to the steward's chambers from her memory of visiting before. Everyone she passed noticed her. A few nodded. Others bowed. And everyone stared, not certain what to make of her. She was rather conspicuous with her loose hair and shiny new armor.

Kay was relieved to find Maxwell in his office.

"Ah, Sir Kaylen." The thin man inclined his head. "What can I do for you?"

"I'm here about the reward. I left direction for it to be given to Sir Hugo of Glea, but since I'm alive, I will no longer be needing his service."

"Very good." The steward shuffled a few things on his desk. "I shall correct that."

After a beat of silence, Kay prompted, "I can collect it now."

"I don't have it ready currently, as the month window has time yet, but I'm certain we can arrange it all." He cleared his throat, and Kay knew she was dismissed.

"When?"

The steward arched an eyebrow. "It will be done timely."

People always got strange about money, particularly the wealthy. Kay knew it was viewed as unseemly, but she wasn't going to let this man's discomfort keep her from her reward. "Shall I come back tomorrow?"

"I am not certain—"

"I'll be back tomorrow."

Kay left, frustrated by the interaction, and unsettled by the nagging panic that she would never see that reward.

You may reach for the stars, but the stars always fall...

Her steps slowed, not certain what she should do. So she wandered onward, more than a little lost again already. This dark palace was a maze.

She spotted the guard who had been with Eliza last night. He straightened, his eyes quickly taking in her armor, which matched his, and his mouth tightened. "Sir Kaylen."

"Sir Grimhook, isn't it?"

He nodded tersely.

"Is Princess Eliza inside?" Kay peered into the room glittering with candles.

Eliza was seated in a comfortable chair, an open book on her lap and a stack of more leaning precariously past the arched velvet back. She looked up and her face instantly brightened.

Kay stepped into the library, her earlier frustration forgotten as Eliza smiled. "Are you reading philosophy?" Kay asked.

"Can't you tell?"

Kay picked up a heavy book, its binding cracking with age. She flipped through it, having a hard time deciphering the tight, looping scrawl. Kay could read, but it wasn't a great skill of hers.

"It's all so interesting," Eliza said earnestly.

"I'll take your word for it."

Eliza laughed, setting her book aside and standing. "As I recall, you rather liked my philosophical arguments." She lowered her voice, sending shivers through Kay's limbs.

Tempting Kay to press Eliza against the bookshelf and lift her skirts, like her eyes were begging her to do.

Kay cleared her throat and looked away. "Your arguments can be quite compelling."

Eliza reached out and ran a hand down Kay's new breastplate.

Kay's heart stopped and she grabbed Eliza's wrist, glaring at the bandage. "What happened?"

"I'm fine," Eliza assured her quickly.

"What happened?"

Eliza bit her lip. "I attacked a tapestry."

"A tapestry?"

Eliza nodded.

"Well, did it deserve it?"

Eliza snorted. "It sort of did, actually." Her smile died. "It was about the lost princess."

Kay pressed her lips to Eliza's palm, tracing the edge of the finespun gauze, holding Eliza's newly damaged hand with her own healed one. "It seems it fought back. Does it need any more vanquishing?"

Eliza stepped closer. "Why? Would you do it for me?"

"Just say the word." Kay's pulse beat too fast. Eliza's skin beneath her thumb was mesmerizingly soft.

Eliza's smile shone brighter than the hundred candles as she ran her eyes over Kay. "At least you're dressed for the part. The smiths worked fast. You look very dashing."

"It's a bit much for walking around the palace, but I thought it might help."

"Help what?"

"Nothing. It's fine."

When Kay stepped back, Eliza kept hold of her hand. "Don't lie to me, Kaylen."

Kay sighed. "The steward didn't have the funds ready."

Eliza was still frowning. "You will get what is owed to you. I promise."

"Don't worry about it. I'll try tomorrow."

Kay glanced around the library, needing to talk about something else. "How big is this place?" She couldn't tell what was wall and what was shelf.

"It goes on a long way." A playful look lit Eliza's face. "I recall a section I particularly enjoyed when I was fifteen. Want to see?"

Eliza looped their arms together and led her deeper into the labyrinth of shelves, up a few steps and down on the other side. Stopping at one of the few clear walls, Eliza stood on her toes to pull down a slim book from the top shelf and handed it to Kay.

Kay flipped to a random page and nearly dropped it.

"El!" Kay hissed.

Eliza sparkled in mischievous delight. "Are you scandalized, Sir Kaylen?"

Kay huffed out a laugh, cautiously reopening the book. "Certainly surprised. How does a princess know exactly where this is?"

"I was bored one winter and decided to catalogue all the sections. This library has *everything*. This one came in rather handy."

"With the second-born Uvarian princess in the garden?"

"Yes, exactly."

Kay considered the erotic illustration on the current page. "I don't think that position is quite possible."

Eliza hooked her finger over the top of the book, angling it toward herself and tilting her head. Then those fingertips left the page to dance over the back of Kay's hand.

Eliza hummed softly, liquifying Kay's insides. "Shall we find out?"

CHAPTER 30
Scandalous

K aylen was irresistible, and Eliza didn't want to resist.

"Please," Eliza breathed, any well-reasoned arguments fleeing from her head. "Want me."

That raw request seemed to work fine.

Kaylen backed Eliza into the corner between the shelf and the wall. She was all hard surfaces in her armor. When Eliza ran her hands over the sculpted metal covering Kaylen's chest, Kaylen didn't protest. It wasn't quite what Eliza wanted—it wasn't Kaylen's skin—but it was more than Kaylen had given her before. With her eyes closed and Kaylen's open mouth on her neck, Eliza could almost imagine what Kaylen felt like beneath the metal.

Kaylen skimmed along Eliza's neckline before tugging it down, her roughened hands slow and gentle. It was wonderful and terribly frustrating. Eliza sank her fingers into Kaylen's hair, and that worked even better.

Kaylen pressed her harder into the bookshelf, bunching up her skirts. Eliza writhed, seeking contact and gasping as the smooth, cold metal encasing Kaylen's strong thigh touched the sensitive skin of her own. Eliza pushed closer, seating herself on Kaylen's leg as her knight gripped her tighter.

Eliza ground down and whined in pleasure.

"Shhh." Kaylen slid one hand up to brush over Eliza's lips.

Before Kaylen could retreat, Eliza captured two of Kaylen's fingers between her teeth.

"Fuck," Kaylen whispered, breath ragged, but she didn't pull away. Instead, she shifted so she could urge Eliza faster. Eliza hummed.

The metal between her legs was slick and warming from her movements. A book thudded as it toppled over on the shelf behind her.

Kaylen brought her lips against Eliza's ear, her wild hair brushing over Eliza's flushed, exposed breasts. Kaylen pulled her fingers from Eliza's mouth and slipped down past Eliza's own curls. "Look at you, darling. Painting my armor for me."

Eliza trembled at the words.

But it was Kaylen's breathless confession that undid her. "I've always wanted you."

Eliza clamped around Kaylen's thigh, shuddering as her pleasure crested. The world spun, blinking in and out between nothing and pure delight.

Kaylen's arms and the uneven wall of books caught her. Eliza dropped her head back and breathed in dust, old leather, and Kaylen.

Kaylen eased her hold, and as Eliza reluctantly released her wobbly legs to stand, she winced from where a buckle had rubbed the delicate skin of her inner thigh. She hadn't noticed, but Kaylen noticed now. Eliza tried to hide it by dropping her skirts, but Kaylen stopped her, pushing the fabric back up to inspect the inflamed spot.

"Don't even think about apologizing," Eliza panted.

Kaylen knelt and pressed her lips to the minor injury instead. Eliza's weak knees gave up and she crumpled. They ended up as a tangle of velvet, metal, and sticky skin in the corner. Kaylen chuckled and Eliza let out a loud, helpless laugh.

With an achingly tender expression, Kaylen pulled Eliza's mouth to her own for a lingering kiss.

Kaylen wasn't pulling away yet, and Eliza clung to her, a desperate hope filling her.

"That was far better than any illustration in a book," Eliza whispered.

"Even the inverted one?"

"No book could compare to you."

Kaylen stilled. "Eliza, I..."

"What?"

"...should let you get to your reading."

The familiar sting consumed Eliza. Not only did it hurt on its own, but it was also a reminder of what was to come.

"But do you have to leave anymore?"

Kaylen frowned at the partially constructed thought Eliza blurted out.

"Because you are a knight of Alludan now," Eliza clarified. "Might your duties keep you here? At the palace? In the capital?"

Kaylen was quiet for a moment. "I'm not certain what the king will expect. I wasn't exactly given a lengthy description yesterday. But when the ball is over, I'll go home. And as long as I can stay there, I will."

Eliza nodded. She understood that, and wanted Kaylen to be able to. And at the same time, she loathed it because Eliza selfishly wanted to keep her. The prospect of their parting seemed so final. So much of an end.

"But you'll have to come back sometimes, right?"

"Probably."

Eliza had an idea. It wasn't a solution, but it would be a wonderful surprise. She smiled, warmth of hope and new possibilities spreading through her as she disentangled herself from Kaylen and they stood.

Eliza used the hem of her shift to clean Kaylen's armor as Kaylen tucked a few flyaway pieces of Eliza's hair behind her ear.

"Will you dine with us again tonight?" Eliza asked, taking Kaylen's arm and leading her back through the library.

"I doubt I'll be invited."

"I'm inviting you."

Kaylen's smile was off. "I think you should spend some time with them on your own."

Eliza sighed. "My father won't speak with me in private, so I doubt he will with company. But I'll try. Oh, and I'm having your room moved."

"I like my room fine."

"I don't want to wander through half the palace to get to you at night."

"We shouldn't sleep together anymore."

Eliza pouted. "Why not?" She wouldn't waste her precious time with Kaylen by sleeping in another bed.

"It's scandalous."

"We've already established I'm scandalous."

"I'm certain everyone already knows you were there last night."

"Well then, if everyone knows, there's no harm in doing it again. Philosophically."

Kaylen snorted. As they approached the library doors, Sir Grimhook gave them a suspicious look.

"Enjoy your reading," Kaylen said, taking Eliza's hand and brushing the barest of kisses to the back. And she was gone, leaving Eliza tingling and happy. And stomach swooping with dread that she was hurtling toward the edge of something she wasn't prepared to face.

KAY'S HANDS SHOOK AS she removed her armor back in the safety of her room. She could still feel Eliza writhing against her. Kay hadn't allowed herself to find her own pleasure since she met Eliza, but it curled through her, growing more insistent with each unwise encounter they had.

Kay's hands got as far as her lower belly when she stopped herself. It would be too much. Her box was already too small for everything she was keeping inside it. She didn't think she could add this too.

So instead, she washed herself quickly and briskly with frigid water from the wash basin.

Deciding to make use of her stocked writing desk, she scratched out a letter to Sir Hugo. The words fell strange and stilted from the quill, but they would do. She needed to tell someone what had happened.

Then she had the dilemma of what to do with the letter. The bell to ring for a servant felt far too invasive, so Kay tucked the note into her pocket and went in search of someone. The palace confused her, all the halls appearing the same, with too many levels, but she eventually found and delivered the letter into the hands of a young page who looked competent, and who eyed her too curiously.

When she got back to her room, it was occupied. The maid whom she had asked for directions from earlier stood inside, along with several others, who were looking around confusedly.

"Princess Eliza has arranged for you to be moved, sir," the maid said. "But we cannot find any possessions to move."

"I only have these." Kay gathered the stray bits of armor she'd laid out on the bed, her body heating at the sight of her leg guard. "Where shall I go?"

"We can carry those, sir."

"I've got them."

Kay followed her along the hall.

"I'm Amber, by the way. If you need anything," the young woman said.

"Thank you, Amber."

"Is it true you were a soldier in Glea? If you don't mind me asking."

"Um, yes. That is true."

"I believe you are the first lady knight of Alludan in two generations."

"Oh." Kay swallowed. "Yes."

"And to think, you were the one of all of them to be victorious! To slay the beast and rescue the princess!"

"I didn't exactly—" Kay bit off her protest as Amber opened a door into a grand bedchamber. Bright and airy in contrast to the rest of the palace, it overlooked the garden rather than the wall and city, and simply screamed of wealth. The room Kay had stayed in last night was rich and elegant, but this was luxurious.

"Perhaps I should stay in my old room," Kay said. "Or another one that's less...white."

"This was the one Princess Eliza insisted on."

Of course she had. A confusing mix of affection and discomfort mingled in Kay. She belonged in this room even less than her old one.

Kay set her armor pieces on the sofa, afraid the weight of them might crush the perfectly flocked velvet as Amber left her alone.

Kay stared at them. Unfamiliar and shiny. Then she stared at the opulent room.

What was she supposed to do now?

CHAPTER 31
Untrustworthy

Eliza drifted along the halls in late afternoon, no real purpose to her steps. A new guard had replaced Sir Grimhook and trailed after Eliza as her feet carried her on the habitual path to the royal wing.

She lingered at the junction to the short hall toward her old room. She'd been told it was repurposed, though not what for.

The hall was silent, most of the doors leading off firmly shut. She peered through an open one she passed, only to find the room empty, the windows shuttered.

Her door was the last one, the wood around the opening carved with patterns of songbirds among roses. Eliza's fingers traced them briefly. She'd forgotten about them, this tiny detail that had seemed so benign when she was young. One of many. When she tested the sculpted iron handle, it stuck. At first she thought it was locked, but she shoved harder, and the door reluctantly swung inward with a heavy creak.

The space slammed into her, along with the dust.

Everything was as she had left it, down to the pretty blue runners over the floor, which were rotting now, their edges frayed and chewed.

The unmade bed lay rumpled, and Eliza shivered at the sight of where the blanket had been kicked off when she'd struggled.

No one had been in here. Except for the mice. A few skittered at the edges of the room, fleeing from her presence.

The room hadn't been repurposed. It had been shut away. A morbid shrine to the lost princess—except everyone knew exactly where she was.

Eliza turned abruptly and slammed the door. Her heart raced as she hurried away. She shouldn't have looked.

The hall spilled into another, and she descended the stairs to the next level, toward the bridge that would take her back to the central keep.

The sound of a young woman laughing and cooing slowed Eliza's steps. A nursemaid stood in a sunny room, rocking a bundle in her arms while speaking softly and lovingly, as people always did with babies.

The maid looked up, her eyes widening but her smile remaining when she saw Eliza.

"Your Highness!" The maid bounced the baby higher. "Your sister is in a fine mood today."

Eliza pushed open the door farther and stepped inside, peering with more interest at the bundle. Princess Annabelle looked like any other baby to Eliza.

"Her Highness has woken from a nap. Would you like to hold her?"

"Oh, I'm not sure if..."

Eliza instinctively reached up to clutch the baby as the maid deposited her into Eliza's arms. "Make sure to support her neck, Your Highness."

"Right." Eliza carefully cradled the delicate, mostly bald head. So fragile. "Hello there," Eliza whispered.

Chubby hands that hadn't quite learned to work yet grasped, and dark eyes squinted up. Eliza looked back at her half sister. Perfect and tiny and innocent.

And for a terrible moment, Eliza despised her. She was gripped by a sudden, irrational envy of the happy, days-old princess with a whole life ahead of her, full of so much possibility. Annabelle had so much time. Eliza's time had been stolen from her.

Would Annabelle get a swan one day when she asked? Would the musty remnants of Eliza's room be swept away and replaced with new pretty silks for a new pretty princess? Would Annabelle grow up pampered and sheltered, and never be forced to realize it?

Eliza's eyes grew damp, the resentment dulling into sadness. She hoped Annabelle would have all those things.

"What are you doing?"

The queen stood in the open doorway, face paling as she stared at Eliza.

"Give her back. Now!" The queen's voice rasped and pitched with panic as she reached for the child.

Eliza let go at once. "I wasn't—"

"Get back! Get away!"

Eliza hastily retreated as the queen held her daughter to her chest and glared with alarming ferocity at Eliza. Princess Annabelle began to fuss, her wail piercing.

"I didn't mean any harm." Eliza backed out of the room.

The queen turned to the shocked and confused nursemaid. "You are dismissed. Permanently."

"But, Your Majesty, please..."

"Leave. Everyone leave!"

The stricken maid and Eliza left, the sound of the queen breaking down echoing after them.

Eliza ran back toward her wing. She shook from the queen's reaction to her. From her fury. Eliza hadn't done anything wrong, but it felt like she had.

Eliza knocked on the door of the room she'd asked Kaylen to be put in, intensely relieved when Kaylen's beautiful face appeared.

After one glance at Eliza's expression, Kaylen pulled her into a hug. Eliza sank into her, better at once. What was wrong with her? She couldn't need Kaylen this much.

"What happened?" Kaylen asked.

Eliza stepped deeper into Kaylen's room to get away from the guard, who was staring at them askance, but he followed.

"You may leave us," Eliza told him.

"I must stay with you while you are out of your room, Your Highness. Sir Grimhook's orders."

"Well, I'm ordering otherwise."

"He has orders from the king, Your Highness."

Eliza flashed with anger and his eyes went wider with fear.

It wasn't his fault, and she didn't want to get another innocent person fired today because of her.

"Fine." Eliza took Kaylen's hand and dragged her down the three doors to her own room, pulling Kaylen inside and shutting the door firmly in the guard's face.

Kaylen hugged her again as Eliza stumbled to explain what had happened.

"The queen is likely threatened by you," Kaylen said, rubbing Eliza's back.

"They really didn't think I would ever return." Eliza hadn't been in the palace for a full day, and she already wished she had never come. "It's like my life ended when I was taken from here and put in my tower. I ceased to exist in the world. And the world doesn't want me back."

"Then the world doesn't deserve you," Kaylen said, her expression fierce.

Eliza sighed, her insides melting for this wonderful woman. "I didn't mean to interrupt you," Eliza said, only now realizing Kaylen's feet were bare against the rugs. Eliza was so selfish. So needy. And she felt worse than she had earlier.

"It's fine. I was trying to nap, in that way-too-fancy bed. Why did you have me put in that room?"

"Because it's close to mine. And I wanted you to have it."

"It's too much."

Kaylen looked down, so Eliza framed Kaylen's face, holding until Kaylen eventually met her eyes. "I'd give you so much more than a nice room, Kay. If I thought you'd let me."

Kaylen surged against her, gripping Eliza like she'd never let her go. This kiss wasn't like their others. It was harder. Wilder.

Thrilled, Eliza met her as wildly, ready for whatever Kaylen would give.

Nothing, apparently.

Kaylen wrenched away, ramming space between them. Space Eliza hated. Kaylen had so much love inside her, and Eliza only got sips, when she craved to bathe in it. To drown.

The burning in her eyes returned.

"Maybe I should take a nap too," Eliza said, instead of admitting the truth—that she was afraid she was falling in love with Kaylen. That she was already head over tickled toes in love with her.

Kaylen nodded jerkily, her breathing faster than usual as she slipped back out past the guard, whose eyes tracked her down the hall as well. Eliza wanted to follow her. Forever.

IT WAS A HARD THING, to say no to Eliza. But Kay managed it when Eliza came by to convince her again to join her for dinner. Kay wasn't sorry for missing it, only for missing Eliza.

Amber knocked on her door soon afterward. "Her Highness says to bring you something to eat, sir. What would you like?"

Kay glanced around the pristine white room. "I'll come to the kitchen and have whatever is left over, or ready."

Amber's eyes widened. "If you wish."

As when Eliza had led Kay through the sprawling kitchens during their arrival yesterday, the space hummed with activity and warmth, delicious smells and a few less pleasant ones. Kay's shoulders relaxed somewhat. She had left her armor and chainmail in her room, and her simple clothes blended in more here.

"There is a staff table here, but perhaps you'd like something quieter?" Amber said.

"This is fine. And really, I'll take anything. But nothing to drink."

Amber gave her an uncertain smile and nodded, leaving Kay to seat herself at a long wooden table where several others were taking meals. A trio played a game of dice at the other end. The clatter of carved bone against wood and their quiet banter and outbursts of mostly good humor cut through any awkward silences.

A middle-aged man up the bench gave Kay an assessing look. "Haven't seen you before. I'm Gill." He leaned over and offered his hand.

"Kay."

"When did you get here?"

"Yesterday."

"And where are you at?"

Kay understood what he was asking but wasn't certain how to reply as Amber returned with two platters of food.

"Here you are, sir," she said, sliding one in front of Kay. "I hope you don't mind if I eat as well."

Gill's gaze sharpened on Kay. "Sir?" He looked closer. "You're not the new lady knight everyone is talking about, are you?"

"It would seem I am."

Gill tilted forward in a bow. "Forgive me, sir. I hope I did not offend you by addressing you so informally."

"Of course not. I was Kay long before I was Sir Kaylen."

"She was once one of us," Amber said, smiling shyly at Kay as she sat across from her.

Kay forced an answering smile and dove into her meal. The stew was thick, hot, and rich. Delicious. Eliza would have liked it too. Kay doubted Eliza was eating anything so humble.

Kay needed to stop thinking of Eliza everywhere she went.

Kay had learned to control her thoughts of home while away. Why was it so difficult to do the same with Eliza? With more time and distance, Kay would get there. Sleeping in the same bed each night was not helping. Kay was already far too wrapped up in the woman.

"So how did you do it?" Amber asked.

Kay used the crusty bread to gather the last morsel of stew from her bowl, which was gone too quickly. "Do what?"

"Rescue Princess Eliza? Knights have been trying for years. Tell us the story!"

"I was lucky."

Amber waited expectantly as Kay glanced over to see Gill watching her quizzically as well.

"I know you probably can't admit it here," Amber said, lowering her voice and leaning closer. "But is it true you secretly married the princess?"

Kay choked on her bread. "What?"

"And did you save that wagon of orphans from ruffians in the borderlands?"

Kay stared at her in numb horror.

"Your reputation precedes you, sir," Gill said, tucking into his pot of sweetened cream. "I have heard already five different accounts of where you stayed in Alludan city. Everyone and their brother saw you."

"We didn't even arrive to the city until yesterday morning," Kay protested, the soup in her belly roiling.

As the news of Eliza's return spread, so would the rumors. Of course, a lady knight would have drawn attention. Kay thought back to all the places where she had claimed Eliza as her wife.

"I did not marry the princess," Eliza stated, the thought tugging uncomfortably at her skin. "Surely people don't believe that."

Kay glanced between Gill and Amber. Amber blushed, and Gill looked skeptical. And both were unapologetically curious.

"Are things much different around here now Her Highness is home?" Kay asked, redirecting away from that frighteningly delightful notion which Kay could not afford to indulge.

"Well, no one is quite certain what will happen with the lineage," Amber answered. "Princess Eliza was crowned first heir before she was captured, of course. But Princess Annabelle was crowned first heir upon her birth, so now that the elder princess is back, we don't know what the king will do with two equally recognized successors."

Unease ladened Kay's insides. She wondered if Eliza knew that about Princess Annabelle. And it likely explained the queen's meltdown.

"No matter what the king decides, each will have their supporters," Gill added, chewing methodically through his heavily buttered roll. "Many would prefer Princess Eliza, as with the king's age, an older heir is comforting to have."

"Do you remember her from before?" Amber asked.

"I sure do. I've been here since I was a boy. Her Highness was always a sweet girl, if a bit pampered. As she should have been."

"You were here when the former queen died as well?" Kay asked.

Gill nodded seriously. "The king changed that day. He has never been the same. And less than a month after his wife died, he lost his daughter too. I hope Princess Eliza's return will bring some light back to him."

Kay stood, grabbing her tray. "Where shall I take this?"

Amber jumped to her feet. "I'll take it. Shall I walk you back to your room?"

"I can find the way. Enjoy the rest of your meal."

Kay nodded to Amber and to Gill, and fled before they could tell her any more absurdly false claims about herself.

She had felt better in the humble rumble of the kitchen, until they realized who she was. She didn't belong there anymore, and neither did she belong in the room she closed the door of.

The hearth glowed merrily, turning the white room to warm golds and shadowy blues. Despite it being too early, Kay stripped down, cleaning up again with the cold water in the washbasin. The sheets were soft and cool as Kay slipped between them in her undershirt, worried she would somehow stain or damage them with her callused hands and sun-roughened skin.

She was failing miserably to sleep when her door creaked open. Heart spiking, her body forgot her surroundings and instinctively tensed to reach for the knife resting on her bedside table.

"Kay?" Eliza's whisper cut through the darkness and Kay's racing pulse steadied only moderately.

"I'm here."

Eliza's form glided toward her and the bed dipped.

"What are you doing?" Kay asked. "I told you we shouldn't sleep together."

Eliza was quiet for a moment. "Do you really want me to leave?"

Kay should say yes. "You probably should."

Eliza's hands found Kay's face in the darkness. "Says who?"

When Kay helplessly kissed Eliza back, she tasted salt. "Have you been crying?"

"Sorry." Eliza wiped at her face with her sleeve, and Kay dabbed at the other, hating Eliza's tears.

"Was it dinner?"

"Dinner barely happened. Neither of them would look at me. It was like I wasn't there. Did you go somewhere? You weren't here when I came by."

"I ate in the kitchens."

"I told them to bring you something."

"I didn't want to be a bother."

Eliza's grip tightened on the back of Kay's neck almost painfully. "You are not a bother, Kaylen. You're so far from one, it's laughable. I want to shake you sometimes because you refuse to see it."

"And you think shaking me would help?" Kay bit out more harshly than she meant. "They asked me how I did it—how I rescued you. You should hear the absurd stories already circulating. They think I'm some hero."

"Because you are." Eliza's kiss was bruising as she straddled Kay, shoving her onto her back. "You're mine," Eliza whispered, capturing Kay's earlobe between her teeth as she wrapped her fingers through Kay's hair and tugged. Kay went rigid with desire. "Hold me down again. Please."

Kay cursed, kicking the expensive bedding away to get to Eliza. Eliza released a breathy giggle, and Kay lost herself. She pinned Eliza to the mattress. Eliza's thigh pressed between her own as Kay's shirt rode up to her waist. They moved together, like wind through grass, like falling snow on bowing branches. Inevitable and natural.

Building pleasure spiraled from the straining roots of Kay's hair to her toes. She almost kept going. It would take nothing at all to find release.

Kay wanted this woman so badly. And Kay couldn't have the things she wanted.

She scrambled off the bed, tripping on the tangle of silky bedding before colliding with the windowsill and climbing into the corner of the charming seat there. Trying to get away. Afraid she would return.

"I can't." Kay wrapped her arms around herself and leaned against the cold stone wall, needing it to take some of the heat inside her away. She was in so deep with Eliza, Kay wasn't sure it was worth fighting it anymore. And that was a treacherous thought.

Kay hid her face between her knees, more of a coward now than she'd been facing her own death. "I can't tonight. Will you forgive me?"

"Forgive you," Eliza echoed, her voice thick. "You really are infuriating, you know."

The words sliced through Kay's skin and she squeezed her eyes shut tighter, forcing down the tears she didn't want.

Trust the land 'neath your feet, for it grew you up strong...

Fingers wove back into Kay's hair, gentle and soothing this time. Kay peeked up at the outline of Eliza, who perched on the window seat in front of her.

"Do you honestly think I'm angry with you?" Eliza asked.

"I don't want to let you down," Kay admitted. "To disappoint you."

"I kind of wish you would. You're so responsible all the time it makes me feel bad about myself. I wish you'd do something selfish for once. What do *you* want, Kay? If you could have anything—do anything—what would it be?"

"I'd go home," Kay said without hesitation. "And I'd—" Kay couldn't finish that thought. *And I'd take you with me.*

"I can sleep in my own room tonight. If you want me to." Eliza sounded unsure.

Kay's heart thrashed. "Stay."

The word slipped dangerously from her mouth, and she couldn't take it back.

Eliza hauled Kay up, wrapping her arms around her and simply holding.

"I'm sorry," Kay murmured.

Eliza sighed. "I know you want to be perfect. And I appreciate that. But I don't want you to be perfect, Kay. I just want you to be real. Like this. With me. Because even though you aren't the only person I know anymore, you're still my favorite."

Her words were too much, and Kay buried her face in Eliza's neck in reply. Inhaling her.

"Come to bed," Eliza whispered. And Kay ached to hear that every night for as long as her ears worked.

She was in so much trouble.

CHAPTER 32
Distractions

The invasion occurred just past dawn. Eliza had barely, reluctantly returned to her own room when a brisk knock was followed by the entrance of Marianne the dressmaker and a trail of maids carrying swatches of fabric.

Marianne was a tall, handsome woman with firm hands and disapproving eyebrows. Eliza rather liked her.

"The king says you must have gowns, at least ten. So what do you like? I recommend warm colors, but if you insist on blue, I suppose I cannot say no."

"I like warm colors," Eliza agreed.

"Good." Marianne's eyebrows briefly turned approving, before they dropped again.

Eliza's gaze shifted over the overwhelming selection of fabrics, catching on black silk embroidered with pink flowers. It wasn't the same pattern as the gown Layla had worn, but it reminded Eliza of it.

"I can work with black," Marianne sighed, following her gaze. She held the fabric against Eliza's chest, nodding. "It won't wash you out. Shall I set this one aside for you?"

Eliza turned to the door, wanting to fetch Kaylen and ask her opinion. But Eliza stopped herself. She couldn't lean on Kaylen forever. She could do this on her own.

"Yes, do," Eliza said.

Marianne stayed all morning, laying out fabrics and sketching designs for Eliza to look over. Eliza was unreasonably proud of herself by the time Marianne swept out, promising her the first gown the following afternoon.

Exhilarated by making her own choices, even if they were unimportant ones, Eliza resolved to find her father and make him speak to her. Kaylen wasn't in her room, and it only somewhat punctured Eliza's determination.

The king was just approaching his audience chamber when Eliza rounded the corner.

"Father?" she called, quickening her steps.

He stiffened when he saw her and turned away. Eliza's feet faltered, but she forced them to keep going. Several members of his council were with him, and their eyes skittered away as they hastily followed the king into the room beyond. The blatant dismissal pricked at Eliza's skin. Before she could reach the door, a well-dressed young man emerged and blocked her path.

"Your Highness." He bowed deeply. "His Majesty has charged me with your tutelage."

"My what?"

"With your long absence, there is no time to waste."

Resentment blotted out the confusion. "And in what subjects has the king determined I am particularly lacking?"

The man sputtered. "I am certain you are not lacking, Your Highness. Though a refresher is always helpful. I shall first need to assess a baseline of what you recall from your time before."

The last bit of Eliza's pride from that morning evaporated. How silly of her to have been proud of choosing some fabric. "I'm going to walk in the garden. You can join me if you must." Eliza begrudgingly led the way outside, leaving her father and his pointedly shut door, trading the oppressive stone walls for open sky, rustling trees, and flowers approaching the end of their season.

"Shall we start with the basics, Your Highness?" the man asked.

"Yes, lets. What is your name?"

"Oh." He blushed slightly. "Lord Emery, Your Highness."

"And what are your qualifications, Lord Emery?"

"I, um..."

Eliza eyed the young man, likely only in his early twenties. "My father has hired you to mind me."

His blush deepened. "I would not say that."

A waft of wonderfully frizzy hair stuck out from behind a shrub, and Eliza's steps quickened. Kaylen sat on a bench on the side of the path, a clump of reeds in her hands as she twisted them, wrapping around Eliza's heart. But as Eliza watched, Kaylen released one half, and the forming figure unraveled. Kaylen clutched the reeds, her head bowed, but didn't move to fix it.

"Why did you stop?"

Kaylen jerked as she dropped the reeds and stood. "Good morning." She tilted forward in a stiff bow, and Eliza hated it.

"Why did you stop?" Eliza repeated.

It took a moment before Kaylen met her eyes. "She's too old for dolls." Kaylen's face twitched and she looked away again, clearing her throat.

Eliza reached for Kaylen to hug her. To hold her. But Kaylen stepped back.

The quick rejection was like an ice shard pierced into Eliza's breast, widening the prick her father had left earlier into an open wound. So Kaylen would hold Eliza when she was upset, but Eliza couldn't comfort her in return?

"Are you Sir Kaylen?" Lord Emery asked, sounding keenly excited by the prospect.

Eliza had forgotten about him already. She tried to rein in her hurt. She didn't want to cry in the gardens today.

Kaylen bowed again. "And you are...?"

"This is Lord Emery. My new babysitter," Eliza announced bitterly.

"Tutor," Lord Emery corrected.

Kaylen nodded, her gaze returning to Eliza finally. "You told me in Rosewood that you wanted to learn all you could."

Eliza's angry defiance deflated a little. If she truly thought about it, having a tutor to ask endless questions of wouldn't be such a bad thing. "I suppose I did."

"An education is something many do not have."

Eliza's cheeks burned. Her princess was showing again.

Kaylen stopped right in front of Lord Emery. He squirmed beneath Kaylen's careful, intense assessment. "I trust you have the best intentions, my lord," Kaylen said, her words quiet but a threat hanging behind them.

"Of course," Lord Emery said, nodding vigorously.

"Will you join us?" Eliza asked Kaylen. "At least for today?"

"Perhaps I shall," Kaylen murmured, still watching Lord Emery. "Just for today."

KAY WAS ABOUT READY to snap the fine quill in two. The damned songbird outside her window kept moving. Not that her pathetic attempt to capture its likeness would have gone any better had it been stuffed. The lines were coming out entirely wrong, and not at all how she meant.

It was a stupid idea anyway. But during Eliza's morning lessons today, Lord Emery focused on drawing. Kay had sat in the room—just to keep an eye on the young lord and ensure Eliza felt comfortable, despite it being their third day together—and listened. Then she'd watched Eliza's talented hands easily create several masterpieces. She'd also watched Eliza's adorable furrow of concentration, and the way she bit her lip. And her smile as she looked proudly at her work. And how her smile brightened at Lord Emery's enthusiastic praise.

Now the lesson was over for the day, and Kay had no excuse to linger. Desperate to do something that wasn't murdering elusive stewards or sulking and avoiding the only person she yearned to see in this place, Kay had thought to try her own hand at drawing. What Lord Emery had said about the principles made sense at the time. Kay was struck by an absurd fantasy that she might discover she possessed some natural talent of her own, and it would impress Eliza.

As it turned out, Kay did not.

"Let's go into the city," Eliza said, breezing directly into Kay's room.

Kay knocked the inkwell, spilling it as she hastily hid the humiliating attempt. Kay swore, dabbing at the desk with a rag.

Sir Grimhook cleared his throat pointedly from the doorway.

"Is everything all right?" Eliza asked, coming closer, and Kay abandoned the mess, stepping to meet her.

"Fine. Everything's fine."

Eliza's lips curled. Last night had been a bad one for her, and Kay loved to see the nightmare's shadows chased away by Eliza's smile. "So I see. Let's go into the city," she repeated.

"Why?"

"Because I'm tired of reading. And of my room."

"Is that safe?"

"It is *not* safe," Sir Grimhook cut in firmly.

Eliza crossed her arms. "I used to visit the city when I was younger."

"Those were different times. If you need something, we will send someone to fetch it for you."

Kay was impressed by Sir Grimhook's ability to withstand the look Eliza gave him without cowering. "I won't be unguarded. I will have you with me, and also Sir Kaylen." Eliza turned a very different look on Kay. "Please?"

Kay was so weak for her. "Where in the city?"

"Anywhere. Let's just get out of here for a while." Eliza captured Kay's hand, the sad, desperate gleam in her eyes stealing Kay's resistance. "Won't you come?"

"Of course."

Eliza grinned and pressed a quick kiss to the corner of Kay's mouth. "I'll go put on Della's boots. Meet you by the stables."

AS SOON AS THEY PASSED through the palace gates, Eliza breathed easier. The tightness loosened and her shoulders relaxed. The palace was enormous compared to her tower, but she'd woken that morning from another dream of the darkness chasing her down the stairs, catching her and returning her to the top over and over. She needed to remind her body that she wasn't trapped.

Lord Emery's lessons in the mornings helped. The young man turned out to be quite intelligent, and barely belittling at all. The histories and alliances of the kingdoms were interesting to learn more about. Eliza had to admit she enjoyed the time in her room with musty books and maps. Especially because Kaylen was there. Kaylen didn't participate, but she listened and watched carefully, and that made Eliza happy.

Tipping her head back, Eliza relished the sun on her skin.

This trip into the city was also an excuse to be with Kaylen, who rode beside her. Eliza wished they shared a horse, although this way, Eliza could admire Kaylen in her armor. She looked utterly scrumptious, as always.

Sir Grimhook was there too, of course, as well as two more knights Sir Grimhook had summoned. Eliza begrudgingly accepted their presence, though she would have rather only had Kaylen with her.

The nearest houses pressed against the steep slope dropping away from the palace walls, with walls and gardens of their own—residences for the powerful who were eager to prove it. The few people on the road paused and turned to stare at them, dropping quickly into deep bows as murmurs of "Your Highness" followed them.

The city grew all around the palace, and Eliza wanted to be in it, not on the thoroughfare. She turned her horse onto a lane that wove into a clean, affluent square. Their hooves echoed off the cobbles as Eliza pressed on, the streets narrowing and growing more practical. Kaylen stayed at her side, their legs occasionally brushing.

"Is there something you are looking for?" Kaylen asked quietly.

"This." Eliza hauled her horse to a stop in front of a cheery bakery, the eaves drooping but the window boxes stuffed with flowers.

Kaylen reached to help Eliza dismount as Sir Grimhook did the same on her other side. Ignoring the man, Eliza took Kaylen's hand and then looped their arms together.

As they piled through the door, creaking armor drowned out the tinkling bell. The elderly woman behind the counter and three customers all stared.

"Your Highness!" the owner gasped, but her attention riveted on the woman beside Eliza. "And Sir Kaylen?"

The other customers pressed against the walls in the small space, whispering excitedly and making no move to leave, staring raptly between Eliza and Kaylen. It was somewhat jarring to be recognized again.

Perhaps this had not been Eliza's best idea.

She quickly scanned the selection of baked goods. "Which would you like?" she asked Kaylen.

"They all look wonderful," Kaylen answered politely, but her mouth was tight. "I ate before we left."

"Then how about something for dessert?"

"Whatever you would like."

Eliza had hoped this outing would bring them closer again and remind them of their journey here, but it seemed to be setting Kaylen more on edge. Eliza hastily ordered a few random things that looked sugary.

"That'll be three pence," the owner said breathlessly, her eyes returning to Kaylen. Everyone else also looked expectantly at a rigid, silent Kaylen.

Eliza should have tracked down some pocket money before setting out, but she'd been too eager to leave. She opened her mouth to say she would send payment later when Sir Grimhook appeared and placed the requested coins on the counter.

"Thank you, sir. The crown shall reimburse you," Eliza said.

"No need for such a small amount. It's an honor, and the least I can do, Your Highness," Sir Grimhook said, throwing a knowing smirk at Kaylen as he turned away.

Discomfort and annoyance tugged Eliza back out the door. This wasn't how today was meant to go. She didn't want the pastries anymore, wrapping them in her handkerchief and tucking them in the pocket between the folds of her skirt.

She'd proven to herself she could leave the palace. Now she was eager to get back.

The street was shockingly busy, a small crowd gathered around the knight who'd remained outside with the horses.

"Your Highness!"

"Sir Kaylen!"

Kaylen's arm slipped protectively around Eliza as she led them to the nearest horse.

This whole trip had been a terrible plan.

KAY RODE AS CLOSE AS she could beside Eliza. People pressed around them, not an angry mob, but a curious one. And they weren't only focused on Eliza. Many were also staring at Kay. Their attention made her tense shoulders tighten more.

Sir Grimhook maneuvered his horse in front of them to clear a path. He glowered at the milling crowd. "Move! Make way!"

They turned back up the street they had arrived down. The palace loomed above them, not far away but too far following the maze of streets.

Sir Grimhook pushed ahead, and they did their best to stay close.

Against the shifting throng, a slim figure darted through the corner of Kay's eye. Moving too fast.

Kay was already halfway out of her saddle when the stranger leapt in front of Eliza's horse, seizing the reins and ripping them from her hands. The animal jerked and reared.

Eliza clung to its mane for a suspended, heart-stopping moment, and Kay launched herself sideways.

They crashed into the street. Kay rolled on top of Eliza, bracing for the impact of hooves. When none immediately crushed her, she pushed up to her protesting arms and knees, still covering Eliza as much as she could.

Eliza stared up in shock, one hand pressed into the center of Kay's chest and the other curled around the nape of her neck in a death grip.

"Are you hurt?" Kay asked as her own heart sprinted away.

Eliza shook her head.

The snorting horses and chaotic sounds around them rushed into Kay's ears.

"Get back! Give them space," ordered the two knights who flanked them, doing their best to keep the renewed crowd away.

"Can you stand?" Kay asked.

"I think so."

Kay helped Eliza up, smothering the sharp pain in her left side, which had caught their fall. She collected Eliza's crown from the cobbles, forcing her hands to steady as the moment of danger rushed through her. Kay smoothed Eliza's hair, replacing and securing the clasped pins that held the crown in place, the small task calming them both. Eliza smiled tremulously, still clinging to Kay, her fingers looped through the straps at either side of Kay's breastplate. They were standing far, far too close together.

Sir Grimhook shoved his way over, gripping a dirt-covered young man in one hand and his sword in the other.

"This is the scoundrel. May I dispatch him, Your Highness?" Sir Grimhook asked, a hard, eager look in his eyes that Kay didn't like. Kay too was furious at the stranger for putting Eliza in danger, but she also recognized the desperation that came on the other side of hopelessness, and he wore it all over. She looked to Eliza for her decision, as the crowd around them hushed, waiting too.

"Why did you do that?" Eliza asked the young man directly.

He kept his gaze on the ground and shrank more. "For the horse, Your Highness."

"You could have killed the crown princess," Sir Grimhook growled, his grip twisting.

Eliza met Kay's eyes for a moment. "But I am fine," Eliza stated, pulling her shoulders back and raising her chin. "Let him go."

Sir Grimhook scowled. "Your Highness, may I suggest we at least hold him and let your father—"

"You may not suggest it. I said to let him go." Eliza's tone rang with authority as she stared steadily at Sir Grimhook. She was staggering, and Kay's knees begged to fall for her.

Sir Grimhook roughly released his captive, who stood motionless as if not trusting he was free, before dashing sideways and disappearing into an alley.

Eliza looked around at the shocked, murmuring crowd, and smiled. "All is well. Please continue your day."

The intensity of the murmurs increased as Kay helped Eliza mount and swung up behind her, not about to let her out of reach again. Kay never wanted to let her go.

Which was why Kay silently vowed to do better about keeping her distance, once they were safely back inside the palace. No more decadent mornings of lessons that weren't for Kay. Kay held Eliza now as her knight, but she longed to hold her forever as something far more. That was impossible, and Kay would not let herself dream of it.

But until then, Kay wrapped her arms tighter.

CHAPTER 33
Alliances

Eliza lurked in the midmorning gloom outside the king's study. She was officially done being ignored. If the world had forgotten about her, she would remind it.

Even after her disastrous expedition into the city, her father had not summoned or spoken to her. Kaylen was absent from Eliza's lesson yesterday morning too. When it became clear Kaylen would not be returning today either, Eliza feigned a headache and sent Lord Emery away.

Now she watched Maxwell, the annoying steward who was delaying Kaylen's reward, approach along the hall. Eliza intercepted him before he reached the door.

"Your appointment has been postponed," she told him. Her princess was out and ready to battle.

"Your Highness, forgive me but—"

Eliza raised her chin and stared him down.

He stepped back. "Of course, Your Highness."

Eliza turned to Sir Grimhook. "Don't let us be interrupted." Then Eliza pushed through the door and closed it behind her.

The king was not expecting her any more now than he had when Eliza appeared in his hall. He stared at her with something that could only have been called dismay. It stung, and her princess immediately wanted to hide behind her own skirts.

"I wish to speak with you," Eliza said, regathering her resolve.

"I have an appointment."

"You have an appointment with me right now."

She walked forward into the room and the king swallowed. He was seated in his ornately carved chair behind his expansive desk, and still leaned back. To get away from her?

"I'm not contagious," Eliza said sourly. "I'm your daughter. Remember?"

"I remember."

"Do you?" Eliza slunk over to an arched window, not seeing the land that stretched and folded beyond. Her heart hammered uncomfortably as she looked back at him. "The witch, Layla, is gone. She succumbed to the sickness. Did you know that?"

The king did not answer, so Eliza plunged on.

"She told me something quite interesting before she did."

Her father shifted. "I don't wish to discuss this with you."

"She told me that she was hired to kidnap me. Why would she have been hired, Father?"

He gripped the arms of his chair and looked...frightened. "It isn't like what you think."

"Then tell me what it is like. Did you hire her?"

"I was trying to protect you," he whispered.

"From what?"

"Didn't your precious witch tell you that too?"

Eliza hesitated. "Was it because of Mother?"

He watched her with haunted, wary eyes. "Do you have it too, then?"

Eliza frowned. They seemed to be having two separate conversations. "Do I have what?"

He flinched.

"Stop hiding things," Eliza demanded. "*Please*. Just say it clearly."

"The sickness."

Eliza stared at him. And he stared back.

"You think I'm a witch?" Eliza asked, incredulous. She laughed, but it caught in her throat.

He didn't deny it.

The stone casement of the window at her back was cool against her fingers as she gripped it, and the implication of what he was telling her, through his words and silence, sank in.

It made no sense. Yet as she thought about it, perhaps it did, in an awful way.

"Mother wasn't killed by a malignant, was she?"

The king shook his head slowly.

She had *been* the malignant.

"No," Eliza managed. "No, of course I'm not a witch." Eliza had never had any special ability at all.

The king did not appear reassured.

"When did you learn? About her?" Eliza asked. There were so many thoughts competing in her head, she couldn't seem to grasp any of them. They swirled around her, but she stood in the calm eye of their storm. For now.

"Shortly after you were born. I was a fool in love and thought she was strong enough, that she wouldn't succumb. We both did."

"Did anyone else know?"

"Of course not," the king snapped. "It would have ruined everything. Especially how it all...ended. As it's often hereditary, I worried you might become like her. You didn't show signs as you grew, but after what happened to her, I couldn't take that chance."

"So you had me locked away." Eliza's chest tightened. "Were you ever planning to tell me? To check if I was?"

"I would not have been able to get to you." The king's face was hard, and Eliza still felt miles away from him, even though she was only steps.

A shield worked both ways. It hadn't been for her protection at all. It had been for everyone else's.

Eliza wished her voice didn't shake. But for once, the king was talking to her, so Eliza asked the questions, even if she wasn't certain she could handle the answers. "If you locked me away, why did you pretend to want to rescue me?"

"Publicly, you were abducted. I couldn't not offer some reward. It's too little to be tempting for most, but it's an honorable way to die for those desperate enough."

Bile burned Eliza's throat at the careless dismissal of Kaylen's life. Eliza also remembered the bits of armor that had once been people. "Why not just kill me and be done with it?"

The king faltered, his eyes shifting away as his hard facade cracked. When he answered, he sounded almost wounded. "Do you truly believe me the sort of man to have my own daughter killed?"

"After eighteen years alone in that tower, I don't think I have any idea what sort of man you were, or are, Father."

The words hung in the silent rift between them, created by time and his decisions. Her heart broke slightly as she realized she may never be able to cross that rift. And if she did, the father she remembered would not be waiting. If he ever existed at all.

"Why did you hire a witch?" Eliza asked, her voice sounding flat.

"I hoped, if you were one also, that another witch might be able to help you. I didn't know what I was doing." His shoulders hunched again, and he looked suddenly even frailer. "After what happened to your mother...I didn't want to lose you too."

"Lose me," Eliza echoed hollowly.

Eliza had never been lost. She was placed very intentionally.

The calm surrounding her broke. Eliza's head spun as she threw herself out the door, startling Sir Grimhook, who clanked after her. The sound grated on Eliza's nerves. It was far too loud. Everything out here was too loud. She needed air. She needed safety. She needed Kaylen.

But Kaylen wasn't in her room. Eliza's panic was clamping its hands around her throat and shoulders, dragging her down.

"Find her," Eliza choked out to Sir Grimhook.

Whatever the knight saw in her face made him pale and he nodded, turning and hurrying away as Eliza climbed into Kaylen's bed, searching for the scent of her. For something familiar in this newly unfamiliar place.

Eliza didn't know how long it was before Kaylen found her there. It might have been moments or days.

"Breathe with me," Kaylen said, appearing in front of her and speaking those same words she had that first day they met. Eliza reached for her shoulders again, this time only covered by cloth.

Falling into Kaylen's beautiful eyes, Eliza was lost. She never wanted to find her way out.

KAY WATCHED ANXIOUSLY as Eliza's heaving chest slowly evened.

"Hi," Kay whispered, brushing Eliza's cheek.

Eliza looped her arms around Kay's neck, clinging like she'd never let go. "All I do is fall apart, for you to put me back together again," Eliza mumbled.

"You put yourself back together. I just get to watch."

Eliza stilled, and then she was kissing Kay.

Caught off-guard, Kay indulged for a few precious moments. "Hold that thought."

Kay extracted herself from Eliza and crossed the room to the open door she hadn't bothered with when she'd seen Eliza struggling to breathe. Sir Grimhook stood in its frame. Kay met his disapproving, warning eyes.

"I'm not supposed to leave her unattended," Sir Grimhook stated.

"You aren't."

Kay shut the door in his face and bolted it before she returned to Eliza, who had pushed up and was sitting on the edge of the bed, her shoulders hunched and head down. Kay knelt in front of her.

"I spoke with my father."

Kay nodded. She hadn't believed the headache excuse earlier.

Eliza kept her eyes on her fingers, which twisted together, her voice barely a whisper. "My mother was a witch."

Kay must have misheard. "What?"

Eliza repeated her statement, but it was still wrong, because it sounded the same. Kay's hands fell limp to her sides as cold dread sank into her gut. Magic was hereditary.

"He asked if I was one too," Eliza mumbled.

"And?"

"And what?"

"Are you?" Kay demanded, reeling back onto her heels, her own panic rearing at the thought that she had brought Eliza to her home. To Ma and Stella. If she had been dangerous this whole time...

Eliza looked up, gripping Kay's arms before she could scramble away. "Of course I'm not. How could you think I am, after what we've been through? I would have done something. Been able to help. Been able to do anything!"

A tense moment passed, Kay leaning away and Eliza leaning in.

And all Kay saw was El. A frightened, confused El. And in that moment, that was the only truth that mattered.

Kay met Eliza halfway, catching her as Eliza crumpled. They curled up together on the floor. Eliza's knee pressed into Kay's elbow and the weight of Eliza's ribs pinched her other, but neither of them let go.

"He never wanted me to be free," Eliza whispered into Kay's shoulder.

Fear pricked at Kay. "Are you safe here?"

"If he truly thought I was an immediate danger, I think I'd already be gone."

But what else would he do? If he'd locked her away before, he could do it again.

"And you are certain you have no magic?" Kay had to know.

"I don't have a witch's unnatural strength. Metal doesn't affect me. I've never heard any voices—fine, I have, but I was lonely, not magical. If I were a witch, I would have been home a lot sooner."

Kay shut her eyes and held Eliza closer. "It'll be all right," Kay promised, but she didn't know that it would be.

"Can I stay in here today?" Eliza whispered. "I'm afraid to go back to my room. To be alone."

"We'll stay right here."

ELIZA SAT ON THE BENCH by the lower pond, on the side her mother always had, trying to remember her.

Eliza couldn't quite picture her face anymore. She'd found a portrait hanging in a hall, but it hadn't stirred recognition in Eliza, despite spending half a day staring at it, surely aggravating a stiff Sir Grimhook.

The knight watched her now. And so did Kaylen. Kaylen sat on the other side of the pond, a book in her hand, but Eliza didn't think she was reading it.

Kaylen had rarely left Eliza physically alone in the two days since Eliza's conversation with her father. And yet Kaylen had retreated even more all the same. She was putting distance between them, and Eliza hated it. But she wasn't certain how to stop it. The only time Kaylen let Eliza close was at night, when Eliza would slip into Kaylen's bed to fall into a fitful sleep. She suspected Kaylen was attempting to wean Eliza off her, and Eliza wasn't taking to it well.

Being inside the palace grew more suffocating each passing day. So here in the garden Eliza sat, free and yet still trapped.

"Your Highness?"

Eliza tore her eyes away from Kaylen.

A stranger stood beside her. His rich velvet kirtle was trimmed with fur despite the pleasantly warm day. He bowed deeply. "May I have the honor of introducing myself again. I am Lord Trimble, and on your father's council."

Eliza nodded absently. "Step thirty-seven."

"Pardon?"

"Nothing." Eliza cleared her throat. She recalled the name, but not the man. "We've met before?"

"Many years ago, Your Highness. I would not expect you to remember."

"Did my father send you to distract me?"

The king was also back to avoiding Eliza again. She'd worked up the courage to attempt cornering him several more times, but he hadn't let her.

Lord Trimble's mouth curved. "No, this visit is entirely of my own initiative. I have been eager to speak with you since your return. About the future."

He sat on the bench, at a respectable distance, but Eliza leaned away. Kaylen wasn't even pretending to read her book anymore, and Eliza relaxed. Kaylen would keep her safe.

"What about the future?" Eliza asked.

"May I speak freely, Your Highness?"

"Most definitely do."

"It may sound harsh, but the truth is that your father will not live forever. And the matter of inheritance, so recently assuaged by Princess Annabelle's birth, is now uncertain again. Not all your father's advisors agree, but please know you have my full support for the crown."

"Why?"

Lord Trimble seemed to consider his answer for a moment. "Practically speaking, you are a much better choice. With your father's age, it is doubtful that Princess Annabelle will be grown in time. And regency is complicated and easily challenged."

Eliza wasn't certain how she felt about being usurped in line to the throne. She thought it probably should have bothered her more. Eliza had never questioned whether she wanted to be queen. It was simply something she knew would happen. But she was learning more each day that she really hadn't known anything.

"Thank you for your honesty," Eliza managed.

"If you need advice on any matters at all, I am more than happy to offer it."

Until recently, Eliza would have likely trusted his open, upfront demeanor. But she was also learning that she couldn't simply trust.

Lord Trimble followed Eliza's gaze. "Your lady knight is certainly popular as well. Very much a woman of the people."

Eliza had heard some of the more outlandish rumors, and enjoyed every single one. Kaylen didn't, however.

"She is certainly an unusual choice," Lord Trimble continued. "But perhaps her rustic charm will serve you well when you take the crown. Even if your father would not approve."

Eliza frowned. "Has my father said so?" What had the king said of Kaylen? Of them?

"It's not my place, Your Highness," Lord Trimble deflected, and Eliza's annoyance flared.

"You brought it up."

"I wonder what your thoughts are on the new trade agreement with Uvaria."

Kaylen had spoken about those agreements in the tavern with the merchant Dillon. She'd said they were choking the markets. "I need to learn more about the situation. But I do believe we should not forget about the people impacted by such deals."

"Very wise, Your Highness," Lord Trimble said a little too quickly. "I would be happy to discuss the particular benefits of the agreements with you in depth, and answer any questions you have."

Eliza stood. "Perhaps another day."

She would rather get Kaylen's opinions first. She imagined Kaylen knew far more about those impacted than this lord.

She headed in Kaylen's direction. The woman met her eyes briefly and then buried her nose in her book. Eliza's heart sank. She thought about stopping or turning back, but she'd already made her destination clear, so she sat on the stone wall that ran around the pond, right beside Kaylen.

"What are you reading?" Eliza asked.

Kaylen flipped back to the title page. "A study of bird migration patterns in Hevalon. Apparently."

"Fascinating."

"Quite. You can borrow it when I am done. Or ask Lord Emery to add it to the curriculum."

"Hmm. I'll think about it."

Kaylen's mouth twitched.

"You may laugh, but I would have eaten that up in my tower. I've always liked birds."

"I've noticed."

Kaylen's dry reply shouldn't have tickled Eliza so much, and she covered her mouth.

"Don't do that," Kaylen said, meeting her eyes.

"What?"

"Don't stifle your laugh. It's beautiful."

Eliza had to catch her breath. "Sir Kaylen, are you trying to make me blush?"

"If you have to ask, I must not be doing a very good job."

Eliza smiled at the echo of her words when she had attempted poorly to seduce Kaylen at that first inn.

Eliza also remembered what Kaylen had done afterward. When she had kissed Eliza's apple-filled mouth in the darkness.

Heat swept Eliza. Though Eliza burned to press the matter of intimacy, she simply needed Kaylen more. Being with her was enough, for as long as she could have her. And Kaylen was already pulling away.

The memory of Kaylen's distress doused Eliza's arousal. She was ashamed of missing what Kaylen didn't want to give. But Eliza did miss it.

Eliza drank in the sight of Kaylen, with her curly hair frizzing and tumbling down in her uneven braid, thinning where Eliza had cut a way a few places.

She realized she'd been staring too long when her eyes started to burn. Because she'd forgot to blink.

"Why aren't you wearing your new clothes?" Eliza asked, running her fingers lightly over the cuff of Kaylen's simple, patched kirtle. She knew the pieces she'd asked Marianne the dressmaker to create for Kaylen had been delivered into Kaylen's empty wardrobe.

"Thank you for the thought. But I can't afford them." Kaylen snapped the book shut, knocking Eliza's touch off her with the movement.

"You don't have to afford them. They were a gift."

"I don't need a gift. I need my reward."

Eliza swallowed past the sting. "Maxwell is still holding it?"

Kaylen sighed, running a hand over her face. "And he left yesterday for an urgent meeting. No one will tell me when he'll be back."

Eliza tentatively reached for Kaylen's sleeve again, rubbing her thumb soothingly over the skin at Kaylen's wrist. Kaylen unclenched her fist and flipped her hand, lacing their fingers together and making Eliza's belly swoop.

"Sorry," Kaylen muttered. "I've been here over a week and still don't have a single ludan to my name."

Eliza squeezed Kaylen's hand. "You will. I promise. Until then, let me spoil you a little. I know you'll look stunning in the green one. I picked it specifically. Will you wear it tomorrow? For me?"

Kaylen's cheeks pinkened and she nodded.

Eliza delighted in the color and reached up before she could think better of it, brushing over Kaylen's warm cheek. "Now who's blushing?"

Kaylen's eyes lingered on Eliza's mouth, but then she sat back, and Eliza's hand fell once more. Alongside her heart.

CHAPTER 34
A Gift

Eliza paced excitedly back and forth, not listening to Lord Emery's lecture as she returned to the window yet again. She'd been at the palace now for ten miserable days and had been waiting for this one since the second.

The king had not been around to object when Eliza ordered the fastest carriage to be sent. If he did object, he could speak to Eliza about it. She would welcome his anger at this point, or any acknowledgment that she existed at all.

But this wasn't about him. Or about Eliza.

This was for Kaylen, whom she missed desperately, despite seeing her each night. Today would help ease the mounting tension in Kaylen's shoulders. Since Kaylen could not go home quite yet, Eliza was bringing Kaylen's home here.

When the first of the four horses appeared through the gates, Eliza whirled.

"Thank you, that'll be all for today," Eliza interrupted Lord Emery, flying out the door and down the hall. She almost stopped by Kaylen's room to bring her along, but she had the surprise all set.

Eliza burst outside as the carriage opened.

Stella appeared first, peering up at the palace with her eyes filling her small face. Ruth firmly took Stella's hand and they both climbed down with the help of a footman.

Eliza barely modulated her steps from a run as she hurried down to greet them.

Ruth clutched Stella close, her eyes widening more on Eliza. She stooped into a bow. "Your Highness," Ruth said. "I had no idea..."

"Please, there's no need for that." Eliza's arms twitched. "May I have a hug instead?"

Ruth stared at her. "Of course, dear. I mean, Your Highness."

Ruth's hug was better than Eliza remembered. Kaylen had obviously learned to give amazing hugs from her mother.

Stella gaped up at Eliza's crown. "It's true? You're a princess?"

"I'm sorry I didn't tell you both. But Kaylen thought it would be safer not to reveal who I was until we reached the palace. Come inside, please."

"Where is Kaylen?" Ruth asked as they entered the palace. Both guests clung to each other, looking around in awe and perhaps a bit of fright.

"You'll see her soon, I promise."

Eliza showed them into the room adjoining Kaylen's, which was decorated with patterns of blues and soft florals. It was pretty, and she thought Stella would like it, along with the other surprises Eliza had arranged.

"I'll go get her," Eliza told them excitedly.

HER LOVELY CHAMPION

KAY RAN THE SHARPENING stone along the blade of her repaired sword. In this quiet corner of the gardens, beneath a large old tree, Kay tucked herself between the roots. Like she used to with the old oak by the brook. Like Stella now did.

Kay's grip faltered and she nearly sliced her hand.

She'd been getting worse at keeping her thoughts away from home. Instead of fortifying as she expected, the walls and compartments in her mind were rotting away. Each day that passed here was harder.

Maxwell had returned yesterday and was still avoiding her, annoyed by her persistence. A victory required different recordings and allocation, he'd said. These things took time, he'd said. He would let her know, he'd said. Kay ground her teeth together as she ran the sharpening stone faster.

The ball was only two days away. Kay had no direction, other than to keep herself away from Eliza, who was the only good thing about this place.

Everything had gone wrong this past month. She wasn't even supposed to be alive. She didn't regret that she was, but her attempts to feel grateful for it rang hollow.

"Sir Kaylen?"

Amber stood nervously in front of her, clutching a parchment in her hand. Kay quickly climbed to her feet.

"You asked me to tell you if I heard any new rumors about you," Amber said, fidgeting with the parchment, and Kay's stomach dropped to her boots. "Well, it's not exactly a rumor, but I thought you should see this."

Several pinholes marred the top of the thick flyer, which was stained by the weather. But the illustration was sickeningly clear. A voluptuous woman wearing armor and a crown stood on the arms of a throne, where a second crowned woman reclined provocatively. *Long live the queens* was scrawled beneath the image.

Kay's stomach plummeted farther, into the ground beneath her.

"Where did this come from?" Kay asked, glancing around, suddenly certain eyes were everywhere staring at it. At her. She barely resisted the urge to slice it to pieces, the corner crumpling in her fist.

"My sister brought it to me. And I'm afraid it wasn't the only one. There have been a few more around the city."

Kay muttered a curse as she rolled up the flyer and shoved it deep in her pocket. "Thank you, Amber. I mean it."

Amber nodded. "I don't think it was meant as an insult, sir."

"It's an insult to the crown. Why would people post this?"

"To show support for you. For Princess Eliza."

"It'll only make things worse."

It was bad enough they called her a hero when she wasn't. How could they flaunt her as a queen? Eliza, yes. But not Kay. The thought of it made her ill.

"There you are!" Eliza's voice cut pleasantly through Kay's troubled mind. Eliza ran toward her down the path, dressed in a sunny yellow today, which complemented her warm skin and rich brown hair beautifully.

"I have something to show you," Eliza said, bouncing on her toes and vibrating with excitement.

"I do too," Kay said darkly, her pocket weighing her down.

"Can it wait? Mine can't!"

Sir Grimhook stood behind Eliza, and he met Kay's gaze with an icy one. The man no longer made any attempt to mask his dislike of Kay.

Kay nodded to him as Eliza dragged her back up the path to the palace.

"Where are we going?" Kay asked.

"You'll see."

Eliza didn't slow until they were in the hallway to their rooms.

"Close your eyes," Eliza demanded.

Kay raised an eyebrow. "Why?"

"Because it's a surprise."

Kay obediently closed her eyes as Eliza guided her forward again. It was disorienting, but she trusted Eliza.

A door opened and someone whispered.

A voice rang clearly. One Kay hadn't heard nearly enough, but she would recognize anywhere. "Ma!"

Kay's eyes flew open, her body already moving toward the sound. Stella rushed to her and Kay gathered her close, the tension and aggravation of the past weeks shattering through her skin like glass and leaving only disbelief. What was Stella doing here?

Kay looked past her frizz of hair to see Ma smiling, tears in her eyes.

"How?" Kay breathed. It was the only word that formed.

Ma looked stunning in a dark blue gown, and Stella wore a pretty new dress of yellow silk to match Eliza's.

Eliza. She watched them from the door, beaming. Glowing.

Eliza had done this.

And fuck it, Kay was in love. Undoubtedly and undeniably in love.

Stella slipped away from her, and Kay struggled to let her go.

"Look at me!" Stella said, twirling around. "I look like a princess! Are you gonna be a princess now too?"

The image from the flyer burned in her mind, and Kay glanced at Eliza again, whose smile faltered. That tore through Kay's freshly open heart. "I don't think so, starling. But you look beautiful."

The gown was a bit too big on Stella's small frame, and the sight of her in it made Kay's throat close. For a terrible, gut-wrenching moment, Kay wanted to tear it off her, and she didn't fully understand why.

Kay pushed back up from where she'd collapsed on her knees as Ma reached for her, hugging her tight. When she pulled back, though, Ma's smile was all wrong.

"What's happened?" Kay murmured, fear threading ice through her veins.

Not again. Not something else.

She looked at Stella, needing to reassure herself that she was here and healthy. Stella was, in fact, grinning and twirling, her attention on the expensive silk draping her small person, finer than any she had ever seen.

"Later," Ma said as she brushed Kay's face with her roughened, cracked hands.

"Is something wrong with the farm?"

"No. In fact, it's probably better than it has been in years." Ma glanced at Eliza. "You did send those people, didn't you, Your Highness?"

"I did. A few to tend and watch it while you are here so you don't have to worry about it. And call me El. Please."

Kay's heart shuddered as Eliza's eyes met hers. Kay feared Eliza could see everything in them.

"I wasn't certain if it was real, when the carriage rolled up," Ma said. "I admit, I almost didn't come, but it was far too grand to be anything other than a true royal carriage." She glanced over Kay, a hint of accusation entering her tone. "And I hear my daughter is a knight of Alludan now?"

"It was all rather sudden," Kay said, her eyes straying back to Stella, who had stopped her twirling and was staring in awe up at the intricately inlaid ceiling.

"Well, I'll leave you for a bit to settle in," Eliza said quietly, touching Ma's arm and slipping from the room before Kay could speak to her.

CHAPTER 35
Hero

Kay sat with Ma on the soft blue sofa as the sky turned to dusk. Stella, exhausted from the nonstop travel, slept soundly already, curled up with only a fluff of hair spilling above the blanket in the massive bed swallowing her.

Kay still couldn't quite believe they were here. And that Ma had actually left the farm.

"Will you tell me what's wrong now?" Kay asked quietly, so she wouldn't wake Stella as she reached for Ma's hand.

"How could you, Kay?" Ma whispered, and the well of sadness and reproach there threatened to shatter Kay again. "You took the king's quest."

Kay's heart tried to race out of her chest. "And I succeeded."

"Did you honestly expect to?"

Kay couldn't lie to her. "No."

Ma's grip tightened and she closed her eyes, but the tears slipped down her aging face.

"I'm sorry," Kay whispered. "But the reward was so much." Not that Kay had seen that reward yet.

"Fuck the reward," Ma said, and Kay was shocked anew that day by the forcefulness in Ma's voice. "I'd rather have my daughter, Kaylen. Do you know how hard it was to learn from everyone else that Sir Kaylen had done the impossible and rescued Princess Eliza? That you'd gone off to die without saying goodbye? And you didn't even tell me. I called the crown princess of our kingdom *El* and asked her to chop carrots in our kitchen!"

Each word sliced through Kay. "I did try to say goodbye. I wrote you a letter. Sir Hugo—"

"The kind man who visited us? Yes, he said he was your friend. And you didn't tell me you borrowed a horse from Lady Velma either. He paid for that too."

Of course he had. "He's a good friend."

"Then tell me, Kay." Ma's voice shook. "If you have such good friends as that. Why would you throw your life away?"

"I wasn't throwing it away," Kay protested. "It was simply the price of what I needed to do."

"Well, it was too high. I know your life has been hard. So has mine. But it isn't over. Promise me—*promise me*—you will never do something like this again."

"I promise."

Ma hugged her, and Kay held her back, regret for Ma's tears sitting heavy inside her.

"Good. Now that that's settled." Ma sat back and pinned Kay with a newly intent look. "About Princess Eliza. Are you two truly together?"

Kay wasn't certain what to say. "No. Sort of. It's complicated."

"Does the king object?"

"I don't honestly know if he does. But I cannot imagine he'd approve."

Ma smiled and cupped Kay's cheek. "I cannot imagine he would disapprove, my dear. Not when you are a hero and the whole kingdom knows your name."

Kay's gut twisted. "They do?"

"Of course they do. I heard it no less than a dozen times on the way here, and we barely stopped at all. How you slew not only the hydra but the witch too."

"I did neither of those things," Kay hissed. "I didn't even rescue her."

"Then what happened?"

"The witch and hydra were both gone by the time I arrived at the tower. I never saw either of them. At least, not there."

Ma watched her for several moments. "You still brought the princess here."

"Well, yes."

"And where would she be now if you had not arrived?"

Kay hesitated.

"Just because there wasn't a lock doesn't mean she was free. So perhaps let yourself acknowledge that you are a hero, even if you didn't have to bloody your sword for it."

Kay sighed. "You sound like Eliza."

Ma smiled. "I like her. I didn't dream I'd ever say that about a princess, let alone meet one. Not that you need it, but I approve. Even if I don't quite know what that would mean."

"It doesn't matter," Kay whispered. "It's impossible. She belongs here. And when this ball is over, I'm coming home."

Ma's eyes filled again, but not with sadness. "Do you promise?"

"I promise."

ELIZA WAITED LONGER than usual to go to Kaylen. She wasn't certain if Kaylen would be in her room tonight. And Eliza was determined that, if not, she would stay away. She'd manage somehow.

She paused and listened briefly at Ruth and Stella's door, but heard nothing, so she continued to Kaylen's.

Eliza knocked softly.

Since leaving the family earlier, anxiety had gnawed at Eliza's insides. Eliza had thought Kaylen was happy, but it had been hard to tell. What if Eliza had made a mistake? What if Kaylen was angry with her for bringing them here without telling her? Eliza should have asked.

The door cracked open after too long.

"May I come in?" Eliza whispered.

Kaylen stepped aside.

"You're alone?" Eliza clarified, glancing around the space.

Her back closed the door with a snap as Kaylen pressed her into it. Eliza instantly flushed with desire. Kaylen was only wearing her undershirt, which did little to stop the heat of her skin from reaching Eliza's.

"El, I—" Kaylen swallowed, and then she shivered, a tiny tremor running through her body, which Eliza felt in her own. "I want you," Kaylen said, the words rough but caressing Eliza's chin and sinking into her belly.

Eliza didn't have to think about it. "Yes."

Kaylen invaded her mouth. Eliza hadn't had Kaylen's lips against her own in far too long. Emboldened by Kaylen's initiation, Eliza slipped her hands down Kaylen's neck and over her shoulders.

Kaylen broke the kiss. Why had Eliza been so careless and ruined it?

But Kaylen wasn't pulling away. Instead, she drew Eliza with her a few steps, spinning and bending Eliza over the low arm of the sofa.

Eliza had come here with the intention of talking. They could talk later.

Her heart tried to fly up her throat. Kaylen's hot breath tickled the back of Eliza's neck as she hitched up Eliza's nightgown, her hands sliding frantically beneath.

Eliza came apart far too quickly, fingernails digging into the plush velvet. She panted, starting to straighten, but Kaylen wasn't done. She pushed Eliza back down, kicking her feet wider.

Eliza grinned at the soft fabric, wanting everything Kaylen would give her.

She pressed herself up into Kaylen's front, where Kaylen was partially curled over her. Kaylen groaned. Teeth brushed the skin of Eliza's neck. Not quite a bite, but a whispered promise of one.

"Yes," Eliza panted. "Do it."

Kaylen bit her lightly. Eliza shuddered again at the slight pressure, her knees giving out from the pleasure.

The sofa and Kaylen's strong arms held her up. Supported her.

Hands gentled and flattened against Eliza's bare belly as she relaxed, delirious and boneless.

Eliza's hairline was damp at the base of her braid. She wasn't sure if it was her own perspiration or from Kaylen's mouth, but the soft hiccup Kaylen muffled evaporated Eliza's smile. She twisted around, her concerns of earlier returning with vengeance.

"What's wrong?" Eliza asked as she kissed the salty skin of Kaylen's cheek.

Kaylen straightened, pulling Eliza up with her. Clinging to her. Eliza clung back and stroked Kaylen's hair because that was all she could do.

"Are you angry with me?" Eliza finally asked.

"Angry?" Kaylen pulled back to look at her through the darkness. Eliza had rarely seen her outside of darkness lately. "Did that feel like anger?"

It had felt incredible. But Eliza still worried. "I didn't tell you. I thought it would be a nice surprise, but, well, it wouldn't be the first time I made a mistake or did something insensitive."

"The last thing you are is insensitive, darling."

Eliza's heart skipped and she smiled again, kissing Kaylen's lips lightly. "Then what are these for?" She brushed over Kaylen's cheek.

"For today."

Eliza waited a few more moments before resigning to the knowledge that this was all she would get from Kaylen tonight. Kaylen had closed herself off once more, and Eliza's chest constricted with sadness.

She drew Kaylen with her to bed. They climbed in together, knees interlocking and feet brushing.

"I miss you," Eliza whispered into the darkness.

Kaylen didn't answer right away, and Eliza's pulse spiked, her scalp growing too tight.

"Me too."

CHAPTER 36
The King's Offer

"Are we ready?" Eliza asked, showing off the gap in her teeth that Kay wanted to stare at for the rest of eternity.

They were going to the gardens this morning, and even the weather seemed to be in a good mood.

"Can we fish in the pond?" Stella asked Kay, so excited that Kay was torn between grinning with her, and weeping.

"I don't think it's good fishing," Kay said. "But we can try."

A knock on the door made everyone turn. A page boy stood there, not much taller than Stella but holding himself proudly, which only accentuated his stature.

"The king wishes to see you, sir," he said loftily, looking at Kay.

Kay glanced at Eliza. "And Princess Eliza?"

"No. Only you, sir."

Hurt mixed with anger flashed across Eliza's face. Stella's smile had also vanished as she looked down, slipping her hand from Kay's.

Kay couldn't refuse a summons from the king, but she nearly did at that moment. "Why don't you all go look for some fish, and I'll come find you when I'm done."

Kay met Eliza's eyes and gave her a small shrug.

Why did Kay feel like she was letting everyone down? "I'll see you soon," she promised, keeping her voice light as it hung heavy in her throat.

Kay hoped the shaking in her hands didn't show as she followed the page through the halls.

The king wanted to see her. Why?

Would he finally ask something of her? Demand answers to questions that should have been given long ago? Or was it about Eliza? About that damned flyer?

The king's study was bright this time of morning with the high, arched windows letting the sun flood in. The king himself paced methodically in front of one, hands clasped behind his back.

"Sir Kaylen, come in. You may leave us," the king told the page, who bowed formally. "First, my steward tells me you are very persistent. This belongs to you."

Maxwell stepped forward and handed Kay an incredibly heavy bag. He looked a bit irked by it too.

"Thank you, Your Majesty," Kay said, ignoring the surliness of the steward, holding the weight tightly, letting it soothe the fears of the past days here. "It is an honor."

The king nodded.

Silence fell.

"Is there anything else, Your Majesty?" Kay asked, uncertain why the king decided to be involved in the transaction suddenly.

"You may leave as well, Maxwell."

The steward scowled but obeyed. The king waited for the door to close, leaving them alone except for Sir Grimhook standing discreetly to the side, looking vaguely eager. It set Kay's nerves on edge again.

The king fixed Kay with a keen expression. "I hear you are close to my daughter. I also hear she has not spent a night in her own bed since arriving. Is that true?"

The floor dropped from beneath Kay's feet, and she scrambled to stay upright. Sir Grimhook's eyes bored hot pricks into her skin. What could she say? She could not lie. "Yes, Your Majesty. And it is entirely my fault, not hers."

The king's eyes crinkled in the first sign of amusement Kay had seen from him. "Oh, I doubt that." The amusement vanished. "You have quite the admiration of the kingdom as well."

Kay shifted uncomfortably.

"I have also heard a disturbing rumor of a marriage."

"It is untrue, Your Majesty," Kay breathed.

"I was not asking if it were true. I am telling you, it is not."

Kay had known the king would never approve someone like Kay for Eliza. But it still felt like she'd swallowed hot coals. And a tiny flicker of impossible hope, which Kay had denied existed, screamed through her as it died. "Of course, Your Majesty."

"I've been in contact with the crown princess of Uvaria. Her younger sister is unmarried, and Eliza will do well there. They had an attachment when they were girls, though Eliza may resist the marriage at first. That is where you come in."

The second-born Uvarian princess. The one Eliza had muddied her skirts and read erotic books with. Dark, unbidden jealousy stoked the coals.

"You want me to end things?" Kay asked, though it was more than expected.

"No, I want you to go with her."

"To Uvaria, Your Majesty?" Kay asked weakly.

"I understand you have a daughter of your own."

"I do." Kay was off balance from the sudden question, her eyes flying to the window, where somewhere beyond, Stella was enjoying the gardens with Ma and Eliza. Without her.

"If you agree to the arrangement, you'll find in these records the deed to a large estate not far from here." The king slid a stack of fine, crisp parchment across his desk. "A prominent position, close to glamours of the capital and court. I will personally arrange the finest tutors for your daughter...?"

"Stella."

"For Lady Stella. She will want for nothing. You may retain your title, though you will need to remain with the princess in Uvaria. And keep her there. Indefinitely."

Kay's world spun. It was more than she'd ever dared to dream of. "May I ask why?"

The king tilted his head, assessing her. "Eliza's return throws into question many things that were set in motion. It is already dividing my council. I've made certain promises that I cannot afford to break." The king fiddled with a gold paperweight on his desk, and Kay suspected that was only part of his reasoning. "Eliza will be happy in Uvaria, and I would prefer her to go willingly. And she trusts you."

"Is this a true offer, Your Majesty? Or an order?"

"Forcing you would not serve my purposes of convincing her. Eliza will go to Uvaria with or without you. But I believe you will find this a most agreeable arrangement for everyone."

Kay stared at the parchment. "When do you need my answer?"

"Eliza will learn of the engagement at the ball tomorrow."

One day. One day to decide the fate of not only herself but everyone she loved.

The king had decided he didn't want his eldest daughter around again, after all. And had chosen marriage instead of a witch's tower. Somewhere far away. Out of sight, out of mind.

Could Kay send Eliza off to that alone? But could Kay truly go and leave Stella again? Perhaps for many years. Perhaps forever.

"Thank you, Your Majesty. I will let you know."

ELIZA COULDN'T STOP her grin when she saw Kaylen approaching along the path. Kaylen had taken to leaving off her armor when around the palace, but had worn it today when Stella asked. Kaylen was breathtaking with her untamable hair wafting behind her and her sturdy strides, shoulders reflecting the sun.

Stella did what Eliza wanted to do, and ran up the path to meet her. Eliza hung back and watched Kaylen's face light up.

"Did you find any fish?" Kaylen asked.

"No!" Stella folded her bony arms. "But Princess El says there's another pond to check. We were waiting for you!"

"I'm here now."

Stella reached a bit hesitantly for Kaylen's hand, and Kaylen mirrored her.

"The pond is this way," Eliza choked through her suddenly full throat.

She met Ruth's eyes, which were shinier than usual. The older woman offered her a gentle, understanding smile and Eliza took her arm, walking with her behind Kaylen and Stella.

"What did the king want?" Stella asked.

Eliza watched Kaylen closely. Her posture tensed. "Just a few matters to clear up about me being a knight. And everything."

Kaylen had been right. She wasn't good at lying. But Stella accepted that answer.

"What happened to your old armor?"

"It was replaced with this. Do you like it?"

Stella shook her head. "I like the old armor better."

"Stella, you shouldn't say that," Ruth scolded gently, looking furtively at Eliza and around.

"Now that you are a knight of Alludan, will you be able to stay home?" Stella asked.

Kaylen's shoulders tensed more. "We'll see."

They reached the lower pond, where Stella clambered up onto the stone wall that ran around the edge. Kaylen kept tight hold of her hand as they circled it, staring into the water together. They looked so alike. And Eliza wanted to keep them both. Ruth, too. She would speak with Kaylen later about it. Their time was running out, and Eliza was tired of waiting. Tired of letting the world shunt her and dictate what happened to her.

"Thank you," Ruth whispered. She was watching Kaylen and Stella as well. "As hard as it is to be away from home, that is worth it." Ruth tilted her head toward the pair. "Don't ruin your gown," Ruth warned hastily, as Stella crouched, the yellow silk skirts a bit too long for her slipping over the rough stone, the hem catching in the pond.

"It's fine," Eliza assured them both. "I have another one for you to wear tomorrow to the ball."

Stella's eyes widened and she looked excitedly at Kaylen. "We're invited to the ball too?"

Kaylen hesitated.

"Of course you are," Eliza answered for her.

"Are we?" Kaylen asked quietly, meeting Eliza's gaze intently.

Eliza didn't look away. "Yes." She was inviting them, even if nothing had been formalized.

"What will it be like?" Stella asked.

"There will be music, and food, and lots of people in fancy clothes. And dancing of course."

Stella frowned. "I don't know how to dance like fancy people." She looked at Kaylen. "Will you teach me?"

CHAPTER 37
Undone

Kay's fingers clumsily unlaced her new green kirtle, pulling it off over her head.

Today had been incredible. They spent nearly all of it in the garden, leaving Kay's skin pink from the sun, and her toes a bit sore from Stella and Ma stepping on them as she, Eliza, and an obliging Lord Emery did their best to show them the basic steps of a few court dances. Kay smiled at the memory of it.

When they tired of that, Eliza had ordered a surly Sir Grimhook to find a fishing hook. Kay had needed to smother her laugh at the look on his face. Apparently, the conversation between Kay and the king hadn't gone as he hoped. And Kay had no doubt he was the one who told the king about Eliza's nightly wanderings.

They hadn't caught any fish, but that hadn't mattered.

But as wonderful as the day had been, it was now over. The ball loomed tomorrow.

Kay's head and heart were jumbled and confused. If she accepted the king's offer, she would never need to say goodbye to Eliza. But Kay had only ever been to Uvaria once, and that had been for blood, not life. It was so far away, which was the whole point.

What could they truly have together there? Kay would be the kept, other woman. Perhaps it was foolish to cling to her tattered pride, but being a princess's mistress rankled the scraps that remained.

Kay could accept and know that Stella and Ma would never lack for anything. Kay wouldn't have to worry if their roof leaked, or if they had enough wood to stay warm. It was the security for them she had always wanted.

The king was right. It made sense to accept.

And yet, the thought made Kay want to throw up. To leave Stella and Ma. To uproot them from home. To take Stella away from her brook.

To watch as Eliza married someone else—a marriage that might become something Eliza would want. And who would Kay be to begrudge her that?

Could Kay stand by as Eliza went to another woman's bed? Would this other princess tolerate Kay's presence? What would happen when Eliza tired of Kay? Would the king revoke what he gave if Kay failed?

Would Eliza ever forgive her for accepting? Would she ever forgive her for refusing?

You may reach for the stars, but the stars always fall back to the land that grew you up tall...

Kay was moving toward the door before she could think about it.

HER LOVELY CHAMPION

The hall was quiet and empty, except for the form of a knight at the end. It wasn't Sir Grimhook tonight, but his counterpart. The king already knew of Eliza's visits to Kay, so she didn't bother to hide her intent. She knocked on Eliza's door.

The soft glow of several candles highlighted Eliza's smile. "I was about to come see you—"

Kay silenced her with a kiss. Eliza opened her mouth at once, eagerly welcoming Kay. The thud of the closing door sent awareness running down her limbs. When she gently nipped Eliza's lip, Eliza released a sharp, delighted gasp.

Something frantic and wild exploded in Kay's chest. She needed Eliza everywhere. Her box was nowhere to be found, and Eliza was spilling all over Kay's insides, wrapping around her heart.

Kay stopped fighting. She had already lost. She loved Eliza one way or another. She would love her tomorrow as well. And she would love her when she had to say goodbye. Kay didn't know if it would hurt more at this point to lose Eliza with or without ever feeling her.

So Kay simply let her heart speak. "Touch me. Please."

Eliza stared at her with wide eyes. "You're sure?"

Kay nodded.

"Do you promise you're sure?"

Kay nodded again.

Eliza's fingers untangled their death grip on Kay's hair, the roots screaming in protest at being free while the skin on the side and back of her neck reveled. And slowly, carefully, as if afraid Kay would change her mind, Eliza brushed her hands over the muscles of Kay's shoulders. They trailed down her arms and slipped to her waist. Climbed up the column of her back and tripped along her spine.

Like a flamewalker through a forest, they left trails of heat behind.

Kay burned brighter as Eliza's fingers danced across her ribs and shaped the weight of her breasts.

Eliza slipped beneath the hem of Kay's undershirt, the cool night air adding contrast to the fire Eliza set. And it wasn't enough. Kay craved more.

Hauling Eliza against her, Kay scooped her up. Eliza's legs wrapped naturally around Kay's waist as she walked blindly. They fell onto the wide bed together, a tangle of sharp inhales and stray elbows, heated skin and shedding clothes. Kay reached between Eliza's thighs, but Eliza caught her wrist.

"Not yet." Eliza pushed Kay's shoulder, laying her back. "I'm not done with you."

The frantic wildness thrashed in pleasure as Eliza swung her leg over and straddled Kay's hips. Her fingertips began their glorious, torturous exploration anew, and then her lips. Eliza followed the scar across Kay's sternum. Then the crook of her elbow. Then the spider lines over her clenching stomach.

Eliza's heavy braided hair dragged, carving through Kay's oversensitive skin. Kay was peeling away everywhere Eliza touched, and soon, all that would be left of her would be a puddle of desire.

Perhaps this was how Kay would die, in the end.

"What do you want?" Eliza asked, her fingers trailing around Kay's knee in a way that was far more arousing than it had any right to be.

"Everything."

Eliza's laughter tickled Kay's belly. "You've never been good at answering my questions."

"Sorry. But I just want you."

Eliza hummed, running her nose along the crease of Kay's hip. "That's an acceptable answer, I suppose." She crawled up Kay's body, settling on top of her, where she belonged. Kay locked her arms around Eliza's back, where they should remain forever. Eliza grinned, and the delightful sight entranced Kay.

Eliza shifted, her knee nudging Kay's wider as her hand slipped between them.

With one brush, Kay was ready to throw herself into oblivion. It was too much, and still not enough. She arched, the curves of Eliza pressing back. Eliza's elegant, talented fingers had barely touched her, and Kay was already breaking.

Eliza was the sea and Kay was her shore. Kay could try to hold her, but Eliza shaped Kay. Moved her. Eroded her.

And Kay was gone, dissolved and washed away into nothing but churning. Sinking. No air.

Eliza held her face as Kay's body reformed and shuddered with the gentling pleasure.

"I love you," Eliza whispered.

Kay wished she were still a pile of sand so she didn't have to hear that. "I—" Kay bit her tongue. "You shouldn't say that."

"Why not? It's true."

"Fuck, El."

"I want you to stay here with me. You and Stella and Ruth."

The blissful, painful pleasure of the moment evaporated. "We shouldn't talk about this now."

"Shouldn't we? When else will we have the chance?" Eliza pushed up on her elbows above Kay, no longer pressing deliciously into her, but caging her in. "You've been avoiding me, like everyone else." Eliza's voice rang with hurt.

"I thought it would be easier."

"It's been terrible and I hate it."

"I hate it too."

"Then stay."

"I can't."

ELIZA STARED DOWN AT her gorgeous, sweet, infuriating Kaylen, her heart threatening to shatter.

"Why not?" Eliza asked. She sounded pathetic to her own ears.

"Your father has plans for me."

"What sort of plans?" A chill ran through Eliza's body. "He's sending you away?"

"Yes."

"Where?"

Kaylen didn't answer.

Eliza sat up. "I'll come with you."

Needing to see Kaylen better, she scrambled from the bed and lit several candles. When she turned back, Kaylen hadn't moved. She was sprawled where Eliza had left her, bare and beautiful and somehow defeated. That wasn't right. Kaylen wasn't defeatable. She was strong and sturdy and always kept going no matter what.

"I'll speak to my father. We'll convince him to change his mind."

Kaylen's bleak expression made every fiber in Eliza's body protest.

"We'll figure it out," Eliza promised.

Kaylen smiled, but it didn't look right. "Yeah."

Kaylen held out her hand, and Eliza took it, only to be yanked off balance. She fell onto her back on the bed with a surprised laugh, Kaylen on top of her.

"And tonight, I want to recreate those illustrations in that naughty book of yours," Kaylen muttered into her ear.

Eliza's thighs tightened around Kaylen's. Being able to touch and feel so much of Kaylen was incredible, their bodies fitting and molding together, skin against skin.

Eliza was still worried, but Kaylen's newly determined hands were chasing the fears into the darkened corners of her mind. They didn't belong here with them tonight.

"Which one?" Eliza panted.

"All of them."

CHAPTER 38
Anything but Her

Eliza fidgeted with her gown as the ballroom filled with people. The formal crown on her head sat heavy, straining her neck. Everyone smiled and bowed to her, curiosity poorly masked behind polite falsehoods. As Eliza avoided the cold queen and shifty-eyed king, she waited impatiently for her favorite people to arrive.

The announcer droned as more and more guests spilled through the door. Until the words Eliza had been listening for rang through the crowd.

"Sir Kaylen, Original Knight of Alludan, accompanied by...guests."

It wasn't only Eliza who turned to stare. The room hushed.

Kaylen's hair appeared amazingly tamed into an elegant pile on her head, as it had been that first dinner here. Yet she wore her armor tonight, not the stuffy gown. She gripped Stella's hand, who wore green velvet instead, and her other arm was looped with Ruth's, in blue. The three looked at the room with matching expressions of faint bewilderment.

Eliza beamed, hurrying to meet them. She resisted the urge to lean in and kiss Kaylen.

"You all look wonderful," Eliza said, meaning it.

Kaylen bowed, her eyes raking Eliza from head to toe, the flicker in them making Eliza's blood hum. "So do you." And Eliza could not doubt that it was true. But Kaylen's shoulders were rigid with tension. Something was wrong.

"Why isn't anyone dancing?" Stella asked, looking at the guests milling around the edges of the dance floor.

"Because we were waiting for you," Eliza answered.

"Can we dance now? Like we practiced?" Stella looked hopefully among the three of them.

Before they could move, Lord Trimble, the lord who had approached Eliza in the garden last week, appeared. "Your Highness, Sir Kaylen." He bowed, and everyone nodded and bowed in the repetitive formality of the greeting. "And this must be your daughter." Lord Trimble eyed Stella, who tucked herself partially behind Kaylen.

"Yes. This is Stella." Kaylen's eyes were tight.

"I hear there are bright things in this young lady's future."

Stella giggled. "I'm not a lady."

Kaylen appeared to be fighting off a grimace.

"I have a son," Lord Trimble said.

"How nice for you," Kaylen replied flatly.

"Who is her father?"

Stella looked between a silent Kaylen and an expectant Lord Trimble. "A no-good wastrel bastard," Stella offered helpfully.

Eliza snorted as Lord Trimble's mouth resembled a fish in air.

"Stella!" Ruth gasped, covering her face.

After a heartbeat, Kaylen grinned down at her daughter. She barely glanced back at Lord Trimble. "Yes, there you have it. If you'll excuse us, we have dancing to do."

Kaylen led Stella out onto the floor, and Eliza looped her arm with Ruth's. After several stares, a few other people joined them so they weren't the only ones. Eliza's chest swelled as they danced the same quad formation they had practiced yesterday, stepping forward and back, sometimes sideways by mistake, joining hands and turning out of rhythm, and eventually back together. It wasn't elegant, and Eliza heard murmuring, probably starting all sorts of new rumors and stories. And she didn't care.

Stella's brow furrowed in concentration as she focused on remembering the steps. Kaylen whispered to her when she forgot, and waited for her to catch up, not allowing the music or anything else to dictate their pace. And Eliza loved her even more.

Stella smiled happily when they finished their clunky, delightful set. "Did I do all right?" she asked Kaylen.

"You did excellent, starling."

"Let's get a drink," Eliza offered, leading them over to the table on the wall, where Eliza had made certain more than wine waited.

When she caught Kaylen's eyes, they were full of something painfully intense. Eliza started to reach for her, but Kaylen went stiff.

A pretty woman glided toward them, her lips stained a deep red, but when they smiled, the expression didn't match her eyes.

"Your Highness," the lady said. "And Sir Kaylen. The whole family is here, I see." Eliza glanced between them all, feeling the tension. And smelled lavender.

"I understand my horse was instrumental in the safe rescue of Princess Eliza. I do hope that will not be forgotten," Lady Velma said loudly with a false smile.

Jealousy flared, but not as brightly as Eliza's anger. "It will certainly not be forgotten how you tried to refuse."

Lady Velma's smile froze on her face. "Your Highness, that's not—"

"It will not be forgotten how you treated Sir Kaylen with disrespect." Eliza's voice rose with her indignation. "It will not be forgotten how you disregard the state of your properties and prey on those in need."

Someone cleared his throat and suddenly the king was standing beside her. "That's enough, Eliza."

Oh, so she existed now? It was disarming to have him look at her, and she was so surprised, she allowed him to steer her away from the center of everyone's attention.

"You are making a fool of yourself," the king said sternly.

"Am I? Perhaps you should have me locked away for another twenty years."

The king threw her a sharp look. "I do have something to say to you later. But you are not in a place to hear it."

And he was gone as suddenly as he had arrived, and Eliza was as aggravated as she had been.

She turned but didn't see Kaylen anymore. As Eliza moved along the edges of the room, looking for her, a conversation from the approaching alcove slowed her feet.

"I cannot believe anyone actually supports her claim. She's entirely unsuitable. The kingdom was safer before she made a mockery of it. Uvaria is hardly far enough."

Eliza's stomach tightened. It was the queen's voice.

"And as for that excuse of a knight of hers...what a disgrace. And thankless too. But it matters not. Soon, we'll be able to breathe again. After tonight, they will both be gone for good. One way or another."

Both gone?

Eliza stepped toward the alcove to demand the queen explain what she meant when the announcer's voice rang out with a familiar name. It took a moment for Eliza's mind to recognize it, and then she halted.

"Her Royal Highness Princess Helena of Uvaria."

The years looked good on Helena. She glided into the room, just as beautiful as Eliza remembered and possessing that natural regal poise Eliza always envied. Her honey hair caught the light, twisted up above an elegant neck. As her eyes landed on Eliza, Helena smiled, coming straight to her. Eliza recovered from her shock enough to return the deep curtsy. Helena smiled brighter and took Eliza's hand, squeezing it tight.

"Hi, Liza."

Eliza had forgotten Helena used to call her that. "What are you doing here?" That was probably not the best way to greet her old friend, but Eliza was too flustered by the evening.

"I'm here for you, of course. I was touring the north with my sister when we heard from your father, and I had to come."

"Oh." Eliza glanced around the room, searching for Kaylen.

Helena drew her nearer. "Will you dance with me?"

A slow partner dance began, and Eliza let herself be pulled to the floor. When they were younger and would practice together, Helena's touch had made Eliza's heart race. Helena's hold was still competent, but Eliza's heart remained notably calm. All Eliza could think was that she wasn't Kaylen.

"How have you been?" Helena asked, and Eliza couldn't help her short bark of laughter. Helena's face pinkened prettily as she joined in. "That was a poor question."

"The past few weeks, I have been well indeed," Eliza settled on, her body flushing when she caught sight of Kaylen finally, standing on the edge of the dance floor.

"Yes, I've heard all about your Sir Kaylen," Helena murmured, following Eliza's gaze. "Don't worry. I don't mind."

Eliza frowned. What would Helena mind about her?

"She will have her own suite. Separate from ours."

Eliza stopped dancing and Helena nearly stumbled. "What are you talking about?"

Helena smiled in an understanding way, and it irked Eliza because Eliza was the one who didn't understand. "Let's step outside."

HER LOVELY CHAMPION

KAY WATCHED THE SECOND-born princess of Uvaria take Eliza's hand and lead her out onto the terrace. The sight scraped down the inside of her skin and she shivered.

"Why aren't you dancing with the princess?" Stella asked.

"The princess has many guests to dance with."

Like second-born princesses of Uvaria. Not common-born, twice-knights.

Everyone seemed to greet Kay, and those who didn't stared. She was getting tired of avoiding them. It had never been like this before. Kay had received plenty of looks in Glea, but she hadn't been noteworthy.

Stella yawned, swaying into Ma's side.

"It's getting late," Ma said, looking exhausted herself despite arriving not long ago. She ran her hand over Stella's hair. "How about we go back to our fancy room and get some sleep?"

Ma met Kay's eyes, and Kay knew she saw her pain.

"We don't belong here, anyway," Ma whispered.

None of them did. Stella had only been allowed because of Eliza. Stella would likely never see anything like this again. And as Kay glanced around the crowded room, she didn't feel sorry for it.

Kay wished she could leave with Ma and Stella, but she couldn't yet. She had to speak with Eliza first.

Kay's hand drifted to her pocket where the pathetic bundle of ribbon-tied parchment weighed her down.

"I'll be up when I can," Kay managed.

As Ma and Stella slipped away to freedom, Kay prowled the edges of the room, avoiding eyes as her attention was drawn repeatedly to the terrace.

They certainly were taking their time out there.

Acid filled her mouth.

They *should* take their time. Kay tried, and failed, to want this for Eliza.

ELIZA STARED AT HELENA'S pretty, hopeful face and tried to make sense of her nonsensical words. "Marry you?"

"I know we'll be happy. We used to have fun together."

They had. But they weren't those people anymore.

Eliza's immediate response was an emphatic "no" until Helena had mentioned Kaylen again.

"And you are certain about Sir Kaylen?"

Helena nodded. "Your father has already spoken to her about it. I understand you care for her. I won't ask you to break things off. I only hope someday you and I might also have something."

Eliza thought back to Kaylen's words last night. *Your father has plans for me.*

Alongside the sinking dread at the prospect of it, hope crept through Eliza. Could it truly be possible? Was this her way to have Kaylen?

Eliza had always known she would be expected to marry. And here stood a woman she used to care for, who wouldn't take her from Kaylen. Eliza's heart screamed at her to say no. But her rational head was considering it. Was she truly considering it?

Her father would be pleased. Eliza wished she didn't care what he thought, after everything, but the child in her who had been stolen from this palace still did.

"I know it's all rather sudden." Helena took Eliza's hand again, running her fingers over the back. "But I'm leaving tomorrow again already to rejoin my sister and return home, and your father wishes you to come with us. Will you?"

Would she? "I must speak to Kaylen."

Helena's hopeful smile dimmed. "Of course." She lifted Eliza's hand to her lips and pressed a soft, lingering kiss to it. "Speaking of..."

Kaylen stood in the doorway to the terrace, outlined by the glow of the ballroom. Eliza's whole body warmed, and she hastily withdrew her hand from Helena's.

"I'll leave you two," Helena said smoothly.

Kaylen averted her eyes and inclined in a stiff bow as Helena glided past. Eliza hurried to Kaylen's side, needing to feel her. But when she reached for Kaylen's cheek, Kaylen stepped back.

"What's wrong?" Eliza asked.

Kaylen huffed, and her eyes finally met Eliza's. They burned with something that looked frighteningly like anger. "What do you think?"

"Kaylen?"

"Did you have a nice chat?" Kaylen asked, voice flat.

Eliza swallowed. "A strange one. And one I think you already know about."

Kaylen nodded jerkily. "You will marry her."

The words sounded all wrong, especially coming from Kaylen. Determined not to let Kaylen's mood deter her,

Eliza took Kaylen's hand. "What did my father tell you yesterday?"

Kaylen looked down. "He knows about us." Those words shouldn't have warmed Eliza's insides, but they did. She wanted to be an *us* with Kaylen. "He told me if I agreed to go with you, to convince you, he'd give me an estate. Make sure Stella never needs for anything."

Eliza blinked, processing that. "Well, that's good, right? Stella should have everything."

Kaylen flinched. Eliza didn't know what she'd said wrong. "Don't worry," Eliza assured her. "I'm not angry about you taking his money. I'll go. As long as you are with me, that's all that matters. It's not ideal, but we'll make it work. We'll—"

"I'm not going."

"What?"

"I am not going to Uvaria."

"But you just said...You told me what my father offered."

"And I've refused it."

"Why?"

"It's not an offer I want."

Eliza pulled her hand free from Kaylen's, which was suddenly ice cold. "You don't want me?"

KAY'S CHEST WAS BEING ripped open. "Don't say that. You know I want you."

"Clearly not enough. Are you finally tired of minding me?"

"I've never minded you, El."

"Don't call me that." Bitterness tinged Eliza's voice. "I thought you didn't say it back last night because you were afraid. But now I wonder if you're just a coward, or didn't feel it at all."

Kay couldn't protest. Couldn't confess. Couldn't tell Eliza she loved her madly and this was crushing her soul. "We've always known this would end."

"It doesn't have to." Eliza's angry tone cracked into something far more painfully raw and desperate. "You could come."

Kay looked into Eliza's beautiful eyes and steeled herself against the emotions behind them. "It's not as simple as that."

"Why not?"

"You accused me once of only thinking of the money. But it's never been about that. It's been about taking care of my family."

"And having the king elevate you and pay for everything isn't taking care of them? You'd be a fool to throw away an offer like that. Maybe you really don't know how to be a mother."

The words hit their mark, and Kay reeled backward.

"Fuck, I didn't mean that at all," Eliza mumbled through the hands pressed over her face. "I'm just—"

Kay was too. She grappled down her anger spurred by the hurt, blinking and swallowing until she was able to speak again.

"It would be a way to take care of them. But not in the way I want. And more importantly, not the way *they* want." Stella's whispered words by the brook echoed over and over.

I don't want stars. I want you. Kay's throat clogged again, and she tried to explain. She needed Eliza to understand. "I've never had the option to choose between staying and leaving. I've always said yes to any opportunity because I had to."

"And I'm not an option worth saying yes to."

Kay released a frustrated breath. Eliza wasn't listening to her. "You told me back at home you would've rather known you were loved. Stella shouldn't ever doubt that she is. And I don't want someone else to have to tell her. I've been gone so long. I've lost so much time already. I won't lose any more."

Eliza turned away, hiding her face again. "You've decided, then?"

Kay took a step closer, her body screaming to comfort the woman in front of her. She reached into her pocket and pulled out the shaking, wretched bundle Kay wished she had never made. But Kay was here now, and so she forced the words out. "I have something for you. To take with you."

"I don't want it."

The spiteful words kicked in Kay's teeth. She nodded, though Eliza couldn't see, stuffing the inadequate gift back into her pocket. Just as well. She'd burn it tonight so Eliza would never know the new ways Kay was unworthy of her.

"I would give anything for you, Eliza. Anything but her."

Eliza swayed and Kay reached out on reflex, but Eliza shrugged sharply away from her touch. "Go. You're going to leave, so do it."

What more was there to say? A million things, and nothing at all that would make it easier.

Kay did as her princess ordered. She left.

HER LOVELY CHAMPION

The lights of the ballroom blurred. Her limbs were heavy, her lungs struggling in her ribs. Each step hurt, carrying her farther away from the woman she loved. Kay was breaking her own heart. One day, she might be able to paste it back together again.

Fly, my starling, goodbye.
Goodbye, goodbye, goodbye.
Goodbye, goodbye...

Kay collided with Sir Grimhook's shiny breastplate in the overbright hallway flaring with torchlight. As she blinked through her haze, two more knights materialized on either side of her.

"Let me pass," Kay stated numbly.

"You should have accepted the king's offer," Sir Grimhook said, his eyes gleaming.

The two knights pressed closer, and Kay's dulled instincts flared in the back of her mind to retreat. She held her ground. "Why do you care?"

"We can't have the people's champion running loose in the kingdom, now can we?"

At least Kay's body retained a sense of preservation, and she reactively stepped back as he advanced.

"I'd love to say it's nothing personal, but it would be unbecoming to lie. Your time playing knight is over, Sir Kaylen."

She almost dodged the blow to her face.

CHAPTER 39

Underhanded Dealings

Tears clouded Eliza's eyes as she stared at the late blooms in the garden below her. She sensed that Kaylen was gone, no wonderful presence of her on this lonely, miserable terrace. Darkness smoldered and twisted amongst the roses, the thorns lengthening.

Yet again, everyone besides Eliza had decided her life. Eliza had asked Kaylen to stay, but Kaylen hadn't wanted to. Eliza knew that was an unfair thought, but she was past caring. Nothing was fair in this disaster of a life.

And it got worse as her father approached her.

"Did Princess Helena speak with you?" the king asked.

"She did." Eliza wrapped her arms around herself to ward off the chill that had nothing to do with the weather.

"Once you have time to adjust, you will be happy in Uvaria."

"You have always been so concerned about my happiness." The bitterness from earlier lingered. "You're banishing me again."

"I am offering you a better life."

Eliza scoffed.

"I don't have to defend my actions to you."

"But I'm the one who paid for them. For eighteen years!"

"Don't raise your voice with me."

"Why? What are you going to do? Lock me away?"

"I am the king."

"And I am not my mother," Eliza spat, her vision consumed by her anger and resentment, which burned away even the threatening darkness.

The king took a step back. He was watching her like she was truly dangerous.

He still thought she might be a witch. Perhaps with enough time, he might trust her. Maybe some part of him could still love her someday despite it. But he wasn't willing to give her that time. She only had so much left herself. She wasn't willing to waste it on him either.

"I won't marry Princess Helena," Eliza stated.

"Don't be dramatic. You're just mooning after that ungrateful knight."

Eliza's anger flared again. "That knight is the one person who truly cares about me." Kaylen didn't care about Princess Eliza. She cared about El. And Eliza needed to find her. She headed for the doors back inside.

"Then where is she now?"

Eliza's steps faltered.

Kaylen was going home. Where she'd always belonged. Eliza had yet again made everything about herself. Kaylen wasn't leaving Eliza—she was moving toward her family. Eliza couldn't let them go so easily. And if, in the end, she had to, it wouldn't be like this.

Eliza didn't bother to give her father an answer, since he hadn't given the important ones to her either.

Helena tried to catch her eye as Eliza dashed through the crowded ballroom, a startled knight falling into step behind her.

She raced out the door and toward the hallway that would take her to their wing. Too many layers of skirts constricted, so she scooped them up, not caring who saw, and dashed up the steps as she used to dash up her tower.

Rounding the corner, she stumbled to a halt.

Kaylen stood facing away from her, surrounded by Sir Grimhook and two other knights. Before Eliza could do anything, Sir Grimhook swung.

Kaylen's head jerked back, as one of the others grappled her.

"Stop!" Eliza shrieked, her stunned feet stumbling into motion toward them.

Kaylen turned into the grip of the one holding her, knocking out his legs and dropping as the second lunged.

The scrape and grind of armor rang through the hall as Kaylen disappeared beneath the overbalanced knight.

"Help her!" Eliza ordered the guard behind her.

Kaylen wasn't helpless on her own, however. She fought, not with grace, but with sharp practicality. With a well-placed elbow to a throat, and palm to the nose, she managed to slip away, scrambling to her feet as the other two drew their swords.

Eliza's heart stopped.

Kaylen ducked, deflecting a swing with her bracer before she could draw her weapon, and then dodged back from a second.

Eliza had to do something. They weren't listening to her words. Fine, then. She wouldn't use her words.

She tore the heavy gold crown from her head.

Kaylen jumped back from another swing and was seized from behind by the first attacker, an unyielding arm cinching around her throat.

From the end of the hall, the king's voice rang with authority. "Stop!"

The two henchmen knights paused, turning to see their king, but Sir Grimhook didn't stand down or take his eyes off Kaylen, who struggled against the choke hold. His hard, gleeful look made Eliza's blood run cold, and then hot with fury.

Eliza hurled her crown. It hit Sir Grimhook squarely in the face as he tried to step toward Kaylen. He stumbled back, Eliza's current guard rushing forward to restrain him and more pouring from behind the king.

Eliza ran to Kaylen, who shoved off the confused-looking knight holding her, only to be caught by Eliza as she threw her arms around Kaylen's neck.

Kaylen clutched her back for a moment, her heavy breaths shaking them both.

Blood painted Kaylen's upper lip and chin from her nose. Eliza fumbled in her sleeve and pressed her handkerchief to Kaylen's wincing face, framed by tumbling curls, which had broken free from the exhausted pins.

"You have good aim," Kaylen mumbled through the cloth, her glittering eyes meeting Eliza's. It was only the two of them for a moment, and everything would be fine. Then Kaylen looked away, and the rest of the world returned.

Eliza whirled on the approaching king, stepping in front of Kaylen. She would not let him hurt her. "Did you do this?" she demanded.

"Of course not." The king glowered fiercely as Sir Grimhook was hauled upright, a satisfying crown-shaped indent on his cheek. "Explain yourself."

Sir Grimhook kept his gaze lowered and jaw sealed, until they were all joined by a new arrival. The queen halted. Sir Grimhook glanced up and shook his head.

"Do not tell me you had something to do with this, dear wife," the king said, his tone dangerous.

The queen glared right back. "Someone had to do something. They are both a danger to you. To our daughter."

"I am handling it."

"Not very well."

The king's face twitched, turning pointedly to the crowd of guests gathered behind him, drawn by the commotion. They all seemed suddenly quite interested in the ceiling, floor, or darkened windows. "And you think this public spectacle will make the danger any less real?"

"You are the one making it public," the queen said, her cheeks and eyes bright.

"Oh, your loyalists did that fine all on their own. By picking a stacked fight in a hallway outside a ballroom. And somehow still failing." The king turned a brief, chilling look on Sir Grimhook. "How dare you undermine me." He tilted his chin at several guards at his side. "Take him out of my sight. And escort Her Majesty to her room. I'll be there shortly."

Eliza returned her attention to Kaylen, checking beneath the stained handkerchief, sickened by Kaylen's blood, which had thankfully stopped leaving her.

"You should see the physician," Eliza said, but Kaylen shook her head, looking at the king.

"I shall leave the palace tonight, Your Majesty."

He nodded. "That would be for the best. You will have a carriage, and an apology from the crown for this disgrace. You are henceforth relieved of your duties."

Eliza's heart sank. He was effectively removing Kaylen of the knighthood he'd demanded her oath for. This wasn't Kaylen's fault.

Kaylen captured Eliza's hand and pressed her bloody lips to the back. "Thank you for rescuing me, princess," she breathed.

Then she turned and ran down the hall and out of sight. Eliza's legs screamed to run after her, but she forced them to stay still.

Too much had happened tonight. Kaylen needed to leave, but Eliza couldn't go with her. Not yet. She had to be brave.

It would have been so easy to follow just like this. Kaylen deserved better, and Eliza could do better for her. A plan was already partially forming in her scattered mind, and Eliza needed time to gather it together.

As the darkness crept around her, Eliza took a deep breath and glared back at it. She was sick of it controlling her life as well.

"Here, Your Highness."

A knight held out her crown, one of the tines bent and a few jewels knocked loose, glittering up from the floor. Eliza stared at it for several moments before closing her fingers around the dented metal.

"And you dropped this as well, Your Highness."

"That's not..."

Eliza took the second item. Several pieces of parchment had been tied together with a yellow hair ribbon. Her hands shook as she unfolded them.

The first two pages were wrinkled, like they'd been crumpled and smoothed out again. Eliza squinted at what looked like a very strange fish. A scribble above it labeled it for her: *bird*. Below that were two more slightly less fish-like creatures, resting on what she guessed was meant to be a tree.

The second page held a tangle of crossed-out sentences.

When I'm with you, my ~~chest~~ everything hurts. In a good way.
You smell better than fresh cut hay.
I'll want you until my hair is gray, and then falls out.
Your ~~smile~~ eyes are ~~like~~ remind me of—
Sorry

The final page was undamaged, and held only a few lines written in the same sharp, simple script.

El,

I wanted to give you something. As it turns out, I am rubbish at both drawing and poetry, and I already gave you the only other thing I know how to make. I was going to destroy these, but you told me to be imperfect. So here I am, darling. I hope you are happy, and can forgive me one day. I won't forget you.

Kay

The words blurred.

"Oh, Kaylen," Eliza whispered.

It didn't matter that Kaylen hadn't said it back. Kaylen's heart was smeared all over these pages, far more charming for their faults than the greatest works of art and verse. Eliza had been so cruel to turn them away earlier, and more of a fool for thinking she could let Kaylen go.

"Your Highness?" The knight was watching her with concern. Eliza blinked around to find they were alone in the hallway, everyone else gone.

Eliza pressed the crumpled, beautiful gift to her chest, letting it give her hope. She wasn't certain she could fix this, but she had to try.

"Tell me when the king is free," Eliza instructed the knight. "We have much to discuss."

CHAPTER 40
Stars Always Fall

K ay trailed her fingers along the fence surrounding the field, the weathered wood newly repaired by strangers' hands. The workers Eliza had sent to take care of the farm had made use of their time well. The weeds were gone, the rows tidy, the door hinges oiled, and the woodshed stocked.

They'd only been back two days, and Kay wasn't certain what to do with herself. She tried not to suffocate Stella or Ma, who were getting back into their own rhythm after the shock of being away and traveling for four days in a coach back.

The hammering dread Kay felt for Stella and Ma's safety as they'd left the palace in the dead of night had faded with the days and distance. She'd been so focused on getting them away, it had smothered the rest of her pain temporarily.

Stella had asked no less than eight times that first night and next day why Eliza hadn't said goodbye, and Kay had given a different excuse for each. All had been true, but none had been the truth.

The thought of Eliza was a burn wound branding her insides. Nothing for a moment, followed by a brief flash of pleasant warmth, and then searing pain. Eliza would never fit inside a box again. She'd never truly fit there before. She didn't belong in a box. So the memory of her ran rampant through Kay's mind and body. And Kay only hoped one day she'd learn to live with that.

Kay was staring at nothing when Ma spoke beside her. "It's getting late."

Kay blinked and looked up at the sky. She nodded, turning back toward the house, but Ma stopped her with a gentle hand.

"How are you doing?"

Kay shrugged. "Surviving. Like I always have."

"I know it doesn't seem like it now, but it will grow more bearable with time."

Kay nodded again. She understood the words were true, even if she couldn't feel them yet.

"Do you regret your choice?" Ma asked.

Kay had confessed everything to her on the journey home. Kay regretted losing Eliza. And at night when she was most vulnerable, dreams of holding her again plagued her. But she knew she had chosen correctly, even if that choice hurt more than any pike to the chest. Kay lived with enough regret and resentment toward Finley. She didn't want to resent Eliza. But living without her was fucking hard.

Having Ma and Stella helped. Kay hoped Eliza was coping all right, hating that she couldn't hold her through it.

But Eliza was far stronger than she gave herself credit for. Perhaps she was doing fine. Accepting and looking forward to her new life. Finding comfort in her soon-to-be wife. Kay hoped that was true.

Kay also hoped she never found out, because she was still falling apart.

"Let's go back to the house," Ma said, taking Kay's arm.

A dust cloud rose above the road where a dark carriage trundled up the valley.

"Looks like Lady Velma is returning," Kay said.

Ma made a small harrumph sound. "So it does."

"I'll go speak with her tomorrow. About the land."

Kay planned to purchase it back. They had sold it for less than it was worth, but Kay feared they'd buy it for much more. But she was determined. Now that Kay had no opportunities in Glea and had been essentially banished by the king of Alludan, Ma would get her wish. Kay would stay and work the land until the remaining ludans ran out. And then...then she would figure something out.

Everyone in the kingdom seemed to know her. Or at least, they knew a distorted version of her, so she wasn't certain what sort of work she might be able to do. But for now she would stay, and perhaps with time, people would start to forget again.

The carriage did not turn from the main road toward the manor. It rumbled onward, heading in their direction. Kay and Ma both quickened their pace. What did she want now?

They reached the front of the house as the horses did, clomping and snorting to a stop.

"I'll deal with her," Kay said. "I don't imagine it'll be pleasant. Make sure Stella doesn't hear."

Ma squeezed her arm. "Call for me if you need me." Then she hurried to their door, where Stella stood with her eyes wide.

Kay straightened her shoulders and faced the carriage as a footman in royal livery jumped down. Kay frowned. Since when did Lady Velma have access to royal footmen?

Kay's whole body flooded with delight at the sight of Eliza. She looked achingly wonderful in a blush-pink gown, the same color she had worn the first time Kay had seen her.

They stared at each other. Kay longed to rush forward, gather Eliza in her arms, and never, ever let go.

"What are you doing here?" Kay asked instead.

Eliza visibly swallowed. "Several things, actually." She shifted nervously. "First, to give you this." She held out a scroll of parchment. It trembled in her hand, and didn't fare any better in Kay's as she took it, trying desperately to ensure their skin didn't touch. Kay didn't think she could survive that.

"What is this?" Kay glanced at the looping lettering.

"Lady Velma's Embers Hollow estate and all of the property she owned in this valley."

Kay recognized her own name on the page and snapped her gaze back to Eliza. "What did you do?"

"She has been compensated. And relocated. Permanently. It's all yours."

Kay stared at her in disbelief. "Mine."

"And your descendants'. Stella is named specifically. And it's already signed by royal order and done, so you can't argue you don't deserve it or whatever you are about to say."

Kay hadn't gotten that far. She was stuck on the fact that Eliza was here.

"Why?" Kay croaked.

"Well, so you won't ever have to deal with her again. And also, selfishly, I don't fancy having her as a neighbor."

Eliza bit her lip, and Kay's heart shuddered. Had she heard that right?

"I've refused the engagement and abdicated my claim to the crown," Eliza explained in a rush. "I'm no longer Princess Eliza. Well, I suppose I still have it as an honorary title, but it doesn't mean anything anymore. I'm simply Eliza now. And I know it's presumptuous of me to come here like this after those things I said to you. I'm not expecting anything. But I'm not going to Uvaria, and I'm not going back to the palace. All I'm asking for is a chance. I want to stay here. With you. With all of you. If you'll have me. You don't have to answer me now. I just—"

They collided with the side of the carriage, the parchment sealing their future pinned between them. Kay covered Eliza's mouth with her own, ravenous after a whole week without her. Kay hoped they never spent so long apart again.

Eliza laughed and Kay buried her face into her neck, inhaling as the joy seeped into every corner of her being.

"You are truly here?" Kay asked, afraid to believe it.

"I'm here."

"And you're sure?"

"I'm sure."

"Do you promise you're sure?"

Eliza huffed, half exasperated and half still laughing. "I traded my crown for the chance you'd say yes, Kay. If that doesn't convince you that I mean it, I don't know what else to do." She cupped Kay's cheeks, meeting her eyes. "We've both lost so much time to other people's whims. Let's make the most of what's left together. Let's start something for us."

Kay pressed their foreheads together. "I should have said it back. I've loved you since you refused to take both my boots, I think."

Eliza threaded her fingers into Kay's hair. "Just tell me more often now to make it up to me."

"I love you." Eliza's eyes crinkled and Kay kissed her again, repeating her sentiment. "I love you."

"I know." Eliza sparkled. "You drew me a fish-bird."

Kay cringed. "You found that?" Kay had lost it during her hasty departure from the palace.

"I did."

"I'll practice and make you a better one someday," Kay promised.

"It's a very admirable fish-bird for your first try, but how about I do the drawing, and you make the dolls?"

"That sounds reasonable." It had been too many moments since Kay had tasted Eliza's lips, so she remedied that. "This won't always be easy," Kay warned.

"I know that too. And here I am."

Here she was. The woman Kay loved. It was far too overwhelming to comprehend. "I'll do my best to make sure you don't regret choosing us."

"I'll never regret you."

Kay's eyes stung as her chest overflowed. "Stay."

"Is that an order?" Eliza whispered, grinning.

"If you want it to be."

"I do."

"Then stay forever."

"I think I will."

EPILOGUE

Three Months Later

"What are you thinking of?" Kaylen murmured into Eliza's ear as she came up behind her, wrapping her arms around Eliza's waist where she stood in front of the tall window overlooking the valley.

Eliza's heart swelled, happier than she'd ever been. "You."

Kaylen hummed. "You've always been excellent at answering questions."

Eliza laughed and continued to stare at the simple wedding band on her hand, which Kaylen had placed there today. Leon had made it for her, along with Kaylen's matching one. Leon and Della and everyone else were waiting downstairs. But right here and now, it was only Eliza and Kaylen in their new room, which was in shambles like the rest of the house, with half the dark paneling already torn down to make way for something brighter.

It was the worst time of year for a house renovation and a wedding, with the snow newly blanketing the earth, but neither of them had been willing to wait. So they hadn't let a minor thing like the weather stop them.

"You're gorgeous in this gown," Kaylen breathed into Eliza's neck, making her shiver with pleasure as Kaylen's hands slid over the pink silk of Eliza's waist and hip, bunching it up. "I've been dying to take it off you all day."

"Isn't it customary to wait for the wedding night? It's only afternoon," Eliza managed, desire curling her toes.

"I don't wanna wait."

"Then don't."

The hem grazed her calf when the clattering of small feet outside broke the tension. The door banged open. "Ma!"

Eliza's skirt swished back down as Kaylen puffed a heated sigh into Eliza's neck. "We might need to work on that," she muttered. Then she stepped back and they both turned.

Kaylen met Stella at the center of the room, pulling her into a quick, tight hug. Even after several months together, they always hugged or touched in some way when they met, even if it had only been half a day since they had seen each other. Eliza hoped they never stopped.

"What is it, starling?" Kaylen asked.

"Sir Hugo has started eating the dessert and the new housekeeper is about to faint!" Stella announced happily.

"And I imagine that is the point." Kaylen glanced at Eliza with a soft smile. "I suppose we should go stop him and reassure Miss Amber."

"Or we could not stop him and simply serve dessert now," Eliza countered, joining them.

Stella smiled up at Eliza, almost shyly. "What should I call you now?" Stella asked.

"Hmm, that's a good question. What do you think?"

Stella considered seriously for a moment. "Well, I can't call you Ma because Ma is Ma. But it feels odd to call you El." Stella's face lit up. "Mel! I'll call you Mel!"

"I'd like to be Mel."

Stella looked at Kaylen. "What do you think?"

Kaylen's eyes shone. "I think that sounds perfect."

The three of them went downstairs and into the chaotic, hastily swept, and bare-walled drawing room, filled with the tiny party they had invited. Ruth looked stunning in the new gown they had commissioned for her, standing beside Sir Hugo in the corner, who was holding a forgotten pastry as he stared, enraptured, at Della's sister, who was completely ignoring his existence. Not everyone was ignoring him, however.

"You did not say another knight of Glea would be here," Leon said to Kaylen as she watched Sir Hugo warily.

"Is that a problem?" Kaylen asked, but then suddenly narrowed her eyes. "I finally remember you. Sir Galeon, right?"

Leon gave Kaylen a hard look. "I think it's time for us to leave."

"Please don't go. If you say you were not a knight, then you were not. But you will continue to be a friend no matter what name you use."

After another tense moment, a smile tugged the unscarred side of Leon's mouth. "Thank you, Sir *Kay*." Leon looked at Eliza and nodded. "Your Highness."

"El," Eliza corrected.

Later, when Eliza's arms ached from hugging and her cheeks were sore from smiling, Sir Hugo cornered them.

"Since you did not allow any toasts earlier, I have something to say to you, you merry married mule," Sir Hugo told Kaylen.

Kaylen grinned, tucking Eliza into her side, where Eliza had happily stayed all day. "What is that, you dessert-destroying dastard?"

"Simply that I am incredibly glad you were so much of a fool that you refused an unrefusable offer from a king."

"I agree."

Sir Hugo pressed a hand to his chest and looked around before leaning toward Eliza. "I do believe someone has done something with your true wife, for she never simply agrees with me."

Eliza laughed. "Really? I find her quite agreeable."

"Well, that's because her foolishness is all for you."

"I also agree with that," Kaylen said.

"What have you done with my friend?"

The day was perfect. It didn't matter that the walls were barren, or that they couldn't go out into the garden or lawn because it started snowing again. Or that everyone ate the dessert before the main meal. Eliza and Kaylen were making a life together here and now, and with the people they chose. With the people they loved. And Eliza, former crown princess of Alludan, was finally free.

From the Author

You have reached the end of this second story in the Sapphic Lady Knights series! If you have not already, you can read Della and Sir Galeon's story in *Her Pretty Knight*. Please visit my website at mariahraebirch.com for more information and to join my newsletter, or connect with me on social media @mariah.rae.birch most places.

I hope you enjoyed reading *Her Lovely Champion* as much as I enjoyed creating it. If so, I ask that you take a moment to leave a review online where you received this copy, or your preferred site. Reviews really help independent authors.

Thank you for giving these characters life by reading!

With love,

Mariah Rae

Acknowledgments

Thank you to everyone who helped make this story possible. First, to Chris, for continuing to provide loving support for my writing. To my critique partner, editor, and friend, Ivy L. James, for cheering me on and improving my craft. To the other writers turned friends, who have encouraged and supported my fledgling career. And to readers like you.

Thank you.

Don't miss out!

Visit the website below and you can sign up to receive emails whenever Mariah Rae Birch publishes a new book. There's no charge and no obligation.

https://books2read.com/r/B-A-MDXKC-BGWIF

BOOKS 2 READ

Connecting independent readers to independent writers.

Also by Mariah Rae Birch

Sapphic Lady Knights
Her Pretty Knight
Her Lovely Champion

Watch for more at https://mariahraebirch.com.

M A R I A H   R A E
B I R C H

About the Author

Mariah Rae quit her corporate job in 2022 and wrote a book. And she never stopped.

While her earliest works of fiction and art were plastered boldly to the kitchen walls in her childhood home, it took her another twenty years to gather her courage to share her stories again. Now she writes sapphic tales full of romance and magic.

An artist of many kinds, writing fills Mariah Rae's creative well to the brim. She lives near the mountains with her spouse and furry children. When not writing, she bakes, lurks in nature, and plays games with her small circle of heart family.

Read more at https://mariahraebirch.com.